THE

KEYS

OF

DEATH

a veterinary medical thriller

CLARE T. WALKER

This publication is a work of fiction. Names, characters, places, and incidents are the products of the author's imagination or are used fictitiously. Any resemblance to actual persons, living or dead, or to actual events is coincidental.

Tom Buonincontro designed the front cover, the back cover, and the colophon.

ISBN: 1511772581
ISBN-13: 978-1511772587

First edition © 2016

Also by Clare T. Walker

Startling Figures, volume 1

"These three stories are not just paranormal thrillers. The author combines an imaginative story with a cast of characters who bring the human side of these supernatural events to life."

"...a psychological thrill ride through the dark passages of humanity, with a redemptive twist."

"Smart, memorable, and chilling."

"These tales contain the best elements of mystery, science fiction and fantasy."

Coming in 2016

Startling Figures, volume 2 — three more stories of the paranormal.

Lonely River — a veterinary medical thriller.

CONTENTS

And Death Shall Be Their Shepherd

JULIUS LAY IN THE BUNKHOUSE on a thin mattress, stiff from the wooden bed slats that dug into his back. He stared up at the slats of the bunk above him and pretended to sleep.

When he had lived with his mother in a round hut with an earthen floor and a thatched roof, a mosquito netting had protected him from the night insects. Here in the bunkhouse he and the forty other boys often fell asleep exhausted from futile attempts to slap away the whining mosquitoes.

Tonight, though, Julius would not sleep. Tonight he had a puzzle to solve.

He waited. All around him he heard the gentle, rhythmic sighs of deep sleep. Talk and music blared from the radio in the men's break room.

Moments later, the radio went silent. The men chattered, doors opened and closed, boots crunched on the hard earth as the men went around the compound to conduct their nightly bed check. Keys rattled in the door to Julius's bunkhouse. The door opened and moonlight streamed in.

The shadow of a man crept along the floor, up one row of beds and down the other. Finally, the door closed and the key snapped the locking bolt home.

Twenty minutes later, the silence was absolute.

Julius slid off his bunk and crawled under it. Months ago he had noticed that the bunkhouse was shoddily constructed. The exterior walls were long, wide planks set vertically and nailed top and bottom. The bottom nails were simply hammered into the floor framing. Working from underneath his bunk, Julius had pried the floor nails free and pushed the bottom board outward. Over several nights, he had fatigued the board so he could push it out enough to squeeze through. No one ever inspected the barrack buildings carefully enough to notice two missing nails.

He had made numerous forays around the compound at night and had always been able to return undetected.

Now, Julius pushed the flat of his hand against the bottom of the loosened board, pushed it out, and squeezed through the space headfirst. If anyone were watching from outside, it would look like the building were giving birth to a dry, scrawny calf. He caught himself with both hands, then eased the rest of his body out, barking his shins in the process.

He crept along the length of his bunkhouse and looked both ways before crossing to the next building. He repeated this process twice more until all he had to do was cross a short span of open ground to reach the fence line. During his after-hours reconnoitering missions Julius had determined that a direct line to the southeast corner would lead him across too much open space. The best way to remain unseen by the night guards was to follow the fence line.

Going the long way round was tedious, but more certain to succeed. He also decided that since the moon was full and high, he would crawl along the fence. It would take more time, but if he were caught, he would never get another chance.

What puzzled Julius were the fires that raged at the older boys' compound, which was southeast of this one. He knew its location because he had observed carefully when the truck came to pick up the twelve- and thirteen-year olds and take them away. He had watched the dust trail as the truck bumped down the south road, then turned to the east and disappeared behind a hill.

His friend Jonathan Ngebe, who had gone to the older boys' compound many weeks ago, had boasted that they would learn to shoot guns, make bombs and drive trucks, not just swing machetes like Julius and the younger boys. He wondered why the older boys went to a new location? Were they not *all* training to be soldiers in Mr. Kony's army?

One night, exploring near the southeast corner of the fence, he heard bursts of machine gun fire coming from the direction of the older boys' compound. Moments later, again in the southeast, he saw an orange coruscation in the distance, above the hillside, followed by a fainter, flickering light that continued for several minutes. The moon had been bright enough for him to see clouds of black smoke rising into the sky.

This night, as he scrambled on his hands and knees, Julius thought what a surprise Jonathan would get, if Julius could find him. He was confident that the gunshots and the bonfire would occur shortly, as they had every three weeks for the past few months.

The fence loomed twelve feet above him and was topped with tightly coiled barbed wire. Julius was small and agile, but he knew he would never be able to scale the fence without cutting himself badly. The guards would ignore minor cuts and bruises, but a severe laceration would not escape detection, especially if it required stitches. Going over the top was out of the question.

He had also rejected burrowing under the fence; he wanted his means of escape to remain secret, and a huge hole under the fence would not remain a secret for long. He had spent many night-time expeditions walking the fence line, looking for defects that could be easily exploited: a faulty seam in the chain link, an improperly fastened corner, or a loose area at ground level that he could push outward the way he had done with the wall of his bunkhouse.

No such defect existed. Unlike the barrack buildings, the fence was skillfully constructed and well maintained.

Since no defect existed in the fence, Julius had decided he would have to create one, so he began searching for wire cutters. He had tried the door of the tool shed numerous times, but the guards were diligent; the door was always locked.

At last his luck had changed. Some of the men recruited a group of boys to help with a building project of some kind. Julius couldn't ascertain the details of what they were building, but it involved a great many pipes, wires and tools lying about.

No one had noticed when a small wire cutter disappeared.

Julius reached the southeast corner of the fence. A few nights ago he had hidden the wire cutters under some dirt and gravel near a metal fence post. He uncovered it and tried cutting the bottom chain link. He had to squeeze the handle of the wire cutters together with both hands, and for a moment he was afraid he wasn't strong enough, but at last the wire sprang apart with a satisfying *snick*. He worked his way up the fence. His hands ached and sweat dripped into his eyes. After severing five links, he pushed at the corner and created a gap.

He squirmed through and pushed the corner back into place. On the outside of the fence, glinting in the moonlight, was a metal plate, affixed to the chain link. He couldn't read, so the words stamped onto the plate were meaningless to him, but he knew a few letters of the English alphabet. On the plate, a block capital A formed a stylized image of Mt. Kilimanjaro, the famous mountain peak in neighboring Tanzania.

Julius tucked the wire cutters into his pocket and set off.

The ground sloped gently upward, and he followed the terrain about a quarter mile, until he crested the hill. When he reached the top he paused to catch his breath. He was glad for the moonlight; without it he wouldn't have been able to see the cluster of buildings in the distance. He set off down the hill through the bush.

Julius had been born out here, in the wilderness of northern Uganda, somewhere north of Gulu. His mother, who was fourteen years old when he was born, had been a first-year student at a girls' boarding school near Gulu when she and twenty of her schoolmates were abducted into the bush by a party of rebels in the Lord's Resistance Army. She and four other girls became the wives of Captain Marcus Apire. Mere weeks after her installation into the Captain's household, she became pregnant. She gave her first son three names: the Christian name Julius, after the revered former president of Tanzania, Julius Nyerere; the Acholi name Okene, which means "alone," because his mother was sad to be separated from her family; and the Swahili name Abayomi, which means "brings joy," because he was the only joy his mother found in captivity.

Despite his rough beginning, Julius's earliest memory was one of total comfort. He remembered being two or three years old, lying in his mother's bosom, his stomach full of *otwoya* and *kwon*. He listened to the traditional stories about how Spider came to live in dark corners, or how Dog abandoned Jackal for the warmth of Man's fire and the leavings from Man's feasts, or how Anansi the trickster was himself tricked by his friend Onini. He had many such stories in his head, so exactly which one was being told to him during this memory, he could not remember.

What he did remember was the softness of his mother's body, her wrap draped over him, the cheerful light of the fire, the soothing voice of the storyteller. "Listen, my people, as I tell you of a little, little thing, that happened long ago."

Those are the words that stayed with him. *A little, little thing that happened long ago.* And now, five, maybe six years later, he thought of himself as a little, little thing that happened long ago.

From his first memory, Julius would work his way forward in time, tracing his history, such as it was, for at only nine or ten years old he had very little history. A memory that often came to him was his mother's cooking. She was forever cooking, squatting before the fire, stirring something in a pot, peeling sweet cassava root, or shelling groundnuts. His mother made the most delicious groundnuts. She would roast them over the fire, salt them, and store them in a jar.

Julius also had vague memories of being in a bright room in a comfortable bed with white sheets, while men and women bustled around looking at their clipboards.

A little, little thing that happened long ago.

Whenever Julius came to this point in his catalogue of memories, he wanted to stop. In his imagination he would continue to sit by the fire and eat the delicious food his mother cooked, sleep in their snug little house protected by a mosquito net. He would go to school with the other children. He would go to Makerere University and become a professor, maybe go to Europe, Asia or the United States to teach.

Instead, he was torn away from his mother, stuffed into a truck, and driven to this compound, where he marched and worked and swung the machete, and ate and slept.

Julius reached another high fence topped by a snarl of barbed wire. Unlike his own compound, the vegetation around this one had not been cleared, so he had excellent cover in which to walk the fence line and look for a place to enter.

He chose a spot along the western boundary, next to a tall tree, so that it would be easy to find from inside the compound. He cut through the links and slithered through the fence, grasping tufts of wiry grass to pull himself through.

Julius reasoned that the older boys' compound, like his, would have a large open space for military drills. That would be the most likely place to stage a bonfire. He scooted across ten yards of hardscrabble and paused at the corner of a wooden building just like the ones in his compound. After skirting the length of it, he peered around the corner.

Another row of bunkhouses. And beyond that, another row. This compound was much larger than his. He hesitated, reluctant to plunge into this maze of barrack buildings and risk losing his way back to the western fence line. A glance over his shoulder reassured him that he could still see the tall tree, but if he penetrated too deeply into the complex, he worried that it might disappear from view.

He heard a group of people approaching from within the maze of barracks. A commander was the first to appear, wearing boots, military fatigues and a peaked cap. He walked backward, training an automatic weapon on a target. Two more armed soldiers appeared, and then a group of about thirty boys. The entire procession turned the corner and continued marching, down the dusty path between the buildings where Julius was hiding. More soldiers flanked the boys, and two more walked behind them. The soldiers surrounded the boys, herding them like a flock of sheep. The soldiers were alert, tense. If one of the boys strayed even a few steps away from the group, the nearest soldier would issue a hissed warning, raise his gun and prod the boy back in line.

Julius's skin crawled as the boys approached. Their faces were without expression. Their eyes were wide but appeared to be unseeing, staring straight ahead at nothing. Even the boys who strayed and were prodded back into formation did not shift their gazes or blink their eyes.

Julius crammed himself into the rough planks of the barrack, trying to melt into the building's shadow on the gravel. He nearly gave himself away with a sharp gasp as he recognized his friend Jonathan, whose eyes, too, were blank and staring. In the moonlight, his face was gray and taut like paper stretched over a skeleton.

Heavy boots tramped by not six feet from Julius's face. A few unarmed soldiers followed the gunmen, each carrying a large plastic jug. All the soldiers had machetes hanging from their belts.

After the grim procession turned the corner, Julius followed, keeping low, moving quickly, and staying in the shadows. The soldiers led the boys out of the barracks complex, across a training and exercise yard, then out into the bush. A few moments later they came to a large cleared area. Julius crawled into the scrub at the periphery of the clearing. He turned his head to spit out a mouthful of dust, and found himself eye to eye with a grinning human face. He suppressed a gasp and his whole body shuddered. A drum beat in his ears and his chest.

But it was only a skull, a small one, with a perfect row of white teeth. Just a child.

A little, little thing that happened long ago.

The soldiers stopped, and keeping their guns ready, arranged the boys in a straight line. The line of boys was facing Julius and the soldiers had their backs to him.

The men carrying the jugs approached the line of boys. They went down the line, dousing each boy with liquid. Julius was familiar with this ritual. Joseph Kony had the Spirit, which is what would give him victory in the end. His commanders were given the power to pass this anointing on to the soldiers by the sprinkling of holy water. Sometimes the commanders would apply sacred oil to the soldiers. These talismans would stop enemy bullets and machetes. Julius concluded that these boys were being prepared for battle, which would also explain their trance-like state. They must be embarking on a truly glorious mission, judging by the drenching. Their bodies glistened in the moonlight.

But something about this ceremony unnerved Julius. It was conducted in total silence. Usually before going out to raid a village or ambush an army convoy, there would be much fanfare: singing, exhortations, and of course, detailed instructions. Surely, with such a thorough soaking as this, there would be laughter and joking, flinching as the cold water hit them. But these boys submitted to the baptism without moving or making a sound. They did not even blink as they were soaked from head to toe, the water pouring from them and pooling at their feet. Truly, the boys were in the grip of the Spirit of Joseph Kony, imbued with his Powers.

After dousing the boys, the men with the jugs stepped back while the armed soldiers spread out and took aim. Julius felt his stomach clench as he realized what was about to happen. An instant later, the men discharged their guns and the boys fell. The soldiers walked among the twitching bodies, shooting the ones that still moved.

Julius held his breath. The soldiers swung their guns over their shoulders and drew their machetes. Julius began to cry as they walked among the bodies and hacked any that moved.

When he thought the men could not possibly do more to desecrate his friends' bodies, two other men stepped forward with glass bottles in their hands. The necks of the bottles were stuffed with rags. They set the rags on fire and tossed them onto the pile of mutilated corpses.

An orange flame erupted into the sky as the bodies caught fire. Julius then realized that the men had doused the boys with gasoline, not water. Black smoke towered above the flames. The men backed away, some of them stepping into the vegetation where Julius was hiding, but he did not dare move.

For several hours after that, he stayed still. Even after the fire had died and the soldiers had sifted through the carnage, even after the choking stench of burned flesh had floated away on a breeze, Julius remained, pressed down into the dirt.

When he finally rose, he ran frantically through the bush, heading east. He had left the wire cutters next to the tall tree at the western fence, so he had no option but to go under or over the fence. Even if he were cut to pieces on the barbed wire, it would not matter now.

2

The Most Wonderful Time of the Year

MICHAELA GRIPPED THE PATIENT'S LOWER LEG and pushed it down, bending the knee enough for her to insert a suction tube into the joint space. With a squelch, blood and fluid disappeared, revealing glistening cartilage and ligaments.

Dr. Brightman, standing next to Michaela, peered into the knee joint. "You were right," he said. "The meniscus is torn. Good call."

She nodded. It was a good call, if she said so herself. After slipping on the ice at Thanksgiving, this patient could hardly walk. When he came to see Michaela, the X-rays revealed plenty of abnormal fluid in the knee joint, but even under sedation, with his leg muscles fully relaxed, she had been unable to demonstrate instability in the joint. His response to pain meds was only so-so. It sounded like the cruciate ligament was only partially torn, at worst, but the level of pain pointed to a torn meniscus, the cushioning tissue deep within the knee joint.

Michaela was good at diagnosing, but when it came to surgery, David Brightman could do these things in his sleep. She watched him work. He was amazingly fast. His hands were in constant motion as he removed the damaged portions of the meniscus, flushed the joint, and drilled the anchor holes for the stabilization suture.

At fifty-eight he showed no signs of slowing down—he was too much of an overachiever for that just yet. He was an internationally recognized surgery professor at the University of Illinois vet school, originally from London's Royal Veterinary College. And yet here he was, in Michaela's little animal hospital, doing a simple exploratory and stabilization surgery on a dog's knee. It was a nice way to end the day. Michaela had no more appointments and would close the animal hospital for the evening when this surgery was over.

A radio on the windowsill played Christmas music, and David hummed along. He moved his hands aside slightly. "Suction, please."

She inserted the suction tube once again and cleared the joint of blood and fluid.

David went back to work on the knee joint. "Terry out with the crew today?"

Michaela nodded.

"Better him than me, in this weather," David quipped, although they both knew that Terry loved it out there. Michaela's husband Terry was also a clinical professor at the vet school, but in a much more down to earth capacity than David. Terry went out every day with senior vet students on the Ambulatory and Farm Services rotation. The dirtier and muckier it got, the more he seemed to enjoy it.

Michaela repositioned the knee to provide a bit more exposure, and David worked in silence for a moment. Then he spoke up. "You're awfully quiet."

She smiled. "You know me. I'm always quiet."

David snorted. After a moment, he continued. "You're irked."

"How do you know?"

He just looked at her, and Michaela could tell that beneath his surgical mask he wore his characteristic smirk.

"All right, you win," she said. "I'm irked."

"Why?"

Michaela sighed. "Why is it that every year around Christmas, people are filling my schedule with put-to-sleep appointments?"

"Ah," said David, comprehending.

"It's almost eerie," she continued. "Without fail, you can gauge how close Christmas is by the number of dog and cat euthanasias."

"I know what you mean." He finished tightening the stabilization suture around the joint. "The annual yuletide parade of death. The ancient Irish Setter's incontinence is barely tolerable by the immediate family, but now they're having visitors for Christmas. Or, the seventeen-year-old cat's daily vomiting is bound to cause some bother if she upchucks all over the carpet in the guest bedroom."

She nodded, and despite the grim subject matter, she couldn't help smiling, enjoying her old professor's acerbic British humor.

"Then of course," he said, "*after* the holidays it's the ones who forgot to die. Really should have been put down months ago, but they just wanted to give blind, arthritic Toby one more year to aimlessly circle the Christmas tree."

Michaela laughed, then sobered immediately. "If it didn't involve the death of a living creature, I suppose it would be amusing," she said.

David cocked his head, a touch of concern in his eyes. "How many have you done today?"

"Five."

"That's enough death for anybody." He shook his head. "Why do you think I got out of private practice? I hardly ever have to deal with that anymore."

"One of them was yours, actually, David."

"Really?"

"A little Welsh Terrier, ten years old. You did an experimental heart procedure on him when he was a puppy."

David raised his eyebrows and nodded.

"For the past few months he's been in kidney failure, and he just stopped responding to the treatment. The poor guy got sicker and sicker..." Michaela shrugged.

"And it was time," David concluded.

She nodded. "He was a sweet little dog."

David began closing the joint capsule. After that he would stitch up the subcutaneous tissue, then the skin. "Just keep reminding yourself why you got into this in the first place, Michaela. You have to find your own reason for getting up in the morning."

Before she could respond, the voice of Abby, the hospital receptionist, came from the intercom on the wall. "Dr. Collins, there's an emergency in room two." The intercom went silent for a moment, then they heard Abby's voice again: "Better bring the crash cart."

David and Michaela exchanged a glance.

"Off you go," he said.

Michaela exited the surgery suite, pulled off her gloves, cap and mask, untied the surgical gown, and slipped off the surgical shoe coverings. She grabbed her lab coat and put it on over her scrubs.

Finally, a chance to save a life instead of ending one.

A few steps down the hallway brought her to the treatment area, the bustling nerve center of the animal hospital. A bank of cages lined one wall, in the middle of the room there were work centers and procedure tables, and on the wall opposite the cages were five exam room doors—far too many exam rooms for a one-doctor practice, but Michaela had insisted that the architect leave plenty of room for the practice to grow. Someday she would have enough veterinarians working for her to make full use of all the rooms.

She lifted the animal's medical file out of the rack mounted to the door of exam room two and flipped it open.

New client. Local address. Two-year-old female spayed Labrador retriever named Rosie. Reason for visit: *Put out of misery.*

Michaela raised her eyebrow at that.

She knocked on the door and pushed it open. Two women stood by the exam table, trying to hold down a large yellow-haired dog as it struggled.

"Easy, girl," one of the women said.

The dog writhed on its right side, trying to get up, whining, its left eye darting. Red-tinged foam spilled from the mouth. Blood smeared the dog's tawny fur and the stainless steel table.

Michaela stepped forward and lifted the dog's upper lip. The gums were bluish pink and tacky to the touch. She pressed the gums with her finger, released it, and watched the white area left behind to see how long it took for the color to return. Three and a half seconds. Not good.

She looked up. "What happened?"

The two women looked at each other. One was tall, with fair skin and freckles. The other was shorter, Hispanic, with long, dark hair.

The Hispanic woman spoke. "She was hit by a car," she said. Her voice shook. "The wheel went right over her. The driver just took off."

Michaela shook her head. It made her sick that someone could run over an animal and just keep going.

She continued her examination. When she lifted the dog's head, she felt the sickening sensation of bone grinding on bone beneath the skin—the bone around the right eye was fractured and blood oozed from the eye socket.

The Hispanic woman spoke again. "She's in a lot of pain. Can't you just put her down?"

Michaela lifted her eyes and took a good look at the women. Both were in their twenties. The Hispanic woman, who had done all the talking so far, was heavyset. The tall woman was slender, with short red hair sticking out from under a navy blue Fighting Illini ski cap. Each woman wore snow boots and a heavy winter coat.

The dog was struggling to breathe. Her mucus membranes were taking on a sickly blue cast—cyanosis. Michaela stepped back to the sink and washed the blood off her hands. "This is bad," she said, "but I think I can help her. I'll have to hurry though, get an IV going, treat her for shock—"

"No!" the Hispanic woman said, sharply. She looked up at the other woman, and they exchanged a frightened look. "I'm sorry," the woman said, "but she's in too much pain. Can't you just put her down? We don't want to see her suffer any more."

Michaela took a deep breath and quickly ran through a mental list of the most serious likely injuries. All of them were extensive, life-threatening, and painful: hemothorax, diaphragmatic hernia, flail chest, pneumothorax, ruptured spleen and liver, broken spine and pelvis. Treatable, but only at great cost. Perhaps that was a factor for these women. The initial diagnostics and critical care alone would rack up a bill of several thousand dollars. If any major bones were broken there would be costly orthopedic surgery on top of that.

The dog had stopped trying to get up and was now lying rigid, exerting incredible effort just to breathe.

She stroked the dog's head. They were right. It was the owners' choice to accept or decline her medical recommendations. Every veterinarian took an oath promising to ease animal suffering, and this dog was suffering terribly. The medical file was in order. One of them had signed the Euthanasia Consent Form. Method of payment: cash.

She looked up at the two women. "I'll be right back."

Michaela left the room and went to the controlled drug cabinet in the treatment area. She unlocked it, took out a bottle of sodium pentobarbital and drew up eight ccs into a syringe.

Two veterinary technicians passed nearby, carrying the knee surgery dog toward the treatment area. David was right behind them, pulling his mask off and removing his surgical cap. He took note of what Michaela was doing, but offered no commentary.

She returned to the exam room with the syringe and a tourniquet. "You're welcome to stay, but you don't have to," she said. Not everyone was comfortable witnessing the death of an animal, and Michaela always gave people the option of stepping outside for this part.

Again, the Hispanic woman spoke for the two of them, and her voice quavered. "We'll stay."

"Have you ever seen an animal put to sleep before?" Michaela asked.

"Yes," they said, together.

She slipped the tourniquet around the dog's left forelimb and tightened it just above the elbow. Then she paused and put her hand on the dog's head. She stroked her ear. The dog looked up at her, but remained motionless. "It's okay, girl. It'll all be over in a minute."

Michaela uncapped the needle, grasped the dog's paw in her left hand and held the syringe in her right. She pumped the paw and watched the cephalic vein rise beneath the skin.

She inserted the needle into the vein, then pulled back on the plunger of the syringe until a plume of purple blood flowed into the barrel. She loosened the tourniquet and depressed the plunger. The euthanasia solution flowed into the vein.

"Good girl," Michaela murmured. "Easy now."

The Hispanic woman stroked the dog's head. "It's okay, Rosie," she whispered. "It's all over now, sweetie."

In a few seconds, the syringe was empty and the dog was still. The agonized breathing had ceased. Her eyes stared straight ahead, pupils wide open. Michaela withdrew the syringe from the vein and placed it on the counter behind her. She took her stethoscope from around her neck, fitted the earpieces into her ears, and placed the bell against the dog's chest.

Silence.

"Is she gone?" the Hispanic woman asked.

Michaela looked up and was not surprised to see tears running down the woman's face. She took a box of tissues from the countertop and placed it on the exam table. She touched her finger to the dog's cornea: no response. "Yes. She's gone."

Both women took a tissue from the box and wiped their eyes.

The taller woman spoke for the first time. "Doctor, are you absolutely *sure* she's dead?"

Michaela heard a note of intensity, an urgency that she'd never heard before in this situation.

"I'm sure, yes."

"Can you make absolutely sure?" the Hispanic woman said.

"What do you mean?"

"Can you get an EEG tracing?"

Michaela blinked. An electroencephalogram was an advanced piece of equipment. Most general veterinary practices didn't even own one.

"A heart monitor, at least," the tall woman said.

"A heart monitor? Honestly, it's not necessary. There's no heartbeat, no corneal reflex, no respirations."

"We would really appreciate it," the Hispanic woman said, with a glance at her taller companion.

Michaela left the exam room, trying to shake off a wave of irritation. But it was late and she didn't feel like arguing.

She went into the surgery room and retrieved the cart with the anesthetic monitoring equipment: pulse oximeter, respiration monitor, and ECG machine. She unplugged the equipment and wheeled the cart to the exam room door.

Rising up onto her toes, she looked through the peephole. Normally she didn't use the peephole to spy on her clients—only to see whether a room was occupied or not without having to barge in. But this time, she looked through and watched the women for a moment. They were conducting an examination of their own. The taller woman pressed her fingers into the groove in the inside of the rear leg, feeling for a pulse. The Hispanic woman was checking the left eye with a penlight.

Michaela's husband Terry came around the corner, wearing his winter coat. He was red-faced from the cold. "Hi, hon," he said. "What's going on?"

She shook her head, a gesture that said, "Don't ask." She pushed open the door and wheeled the cart in, deliberately taking no notice as the Hispanic woman hastily put away the penlight.

Michaela plugged in the ECG machine, unwound the leads and attached them to the dog's limbs, one just above each elbow, the third just above the left knee.

She switched on the ECG. A green, horizontal line appeared on the monitor. She let it run for thirty seconds. "She's gone," she said. "I'm sorry for your loss."

The Hispanic woman stroked the dog's head gently. "Good bye, Rosie," she said, her voice catching and tears filling her eyes. Again, she exchanged a glance with her companion. Then she turned to Michaela and extended her hand. "Thank you very much, Doctor. Merry Christmas."

"Merry Christmas," Michaela said.

The taller woman also shook her hand and wished her Merry Christmas, then they left the exam room. Since they had already paid, they headed straight across the empty waiting room and out the front door.

Abby, the receptionist, piped up from behind the front desk. "That must have been a tough call."

Michaela nodded. It never felt right, putting an animal down when she knew what was wrong and how to fix it. Terry worked with livestock farmers all day, who routinely made life and death decisions based on money and practicality. He was used to it, but she hated it when economics came to her door.

She watched through the front window as the two women got into a maroon Subaru wagon. Michaela walked over to the desk and handed Abby the file. "Did they seem odd to you?"

Abby shrugged. "They were upset. Freaked out. People usually are with a hit-and-run." She dropped the file into a wire basket on her desk. "They requested ashes back."

It was not common, due to costs, for people to request "ashes back" on their pets. Most pet owners chose group cremation, which was inexpensive. "Ashes back" meant private or semi-private cremation and the return of the pet's ashes in a special sealed container. A certain percentage of pet owners were willing to pay extra for this added service, since it gave them a tangible keepsake of their pet.

"Go ahead and lock up, Abby," she said. "I'll get Terry to help me bag this one."

Michaela met David and Terry back in the treatment area.

The surgical patient was bandaged and recovering from anesthesia. David had changed into his street clothes and was preparing to leave. "Right. I must be off. Back to the veterinary college to be stimulated by young minds who don't know a cat's anus from their own." He looked at Michaela. "Any better?"

Michaela shrugged.

David looked at Terry. "I think you need to take her home for a healthy dose of Christmas cheer."

Michaela felt her cheeks flush. "I'll be fine, David."

"If you say so." He shook Terry's hand and gave Michaela a gallant kiss on the cheek. "Good night, you two. Happy Christmas." Then he donned his wool overcoat and swept impressively from the room.

Terry looked puzzled. "What'd I miss?"

"I'll tell you later. Could you do me a favor and help me bag the dog in room two?"

"Sure."

Michaela went back to the exam room. The dog lay on the table, surrounded by congealing blood. Its fur stood up in red spikes. She put her hand on the dog's head and stroked its left ear, thinking. Something wasn't right about this case.

"Rosie," she murmured. The skin on the inside of the earflap was soft and pink.

Then it hit her. While obviously the victim of a serious trauma, Rosie lacked one of the telltale signs of being struck by a vehicle. Usually, hit-by-car victims had dirt on them. Abrasions embedded with gravel. Leaves and sticks in their fur, and in the winter, snow and slush—evidence of having been thrown violently to the pavement, possibly dragged across it, and then ejected onto the side of the road. Rosie was covered in her own blood, but otherwise clean.

Terry came into the room with a bright blue carcass bag.

"Can you help me flip her over?" Michaela asked.

They turned Rosie over onto her other side.

"Whoa," Terry said.

Michaela looked at him. "I guess she wasn't hit by a car."

Like her left side, Rosie's right side showed no signs of vehicle trauma: no dirt, no road rash. But on the ribcage were two distinct, circular holes, each oozing with fresh blood.

Gunshot wounds.

3

Deception

MICHAELA CURSED UNDER HER BREATH, angry that she had been so easily misled. The two women had been trying to hold their dog down on *this* side, and had cut Michaela short during her examination. They didn't want her to see these bullet holes. "Let's take some X-rays," she muttered.

"I'll go set it up." Terry left the exam room and headed for X-ray.

Michaela went into the reception area. She retrieved Rosie's file from the wire basket on Abby's desk, then went to the office and got her digital camera. She brought it back to the exam room and took a wide shot of the dog on her left side, then close-ups of each gunshot wound and of her mangled eye socket.

Terry returned with a gurney. He helped Michaela flip Rosie over, and she repeated the photographs on the other side. She took a close-up of the left rear leg, which, upon closer examination, appeared severely swollen and bruised.

Then, together, they lifted Rosie onto the gurney and wheeled her to X-ray.

*   *   *

Later, in the office, Michaela pulled up the digital radiographs on the computer monitor.

She started with the skull and skeleton. The facial bones on the right side, including the zygomatic arch, were shattered into several pieces, and the maxilla—the upper jaw—was broken almost clean through at about the level of the large premolars. Interestingly, the lower jaw also bore evidence of trauma, but not recent. The right ramus of the mandible had evidence of a healing fracture. The left rear leg bore comminuted fractures of the femur and tibia. In addition, the tibia also had evidence of a previous fracture.

The chest X-rays revealed an incidental finding of a pet identification microchip in the subcutaneous tissue over the shoulder blades, and as expected, both air and fluid in the chest. But right away Michaela saw something she did not expect: *four* metallic densities.

"Four bullets," Michaela said to herself. But only two entry wounds.

Rosie had been shot in the chest before—and survived.

The abdomen looked normal, showing good detail of all the internal organs. No sign of fluid build up, making hemorrhage into the abdomen unlikely. But there was a lozenge-shaped, metal density in the liver. Another bullet?

Michaela squinted and leaned in for a better look.

She jumped as Terry appeared in the doorway. "Bagged and tagged," he said.

"You put her in the freezer?"

"Yep."

"Thanks, hon."

The freezer in the animal hospital was a large walk-in unit, dating back to the days when the building had been a meat processing facility on a family farm. It had a loading dock entrance to the outside; if Michaela went on a house call put-to-sleep appointment, she could drive her truck right up to the dock and carry the body in with ease. The cremation service also appreciated how easy it was to pick up the deceased animals.

Michaela thought bitterly that it was standing room only in there at the moment.

Terry stepped all the way into the office and perched on the corner of Michaela's desk. He stretched out his hand toward her. "Need anything else?"

She took his hand. "No, I'm good." Terry's hand was dry, chapped and roughened by the harsh winter weather, but it was warm and his grip was strong.

He gave her hand a squeeze.

Michaela stood up and put her arms around him, and he enfolded her in his. He smelled good, cotton flannel and pine, freshly showered after a day in the muck and mud of the farms. She sighed and leaned into him. She could stay like this forever.

"Heard you had a rough day," he said. "Five put-to-sleeps?"

"Six, counting this one," she murmured into his shoulder.

"That is rough."

She looked up at him. "Might be a new record." She felt tears coming, and she bit her lip.

Terry's face softened. "Oh, sweetheart," he said, as he drew her in close again.

Michaela wiped her eyes. "Look at me. Crying over other people's pets."

"Hey," he said, taking her face into his hands. "I'd worry about you if you weren't." He searched her features in that knowing way of his. "What's really going on?"

Michaela sighed. "Terry, why do we put all this effort and heartache into animals?"

"What do you mean?"

"David Brightman is double-boarded in cardiology and surgery. Imagine what he could be doing if he were a human cardiology and surgical specialist. He could be out there saving babies with heart defects. And instead he's spending all that skill and expertise on people's pets. Dogs and cats that only live for ten or twelve years. Fifteen or sixteen if you're really lucky. Sometimes it just seems like a waste of talent and resources."

Terry frowned. "What's gotten into you? You *are* helping people. You can't tell them how much to love their pets or how much money to spend on them."

"I know, but it's not just that. We save them. We cure diseases. We mend broken legs. And then, because they're peeing on the rug, we put them to sleep. Kill them, in a word. Does that make sense?"

"Is this because of all the Christmas put-to-sleeps?"

"Yes it is! Case in point: that Welsh terrier I saw today. Jasper."

Terry nodded, recalling the case. "That was one of David's."

"Right. He did this fabulous surgery on it, incredibly complex and cutting edge. He was transposing arteries and rerouting blood flow—it was incredible. And now here comes Jasper, ten years later, being put down for something completely unrelated. Those people spent thousands of dollars on that dog. Was it worth it?"

Terry shrugged. "Jasper was a great dog, and they enjoyed him for ten and a half years. If it was worth it to them, it should be worth it to us."

Michaela's thoughts returned to Rosie. "I knew how to help that dog just now. But the owners didn't want to." Michaela shook her head helplessly. "Sometimes I wonder if I'm doing any damn good at all."

He smiled, then leaned toward her and kissed her. "You are." He kissed her again, warmly, then passionately. "Let's go home for that healthy dose of Christmas cheer."

Michaela smiled. "I'm just finishing my notes on this case and I'll be home. You could stay and watch but that would be boring."

"True." He kissed her, but quickly this time. "See you back at the house." He shrugged on his coat, hat and gloves, and strode out of the office with a wink.

Michaela returned to her desk. Terry had forgotten his keys. She waited, and a moment later he reappeared and scooped them up. He gave her another kiss. "Really leaving this time. 'Bye."

"Love you," she said.

After he left, Michaela flipped open the file and shook her head. Her notes were non-existent. She had been so distracted by the dog's condition and the two women's odd behavior that she had neglected to write anything in the medical record. It contained only the most basic information:

Signalment: a two-year-old spayed female Labrador retriever.

Owner: Adriana Smith

Address: 78 South Grant Street, Champaign, Illinois.

The phone number was local—the 217 area code.

Reason for visit: "put out of misery."

Michaela took her pen out of her lab coat pocket and wrote in the record. *The patient presented to the animal hospital in good nutritional condition, alert and aware of its surroundings, responsive, laterally recumbent but struggling to right itself. The patient was in respiratory distress.*

She paused. How was she going to document the rest of this? She hadn't even taken the dog's vitals. In fact, looking back at her performance in the exam room, she had conducted only a cursory examination of the patient, noting its injuries generally but not with any kind of clinical precision. No wonder she hadn't seen the gunshot wounds. She had been shocked by the dog's appearance and had picked up on the women's distress, allowing them to drive the outcome of the case. She should have at least stabilized the dog and conducted a thorough examination. IV catheter, fast saline drip, shock doses of corticosteroids, flow-by oxygen. Pain medication. Then, she and the owners could have discussed the options more calmly.

That was the point. They didn't want her to discover that their dog had been shot.

Shot by whom? Michaela wondered.

"Face it," she berated herself. "You panicked." She had been tired. Fatigued at the end of a long day at the end of a long week at the end of a long month.

And now the dog was dead.

She jumped at the thump of the building's furnace switching on. She picked up her pen and began to write again. *The patient's mucus membranes were muddy and tacky, CRT 3.5 seconds. Epistaxis from both nostrils and hemorrhage of frank blood and foam from the mouth were evident.*

Michaela looked up sharply at a loud banging sound. She listened for a moment and then heard it again—a heavy, metallic thud, like a garage door slamming shut.

"Terry?" she called. "Is that you? Hello?"

She put down her pen and stood up. For a moment, she heard nothing, then suddenly the loud bang again.

Her mind raced. She recalled that at least twice the two women had exchanged a significant look. They must have known about the gunshot wounds. Or even been the ones to inflict them. Had they been planning all along to come back? Pretty elaborate set-up for a ruse, not to mention brutal. Who would deliberately shoot their own dog as an excuse to come inside and case an animal hospital? If they were planning a break-in they would come back when nobody was around, not when Michaela's car was still in the parking lot.

She left her office. An exit light over the back door was the hallway's only illumination. Michaela paused and watched for approaching shadows, then crept into the hallway and around the corner toward the treatment area.

One of the hospitalized patients, a Schnauzer puppy Michaela had spayed that morning, heard her coming and woofed. "Quiet, girl," Michaela whispered.

Michaela jumped as all the dogs in the boarding kennel started barking. She walked across the treatment area, past the exam rooms, and into the hallway leading to the back of the hospital.

She rounded the corner and froze. The door to the walk-in freezer was wide open. The door to the kennel had also been pushed open. Michaela could see into the two runs that were directly in front of the doorway. The dogs were silent now, ears up, tails straight out, their attention riveted on whoever was in there with them. Then each lowered its ears and backed away, hackles rising.

Michaela saw a shadow on the floor of the kennel, approaching from the right.

She backed away from the doorway. She reached into her lab coat pocket, fishing for her cell phone, ready to call 911.

Then, into the open doorway stepped a yellow-haired dog.

It was Rosie. She stood on three legs, her left rear leg hanging uselessly, the toe dragging on the floor. Her body was smeared with dried and fresh blood, and her right eye was bleeding and swollen shut like a prize-fighter's.

The dog took two hobbling steps forward. Michaela cried out and dropped her cell phone as she backed into the wall.

The words of the women in the exam room came back to her. *Are you absolutely sure she's dead?*

4

Christmas Cheer

MICHAELA STARTED HER TRUCK. The clock on the dashboard said 11:30 PM. She sat for a moment, watching the wipers sweep snow from the windshield, still shocked at what had happened.

The dog had been dead. Michaela had given it the correct dose of euthanasia solution. She had hit the vein cleanly, and she was certain no perivascular leakage had occurred. No heartbeat. No respirations. Absent corneal reflex. Flatline ECG. Clinically dead and sealed in a heavy-duty plastic bag, tagged for cremation, and cooling in the freezer for an hour and a half.

Body bags, marked with bright green tags, lined the walls of the walk-in freezer, but Rosie's body bag had been in tatters. The gurney lay on its side and the door of the freezer was wide open. Rosie must have thrown herself repeatedly at the door, hit the crash bar just right, and then escaped.

It was a veterinarian's worst nightmare.

Michaela pulled out of the parking lot. Snow fell—large, heavy flakes, falling softly, straight down. The kind of snow that made it seem warmer and more pleasant outside than the actual temperature would indicate. It was piling up quickly. Snowplows and salt trucks crisscrossed the roads in the distance. The snow was a few inches deep already, but her Ford F150 moved easily over it.

Michaela reached her house in fifteen minutes. The Christmas tree glowed in the front room, and the flickering shadows and light of the TV played upon one wall. She pulled around to the garage, which was attached to a short breezeway they used as a mudroom. She hit the garage door remote, and drove in.

Terry's battered Jeep was there, pulled in a bit too far and partially squashing one of the garbage bins against the front wall of the garage. She tried to extricate it, but it was hopelessly stuck.

She stamped snow off her boots and removed them. As quietly as she could, she entered the house and crept into the darkened mudroom. She stroked the cat, Rooster, who was sprawled, purring, in his favorite spot on top of the dryer. Under Michaela's hand the cat rolled over onto his back, stretched and yawned luxuriantly, and blinked at her with his left eye. Rooster's right eye was long gone; Michaela had removed it when he was a kitten, after it had been irreparably damaged during a fight with some unknown adversary.

Michaela's Boxer, Tripod, clicked across the kitchen linoleum to greet her. He hobbled up ably on his three remaining legs, wagging his stumpy tail so hard he nearly upended himself. "Settle down, boy," she said, then rubbed his ears and slapped his sides. "Wanna go outside?"

Tripod spun around and jumped at the back door. Michaela opened it, and he launched himself into the yard, cavorting in the snow. Michaela pulled the door shut and went to find her husband.

In the living room, she found the TV on and a rumpled Chicago Bears fleece blanket on the couch. For some reason

Terry often left the TV on even after he went to bed. Michaela thought it was because he couldn't stand the silence in the empty house.

She picked up the blanket and folded it. On the TV screen, Luke Skywalker battled Darth Vader in *Return of the Jedi*. Michaela watched for a moment. She had never been too fond of this ending—Darth Vader turning out to be a good guy in the end. Deathbed conversions always irritated her. She understood that they could be sincere, in theory, but it didn't seem fair, that someone who had spent his life dedicated to evil could, moments before his death, realize his error, confess his sins, and get into Paradise free and clear, when there were so many people actually trying to do good their whole lives. In her more cynical moments, Michaela would ask herself if it was not better to simply do whatever the hell you wanted, with a view to repenting at the last moment.

She wondered what her cousin Brendan would say to that. He certainly had personal experience of doing whatever the hell he wanted, although now he undoubtedly had a scripted soliloquy of theologically correct answers.

Michaela tossed the blanket onto the couch, turned off the TV and went back to the kitchen, scolding herself for expending yet more mental and emotional energy on her cousin. It still bothered her that the mere memory of him could set off the fight or flight response within her. Did a deathbed conversion put right all the damage? Did it bring the dead back to life?

She let Tripod inside, and sidestepped quickly to avoid him as he clattered through the kitchen. She heard him bound down the hallway to take his usual position at the foot of their bed.

Michaela stopped in the bathroom to brush her teeth, and then went into their bedroom. Terry was asleep. She got undressed and slipped under the covers.

He stirred and opened one eye, blearily. "What time is it?"

"Just after midnight. Sorry."

"S'alright."

She moved in close and kissed him. He responded by drawing her in to his chest. Michaela sighed and relaxed into the warm refuge of his body.

He murmured into her hair. "Where've you been?"

"Where no veterinarian has gone before."

"What?"

"You're not going to believe this."

Terry grunted.

"Remember that dog? Rosie?" Michaela continued. "The one who was shot? The one you put in the freezer?"

"Yeah."

"Would you believe she's alive?"

That got Terry's attention. He pushed himself up onto his elbow. "Alive? How?"

"I have no idea." Michaela recalled with grim irony what she had written in Rosie's record to describe it: *Approximately ninety minutes after apparent clinical death, the patient was found to be conscious and ambulatory, having extricated itself from the body bag and the holding freezer.*

"Holy crap," Terry said. "What did you do?"

"What I should have done in the first place. I started an IV and treated her for shock and pain. Then I cleaned her up. Put a big Robert Jones bandage on her leg and wrapped her chest. When I left she was fast asleep."

"What a trooper," Terry said.

Michaela scoffed bitterly. "It's not funny, Terry. How am I going to explain this to the owner?"

"Did you get hold of them?"

"No. Bad number."

"That's a big surprise. They lied about her being hit by a car. If you asked me, I'd say they were the ones who have some explaining to do."

"It's not a phone conversation I was looking forward to anyway." Michaela mimed putting a phone up to her ear. "Hello, Mrs. Smith? If that is your name?"

Terry gave a short laugh.

Michaela continued. "I figured out that you lied to me and that your dog was shot, not hit by a car. And, by the way—surprise!—she's still alive."

"Look on the bright side," Terry said. "It's not every day you get a do-over."

"And this time I did everything I could for her."

"Do you think she'll live through the night?"

"I don't know," she said. When those two women brought Rosie in, she had already been in shock and near death. Then Michaela had given her eight ccs of sodium pentobarbital. "She shouldn't be alive right now."

Terry rested his hand gently on her hip. "At least you made her comfortable."

Michaela knew from experience that if she weren't careful, she'd be awake all night, going round and round in her head thinking about what she could have done, what she should have done. But agonizing over cases had never helped before, and she knew it wouldn't make a difference now. She had done all she could. She would have to leave it at that until tomorrow. With an effort, she pushed it out of her mind.

Terry was still propped on his elbow. His pillow-tousled hair stuck up in a funny way, so she smoothed it down. He took her hand in his and kissed her fingers.

Michaela marveled at her good fortune. Her husband was always forgetting things, he was a bit untidy, but the joy and spontaneity he brought into her life counterbalanced her seriousness in a way that helped her keep her sanity.

In the morning, it would be fun to see his reaction to the night-time snowfall. He was like a big kid. He loved to hurtle down hills in a sled, strap on snowshoes and stomp around, or whip snowballs at telephone poles. After a fresh snowfall he would often go outside and shuffle around the back yard, creating a giant maze in the snow, complete with dead ends, false trails, and giant curlicues that spiraled into their centers. He would come inside, red-faced, and implore Michaela to go outside and navigate the maze. She didn't always have the patience or the time to complete the entire thing—sometimes she cheated and jumped out of a dead-end instead of back-tracking to its beginning and choosing another route. Usually, Terry would run the maze with her, doing the spirals all the way in and all the way out just for the fun of it.

He also loved to build snowmen. He had already built three this year. He always made likenesses of Michaela, himself, and Michaela's mother, Alicia. They got costumes and props, too, and this year Michaela's wore a white lab coat and an old stethoscope, Terry's double a cowboy hat, holster and gun, and Alicia's a gray wig, glasses, and a blender.

Terry was *her* reason for getting up in the morning.

She eased him onto his back.

He smiled up at her. "Does this mean you're ready for your healthy dose of Christmas cheer?"

5

Caught Up

JULIUS STOOD OUTSIDE IN THE SNOW, watching it fall silently from the darkness above. In the absence of snow, the night was black out here in the country. But when there was snow on the ground, clinging to the trees, and falling from the sky, the air was suffused with mysterious light. This was his second winter in America, and still he wondered at the light. He reasoned that it must be reflected, bouncing off the snow. But reflected from where? The moon and the stars were veiled, the motion detector light in the parking lot had powered down, yet he could see well into the distance.

His arrival in wintertime last year had been his first experience of snow and cold. It made him appreciate the beautiful tropical climate of Africa all the more. If Africa had a climate like this, and he had made his escape from the compound in winter, all those years ago, he would have died of exposure within hours. He nearly *did* die, not from exposure to cold, but of dehydration. For days, he had stumbled aimlessly, with no idea where he was going, until he finally crawled out of the bush onto the Gulu-Kitgum road at dusk.

He had been surprised to find himself surrounded by people, mostly children and their mothers, stooped beneath heavy packs or straining behind rough-wheeled carts. The flow of foot traffic was one-way, and the red earth of the road was barely discernible beneath the feet of the travelers. As the saying went, there were so many people that if you tossed a grain of sand into the air over their heads, it would not be able to find its way to the ground.

He was exhausted, but few of the travelers did more than glance at him, because, in truth, he looked no worse than they.

He approached a woman balancing a jug on her head and pulled at her sleeve. "Please, can you help me? Have you any water to spare?"

The woman quickened her pace. "I have nothing to spare, child."

"But I have just come from the bush."

The woman turned her eyes toward Julius. "From the bush?"

"Yes."

"All alone?"

"Yes."

The woman slowed, narrowing her eyes. She called to someone in front of her. "Nicholas!" A man a few paces ahead, pulling a two-wheeled cart behind him, turned around at the sound of his name. "This boy says he has just come from the bush," the woman said.

People within earshot turned to look or drew up near the woman and Julius. Two children, one about five years old and the other about seven, ran up and looked at Julius shyly from behind the woman.

Nicholas leaned his cart against his hip and addressed Julius. "When?"

"Just now," said Julius. His throat was so dry it felt caked shut and his voice sounded harsh in his throat.

The woman spoke. "He was asking for water. I did not believe him when he said he had been in the bush. I thought he was just begging."

The little group soon became a big one as curious onlookers stopped to see what was going on. The dust of the red, hard-packed earth stirred around their ankles.

Nicholas reached into his cart and pulled out a bottle of water.

Julius took it and gulped half the bottle. He peeked at Nicholas, who gestured for him to continue. Julius drank more. Then he whispered, "Food?" He swayed on his feet.

The woman took the water jug from her head and set it down. Nicholas picked up Julius and carried him to the side of the road away from the foot traffic. The two children followed their mother.

Nicholas had a box of crackers and some dried fruit. He gave some to Julius, who ate them eagerly. "What is your name?"

"Julius Abayomi."

"What village are you from?"

"I am from no village. I am a soldier in the army of the great Joseph Kony."

Nicholas and the woman looked sharply at each other. The woman drew her children closer.

"What are you doing here?" Nicholas said.

"I escaped."

"Then you are no longer a soldier of the LRA. If you have escaped, don't you know what Kony's men will do to you if they catch you?"

Julius nodded. Back in his compound, two boys tried to run away. Both had been caught. In order to demonstrate the consequences of trying to escape, the commanders had cut off the lips and ears of one boy, and hacked off the fingers of the other boy.

Nicholas spoke again. "How old were you when the men of the LRA came to take you away from your village?"

"I was never taken away. I lived with my mother until it was time for me to go to the training place and learn to fight."

Nicholas looked at the woman. "He was born in captivity." Then he spoke to Julius again. "How did you escape?"

Julius told them about loosening the board in the barracks and stealing the wire cutters. Frightened and unsure, he omitted the part about Jonathan and the other boys.

The woman spoke up. "We should take him to the sisters." In response to her husband's nod, the woman said, "Julius, my name is Imena Abuja. This is my husband Nicholas. Do not be afraid. We are going to take you with us to Gulu."

They returned to the road and joined the stream of foot traffic. Imena told Julius that her sons' names were Martin and Dennis.

When they crested a hill, Julius looked at the long line of travelers flowing down the slope and then up to the top of the next incline. Beyond that he could see more people moving along. Behind him, the road was packed with yet more people.

"Where are all these people going?" Julius asked.

Nicholas answered. "We are all from the villages around Gulu. But we cannot stay in our villages overnight."

"Why not?"

"It is not safe."

"Why is it not safe?"

"The soldiers of the Lord's Resistance Army come and attack us. They take our little boys away to camps to train in Mr. Kony's army. The women and girls they give as wives to their commanders." Nicholas paused. "And the rest they kill. All of Acholi is under the bloody booted heel of Joseph Kony."

When they arrived in Gulu town, Nicholas found a place for his family under a shop front overhang. He and Imena unpacked blankets from the cart and spread them out. They allowed Julius to lie down with them. In the bush, Julius had slept on the ground, fitfully, and only when total exhaustion overrode his fear. That night, wrapped in a blanket, with warm bodies all around him, he experienced more comfort than he had in days, and more companionship than he had experienced in months. Even though all around him was the noise of children coughing and adults talking, Julius had fallen deeply asleep within seconds.

The next morning, as the sun rose, Nicholas had shaken Julius gently. All around them, the families were stirring. Imena and the other children were already awake. Imena rolled up the blankets while the children ate millet cakes.

Julius groaned and rolled over. He wanted to sleep.

He heard Nicholas's voice, murmuring softly.

Then he heard a new voice, a woman. "It is a miracle he is still alive. Thank you for coming to get us." Julius felt the woman kneel down next to him and put her hand on his shoulder. "Julius. Come, child, wake up."

Julius opened his eyes and yawned deeply. He sat up. The woman addressing him was an Acholi woman, dressed in traditional garb but wearing a type of headdress he had never seen before. "It is time for Mr. and Mrs. Abuja to return to their village."

"Am I not going back with them?" Julius asked.

The woman shook her head. "No. You will come with us. We have a place for you to stay." Behind her was another woman, dressed the same way, but she was white.

Julius stood up.

Nicholas came forward and shook his hand. "God be with you, Julius."

Imena hugged him. "Good-bye, Julius. You will be safe now."

The woman with the headdress prompted Julius to thank the Abujas for their kindness. Then she took his hand and led him off the wooden stoop. He turned and waved over his shoulder. Imena's children waved shyly back at him.

On the street, people laden with packs were already vacating their sleeping places and taking the Gulu-Kitgum road back the way they had come.

"Where are they all going now?" Julius asked.

The black woman with the headdress answered. "They are returning to their villages."

"Where are we going?"

"We are going to the St. Peter Claver Rehabilitation Center, here in Gulu. I am Sister Mary Emmanuel, and this is Sister Mary Margaret."

"Will we have breakfast there?"

The sisters both laughed. "Indeed, yes," Sister Mary Emmanuel said. "We are blessed to have plenty of food at the moment."

The St. Peter Claver Rehabilitation Center was ten minutes away on foot. Everywhere they went, they met people leaving town, heading out into the countryside.

"Do the people walk into town every night to sleep?"

"Yes."

"And do they return every day to their villages?"

"Yes."

"Why do they not just stay in Gulu?"

"Because there are no houses for them. They have no place to keep their belongings. And because their farms are out in the country. They must return every day to work their farms and care for their households, but they cannot stay there at night. That is when the rebels come. They are trying to overthrow the government of Uganda. But surely you know this, Julius?"

"I know that I was training to fight the enemies of Joseph Kony."

Sister Mary Emmanuel and Sister Mary Margaret exchanged a glance.

The St. Peter Claver Rehabilitation Center was surrounded by a high stone wall and accessed by a solid metal gate. Inside the dirt compound were several low buildings with covered cement stoops. Between two of the buildings, seated on benches under a canopy, a large number of children were eating.

Many of them took note of Julius, but were too busy emptying their breakfast bowls to pay much attention. Sister Mary Emmanuel brought Julius to a man she called Mr. Otoye.

He grinned broadly at Julius. "Welcome, young man. You must be hungry." Julius tried not to stare, but Mr. Otoye had no fingers or thumbs, only scarred, misshapen stumps. He guided Julius to a stack of metal bowls and spoons, and put him in line after the other children who were waiting for their breakfast.

Two older boys scooped porridge from a large pot into the bowls as the children filed past. When Julius received his steaming bowl, he squeezed into the first bench he came to and ate the porridge so fast he didn't taste it. A wide-eyed boy next to him wordlessly handed Julius what remained in his bowl, and watched Julius finish it.

Then, for the first time in many days, Julius had thought of his mother. Tears coursed down his cheeks, but he had not been ashamed, for he had not been the only child crying into his breakfast.

A freezing gust of wind blew snow into Julius's face, jolting him out of his reverie. Beyond the parking lot, on the other side of an expanse of empty snow, a grove of trees swayed in the wind. The skeletal limbs of the bare maples and oaks mingled with the green and snowy firs, hollies, and giant yews. As winter progressed, the evergreen boughs, weighed down with snow and ice, drooped toward the ground, the lowermost branches brushing the blanket of needles and leaf mold, becoming slowly entombed in the ever-growing drifts of snow.

Jacob Otoye and the sisters at St. Peter's had saved Julius's life. He had promised to repay them someday. In fact, if all went according to plan, he would not only be able to repay his benefactors, he would be able to repay his enemies.

His handheld tablet computer chimed gently. Julius pulled it from his pocket and looked at the screen. A text message read, PROBLEM. He allowed himself a wry smile. Being an expert in computers had paved the way for his presence here, but it made his co-workers lazy. Still, it was pleasant to be highly regarded.

He pressed his key card to the security panel next to the door. When it clicked, he pulled the door open and went inside. A verse of scripture came to him, one he had learned from the sisters at St. Peter's: *pray that your flight not take place in winter.*

6

Wounds

ALICIA COLLINS STOOD AT THE STOVETOP in Michaela's kitchen, making her traditional Christmas Eve four-burner breakfast and waiting for her daughter to wake up. A radio announcer intoned, "News from the Middle East: a border skirmish in the Golan Heights."

"That's news?" Alicia said to the radio. She flipped a piece of French toast and pulled her tablet computer closer to her on the countertop and read the headlines.

"Yet another Illinois governor frog-marched to the police station on corruption charges." She snorted. "No surprise there." She tapped the headline and read the story.

Alicia loved her tablet computer. If she missed her favorite talk radio programs, she could download them from the websites and listen to them while she was driving, gardening, sewing, or on the rare occasions when she cleaned house. Her car had a device dock so audio could be piped into the speakers. Several years ago she had transferred all her CDs to her computer, then uploaded them to an online server. She ran a paperless house, too—she scanned all her important papers and kept them on her computer in an electronic filing cabinet app, all backed up online.

Alicia smiled at how a tech savvy old woman like herself could have produced a daughter who was a highly skilled veterinarian, but could barely operate her cell phone. Michaela still had a flip phone, for goodness' sake. It was so obsolete it couldn't even download apps.

Alicia moved the French toast to a plate, dipped another piece of bread into the egg mixture and slapped it onto the sizzling griddle. She turned to see Michaela in the doorway, in pajamas and socks, smiling sleepily.

"Merry Christmas, sweetie," Alicia said.

"Morning, Mom." Michaela padded into the kitchen and poured herself a cup of coffee.

The French toast was done. Alicia removed it from the pan and transferred it to a waiting plate in the warming oven. She put the spatula in the sink. "French toast?"

"Absolutely." Michaela sat down at the kitchen table. She rubbed her eyes and yawned. "When did you get here?"

"About an hour ago. Terry said you got in late last night."

"About midnight," she replied.

Alicia set the butter and maple syrup on the table. "Let me guess. Gastric dilatation volvulus?"

Michaela smiled. "Nope."

Alicia had talked to her daughter about many of her cases and had even helped out at the animal hospital during emergencies, when Michaela was just starting the practice. "Urethral obstruction?"

"Nope."

"Not a hit by car?" She set a pan of hash browns on the table.

"I don't think so."

"You don't *think* so? Isn't that usually pretty obvious?"

"Usually, but that's not the whole story," Michaela said.

Alicia divided up the French toast onto two plates, retrieved bacon from the oven, and brought a bowl of fruit salad to the table. She poured hot tea into mugs and transferred fried tomatoes from a frying pan to the plates.

Michaela whistled. "You've been busy this morning. Did I sleep that late?" The clock on the microwave read 9:30 am.

"Broken leg?" Alicia said.

"Good guess," Michaela said. "And that *was* one of the patient's presenting conditions. But there's more."

"I give up."

"Gunshot wounds."

Now Alicia whistled. "You don't see that every day. Dog or cat?"

"Dog. And believe it or not, she's fine."

"That's good." Alicia let Tripod in and straightened the doormat. She turned off the radio and sat down at the table. "Shall we say grace?"

"If you insist," Michaela said.

Alicia looked sideways at her and pursed her lips. "In the name of the Father, and of the Son, and of the Holy Spirit," she said.

"Amen," they said together, then: "Bless us, O Lord, and these thy gifts, which we are about to receive from Thy bounty, through Christ our Lord. Amen. And may the souls of the faithful departed, through the mercy of God, rest in peace. Amen."

Alicia crossed herself at the end of the prayer, but noticed that Michaela did not. "You okay, sweetheart?" Alicia ventured.

Her daughter nodded.

Michaela had been in a funk lately. Alicia hoped she'd cheer up by tonight.

When they finished eating, Michaela helped Alicia clear and wash the dishes. They were both standing at the window, looking outside at the back yard. Suddenly Michaela stiffened. "For crying out loud," she muttered. She shook dishwater from her hands and grabbed a towel.

"What is it?" Alicia asked.

Michaela shook her head and gestured vaguely toward the window.

Alicia looked out and barely restrained a groan; Terry had built a new snowman and had dressed it in a black Roman collar and cape. "Michaela—" she began, hurriedly drying her hands.

"Don't even start, Mom," Michaela said on her way out of the kitchen.

A moment later, Alicia heard the shower running.

The radio announcer returned to the story about violence at the fence that bordered Israel's territory on the Heights. She shook her head and clucked. Alicia often caught herself despairing over the situation in the Middle East because resolution seemed so impossible. But then she had to remind herself that Northern Ireland had been the same way. Her husband Sean had grown up there, in Belfast, right in the thick of the Troubles. He believed it was his duty as a Catholic to hate Protestants. The Protestants played their part and dutifully hated him back. Alicia had never been able to understand this intractable bitterness, this deep-seated resentment that seemed to be in their DNA. Then again, she had grown up in the farm country of central Illinois. The only controversies here were corn versus soybeans, and the Fighting Illini versus the Redbirds.

Alicia had met Sean, all those years ago, when they were both students at the University of Illinois. He was an angry young Irishman, an exchange student to America. But four years of bucolic stability had eventually softened him. Going to class, studying in the library, cheering at Illini games—no bombs, no bonfires, no British soldiers roaming the streets with their fatigues and semi-automatic weapons. Sean had given up his hatred, but Alicia often wondered what would have become of him if he had stayed in Belfast, like his brother J.J. and his family.

Michaela had no siblings, so Alicia and Sean brought her to Ireland every year to visit J.J. and Viola's kids. They had become close. One summer Michaela arrived in Belfast with everything she and her cousins needed to play veterinarian: white lab coats, toy stethoscopes, pretend medical supplies. Nina acted as her veterinary assistant, while Brendan and Joey brought her a parade of sick stuffed animals. Michaela was only ten at the time, but she had her whole life planned out, including the details of her own animal hospital. Alicia was proud of her daughter. She was well on the way to fulfilling every one of her childhood dreams. But the past still haunted her.

Michaela reappeared, wearing her coat.

"You're going back to the hospital?" Alicia asked.

"I have to check on that dog. And David has a surgical patient going home." Michaela stood in front of the kitchen window, zipping her coat.

Alicia nodded. Then, carefully, bracing herself for her daughter's response, she asked, "Are you and Terry coming to Midnight Mass tonight?"

But Michaela hadn't heard. "Why the hell did he do that?" she demanded, looking toward the snowmen in the backyard. "Is he trying to bait me?"

"You know the answer to that question. Terry's about as spiteful as a Golden Retriever puppy."

"And he has about as much tact."

Alicia spread her hands. "You knew that long before you married him."

Tripod looked up at them anxiously as he paced around the kitchen between Michaela and Alicia.

Alicia's voice was measured and quiet. "When are you going to let it go, Michaela?"

Michaela's face was flushed and her eyes were hard as flint. "Someone in this family has to hold onto the truth and hold Brendan accountable," she said.

"If you insist," Alicia said with pointed emphasis. "But I doubt Terry meant to goad you with a snowman effigy to your estranged cousin."

The unintended humor of this remark must have taken Michaela by surprise, because she allowed herself a half smile in spite of her palpable resolve to stay angry.

Alicia sighed, relieved that the tension had been broken. She watched Michaela pull on her boots and grab her keys to leave. As the door closed behind her, she prayed for the same kind of heart-changing Divine Intervention for her daughter that God had seen fit to bestow on her husband. In Northern Ireland, the Troubles were over. But in her own family, the Troubles continued.

* * *

On the way to the animal hospital, Michaela felt her anger simmering. Everywhere she went, she was oppressed by reminders of Brendan.

She missed Ireland and those summers in Belfast. Her parents always arranged side trips to the South so that she and her cousins could experience Ireland without the threat of bombs and fires, without British soldiers in green camouflage and checkpoints and those parades that always turned into giant street fights or worse. But she never told her parents that she actually preferred the North because, as a child and especially as a teenager, she thought it was more exciting.

Still, years ago she had vowed never to return to Ireland, for the express purpose of never setting eyes on her cousin again.

Then, after fornicating his way across Europe for two years, Brendan had apparently repented of it all and entered the seminary in Peoria. Of all the places he could have come to do his holy man of the desert routine, he had chosen central Illinois. His dear old Aunt Alicia had welcomed him back like a prodigal son. Michaela had never been able to understand that.

Michaela pulled over and got out of her truck. The straight country road was devoid of traffic, the air was cold and bracing, and the morning winter sun low and bright in the sky.

A vast, flat expanse of snow stretched from horizon to horizon. A few trees stood majestically in the distance. They looked as if they were made of glass. It was stunning. Beautiful. A few feet away was the pasture fence, transformed into a glistening work of art by ice and snow clinging to every wire. Brown tufts of grass, also swathed in snow, broke through the surface. Black-faced sheep, their fleece sparkling, milled about the fence. They looked at her and bleated plaintively.

The open landscape was one of the things Michaela loved about central Illinois. Watching weather systems rise and rumble overhead. Being able to see, in the distance, an entire freight train from engine to caboose. Catching every earthy smell on the wind that raced across the cropland.

Above her, the sky was blue and perfect, unmarred by clouds. Two hawks rode high in the air, one turning in quick, tight counterclockwise circles, the other in large, lazy clockwise loops.

By the time Michaela pulled into the animal hospital's driveway, she was in better humor and had made up her mind not to mention the snowman to Terry. It was Brendan she was really angry at, and she decided it wouldn't be worth it to start a fight with Terry over something he obviously meant as a joke.

The clock on her dashboard said 11:15. The animal hospital was officially closed, but she had arranged to send David Brightman's knee surgery home at one o'clock. There would be ample time to check on Rosie.

Terry was working his way across the parking lot with the snowplow mounted to the front of his jeep. He killed the engine and got out.

"How's she doing?" Michaela asked, following Terry inside to the treatment area.

"See for yourself."

Rosie stood in her cage, wagging her tail. The swelling and edema around the right eye had subsided and her mouth lolled open in that happy dog grin.

Michaela opened the cage and stroked the dog's head. Rosie responded by licking her hand. "Terry, can you grab a leash? I want to change her bandages." Michaela stopped the IV fluids, then removed the tape securing the fluid line to the dog's foreleg. She removed the needle from the injection port and capped it. Finally, she flushed the catheter with heparinized saline to prevent clotting.

Terry returned with a hospital leash and looped it over Rosie's head. "Come on, girl."

"She's maneuvering pretty well with that bandage on her leg," Michaela observed.

"And you thought you weren't doing any damn good," said Terry, with a laugh.

"I didn't do anything, Terry." Michaela knelt down next to Rosie and inspected her bandages. They were all clean and intact. She fished a bandage scissors out of her lab coat pocket, inserted the blunt lower blade carefully under the taped edge of the chest bandage, just behind the dog's shoulder blade, and expertly split the bandage from front to back. She peeled it away carefully, then removed the no-stick gauze pads from the site of each gunshot wound. Last night, the wounds had been fresh and bleeding, but now the bleeding had completely stopped.

"That's unbelievable," Michaela said.

She removed the padded wrap from the dog's broken left rear leg.

"Did you do surgery on her last night?" Terry asked.

"No. Just standard wound care and stabilization. That's all."

The bruising of the left rear leg was unchanged, but the swelling had gone down. Gently, Michaela palpated the leg from hip to hock. Rosie didn't object, but stood rigid. Everything seemed to be fine.

More than fine. Rosie's condition was remarkably improved, much more than expected.

Terry held Rosie in place while Michaela replaced the chest wrap and the leg bandage. When he tugged gently on the leash, Rosie followed him obediently across the treatment room. Michaela walked behind them, observing Rosie's gait. The dog was hampered by the bulky bandage, but appeared to be bearing some weight on the broken leg.

Terry opened the back door of the hospital and led Rosie into a covered outdoor exercise area. The dog immediately squatted on one leg to urinate, then walked a few paces to relieve her bowels. Everything appeared normal.

Michaela knelt down and examined Rosie's facial injuries. The white of the right eye was severely bloodshot, the cornea slightly clouded, and the eyelids swollen—but, incredibly, she was able to blink and move her eye normally.

She had no idea what to make of this. "It's getting cold," she said, standing up. "Let's go back in." Michaela had nearly reached the back door when she realized Terry wasn't following her. She looked back.

He tugged gently on the leash and frowned.

"What's going on?" she said, returning to his side.

Rosie was frozen in place, and her eyes were blank. From many years of close association with dogs, Michaela knew that their eyes could be expressive, with an emotional repertoire as varied as that of humans. Joy. Loving trust. Mischief. Playfulness. Nervousness. Terror. Abject hatred. But Rosie's eyes were expressionless as she stared straight ahead, unseeing, unblinking, like a machine that had been switched off.

Michaela shuddered. With a jolt, she saw that something else was wrong. "Terry, she's not breathing."

"What?"

"Watch." Rosie's mouth was open, as if she were panting, but her ribcage was motionless.

Terry swallowed. "What the hell…" he mouthed.

Like a machine being switched on again, Rosie blinked, shook her head, and began to pant softly. She turned to look at Michaela and Terry. The three figures stood immobile in the cold, their breath rising like plumes of white fog.

7

Resurrection

WHATEVER HAD AFFLICTED ROSIE, she snapped out of it. She blinked and turned her head, refocused her eyes, and gave a quick wag of her tail. Michaela looked at Terry. "She must have had a partial seizure," she guessed. The blow to the head, heavy enough to break bones in the face, must have caused some brain trauma.

They went back inside and took a complete set of X-rays. Last night Rosie had been drowning in her own blood, yet this morning she was fine. It didn't make any sense.

Just as they finished taking the X-rays—at one o'clock sharp—David Brightman's knee surgery client arrived to pick up his dog. Michaela went over the aftercare, set up the recheck appointments, and collected the payment.

Terry came in. "I put her in one of the big runs, gave her some food and water." He picked up Rosie's chart and flipped it open, then reached over her shoulder to the computer keyboard and typed in the URL for a directory assistance website.

He typed "Adriana Smith" and "Champaign, IL" into the search fields.

No entries found.

Terry clicked to a map website. He typed the address into the search window—78 South Grant Street, Champaign, IL—and clicked enter.

No such address.

Michaela and Terry looked at each other. "Are you thinking what I'm thinking?" he asked.

She nodded. "We've been had." This wouldn't be the first time someone had given false identifying information to avoid paying the vet bill.

Except these owners had paid up front, in cash.

"Too bad we can't get hold of them," Terry grumbled.

Michaela agreed. "I think *I'd* want to know that my dog was still alive." She drummed her fingers on the desk.

"Let's look at the X-rays," Terry said. He opened the program and called up the dog's films on the monitor.

One by one, she and Terry compared the films from the previous night to the ones they had just taken. The skull X-rays showed that the maxillary and facial bone fractures were unchanged. As expected, the severely fractured left rear leg was still the same. One bullet in the abdomen and four bullets in the chest, as before, but, incredibly, there was no sign of air or fluid in the chest. How could this be?

Terry pointed to a small metallic density above the shoulder blades. "Is that a microchip?"

Of course. Michaela had forgotten about that. She grabbed a microchip scanner off the desk. The microchip registration would lead them straight to the real owner. It hadn't occurred to Michaela until that moment, but maybe the dog didn't belong to Adriana Smith at all.

With scanner in hand, Michaela pushed open the door of the boarding kennel. Immediately, she sensed something was wrong. Usually, anytime anyone entered the boarding area, the dogs would start barking. Today, Michaela and Terry were greeted by complete silence.

From where they stood, they could see into several dog runs. Each was occupied by one dog, crouched in the far corner, head low and ears back, food and water bowls full, the contents untouched.

Then they came to Rosie. She stood in the middle of the run, looking at nothing.

Michaela opened the door of the run, and once again Rosie snapped to consciousness, looking up at them and wagging her tail. Michaela turned on the microchip scanner, and ran it over the dog's shoulders. The scanner beeped and recorded a number: SGG-068-19H5-7465-87Y.

She squatted down next to Rosie and rubbed her ears. Rosie responded by turning to lick her hand. "She seems fine now." She took Rosie's head in both hands and looked into her eyes. Instead of black pools of nothingness, like before, they were now warm and expressive, full of life, expecting nothing but good things. "What do you think, girl? Should we run your number and find your people?" Rosie opened her mouth and panted into Michaela's face.

Michaela stood up. "Let's bring her with us," she said, looping the hospital leash around Rosie's neck. "I want to watch her and see if she has any more episodes."

"Plus she's creeping out the other dogs," Terry said wryly.

She turned and looked at him, amused. "What do you mean 'creeping them out?' "

Terry shrugged.

Michaela scoffed. "Her strange mentation is due to brain trauma."

"If you say so."

They returned to the treatment area with Rosie and coaxed her to lie down on a blanket.

The microchip number gave no indication of which company the chip belonged to, so they would have to go down the list until they found the one the owners had used to register Rosie. At the computer workstation, Michaela typed in "pet microchip companies."

One result looked promising: a master look-up site that asked for the number and spat out the company the chip was enrolled with. After entering Rosie's number, Michaela got no match. However, the site did provide a long list of possible companies and their phone numbers, including a few companies she knew of—the ones whose microchips most veterinary hospitals carried and recommended to their clients.

Michaela contacted all the companies on the list, but none found a match for Rosie's number.

A dead end. She looked at Rosie. She was lying down, head on her paws, apparently sleeping. Terry was at one of the other computer work stations, playing a game of solitaire.

"The microchip is a bust," Michaela declared.

Terry snorted.

"This dog is definitely not dead," Michaela said, musing aloud. "And she's definitely not dying. Those two women wanted me to euthanize and cremate her, and return the ashes to them."

"But there's no way to reach them to tell them what happened," Terry finished.

"I think we'll just have to hold onto her and see if they contact us," Michaela concluded. She stared at the computer monitor as the screen saver cycled through a montage of cat and dog images.

"Michaela," Terry said. His voice was strained. "You might want to rethink that idea."

She looked at him, then followed his concerned gaze.

Rosie was on the floor as before, on her chest, but her head was up. She looked like a statue, staring into an invisible distance, as before. Her head tremored slightly—she was definitely neurological.

Then, with each exhalation, a horrible sound issued from her throat, similar to the dysphoric vocalization of a surgical patient waking up from anesthesia. To the untrained ear, it sounded like an animal in agony. Michaela routinely tranquilized any dog making this sound during its recovery, because clients at the animal hospital found it so disturbing.

The sound Rosie made was even worse. It was a howl, a cry, and a groan, the rattling breath of a creature in the throes of death. The dog was completely unaware of its surroundings, eyes blank, jaw slightly dropped, head quivering. Michaela had never seen anything like this. The trauma to Rosie's brain must have been severe.

Michaela leapt from her chair and got the euthanasia solution from the lock box. She filled a ten-cc syringe, enough to humanely dispatch a dog twice Rosie's size. She crouched down next to Rosie and had the needle poised above her foreleg, ready to insert it into the catheter's injection port.

"Wait," Terry blurted. "I'll be right back."

Michaela turned and saw him run into the surgery suite. Rosie's whole body was shivering now, a terrifying wail escaping from her throat. Terry hurried back wheeling the ECG machine on its cart.

"What are you doing?" Michaela's throat contracted and tears stung her eyes.

Terry put a hand on her shoulder. "Give me a sec." He trotted around the corner to the office, then reappeared a moment later with the camcorder. "We should document everything this time," he explained.

Michaela immediately agreed. She had acted rashly last night, and she was about to repeat her mistake in her haste to put Rosie out of her misery for the second time.

Terry pressed record on the camcorder and set it on a small step stool.

Michaela's skin crawled and her face was hot, her heart pounding in her ears. She brushed away a tear and flushed the IV catheter with heparinized saline. Meanwhile, Terry quickly connected the ECG leads to Rosie and turned the machine on. The ECG beeped softly with each heartbeat and the machine spat out a ribbon of paper containing a normal ECG tracing.

Her hands shook, but Michaela managed to insert the needle cleanly into the catheter's injection port. She emptied the syringe, and as the euthanasia solution flowed into Rosie's vein, the vocalizing stopped. Rosie lowered her head. A second later she stopped breathing. Her pupils were wide open.

The ECG flat-lined. Michaela touched a button and silenced the monotone whine of the machine. ECG printout tape continued to whir out of the machine and pile up on the floor.

Terry and Michaela stared at the dog. She was still, except for tiny muscle tremors along her flank and rear legs. After a few seconds even those stopped, and she was motionless.

Terry sighed heavily.

"Time of death..." Michaela checked her watch. "1:27 pm."

They sat together on the floor, Michaela cross-legged, with Rosie's file next to her. She recorded the amount of euthanasia solution used and the time of death. She checked the spool of ECG printout paper; it was almost full.

"Are you okay?" Terry said.

She leaned into him, and he put his arm around her shoulder. "Yeah. Thanks."

He nodded and they resumed their vigil. Slowly, Michaela's heart rate returned to normal.

Terry glanced at her. "Are you going with us to Midnight Mass tonight?" he asked, with a studied effort to keep his voice neutral.

Michaela's heart rate spiked again, but for a completely different reason. "Why is everyone hounding me about going to Midnight Mass?" she said hotly.

"Okay, okay," Terry said. "Sorry I mentioned it. I just don't think it should be too hard for you to pull yourself together and play nice once or twice a year."

Michaela stood up and took several steps away.

After a moment, Terry said, "I'll go finish plowing."

"Good idea," Michaela said tersely.

He climbed to his feet, found his coat, hat and gloves, and headed outside.

Rosie hadn't moved. The pile of ECG printout was voluminous, so Michaela found the end and rolled it up neatly. She went to the office and brought back a comfortable office chair. After what had happened last night, she was determined to keep Rosie directly in sight.

What in the world had happened to this dog? Her injuries seemed random and incongruous: hit in the head and rear leg broken, with no outward indications of the most common cause of such head-to-toe damage—vehicular trauma. And the gunshot wounds. Nothing added up. Had Adriana Smith and her friend done this to their own dog? If so, why? And if their intention was to kill, why didn't they just finish the job themselves, instead of bringing Rosie to the animal hospital expecting Michaela to do their dirty work?

She shook her head. This was crazy. A bad phone number and address didn't equate to animal abusers on the run. People move, they switch mobile phone providers, they write things down incorrectly when they're under stress.

But something else wasn't making sense. They demanded proof of clinical death. Did their insistence have anything to do with the fact that Rosie had been shot in the chest before and survived? And they had been cagey, frequently exchanging significant, nervous looks. What were they afraid of?

Those eyes. That gut-wrenching sound. Michaela's instinctive reaction had been exactly the same as Adriana Smith's—put this dog down. Now. But was it because Rosie was suffering? Or was it because Rosie terrified them?

Looking at Rosie lying on the floor, a childhood memory came back to Michaela. She and her parents had gone with some other tourists on a fishing expedition in New England. They had caught a small shark, hauled it aboard, left its shimmering form gasping on the deck of the boat and watched it die from a safe distance. The skipper of the boat had instructed that under no circumstances was anyone to touch the creature, even if it appeared to be dead. She remembered the gruff fisherman's exact words: "They can come back to life like cartoon characters. You'll find yourself up to the elbow in its mouth."

The shark's open jaws bristled with deadly looking teeth, and its gills gaped rhythmically as it tried to breath. But Michaela remembered those eyes most of all: they were lidless, devoid of expression, black and gleaming as obsidian. Staring into that creature's eyes, she gazed upon nothing but emptiness. She felt that if she did not shake herself free, those eyes would draw her down into a deep place from which there was no escape.

She looked at Rosie's dead eyes and shuddered. Her condition was unchanged. Michaela pressed the audio button on the machine and listened for a moment to the soft, monotone trill of the flat-line.

She thought back to the previous night. The two women had brought Rosie in at about seven o'clock, and she estimated that she had completed the euthanasia by half past. She and Terry had X-rayed the dog, cleaned up, and prepared the body in about an hour.

Terry came in, snowy and red-faced.

"What time did you leave last night?" she asked him.

"8:30 or so."

Michaela began thinking aloud: "Then I went into the office to write up the chart." Thirty minutes later she heard the banging of the walk-in cooler door and then discovered the dog. About an hour and a half from time of death to...what? Recovery from unintended anesthesia? Reanimation?

The owners—or whoever they were—had behaved suspiciously. They were deathly afraid that putting Rosie to sleep would not work.

After what she had seen last night, and the way the dog's life-threatening injuries had resolved, Michaela had her doubts, too.

But there Rosie lay, utterly still. She checked her watch. It was 2:58 pm. The ECG machine was still churning out a strip of paper with a single unbroken line straight down the middle. She sighed. This was ridiculous—Rosie had been lying there dead for an hour and a half. She was letting her imagination run away from her. It was Christmas Eve and they had things to do.

She looked at Terry. "I'm sorry I snapped at you just now."

"It's okay." He cleared his throat. "So are you coming tonight?"

"I haven't decided yet," she replied. She nodded toward Rosie. "Could I trouble you for a body bag?"

He grinned. "Coming right up. Want fries with that?"

As if on cue, the machine beeped.

"Please tell me that's an equipment malfunction," Terry said.

Michaela crouched down next to the dog, staring at the monitor. Nothing but a flat, green line. She grabbed the printout and found what the machine had recorded at the time of the beep: a single, perfectly formed heartbeat.

Terry whistled. "This is way too long for residual electrical impulses."

The machine beeped again, and this time Michaela saw the heartbeat on the monitor. Another normal P wave, followed by a QRS complex.

Another beep.

Then another.

"No way," Terry breathed.

The beeps kept coming, and soon the ECG recorded a heart rate of 102 beats per minute.

She and Terry jumped as Rosie took a deep, shuddering breath in, followed by a loud exhalation. A moment later, she opened her eyes, licked her lips, and tried to raise her head. Springing into clinical mode, Michaela lifted the dog's lip: the mucous membranes were pink and the capillary refill time was two seconds. She put her stethoscope in her ears and listened to the dog's heart and lungs: clear as a bell.

The ECG machine spat out the final inches of printout as its paper spool ran empty. Michaela turned off the machine and unhooked the ECG leads. Rosie righted herself to a sternal position, and briefly wagged her tail. Her eyes were alert and responsive.

Michaela whispered to Terry, "I guess we won't need that body bag after all."

* * *

Shortly after three o'clock, Michaela and Terry left the animal hospital, she in her pick-up truck, he in his Jeep. As they pulled out of the parking lot onto the main road, a black Range Rover, parked outside a business across the street, pulled out after them.

It kept its distance and followed them all the way home.

8

A Dangerous Character

Brendan pulled the white alb over his head and shrugged into the sleeves. Facing the mirror, away from the bustle in the sacristy, he whispered the first vesting prayer. "Purify me, O Lord, from all stain, and cleanse my heart."

Behind him, leaning on the counter with the lectionary open in front of her, the lector assigned to the mass was doing a last minute review of the readings. Altar servers came and went, fetching chalice and paten, the cruets, or the finger towels—all the little housekeeping details of preparing for Mass. Through the sacristy door drifted the voices of the choir, working their way through a selection of Christmas Eve preludes.

He took up the cincture and wrapped it around his waist. The old prayer ran through his mind. *Gird me, O Lord, with the cincture of purity, and quench in my heart the fire of concupiscence, that the virtue of continence and chastity may remain in me.*

Then he kissed the hem of the stole, slipped it over his head and settled it onto the back of his neck.

He opened the cabinet where the outer vestments hung. Tonight the priests and deacons would be wearing a set of chasubles reserved for special feast days, white with glittery gold ornament and edging. Brendan's chasuble bore a beautiful embroidered frontispiece picturing the Nativity of the Lord. He draped it over his head and adjusted it over his arms. *O Lord, who said, 'My yoke is easy and my burden light,' grant that I may carry it so as to obtain thy grace.* "Amen," he whispered.

The last item, although not officially part of the vesture, was the cordless microphone. Brendan snaked the microphone cable up and out of the chasuble's neck hole and clipped the mic to the chasuble itself. There was no official vesting prayer for this, but Brendan muttered, "Lord, please let this blasted contraption work properly this evening."

He liked special seasonal feasts and their liturgies, these events that came around every year. They were like the major beats in a perpetual piece of music.

Advent. Christmas. Lent.

Holy Week. Easter. Advent.

These major seasons were interspersed with saints' days, Marian feasts, and special liturgical commemorations like Pentecost, Corpus Christi, All Saints' Day. The minor beats.

Within the minor beats, Sunday after Sunday after Sunday pulsed forward week by week, time moving forward in an infinite line, or around and around like a perfect, ever-repeating circle. Yet it wasn't really like either of these. It was more like a spiral, forever rotating in place and revisiting the same events in one dimension, yet constantly moving onward and upward so that it was different every time. And it seemed to be spinning faster every year. It always surprised him how quickly these seasons came around. Hadn't he just been here a moment ago, vesting for last year's Midnight Mass?

Brendan enjoyed this time right before Mass. He liked the murmuring and the bustling about, the easy camaraderie between ordained ministers and lay people young and old. He liked watching the senior altar servers read the riot act to the youngsters. *Don't scratch your face. Stop messing with the zipper on the alb. And don't spill anything!* It reminded him of his family's little kitchen growing up in Belfast. Too many people in too cramped a space, people stepping over one another to get pots, pans and plates. Scooching the dog out of the way to grab something out of a low cabinet.

It occurred to Brendan that if people would think of the Church that way—as a family—instead of as a business or an institution or a corporation, then perhaps the Church would be the subject of fewer misunderstandings. His experience as a priest had certainly demonstrated to him that the Church thought of itself as a family. His pastor and his bishop were his fathers, and he in turn was a father to his parishioners. He supposed some men and women bristled and chafed against that particular image of authority, but Brendan found comfort in it.

Families could be messy, though. He looked through the sacristy door at the rapidly filling church, wondering if his cousin Michaela were out there. He'd spoken to his aunt, Alicia, and the plan was for her, Terry, and Michaela to come to Mass tonight.

"Ready, Father?" said a voice behind him. It was Father Angelo, the pastor.

"I am," said Brendan.

The lector and the deacons had already left the sacristy. Brendan followed Father Angelo out to the vestibule of the church, where the procession was lining up. Seven altar servers, in their white robes, led the way, cross bearer in front, two candle bearers, and four torch bearers. Then the lector, the two deacons, each swinging a smoking censor, and then Brendan, followed by the pastor.

Brendan loved processions—the incense, the bells, everything.

Father Angelo nudged Brendan and grinned. "I think your fans will be happy to hear you tonight."

"They get to hear my beautiful singing voice anyway." Brendan would be chanting the Gospel, which had required quite a lot of practice. He knew he wasn't a great singer, but he was at least competent enough to chant some things passably. He was also assigned to preach tonight.

"It's that brogue they really want to hear," said the pastor.

Brendan laughed. It was true. His thick, Northern Ireland accent was unusual to his central Illinois parishioners. Most people had only heard the "standard" Irish brogue of the South—"leprechaun Irish," Brendan called it. His heavier accent fascinated them. He joked that he could get up to the pulpit and read the newspaper, and people would sit in rapt attention.

But he was nervous, as he always was on the rare occasions when Alicia persuaded her daughter to attend one of his masses. He prayed for a miracle of forgiveness and reconciliation.

He and Michaela had been close, many years ago. Every summer she came to visit, and they were inseparable. Brendan's little brother Joey was often sick, but all the kids worked around that and managed to have a lot of fun indoors and out.

Poor Joey. When his doctors finally arrived at a diagnosis of leukemia, Brendan and his sister Nina were too young to understand just how dire the situation was. Brendan remembered those months as a chaotic mixture of doctor visits, Joey's prolonged absences from school, his mother often in tears, and his father's robust form diminishing before his eyes.

Despite every treatment, Joey only got sicker. One day his mother went in to wake him for breakfast and discovered that he had passed away during the night. He was only eight years old. Brendan was thirteen. Sean, Alicia and Michaela cut short a side trip to Galway and returned to Belfast.

After the funeral, Brendan had withdrawn upstairs. He sat in the window seat of the room he had shared with Joey, feeling guilty for all the times he had longed for a room of his own. *You've got your wish now,* he thought bitterly. He heard a soft knock on the door and looked up.

It was Michaela. "There you are," she said, coming in to sit next to him. Her nose was red and her eyes were wet.

I will not cry in front of a girl, he vowed silently. But Michaela, even as a little girl, was naturally compassionate and empathetic. She had put her small hand into his, and that was all it took for Brendan to burst into tears.

In the church, the cantor announced the entrance hymn, the music started, and the Midnight Mass procession began. Once Brendan got up to the sanctuary and took his place, he scanned the congregation, looking for his aunt, for Terry, and for Michaela.

The church was so full that he wasn't able to locate them during the preliminary rites of the Mass or during the readings. As he went to the ambo to proclaim the Gospel, he still hadn't found them. They must have decided not to come. In spite of his desire to see them at Mass, he couldn't help relaxing a little when he realized they weren't there. He felt the tension drop away.

It occurred to Brendan that maybe some things would be easier if families thought of themselves as corporations. Official procedures for registering grievances, requesting transfers, disciplining poor performers. Terminating an association. Severing a connection.

The choir finished the *Alleluia* and the church echoed with the final chord of the pipe organ.

"The Lord be with you," Brendan intoned.

The congregation chanted back, "And with your spirit." They knew their part well.

"A reading from the Holy Gospel according to St. Luke." Brendan then traced a small cross on his forehead, over his lips, and over his heart, then on the page of the Gospel. He stepped back and took the smoking censor from the altar server. Holding it up by its gold chain, he raised the censor to eye level and swung it back and forth over the Gospel text. The fragrant smoke billowed around him and rose up to the ceiling. The words of the psalmist came to mind: *Like burning incense, Lord, let my prayer rise up to you.*

At the ambo, Brendan chanted the Gospel, Luke's account of the birth of Christ. He loved this particular chant melody. It was simple and beautiful. The organ accompaniment was moving, especially at the end when he came to the angels' hymn of praise, and the voice of the choir soared as they joined in the refrain: *Gloria in excelsis Deo et pax ad omnia.*

He concluded the proclamation by chanting, "The Gospel of the Lord."

The congregation sang the response: "Praise to you, Lord Jesus Christ."

Brendan lifted the Gospel book to his lips and kissed it. He replaced the book on the ambo and retrieved his notes from a little shelf beneath the book.

He checked his notes briefly, then looked up and scanned the rest of the congregation. Brendan convinced himself that he was glad for Michaela's absence. He was always both afraid to meet her eyes and afraid not to. Which was worse? To see those green eyes flash into his with an angry glare, or to observe their studied aversion and see instead the hard edge of her jaw and the new lines on her face?

He decided to go for it and deliver the "unsanitized" version of his homily, which included things he never mentioned in Michaela's presence.

"When I was a child growing up in Belfast," he began, "my parents gave me the Gospel of Jesus Christ. They were good and holy people, and they raised me to be a good Christian. But, as many of you may know, Belfast, Ireland in the seventies and eighties wasn't the easiest place to be a good Christian." Like a good public speaker, he tried to maintain eye contact, and saw expressions of interest on the faces gazing up at him. "We called it The Troubles. One side wanted Northern Ireland to be part of Great Britain, along with England, Scotland and Wales. The other side wanted Northern Ireland to join the rest of Ireland to the south. It was a political argument made much worse by a long history of religious intolerance. Catholics versus Protestants, with both sides abandoning the Gospel and, to put it bluntly, justifying violence and murder to get what they wanted."

That got their attention. "Those of you who know my story know why I'm telling you this. Despite my good upbringing, I became an angry youth looking for an excuse to lash out. In Northern Ireland at that time, boys like me usually ended up in one of the paramilitary organizations there. Catholics joined the IRA and Protestants joined the UDA."

Throughout his childhood, especially during Joey's battle with leukemia, Brendan's parents had forbidden him to get involved and had shielded him from the Troubles as best they could. But Brendan always thought of the weeks after Joey's funeral, after Sean and Alicia and Michaela had returned to the United States, as the time when he grew up into a terrible anger. In his immature teenage grief, he lashed out at everything but had no focus. He was ripe for recruitment.

One day in the fall school term, Brendan skipped school with two classmates and went to the peace line at Cupar Street, armed with gravel-filled beer bottles hidden in their school rucksacks.

The peace line was a row of abandoned houses that formed a barrier between the Protestants and the Catholics. The windows and doors were boarded up, the roofs collapsing, the walls covered in graffiti. The house they stood in front of sported a huge fist, outlined in black, filled in with the colors of the Irish Republic—orange, white and green. Next to it, in huge block letters, were the words BRITS OUT NOW.

The boys lowered their rucksacks to the ground, next to the smoldering remains of a street-rally bonfire. They dug out their bottles, counted to three and hurled the bottles over the rooftops into the Protestant neighborhood on the other side.

They listened with satisfaction to the sound of breaking glass as their "gravel bombs" smashed against the pavement. They hoped to see similar missiles sailing back over, ready for a good skirmish with some faceless Prods. They were so intent on their visions of a spectacular street fight that they didn't see the tobacconist catapult out of his store and charge at them. He smacked Brendan with the flat of his hand and screamed, "You goddamn hooligans! Get the hell out of here!"

Brendan's compatriot, a boy named Seamus, shouted right back at the man. "Leave off! Or are you a Prod spy?"

"Prod nothing, ye little bastard. I'm the one who has to make me living here, right under this bloody wall, and I don't need the likes of you coming around and starting up more trouble. Go back to where you belong and leave the stupid-arse stunts to the layabouts in the fuckin' IRA!"

The shopkeeper turned to the third boy, a redhead named Tommy Morgan. He snatched the last gravel bomb out of the boy's hand and threw it over the peace line himself.

As an adult, Brendan chuckled at the memory of the fuming shopkeeper stomping and cursing back to his shop, while Brendan and his friends stared in gape-mouthed shock.

They shuffled down the littered sidewalk, still peering hopefully over their shoulders for retaliatory missiles. That could have marked the end of their youthful foray into politics, but a young man, leaning on a brick wall, pushed himself upright and stood in their way.

Brendan and his friends masked their fear with adolescent bravado. The man wore tight black denim jeans, black punk boots, and a leather jacket heavy with thick belts and chrome buckles. His hair was shoulder-length and tousled, and he sported dark sunglasses even though the sky was threatening rain.

Casually, he lit a cigarette, then offered his pack to the boys. Brendan was the first to take one, then Seamus and finally, Tommy. The older man lit the boys' cigarettes one by one. He smirked a little but refrained from laughing as all three doubled over coughing. But they kept the cigarettes, inhaling cautiously every time their coughing subsided.

"You won't get the Brits out like that," the man finally said.

"Oh, yeah?" blurted Seamus. "Who the hell are you?"

"A layabout in the fuckin' IRA."

Bringing his mind back to the present, Brendan continued his homily. "By the time I was fifteen," he said, "I had become expert at living a double life. I was a model student and docile son by day, but in the middle of the night, I slipped out of the house unnoticed. I broke into homes and shops to steal supplies for the war or to set fires. I stole cars and drove them to IRA drop points, where other volunteers rigged them with explosives. Soon I was the one rigging the cars.

"I abandoned everything my parents taught me. The Gospel of Jesus Christ died in me. My violence and my sinfulness killed it."

Out in the congregation, he saw some people leaning forward in their pews, fascinated. "Brothers and sisters, you are looking at someone who was a lost cause. A violent, angry young man who had so anesthetized his conscience that nothing was taboo anymore. So what happened? How did I end up becoming a Christian again, first of all, and then becoming a priest, of all things?

"I hope I don't disappoint you too much when I tell you it was nothin' earth shattering, but it does explain why Christmastime is so dear to me. I'll spare you the details, but my career as an operative for the IRA ended badly. I left Ireland, traipsed across Europe, and ended up in Spain, in a little suburb near Madrid. I arrived a few days before Christmas and was wandering about looking for a room to rent. I happened upon a little procession: a man dressed up as St. Joseph and a woman dressed up as Mary. The woman was pregnant but they had somehow convinced her to sit up on a little donkey. They were just walking through the streets of this little town. No fanfare. No announcements. A small group of people following along.

"As they passed, people's faces would appear in windows, or they'd open their front doors and come out for a look. Their route happened to coincide with mine, so I was following along for a few blocks. Then they came to the parish church and stopped at a life-sized, mock-up stable out front. A real cow and a real sheep were tied up there, and there were a few lads dressed as shepherds hanging about. Mary and Joseph went in, tied up the donkey, and took their places in the scene.

"The parishioners who had come along started singing Christmas carols, and in the yuletide spirit a little old lady grabbed my arm and led me closer, stuffed a dog-eared little Christmas carol book into my hands.

"Turns out that little old lady had a top floor available in her house, which I rented for a while. She didn't speak English very well and I didn't speak Spanish very well, but she just took me under her wing. She had no idea what a dangerous character she was dealing with, but she fed me breakfast and supper, and expected me to pray the Rosary with her family every evening. She dragged me to Christmas Mass, and after that to Sunday Mass every week. My rebirth as a Christian was totally without fanfare. It went unnoticed by everyone around me, except perhaps the dear old parish priest. Can you imagine hearin' the confession of a former terrorist?"

Brendan paused to wait for this to sink in.

He checked his watch. He was often too garrulous in his homilies. This was an important one, though. Every year, he and his brother priests exchanged strategies about how to reach the "submarine Catholics," the ones who stayed out of radar range for months at a time but who surfaced twice a year, at Christmas and Easter. How to draw them back to weekly Mass and the Sacraments. You didn't want to give an insipid, feel-good homily, but fire and brimstone didn't go over too well, either.

"The birth of Jesus also went unnoticed by almost everyone except a few people who happened to be there—the shepherds and a few others who were paying attention."

Brendan pointed to the nativity display in front of the altar. "Look at the cradle in Bethlehem. The Gospel is not just a nice idea or a moral code. The Gospel is a Real Person. The Gospel has hands, and feet, and a heart beating with love for you and me." Then he turned and pointed to the Crucifix above the altar. "Look at the Crucifix. Look at his hands, his feet. His heart. Look at the lengths Our Lord has gone to.

"My dear brothers and sisters, I'm no expert in world religions, but I believe Christianity is unique. Other religions concern themselves with man's search for the divine and his search for religious experience. Christianity is just the opposite. Christianity is about God's search for man. The Gospel has a voice that calls out to us. It has feet that chase after us, hands that reach out for us. And this persistent Gospel managed to catch up with me."

Then, as Brendan paused, he saw them out of the corner of his eye—his aunt Alicia, Terry, and Michaela. His insides lurched and heat rushed to his face.

His aunt was watching him, a little smile on her face, warmth in her eyes, tears streaming down her cheeks. Miraculously, inexplicably, she had forgiven him. And Terry had nothing against Brendan, which spoke wonders for his character, because he'd heard the whole story from Michaela.

And there she was. His cousin. She looked stonily to the front. He had delivered the entire "unsanitized" homily, with no idea Michaela had been there. Brendan was astonished to feel his knees trembling, as if he were a newly ordained priest saying his first Mass.

The last words Michaela had ever spoken to him thundered in his head. *Are you happy now, Brendan? Are you?*

He took a deep breath and went on, hastening to the end. "The birth of Jesus, and his death and resurrection thirty-three years later, is a shout from the Heavens, a declaration of the insane, foolish love of God. He will do anything for you." Somehow he managed to avoid looking at Michaela again. "All you have to do is let Him love you. Let Him change your heart."

Hastily, he made the sign of the cross over the congregation. "May the baby Jesus be born anew in your hearts and in your homes this Christmas, and always."

Brendan crossed the sanctuary and returned to his chair. It took every ounce of self-restraint not to slump forward with his head in his hands, in utter despair. *You bloody fool,* he thought, recalling the words of his homily and throwing them back in his own face: *my career as an operative for the IRA ended badly.* He scoffed at himself inwardly. That's one way of putting it.

The pastor stood and led the congregation in the recitation of the Nicene Creed.

Brendan closed his eyes against what might have been.

After Mass he was standing in the vestibule shaking hands and exchanging Merry Christmases with the parishioners, and suddenly Aunt Alicia was at his elbow. He hugged and kissed her. "How are you, darlin'?"

She kissed him back. "Merry Christmas, Bren. You look more fatherly every time I see you."

"You mean I'm getting old?"

"No, just distinguished," she laughed.

He turned to Terry, who had just come over, "Did you hear that, now? Should I let her get away with that?"

"I think I see a touch of gray there." Terry gripped Brendan's hand and grinned. "Merry Christmas, Father. Way to preach it up there."

"Well..." Brendan fumbled for a response. "Merry Christmas to you," he finally said, lamely. Across the vestibule, Michaela, keeping her distance, looked the other way. He watched her face light up as she smiled and chatted with some people she knew. Perhaps they were clients of hers. She was one of the "dark" Irish: dark brown hair framing an impeccable, fair complexion. She had her father Sean's green eyes.

Michaela turned to greet another person, and Brendan was caught in her line of sight as her eyes inadvertently flickered toward his. Instantly, her smile disappeared and she looked away. He averted his own eyes and felt his heart begin to pound, as a wave of embarrassment crashed over him. Brendan couldn't believe he had just delivered that homily, knowing there was even the slightest possibility of Michaela being there. What was he thinking? A sudden upwelling of emotion surprised him, because he thought he had grown accustomed to Michaela's cool avoidance of him. This time, for no reason he could discern, it felt different.

This time, it felt like death—the death of all his hope. His throat tightened, and he dug the heel of his hand into his eye to stop the emergence of a tear. The seldom-sung fourth verse of a Christmas carol came to him: *sorrowing, sighing, bleeding, dying. Sealed in a stone cold tomb.*

9

Ashes

MICHAELA, TERRY, AND ALICIA spent Christmas Day like Americans everywhere: sleeping in, opening presents, and overeating. Michaela was grateful that Terry and her mother got along so well. There were no in-law problems between them.

The day after Christmas, though, was booked with routine office visits: vaccine appointments, a simple gastrointestinal case, a cat that needed stitches because the owner foolishly tried to cut off matted hair with scissors and had instead cut out a chunk of skin.

Michaela also received a visit from one of her favorite patients, a Belgian Malinois named Crush. He was a police order enforcement dog, which meant he chased bad guys. His handler, Hank Ullman, was an officer in the Champaign PD. He and his wife lived on the same block as Michaela and Terry.

Hank was off-duty, dressed in civilian clothes. "I think he's got an ear infection. He keeps shaking his head and I can see some black gunk in there."

Hank checked the strap on Crush's basket muzzle. Crush had been trained to treat anyone approaching him or his handler as a threat. However, Hank had trained the dog to accept Michaela's examination. The muzzle was only a precaution.

"*Staan*," Hank said. He used the Dutch word for "stand" because, like most police dogs, Crush was trained overseas. American police departments found it easier to teach the human officers a few foreign commands rather than trying to retrain the dogs in English.

Michaela inserted the cone of an otoscope into Crush's ear. "You're right, Hank. His ear canal is red and swollen, and there's so much discharge I can't even see the eardrum." Michaela used a cotton-tipped swab to collect a sample of the discharge, which was dark and tarry. She went to the laboratory and smeared the stuff onto a microscope slide. After she stained it, she looked at it under the microscope and saw hundreds of budding yeast organisms. They looked like purple boot prints, stomping all over the circular microscopic field.

Back in the exam room, she flushed Crush's ear with a medicated solution, then prescribed an ointment to kill the pathogenic yeast.

"Do that twice a day for two weeks, then bring him back and I'll check to make sure the infection is cleared up." Straightforward. Ear infections were one of Michaela's favorite ailments: quick diagnosis and usually an easy solution.

"Thanks, Doc," Hank said. "Crush thanks you, too."

Michaela looked at Crush, who eyed her suspiciously. "I'll take your word for it." She opened the door of the exam room and went out after Hank. His wife Kath and their three kids were in the waiting room.

"Look who's here," Michaela exclaimed. She crouched down and addressed the children. "Are you guys here to help Crush be brave at the doctor's?" Hank didn't allow the children in the exam room when Crush thought he was working, so the best they could do was beg to come along and wait in the reception area. The youngest, six-month-old Charlie, was Terry and Michaela's godson.

While Hank was paying the bill, Kath took Michaela aside. "So?" she said, a conspiratorial grin on her face.

Michaela blushed. "Can't say for sure yet."

* * *

David Brightman stopped by the hospital with lunch: enough pizza for the entire staff. He and Michaela ate in the office. She was quiet, thinking about Rosie.

"I'm thinking about retiring," he said suddenly.

Michaela looked up, surprised. "You? Since when?"

He shrugged. "It's all getting a bit tiresome, isn't it? Perhaps I should pull the plug."

"That's a grim way to put it." She watched him for a moment. "Seriously, what's going on? I thought your personal motto was 'chop 'til you drop.' Why are you talking about retiring?"

"Maybe I've just been woken up in the middle of the night one too many times." He sighed heavily, then gave her a wry smile and appeared to shake off his melancholy. "I'm doing surgery on one of your referrals tomorrow," he said, helping himself to another slice of pizza.

"Oh?" Michaela said. "Who?"

"Fridge."

She nodded. Fridge was a German Shepherd puppy named after the famed 1980s Chicago Bear William "The Fridge" Perry. Michaela had discovered a congenital heart defect—patent ductus arteriosus—so she had sent the family to see David about surgery.

"They told me you're the best vet they've ever had," David said.

"His heart murmur was so loud I could hear it from across the room."

"Oh, come on, Michaela. I'm trying to cheer you up. They absolutely adore you."

Michaela rolled her eyes.

"Good God, I thought all you Americans had loads of self-esteem. What's the matter with you?"

She shook her head and continued to eat.

"All right. Have it your way. You're hopeless."

Michaela stared at the floor, chewing.

"Are you irked again?"

Michaela looked up at him; she had been so lost in thought she had forgotten he was there. He was staring at her with that soft look in his eyes, the one that used to make her heart melt. She pushed the thought away—that was years ago, long before Terry. She wiped her fingers, threw the napkin in the trash, and stood up. "I want to show you something."

She led David through the treatment area, past the bank of cages where the hospital cases stayed. At the moment there was only one patient: a dog with an ear hematoma she had lanced and drained earlier. It was resting comfortably.

The dogs in the boarding kennel were eerily silent, as before. Michaela led the way past them to Rosie's run. She was standing, head slightly lowered, tail down, ears relaxed.

David's voice startled her. "What's wrong with that dog?"

"You see it too?"

"I'd say its mentation was odd."

Michaela laughed dryly at the understatement, remembering Rosie's unnerving stare and empty eyes.

She unlatched the gate, entered the run, and knelt. "Come here, girl."

Rosie looked up, wagged her tail, and took two steps toward Michaela's outstretched hand.

Michaela rubbed the dog's ears, then stood up. "Do you remember when you were here the other day, doing that knee surgery?"

David nodded.

"As you were finishing up I was called out to an emergency."

David nodded again. "And?"

Michaela pointed at Rosie. "This is it."

He shrugged. "Seems all right. Other than looking a bit off kilter." David looked at Michaela. "Well done."

She shook her head. "She was dying. Critical, shocky, cyanotic. Bleeding from the nose and mouth. Fractured facial bones and maxilla. Comminuted fractures of the femur and tibia."

Michaela looked at him to gauge his reaction. He leaned to the side, frowning, getting a good look at the dog's affected areas. "Which leg was fractured?"

"The left rear."

David stepped closer to the cage to examine the dog's leg. Rosie was standing evenly, bearing full weight upon all four limbs. He turned to Michaela. "Anything else?"

"Hemothorax. Pneumothorax."

"Hit by a car?"

Michaela shook her head again. She gently turned Rosie around and showed him the gunshot wounds.

He raised both eyebrows.

"Let me show you something else." She led him out of the kennel area and back into the office, where she pulled up the X-rays on her monitor.

David whistled when he saw the bullets in the chest. "Four bullets," he muttered.

"But only two new entry wounds," Michaela finished. Then she pointed at the bullet in the abdomen. "Plus this."

David stared at the monitor, deep in thought. "Who brought the dog in?"

Michaela summarized her encounter with the two women—their false contact information, their nervous, suspicious behavior. "What do you think?"

He gave a little laugh. "Isn't it obvious? Two lunatics are using their dog for target practice and also bashing it repeatedly with blunt objects."

"David, come on. This is serious."

He nodded. "I know it is. It sounds like an odd case of Munchausen-by-proxy."

"Which is?"

"It's better documented in human beings. A caregiver—parent, grandparent, babysitter—causes symptoms of illness or injury in a child and repeatedly brings the child to the doctor. They crave the attention they get from the doctors and medical staff."

"That's sick. People do that to animals, too?"

"It's not as well documented as a form of animal abuse, but it does exist." He shrugged. "These people got a bit carried away."

Michaela thought for a moment. It sounded like a plausible explanation. It would explain the evidence of previous injury and why they brought the dog to her. But why did they seemed overly concerned to make doubly sure the dog was dead? Maybe they were both so mentally unstable that they were afraid, worried that the dog's ghost would exact revenge upon them or something. Mental illness certainly was a good explanation for the women's behavior.

But it didn't explain everything.

"There's something else," she said.

David looked at her expectantly.

"Would you believe I put this dog to sleep that night?"

"You're joking."

Michaela shook her head. "She woke up and ripped herself out of the body bag."

He took a deep breath. "Well, I have heard of cases where an animal was under-dosed and then woke up."

Michaela was saving the best for last. "I thought of that. So I put her to sleep again. Overdosed her. Took an ECG tracing. And videotaped it." She picked up the video camera and fast-forwarded to the end of the video. "At this point, the dog has been in full respiratory and cardiac arrest for ninety minutes." She pressed play and handed David the camera.

She watched David's reaction as, on the monitor, the ECG started to beep, and then a moment later Rosie started to breath.

He watched Michaela and Terry come into the frame to examine the dog. Then, his left eyebrow registered his astonishment, arching further and further toward his hairline as Rosie sat up.

"Blimey," he said at last.

"Is that all you've got to say?"

"You were thorough."

"I'm open to any suggestions on how to proceed."

"All right. Let's look at it with complete objectivity and clinical detachment." He paused for effect. "You've got two barmy animal abusers on the loose."

Michaela punched him on the arm. "David, stop it! What about the fact that she comes back to life like Wile E. Coyote?"

"Okay. Seriously?"

Michaela looked pointedly at him. "If you wouldn't mind."

"Let me take another look at her."

They went back to the kennel area. This time Rosie was alert.

David peered at the dog through narrowed eyes, his forehead creased. "Ever heard of Lazarus Syndrome?"

"No, but I think I can guess what it is: subjects that are documented as clinically dead coming back to life?"

He nodded. "Once again, more commonly documented in humans. In fact, I don't know of any documented cases in animals." He tapped the metal chain link of the cage door. "In people, it occurs randomly in all types of cases. Attempted suicides. Trauma victims. Heart attacks. Asphyxiation." He paused. "Drowning," he added.

Michaela saw a pained look in his eyes, but before she could say anything, he continued briskly. "In most cases, resuscitation was attempted, abandoned, and the person pronounced dead. Then they just—"

"—woke up," Michaela finished.

David looked at Rosie. She stood quietly, panting normally, looking from David to Michaela as if she were following the conversation with rapt attention.

He continued. "Odd physiological responses to sodium pentobarbital aside, this still has all the earmarks of being a complicated animal abuse case: badly injured dog, loony owners. Here's what I would do. Collect and organize all the records and data. I know a woman who's in forensic veterinary medicine who's also an attorney."

"Really? Where?"

"Indianapolis. She specializes in animal welfare and ethics issues, goes around Indiana documenting animal neglect and abuse cases."

"That's perfect."

"Exactly. Put all your records in order and I'll have her take a look. She can advise you and refer you to her associate here in Illinois."

Later, after David left, Michaela was still mulling over his offer. She could hardly believe her luck, but at the same time she didn't want to just refer it and forget it.

Rosie seemed to drop in and out of a strange neurological state throughout the day. One moment she was fine: bright, alert, responsive, mouth wide open in that happy dog grin. The next moment she was gone, standing there with dull, dead eyes. During a lull in her afternoon appointments, Michaela went to the kennel to check on Rosie again. She was "awake." In fact, it seemed to Michaela that Rosie looked at her with some kind of knowledge, as if she knew that Michaela had tried not just once, but twice, to do away with her.

"Dr. Collins?"

Michaela turned.

Her receptionist, Abby, stood in the doorway. "Guess who's here." She cocked an eyebrow significantly. "That hit-by-car from the other night? They're here to pick up the dog's ashes. Did you call them?"

Michaela hastily left the kennel. She and Terry had decided not to tell the staff what had happened, and she didn't want Abby to get a good look at Rosie and recognize her. "Tried to," she said. "Bad number." She followed Abby back into the treatment area.

Abby looked puzzled. "Are the ashes back already?"

"I'll take care of it. Can you put them in the comfy room?"

"Sure." Abby returned to the reception area.

The "comfy room" was exam room five, specially appointed and furnished like a little parlor. A loveseat and armchair were arranged in an L, with an end table between them. Against one wall was a wooden cabinet with a built-in sink and places above and below for medical supplies. A large area rug covered the floor and softly glowing table lamps bathed the room in warm, comforting light. A wall-mounted clinical light swung out when necessary. Michaela used this room for client consultations and cases that didn't require in-depth treatment, like showing clients how to administer insulin shots to their diabetic pets or subcutaneous fluids to their aged animals. The room was also the best place to deliver bad news to distraught pet owners and for put-to-sleeps.

Michaela had been in this room far too often in recent weeks.

She waited outside the door and in a moment heard Abby say, "The doctor will be right with you." Then Abby came out. "All yours, Dr. Collins."

"Thanks." Michaela collected Rosie's chart, went to the door and looked through the peephole. The same two women were standing uneasily in the middle of the room.

She was about to push the door open and go in, but something stopped her. If she told these women what had happened, she would be obliged to return Rosie to them. If David's theory were correct—that one or both of these women was an animal abuser afflicted by Munchausen-by-proxy disorder—she would be placing Rosie back into a dangerous situation. She turned away from the door and thought for a moment.

Then she had an idea.

Michaela put the chart into the door rack and went to her office. On the floor of the coat closet was a stack of small cardboard boxes. She moved a few boxes from the front and grabbed a larger box from the very back. At her desk, she opened the cardboard box and removed the metal canister. Last year, the holiday euthanasia rush had claimed this dog: a fifteen-year-old, arthritic Golden Retriever. The owner had requested ashes back but had never picked them up, and then the family had moved to Europe. Discarding unclaimed remains was one of the many things on the animal hospital's "to do" list, but was such a low priority that it simply never got done, so every year the stack of boxes in the closet got a little taller.

She took the canister back to the treatment area, knowing that what she was about to do was unethical and possibly illegal, but if these people had done this to Rosie she would sort out the ethics later. She pushed the door open. "Good afternoon," she said, smiling. "Please, have a seat."

"Is something wrong?" said the Hispanic woman, Adriana Smith.

Michaela shook her head. "I'm just glad you're here. We usually call people when the ashes are ready." She watched the women carefully to see how they would react to what she said next. "But your phone number was out of service and we weren't sure how to reach you."

The Hispanic woman managed to maintain her poker face, but the taller woman glanced nervously away.

Michaela handed the canister to the Mrs. Smith. "I'm so sorry about Rosie," she said, unsure of her own poker face.

Mrs. Smith met her eyes. "Thank you for all your help, Doctor," she said. "We're just glad she's not going to suffer anymore."

* * *

The women got up, opened the door and went out. They crossed the waiting room quickly, just as they had done the night before Christmas Eve. They went out into the swirling snow, got into a maroon Subaru, and drove away.

They didn't notice a black Range Rover pull out from across the street and follow them.

* * *

As the last appointment of the evening was checking out at the reception desk, Michaela emptied the pockets of her lab coat, hung up her stethoscope, and put on her winter jacket.

She heard the receptionists and veterinary technicians locking up and calling out their "good nights." Then the side door slammed, and she was alone in the hospital. Headlights flashed in the employees' parking lot before disappearing into the snowy darkness.

Michaela put on her hat and gloves, then went to the back hallway and pushed open the EXIT door. Ducking her head against the frigid wind, she crunched across the snow to her truck. Halfway there she realized that she had forgotten to arm the alarm system.

As she turned on her heel to go back inside, the parking area blazed with light and noise as a vehicle roared to life and switched on its high beams. Michaela raised her hands to shield her eyes. A moment later, the driver's side door of the vehicle opened and a shadowy form appeared.

10

Crash Cart

MICHAELA COULDN'T SEE THE PERSON'S FACE, but she could tell that the car was a dark Subaru wagon, and that there was someone in the passenger seat. "What do you want?" she demanded.

"Where's Rosie?" the woman said.

Michaela recognized the slight Hispanic accent. "What are you talking about?"

"You gave us the remains of a different dog."

"Sorry, but that's not possible."

"We scanned the ashes."

Michaela swore under her breath. *The microchip*. Why didn't she think of that?

Adriana Smith took a step closer. "Dr. Collins, please. Where is our dog?"

Tired and exasperated, Michaela raised her voice. "You lied to me. Your dog wasn't hit by a car. You shot it."

Adriana took another step forward. "We want to see Rosie." Her voice was shaking.

A new voice rang out behind Adriana. "You can't."

Adriana turned around. It was Terry. The steam from his breath formed a wavering halo around his head.

"Please," said Adriana. "Let me see her."

"I said you can't." Terry glanced at Michaela. "I took her home."

"You'd better be telling the truth," Adriana countered.

"Or what? You'll shine your brights on me, too?" Terry snorted. "I think you need to tell us what the hell is going on."

Adriana stood motionless for an instant. Then she returned to her car, opened the driver's side door and turned off the high beams. "If I tell you, will you help me?"

"We'll consider it," Michaela said, evenly.

Adriana hesitated for a moment more, then walked toward her. The other woman—the taller one—got out of the Subaru.

Terry joined the three women in the gentle wash of the low beams. The wind whipped about them.

"Dr. Collins, I'm Adriana Munoz. This is Cori Nelson."

Michaela nodded: Adriana *had* given a false name. She extended her mittened hand to Adriana and Cori in turn, then, indicating Terry, said, "This is my husband, Dr. Adams."

Adriana looked around nervously. "We work for a biotech company called Synthetic Genetics Group," she said.

The wind suddenly stilled. Michaela raised her eyebrows. "And Rosie was a test subject."

Adriana nodded.

"You took her from your facility and brought her here to be euthanized. Why?"

Adriana's eyes darted from side to side. "Dr. Collins, we are in big trouble."

Michaela wanted to hear more, but her fingers, ears, and toes were numb. "Okay, but we need to get out of this cold." She turned and headed toward the door of the animal hospital, followed by Adriana and Cori.

Terry stopped them. "You know what, though, hon? I'm starved. Let's go into town and get some food."

Michaela said, "Where do you want to go?"

"How about The Courier?" he suggested. He turned to Adriana. "You know where that is?"

Adriana nodded. "We'll follow you."

Cori spoke up for the first time. "Just a minute."

Everyone stopped and stared at her.

"Where is all this leading?" Cori demanded. "We want Rosie back. Now."

Adriana looked at her, confused. "What do you mean, 'where is this leading?' We've got to put a stop to this research."

Cori shook her head and started to back away. "I don't want any part of this." She headed for the passenger door of the Subaru.

"But Cori—" Adriana protested.

Cori whirled around. "Look, I'm no animal rights crusader! I'm no activist! And I need this job! I cannot afford to just throw it away. You go with them if you want, but I'm going home."

Adriana looked desperately at Michaela and Terry.

"Go ahead and take her home," Michaela said. "We'll meet you there."

* * *

As usual, The Courier Café in Urbana was crowded and loud. When Michaela and Terry entered, they got stuck behind a logjam of patrons waiting to be seated, but the hostess sorted it out quickly and led them to a booth in the front of the restaurant. The booth had high paneled sides, lending it the privacy of a confessional. As they slid into the booth, a waitress appeared and Terry ordered three coffees. He opened his menu and studied it intently.

Michaela glanced at her menu. She had eaten a lot of pizza and she wasn't very hungry. "Why couldn't we just go inside the animal hospital and talk with them?"

"I told you," he said. "I'm starved. I haven't eaten since breakfast."

She should have known. Terry was such a thoroughly uncomplicated man. He seldom spoke with any level of subtext. She looked at him and chuckled.

"What?" he said.

She shook her head. "Nothing."

"Come on, tell me," he insisted.

"I was just thinking that you had some secret reason for creating this diversion, to get them away from Rosie."

Terry snorted. "Hey, you know me. What you see is what you get." He looked back at the menu for a moment, then glanced sideways at Michaela. "Mick, they really *are* in trouble."

"You don't think Cori's overreacting?"

"No. They work for a biotech company, right?"

Michaela nodded. "Synthetic Genetics," she said, recalling the name of the company.

"Biotech companies spend millions of dollars on research and product development."

"Right," she said. "But whatever they're up to, it's way beyond anything I've ever seen, or even heard of."

"Exactly. They can make a dead dog come back to life. Imagine how much the company has invested in biotech like *that*."

Michaela had to agree. A company doing research like this would be spending not millions, but *billions* to develop their technology, and would not look kindly upon whistle-blowers like Adriana and Cori.

"We're probably going to need a refresher course in genetics just to follow this conversation," she said. As veterinarians, she and Terry had learned enough Mendelian genetics to understand heredity as it related to breeding, and enough molecular genetics to understand gene therapy and other clinical applications. But based on what they'd witnessed with Rosie, this company was into genetic technology far beyond their knowledge.

"I wonder who's behind it?" said Terry. "Who would fund research like this?"

Michaela looked up and saw Adriana arrive. She waved her over. "Hopefully we're about to find out."

Adriana took the bench opposite them. "I'm sorry about Cori," she said.

Michaela sighed. "I don't blame her. Sounds like she really needs her job."

Michaela and Terry waited for the waitress to return and pour the coffee, then launched into their questions. "How about if you start with some background on your company," Michaela began.

"Okay," said Adriana. "Originally, we were a group within a larger pharmaceutical company developing shock and trauma drugs."

"Can you tell us the name of that company?" Terry asked.

"Have you heard of BAP Pharmaceuticals?"

They nodded. BAP was one of the biggest pharmaceutical companies in the world, a multinational corporation with headquarters overseas.

Adriana continued. "Our group inside BAP was called the Synthetic Genetics Group. We were trying to create gene sequences that we could plug into bacterial chromosomes and make them pump out new drugs for treating shock and trauma. When I first started, I had no idea such a thing was possible."

Michaela was familiar with this technology. "They already do it with natural substances. Human insulin is made by bacteria that have the human gene for insulin spliced in. "

"Transgenic bacteria. They do it with all kinds of drugs," Terry added. "The clotting factors to treat hemophilia are made the same way."

Adriana lowered her voice. "Our group obtained additional funding from another source and we broke away as a separate company. We still investigate trauma medicine, but we're way beyond tinkering with bacteria. We've been doing surgical and genetic manipulations on entire organisms. We make it so a trauma victim can essentially treat itself."

Michaela and Terry looked at each other. Now they were getting somewhere.

"The test subjects are genetically altered so their cells secrete patented molecules which arrest the effects of severe trauma: corticosteroids, catecholamines, other tissue stabilizers. Plus a few other cutting-edge molecules that are also patented and proprietary. The developers call it the genetic crash cart."

Michaela wrapped her hands around her coffee mug. "Genetically altered?" she said. "How?"

"I don't know all the exact molecular mechanisms. They isolated the genes for the enzymes that oversee cortisol synthesis and tweaked them somehow into super-genes that code for turbo-charged corticosteroids. The test subjects don't just make cortisol anymore. Their own cells manufacture the equivalent of dexamethasone and PSS."

Michaela exhaled loudly. Dexamethasone and PSS— prednisolone sodium succinate—were *synthetic* corticosteroids, much more potent than the body's naturally occurring cortisol. Standard treatment for shock and trauma involved massive doses of dexamethasone or PSS intravenously, to prevent endotoxemia, stabilize cell membranes, retard cell death.

"Synthetic super genes?" Terry asked.

Adriana nodded. "Made from scratch. 'Just like Mama used to make' according to the geneticist who directs that part of the project. They've got genes that step up the body's normal catecholamine cascade—all sorts of things that crank out in response to trauma."

Terry shook his head in disbelief. "I don't believe this."

Michaela was puzzled. "Why not?"

"You know Jan Mueller?"

Of course. Jan was their classmate from vet school. She was now a molecular biologist, doing research and teaching microbiology to first year vet students. Terry and the other clinical professors sometimes hung out with the researchers—soldiers in the trenches with the theorists in the ivory tower. It was good intellectual cross-pollination.

"Jan and the other egghead researchers would debunk the crap out of this," Terry said. "I ran into her at the cafeteria not too long ago. They were talking shop, saying you can't just plug a string of DNA nucleotides into the genome and then sit back expecting it to make what you want it to make. Not only would you have no guarantee that the new DNA would behave itself, but proteins that genes code for are embedded within cascades, pathways, feedback loops. Plus there's a new thing called epigenetics, where the bits and pieces stuck to the DNA can have huge effects on the way genes are expressed. There's just no way this can be done."

Adriana shrugged and spread her hands. "I have no idea how it works. Cori and I are just technicians." She took a sip of coffee. "Some of the animals also have surgical implants creating redundant branches of major blood vessels. The natural vessels are rigged to shut down if they are transected or damaged, and then blood supply is re-routed to the implants."

Michaela whistled softly in amazement.

"I take it Rosie reanimated?" Adriana asked.

Terry gave a cynical laugh. "Is that what you call it?"

Michaela shushed him.

Adriana continued. "It's beyond belief. But you saw what they did to Rosie." She looked around nervously. "We just couldn't stand it anymore."

"Put aside the theoretical snags for now," Michaela said. "How does this genetic crash cart work?"

"When certain trigger sites are disturbed, the genetic crash cart pumps the shock-arresting substances into the body, the damaged vessels shut down, and the implanted blood vessels continue to function. It's like an automobile airbag deploying when it senses a sudden deceleration."

The appearance of their waitress halted their conversation. She hovered over them, pen poised over her order book. "Are you folks ready to order now?"

Michaela hadn't even looked at her menu. She asked the waitress for a few more minutes. After the waitress left, Michaela turned to Adriana. "We understand the gist of the theory behind the research: a so-called 'genetic crash cart' and a kind of circulatory bypass system that somehow prevents death from severe trauma."

"That actually sounds pretty cool," Terry finally admitted.

"Right," said Michaela, "but at this point, how it works is irrelevant. How the research is conducted is the main problem." She turned to Adriana. "You took laboratory animals and broke their legs, caused blunt trauma to their heads, inflicted penetrating trauma to their chest cavities, and watched them recover miraculously as their physiologic airbags deployed. Some of my details may be off, but am I on the right track here?"

Adriana nodded.

"Then," Michaela concluded, "the work got a little too grisly, even for you."

"The shock-arresting drugs and the arterial bypass systems worked perfectly," said Adriana. "The investigators were able to prevent death in the single event injuries, so they started inducing simultaneous traumas in single subjects. Multiple gunshot wounds, blunt traumas, brain and spinal cord injuries." Adriana hesitated. "That's when the subjects started to die. They called it the 'hard kill' procedure. They wanted to see what it took to kill these guys."

Michaela was aghast. "And this is sanctioned research? Who the hell approved all this?"

"And who funded it?" Terry added.

"I have no idea," Adriana said, lowering her voice again. "But it's got to be dirty money, right? One whiff of this and the regulatory agencies would crack down on it like the wrath of God."

Terry and Michaela both nodded. The government animal welfare regulations were draconian in their strictness, and with good reason. Biotech research of any kind required the use of living animals, and it was essential that those animals be treated as humanely as possible.

Adriana sighed. "Let me back up. At first, they *did* do everything by the book, according to the rules for trauma research. One day they purposely produced injuries serious enough to overwhelm the crash cart—a hard kill—and the subject died, as expected. Then she just...woke up." Adriana paused significantly. "That was not expected. At least, not by me and the other techs."

"Rosie," Michaela said.

Adriana nodded. "Cori and I were on the trauma floor, monitoring the physiologic response to the injuries. It went *way* beyond anything we had ever seen."

"I'll bet," Terry observed.

Adriana took another sip of her coffee.

"And then?" Michaela prompted.

"After Rosie, they started doing the multiple injury hard kills on most of the subjects, looking for what they started calling a 'soft kill,' like Rosie. But Rosie's the only one so far who's ever reanimated. Then they started doing the studies on *awake* subjects—they wouldn't even anesthetize them. *That's* when it got too grisly. Even for us," she finished miserably.

That explained the evidence of previous fractures in the leg and jaw, and the numerous bullets in Rosie's body. Michaela leaned forward. "The next question is this: why did you bring me a mortally injured dog, lie to me about it, and demand that I put it to sleep when you knew what would happen afterward? Was that part of your research, too?"

"We weren't sure it would happen. We hoped it wouldn't happen." Adriana shifted uncomfortably before continuing. "The principal investigators exceeded allowable practices. Rosie should have been humanely euthanized, her tissues collected for analysis, and her remains incinerated."

"Kind of hard to do that when she keeps coming back to life," Terry added, wryly.

"Exactly! He kept—" Adriana broke off and spread her hands helplessly. "He just kept killing her."

"Who's he?" Michaela asked.

"The director who manages that part of the project. He's a geneticist, so he doesn't even need to be on the kill floor, but I think he gets off on it. He especially enjoys the shooting." She shook her head. "We just wanted to put Rosie out of her misery," she continued. "That's why we brought Rosie to you."

Michaela narrowed her eyes. "Why me? There are lots of animal hospitals around here."

"Yours was the first one we came to that was still open that night."

Michaela and Terry glanced at each other. So this was all just dumb luck.

Adriana went on. "We know vets always store dead animals in a freezer until the cremation service picks them up. We hoped putting her body in a freezer would somehow stop the reanimation process."

"It didn't," Michaela said. "You didn't exactly go about this the right way. If you had ethical concerns about the nature of the experiments, there are proper channels. Have you got any documentation at all?"

"No. This was all kind of spur of the moment." Adriana dropped her eyes.

Michaela certainly understood "spur of the moment" compassion—her performance the other night with Rosie was a perfect example. "Do you still have access to the facility?" she asked.

"I don't think so. I haven't even tried to get back in."

Michaela and Terry exchanged a glance. Adriana hadn't tried because she was scared. She hadn't thought this through. If she had, she would have taken her time, gathered enough information to build a case and then gone directly to the authorities. Now all she had were her eyewitness recollections and righteous indignation.

Plus the documentation Michaela had on Rosie.

Michaela asked bluntly, "What do you want to do now? Do you want to see the project shut down?"

Adriana nodded. "Will you help me?"

Michaela finished her coffee. Did she and Terry really want to get involved in a high tech corporate whistle-blowing scheme?

Terry took note of her hesitation. "What's going on, Michaela?"

"I'm just not sure about this," Michaela replied.

"Animals are suffering and we've got the evidence," he said. "We could shut this whole thing down."

"All right. Say we do shut this project down. Who's to say they won't start it right back up again somewhere else?"

Terry raised his eyebrows, surprised. "That is the lamest excuse I've ever heard. That's like saying you refuse to feed a homeless person today because he's just going to be hungry tomorrow."

Michaela sighed and dropped her shoulders.

Terry continued. "What about the animals right under our noses that are going through hell? We can't stop future projects but we can stop this one."

Michaela thought of what David Brightman had said, that this situation had all the earmarks of being 'complicated.' She turned to Adriana and said, "Do you mind?"

"Go ahead," Adriana replied.

Taking the cue, Terry helped his wife out of the booth like a gentleman handing a lady out of a carriage. He guided her to the cashier's station.

Michaela stood close to Terry and kept her voice low. "David seemed to think it was a bad idea to get involved."

"David? He knows about it?"

"He came by today and I showed him everything."

"Michaela, most of the work has already been done. We've got eyewitness testimony from Adriana. We've got photos, videos, X-rays, and Rosie's medical records. It looks pretty straightforward."

She pinched the bridge of her nose.

Terry persisted. "Aren't you the one who's been whining about how you're not doing any damn good? Here's your chance, Mick."

She looked up at Terry. "I've been whining?"

He smiled gently. "Like a two-year-old."

She thought for a moment. "David said he knew someone in animal ethics. A lawyer who specializes in animal abuse cases."

"That's perfect."

Michaela nodded.

"Then come on." He put his arm around her and guided her back toward their booth.

"Terry, there's something else I need to tell you," she said.

"What is it, sweetheart?" He glanced toward the booth. "Uh-oh."

Adriana wasn't alone.

A man stood over their table. He was short and wiry, with neat sandy hair, thinning slightly on top. His boyish features were accented with trendy glasses.

As Michaela and Terry approached, the man grinned broadly and extended his hand. "Garrett Sanger. Pleasure to meet you folks." He spoke in a soft, southern drawl. "I'm one of the directors at Synthetic Genetics Group." He slid into the booth across from Adriana. "I don't know about y'all, but I'm dying for some buffalo wings."

Adriana looked distinctly uncomfortable. Michaela and Terry squeezed in next to her.

Sanger seemed to be aware of the effect of his arrival. "So, what'd I miss?"

Terry scowled. "Nothing that was any of your business."

Sanger laughed. "Well, actually, I kind of overheard what y'all were saying and it most definitely *is* my business. I don't mind our employees sittin' around talkin' in generalities about what we're doing. Groundbreaking work, frontiers of science and all that, but," and he looked at Adriana, "from what I could make out, y'all are violating pretty much every provision of your confidentiality agreement." He smiled unpleasantly.

Adriana set her jaw. "So fire me."

Sanger chuckled again. "That's a given, honey."

"Don't listen to him, Adriana," Michaela said. "There are protections in place for people in your situation. They can't just summarily fire you. Or threaten you in any way." She looked pointedly at Sanger.

Terry eyed him suspiciously. "How did you know we were here?"

"I believe y'all might have a leak in your organization."

Adriana groaned. "Cori called you?"

"Who cares about a leak?" Michaela said. "Between the three of us we've got enough information to shut your project down."

Sanger looked up as the waitress arrived. "I'll have some coffee," he said, "and bring us four Dagwoods, with every-thing." He looked at the other three and winked. "Don't worry. It's on me."

He ogled the waitress as she left, then turned back to the others, drumming his fingers on the table, fidgeting like a hy-peractive child.

Terry was deadpan. "I thought you came here for the buf-falo wings."

Michaela recalled something Adriana had just said. *Just like Mama used to make.* "What exactly is it you do, Mr. Sanger?"

"I'm a molecular geneticist," Sanger replied. "Ph.D'd here at U of I, post-doc with BAP Pharmaceuticals. I stayed on to head up the new company when it branched off. Life story of a biotech geek." He finally stopped twitching and laid his hands flat on the table. "Short and boring."

Michaela and Terry remained impassive.

Sanger raised his hands in mock surrender. "Okay, you got me. I didn't come here for the buffalo wings." He looked at Michaela, Terry and finally Adriana. All trace of down-home good humor vanished. "This project is my life's work."

"Life's work?" Michaela scoffed. "You mean this inhumane, unethical, immoral—"

Sanger broke in. "I'm not gonna sit back and let you two and your new best friend fuck it up."

"Hey!" Terry barked.

"Let 'em bring it, Terry," Michaela countered, her anger flaring. She fixed Sanger with hardened eyes, refusing to be intimidated by his posturing bravado. "We've seen what goes on at your company, and we're going to blow the whistle on you and your project."

She stood up, jostling the table and knocking over a vase. "Not only are we going to shut you down, we're going to make sure you're all prosecuted. You're going to jail for this."

People stared as the three of them slid out of the booth. The astonished waitress came by at that moment with a tray of huge sandwiches.

Michaela pushed the door open and strode to the parking lot. Terry and Adriana hurried to keep up.

"Call me tomorrow at the animal hospital," Michaela said, "and we'll get started on this thing."

"Sounds good," said Adriana. "And thanks." She smiled and headed for her car. "I really appreciate your help."

Michaela unlocked her truck. "Do you believe that guy?" she fumed. "This whole thing makes my blood boil!"

She turned to Terry, who was leaning on his Jeep, smiling broadly and shaking his head in amusement.

"What's so funny?" she said.

"I love it when you put your Irish on."

11

The Breath of Empty Space

GARRETT SANGER FOUND HIMSELF ALONE in the restaurant booth with four heaping sandwiches and an overturned vase in front of him.

He jumped at the voice above his head. "You sure know how to put the fear of God into people."

It was Frank Galton, in all his mustached glory.

Sanger scowled. "How the hell did this happen?" he hissed. "You're supposed to be in charge of security. How did those two even get off the kill floor, let alone out of the building with that dog?"

Galton sat down across from Sanger. "You tell me. I'm a security *consultant*. I have a day job and I can't be in the building twenty-four hours a day. That's why I hire a team to assist me, so when I go out of town for three days I don't come back to a colossal fuck-up. So you tell me, Mark."

"It's Garrett," Sanger muttered. His real first name was Mark, after his father, but as soon as he was old enough, he had dropped the bastard's name and started going by his middle name.

"Whatever you say, *Garrett*. What you just told me indicates that you conducted the kill and then left the floor without waiting for the dog to actually die."

"Oh, I get it. This is all my fault?"

Galton shook his head. He righted the overturned vase and replaced the flower.

Sanger waved his hand dismissively. "The techs know how to document clinical death."

"Which may be fine for a hard kill, but not for a soft kill. You were supposed to be documenting what happened next. You're supposed to be a goddamn scientist." Galton pulled some paper napkins from a dispenser and wiped up the spilled water from the tabletop. "Where the hell did you go?"

"None of your damn business," Sanger snapped.

"Everything is my business when we have a security breach of this magnitude." Galton's voice dripped with contempt. "Garrett, you don't seem to comprehend the seriousness of this situation. The dog has been missing for days and everyone in the place has a terminal case of 'not-my-problem' syndrome."

"Are you going to call the Director?"

Galton shook his head. "We're going to keep this quiet. No one has to know what happened. Especially the investors." He sighed heavily. "Of all the subjects in the entire facility, it had to be *this* one."

Sanger hated to admit it, but Galton was right. As an experimental subject, the dog the staff had named "Rosie" was of inestimable value; she was the only one who had ever reanimated. And she had been in the hands of some do-gooder animal welfare types for three days. He was furious at himself for leaving the kill floor. "What are we going to do now?" he said. "We can't just let them go to the authorities. We have to get her back."

Galton fixed Sanger with an impassive stare, a kind of studied nonchalance that had always driven Sanger crazy. "What do you suggest? Go run them off the road?"

Sanger scoffed. The man was so insufferably calm. He wanted to smack that smug smile off his face.

Galton continued. "The reason you're not in charge of security is that you're too hot-headed, and, if I may, burdened with an overactive libido that makes you a distraction to the members of the staff. Don't worry. I have a protocol in place for dealing with breaches in security."

"A protocol?" Sanger sneered. "I suppose it involves filling out a stack of triplicate forms?"

"Just stick to your test tubes and lab techs, Garrett, but do me a favor and leave the women in *my* group alone. Everything will be fine if you just do your job and let me and my staff do ours."

Sanger glared at Galton, breathing hard.

"There's no need to panic," said Galton. "We know Munoz doesn't have any other concrete evidence."

"We do?"

"Come on. A staff member can't leave Synthetic Genetics with so much as a paper clip in his pocket."

Sanger had to give him that. Every movement in and out of the facility and within the facility was monitored. Employees were not permitted to bring purses, briefcases, or other personal items into the building, nor were they permitted to bring in mobile devices or other electronics. They entered in street clothes, changed into company scrubs, and changed back after their shifts. They hung up their clothes on open racks, knowing they could be and usually were searched daily. Most employees left their personal belongings in their cars, including their coats, unaware that even their vehicles were searched every day. Technically, the searches were illegal, but none of the employees objected—they were so well compensated they were willing to overlook a little thing like the violation of their constitutional rights. They passed through metal detectors when entering or leaving. Only a handful of employees had in and out privileges with 24-hour access key cards. No one could enter or leave the facility without being seen because all movement was continually monitored.

Unless the technician assigned to the surveillance monitors is upstairs in the company lounge screwing the Director of Genetic Research. Garrett regretted it now, but at the time it had seemed like a "now or never" moment, and he had never passed up one of those in his life.

In his opinion, Frank Galton was an incompetent fool, no better than a rent-a-cop. By the time he completed his damn protocol, every detail of the project's research methods would be the next viral video on the Internet.

Galton continued. "After we quiet things down, we'll retrieve the test subject and any documentation those two veterinarians have."

"You heard them. What makes you think they'll back down?"

Galton shook his head. "Trust me, Garrett. The protocol."

The waitress came up to the table and looked from Sanger to Galton, waving the check. "Who gets the bad news?" she asked, awkwardly.

Sanger stood and glared at Galton. "Good luck with your protocol." He spun around and stalked out of the restaurant.

When Sanger reached his SUV, he wrenched open the door, climbed up, and hurled himself into the driver's seat. He slammed the door behind him and cranked the key in the ignition.

He drove out onto University Avenue, heading east toward St. Joseph. As he left the outskirts of Urbana, the busy avenue slowly transformed into a lonely country road designated not by a name, but by a number. After a while he switched the radio off and drove in silence. Sanger had never been in a sensory deprivation chamber, but he imagined it must be a lot like this: surrounded by emptiness, no sound but muted white noise.

Sanger had become a molecular biologist because he believed that the genetic code held the key to everything he advocated. But genetics was moving too fast, even for him. His doctoral thesis was almost obsolete the day it was published. The entire premise upon which he had entered the field was being discredited: the one gene, one protein premise. The idea that the genome was a series of discrete units called genes, each of which coded for one specific protein, like an assembly line that cranked out nothing but the same widget over and over. This whole idea was being disproved, because it turned out the genetic sequence could be edited on the fly by the very proteins that were supposedly just following orders. Multiple genes worked in synergy. Or sometimes they didn't. Extrachromosomal material contributed to the expression of traits. Genes could be read backward and forward, coding for entirely different proteins depending on which direction you went. Genes nested within genes. Individual genes had parts scattered all over the genome. It was so complex it made his head spin.

One day, standing in his lab, he realized that the gene he was looking for very likely didn't exist. At that moment, he had felt the foundation of his professional life crumble beneath him.

He wasn't sure Vic's place was open tonight, but he needed to clear his head, go someplace he could focus, get out of his mental quagmire for a while by honing his physical skills to a hard edge.

He turned around and headed back the way he had come. About a quarter mile before the Salt Fork River he turned onto another county road. Two hundred yards down was a large gray metal building, a former agricultural construction of some kind, but now boasting a large marquee labeled University Gun Club. He pulled into the icy parking lot. Several vehicles huddled near the entrance, but Sanger parked his SUV on the far side of the lot, in the dark. He popped the hatch and retrieved a black duffel bag from the back. The night was clear and bitterly cold, the sky black and salted with a stunning array of stars. He dismissed it all. He knew nothing about astronomy and had no interest in constellations, and he felt the cold creeping through his coat. He crunched across the lot and pulled the door open. Heat and light washed over him, and the acrid smell of gunpowder stung his nasal passages.

He recognized the young woman at the counter, the owner's daughter. She was good looking: perfect teeth, machine-tanned, with shoulder-length blonde hair and tight, low cut clothes. Probably doable, he had often mused, but in the interests of diplomacy with her father he had left her alone. Besides, Vic's latest toy was a sweet, fully automatic 12-gauge shotgun that fired three hundred rounds a minute. That gun was amazing. Last spring, Vic had done a demo for the club in the range out back. He had immersed the thing in water, pulled it out dripping wet, then proceeded to demolish a set of targets thirty yards out. It could cut a solid-core door in half in about twelve seconds. Sanger knew he'd hate to be on the receiving end of that bad boy.

She saw him and smiled. "Hi, Garrett," she said, in that way of hers. "Whatcha get me for Christmas?"

"That depends on whether you've been naughty or nice, sweetheart." Sanger winked at her and put his range bag on the counter.

Another employee appeared from the back room, a tall, beer-bellied, bearded middle-aged redneck named Marty. Even without his NASCAR hat and an American flag screen-printed on his tee shirt, he looked like a walking advertisement for the NRA. "Hey, Sanger," he bellowed. "How come you don't trade in your forty-five for a firearm your girly-man wrists can handle?"

" 'Cause my forty-five'll make a bigger hole in your ass, that's why."

The girl made a face. "Don't listen to him." Then she leaned over the counter and whispered, loud enough for Marty to hear, "He shoots a nine because it matches his other, shall we say, deficiencies."

"Fuck you, bitch," Marty shouted as he disappeared into the back.

"You wish!" she shouted back.

Sanger laughed and pushed the range bag toward her. "My other gun's a Glock, but don't tell him that."

She winked, unzipped the bag, and examined the ammo boxes and other contents.

Her top had a scooping neckline, and as she leaned over to check the bag, Sanger could see part of another tattoo, a vine and roses, on her left breast. It disappeared provocatively into the shadowy region of her cleavage. His eyes flicked up to her face; she had caught him looking. He grinned and drummed on the glass counter.

She smacked her gum, flashing her teeth. She never minded. What were the tattoos and the tanning for anyway?

She fished out the pistol case. "Mind if I handle your piece?" she asked.

"Please do."

Inside the case, his Springfield XD-45 Compact Semi-Auto was packed snugly in a nest of formed foam. She lifted it out, examined the magazine to make sure it was empty, then inspected the chamber. When she was satisfied that there was no round in the chamber, she expertly racked the slide. This always impressed Sanger, because many women lacked the upper body strength to smoothly move the slide on a handgun. Her arm muscles, beneath her smooth, tanned skin, flexed provocatively as she gripped the slide over the top of the barrel with her left hand and slammed it back, simultaneously thrusting the body of the gun forward with her shooting hand.

She repacked the firearm, zipped up the duffel bag and handed it back to him. "Have fun."

Sanger grabbed the bag and walked the length of the gun counter to the range entrance, past a sign that read, "Hearing Protection Required Beyond This Point." Muffled shots popped on the other side of the door. He opened the duffel and snugged his headphones over his ears.

Three other shooters were inside the range. He chose a stall toward the far wall. It was hot. Sweat prickled at the back of his neck and under his arms. The smell of gunpowder was so strong it burned his nose. Vic was always frugal about turning the fans on. He said he went through air filters too fast if he blasted the fans all the time. Some of the other shooters complained, but Sanger actually relished it. The heat, the smoke, the odor. Even the sweat.

He put his safety glasses on and clicked a loaded mag into his gun, then loaded a target onto the holder—a large piece of heavy white paper with a life-sized outline of a human torso, from the hips up. He punched the button to send it sailing down to the other end. He racked the slide to chamber a round, then flipped the safety. The gun was heavy, not at all like he had imagined when he was a kid, playing with toy guns. The textured grip was rough and biting, the barrel slick and smooth. It felt solid and real in his hands, heavy enough to cause his shoulder muscles to fatigue, with a recoil that always sent a jarring reverberation up the length of his arm.

Poised to fire, his heart raced as he took aim. He squeezed the trigger four times in quick succession, striking the target in his favorite pattern: forehead, breastbone, left shoulder, right shoulder.

"Amen," he muttered, curling his lip.

Shooting was physical and tangible, not like the theoretical, invisible work he did all day in his mind and in his lab. What the hell were genes, nucleotides, proteases, introns and exons anyway, when at the range he held pure danger and the power of life and death in his hands?

Sanger had been here, standing in this very spot—after endless, pointless days of going through the motions, simply carrying out the trials just to complete the study that brought in grant money—when something had clicked and he knew instantly what he had to do.

The genetic crash cart wasn't an artificial gene spliced into the mess of the naturally-occurring genome. Sanger had bypassed all that crap with something far more elegant. But time-consuming. It had taken years to construct.

But he had still been devoted to his *real* life's work, the search for the thing that would destroy forever the arguments of the pathetic creationists, the miserable intelligent design crowd.

And when he finally *did* discover it—by accident—it surprised even him.

He expertly emptied the magazine into the target's brain.

A slap of the button brought the target billowing toward him. Sweat ran freely down his back and abdomen, into his eyes and mouth. He licked his lips, savoring the salty taste. He remembered a night years ago, a girl beneath him, a pillowcase that smelled like jasmine, and something else, something musky and arousing. But it was all wrong. Something had gone dreadfully wrong...

He blinked hard, and wiped his eyes. This wasn't helping. Usually shooting calmed him, helped him think. But, instead, he could feel himself becoming more and more enraged as he thought about the project and as old memories intruded.

Sanger was not old, not by a long shot, but he knew he was getting too old to start over. If his project were shut down, it would mean the end of almost twenty years of work.

He ripped the target down and snapped a fresh one in place. He slammed his palm against the button and waited for the new target to reach the end of the range.

So they were going to shut down his project. That lab rat and her roommate, and those animal doctors.

Like hell they were.

An image flashed into his mind: the tantalizing vine and roses tattoo. He wondered, not for the first time, just how far it went and where that vine was planted.

The instant the target stopped, he emptied the clip starting at the navel and ending at the neck, like a surgical blade slicing a body wide open from bottom to top.

He released the third spent mag and squatted down next to his bag. He jammed the pistol, the empty magazines, and the remaining ammo back into the duffel. He snatched the safety glasses and headphones off and stuffed them into the bag too. He jerked the zipper closed and strode to the door.

When he opened the door to the gun store, the cool air hit him and snapped him back to reality. He forced himself to saunter to the counter. To hell with Vic and his bad ass Russian shot gun.

The girl looked at him in surprise. "Done already?"

"Too hot in there for me, honey. Tell your dad to turn on those damn fans, huh?"

She rolled her eyes. "I know! He is such a cheapskate. He's always complaining about how expensive those air filters are."

"Your dad here?"

"Nope."

"What time you get off?"

She fixed him with a mock quizzical gaze. "Eleven. Why?"

Sanger shrugged. "I don't know. I could really go for a beer. Wanna come?"

"Where?"

"Someplace they got sandwiches. I'm starving."

She leaned on the counter, toward him. "I make great sandwiches."

He looked into her eyes and smiled.

Without looking away, she called out, "Hey, Marty?"

"Yo!"

"Hold down the fort for me? I'm gonna go home early."

Marty appeared in the doorway and broke the spell. "Say what?"

She pushed herself away from the glass countertop and squeezed past Marty into the office. She reappeared a moment later with her coat and purse. "I found a hungry waif and I'm gonna go home and feed him."

Marty snorted and shook his head.

Sanger hurriedly put on his coat and followed her out. He glanced back at Marty, who raised a hand toward him, middle finger extended.

To his surprise, though, instead of stepping into the parking lot toward their cars, she pulled his sleeve and led him down a sidewalk alongside the building. The walk rounded the corner and led to an exterior staircase. The banister was swathed in evergreens and red velvet bows. Above, on the landing, there was a miniature pine tree in a pot, draped in blinking lights.

When they reached the top of the stairs, she unlocked the door and they went in. She took off her coat and lit the Christmas tree. The glow of lights revealed a well-appointed studio apartment, all flowers and lace. Couch. TV. Small kitchenette. A bed in the corner.

"I'll be damned," he said, pulling the door closed behind him.

She slunk toward him, unzipped his jacket and slid it off his shoulders. It dropped to the ground at his heels. She put her hands on his hips and shoved him against the door, then moved in, pressing her pelvis against his.

"Ain't you worried about the noise?" he said.

Her lips were parted, exposing her perfect, white teeth. She looked like a feral cat. "Don't worry," she purred. "It's soundproof."

12

Angels and Spiders

WHY, GALTON MUSED, was he constantly surrounded by people who acted on thoughtless impulse? Those two lab techs, spiriting away a critically injured test subject from the kill floor. Garrett Sanger, confronting the whistle-blowers himself, as if the company actually needed his assistance in matters of security, then losing his temper when he discovered that they were not going to be shot on sight. True, Galton always had his weapon with him, but he certainly wasn't going to open fire in the middle of the Courier Café.

Even the way they had all stomped out of the restaurant without paying—first those three and then Sanger—all thoughtlessly impulsive.

Still, Galton had been a good sport. He had paid for the sandwiches, taken them "to-go," and given the waitress a generous tip, plus one of the sandwiches. He gave another sandwich to the cashier. Both of them accepted gratefully.

Cori Nelson's rash phone call to Sanger was unfortunate because it got Sanger involved in security issues. That little twerp, driving around in an SUV he needed a step ladder to get into. He shook his head. That car was emblematic of the pathetic man-child Garrett Sanger was, behind the wheel of a massive intellect, but possessing no discipline, which meant he had no control. He was always getting himself into situations that were too big for him, just like this research project. From what Galton had been able to gather about the biotechnology they were developing, it seemed that Sanger had stumbled upon a solution purely by chance. And now he was a Director, which perhaps was the main reason he was seemingly able to screw every woman in sight. His sexual conquests certainly inflated his ego, but in the end he was still a little man behind the wheel of a vehicle that was too big for him.

Galton already knew what had happened at Synthetic Genetics three days ago. The only thing he didn't know was where the subject was now. According to Cori Nelson, she and Adriana Munoz had taken the dog to an animal hospital, but one of the veterinarians told them he had taken the dog home. This minor problem of uncertainty was about to be rectified.

He crossed the street and approached a black Range Rover, which was idling quietly, yellow parking lights glowing in the darkness. The car seemed to pulse and vibrate with the rhythmic bass of a car stereo turned up way too loud for Galton's taste. He opened the passenger side door and got in.

The young black man at the wheel leaned forward immediately and switched off the stereo with one hand. With the other hand he pulled an in-ear monitor from one ear.

Galton removed a pin from his coat lapel and dropped it into the young man's palm. "Julius, did you get all that?"

"Yes," Julius replied. He placed the in-ear monitor and the lapel pin microphone into a small padded case, zipped it up, and dropped it into a compartment in the Range Rover's center console. "This is a serious security breach. Sanger was foolish."

"Foolish. Yeah, it was that." Galton could think of worse words for Sanger's stupidity. He handed Julius a slip of paper containing the missing subject's microchip number. "What does the chip say? Are they lying?"

Julius pulled a handheld tablet computer from his coat pocket. He clicked to a GPS service on the Internet and entered the chip number.

Galton took back the slip of paper and placed it in his pocket.

A moment later the results lit up the computer screen. "The subject is still at the animal hospital." Julius spoke with a lilting African accent. His English pronunciation was refined and precise. He showed Galton a satellite map of Champaign-Urbana, with a red pushpin icon showing the subject's exact location.

"Alive?" Galton asked.

Julius called up the Synthetic Genetics bioinformatics database, tapped and swiped the screen for a moment, then tilted it toward Galton. An ECG tracing scrolled along the bottom of the screen like a stock ticker, along with the respiration rate. The dog's body temperature was there, too.

"Put a trace on that chip and set it up so that I get an alert if it's moved."

Julius typed more commands into his computer.

Galton watched him carefully. Julius Abayomi had an interesting history: grew up in some kind of orphanage in Africa but turned out to be a computer *wunderkind*. He attended Makerere University in Uganda and completed two degrees in four years, one in computer science and one in business. Now he was a grad student at Illinois, in the College of Business, interning at Synthetic Genetics Group. Galton had tapped him to tackle the surveillance automation protocol he wanted to implement.

But something worried Galton. The young protégé was turning out to be adept at every aspect of the computer system. He seemed to know it all, and for the past few months, the system administration guys had been reporting various irregular but not exactly egregious computer glitches: unexplained CPU activity, disk usage, and traffic over the internal network. But the glitches always corrected themselves quickly. They said it was like glancing out a window and seeing a curtain fall quickly into place, as if someone were secretly watching and taking precautions not to be seen.

Julius finished typing. "Done. An alert to your cell phone, tablet, and office computer."

Galton stroked his mustache, thinking. "I'm bringing in a team to upgrade the whole security system," he said. "Gut it completely and rebuild the internal network from the ground up, revamp the protocol of back-ups to the remote data center, everything."

The young man's eyebrows shot up. "Starting when?" he asked.

"Soon. Before the New Year. A security breach of this magnitude proves our physical vulnerability. I think we need to assume that our computers are equally vulnerable."

Julius nodded. "That is an excellent idea. You can never be too careful. Let me know if I can be of useful assistance."

"I appreciate that, son." Galton pulled the second-to-last sandwich out of the bag and handed it to the young man, who thanked him politely.

"You're welcome. Merry Christmas." Galton got out and went to his own car. He passed a garbage can on the sidewalk and tossed the fourth sandwich into it, along with the piece of paper containing the subject's chip number.

* * *

After Galton left, Julius unwrapped the sandwich and took a bite. This latest development was most unfortunate. Galton's already extreme paranoia had intensified.

An intranet linked all the company's computers together, and the building also contained a roomful of servers housing SGG's data and operating systems. Every night at midnight, data streamed from the servers onto the Internet, backing up the day's work at a remote data center. Vulnerabilities in such a system were always possible. Reconstructing the computer security system was wise. Julius had to admire Galton's strategy.

But it would result in a significant delay in what Julius had come all the way from Africa to do. For the past twelve months, he had been working on the company's surveillance system, but had secretly been installing a suite of computer programs throughout the network. He called his computer programs Sun Angels, after the mythical name of the African meerkat. Meerkats lived in colonies and dug into the red earth with their powerful claws, constructing labyrinthine networks of tunnels and dens, with hidden escape hatches throughout their territory. Like meerkats, the Sun Angels programs burrowed their way past network security measures, hid themselves in niches of memory, and built little trapdoors for getting in and out without detection.

Once the tunnels and trapdoors were constructed, Julius sent in the Spiders. They clung to the Sun Angels with their sticky feet and gained access to the deepest parts of the system. Then the Spiders hopped off and crept into crevices the Sun Angels couldn't reach. In the mythology of his country, the clever trickster Anansi was sometimes depicted as a spider. Just like Anansi, Julius's Spiders always returned from their adventures with much wisdom. When he had used the Sun Angels and Spiders system in Africa, he had been able to discover astonishing things.

Julius's system of computer programs was nearly acclimated to its icy American environs, but it was not truly ready. It was not as elegant as Julius knew it could be, and at this point he could not be sure it would escape detection once it was launched. He had been proceeding under the assumption that he had unlimited time to do his work slowly and carefully.

But the theft of a key test subject from the facility had taken everyone by surprise. It was a random element for which no plan had been formulated.

The night of the subject's disappearance, Sanger had immediately called upon Julius to locate her. The technology of the microchips was highly advanced—all the electronics needed to receive GPS satellite data and monitor the subject's vital signs were packed into a device the size of a grain of rice. This alone would have been impressive, but these chips could also transmit the data, a function normally requiring a device many times the size of a typical identification microchip. But like all such devices, it needed power or it was just an impressive set of inert circuits. The genius of these chips is that they ran on the subjects' own juice, as it were, gleaning all the power they needed right from the body's own electrical impulses. It was ironic because the device wouldn't work if the subject died. Rosie's chip had gone dark that night. Julius and Sanger had both known there was nothing to be done except hope the employees who took her came forward.

The next morning the chip was active again, transmitting live bioinformatics data. In Galton's absence over the Christmas holidays, Julius had considered it his responsibility to at least monitor the situation, so he had followed the subject's chip to the animal hospital, and then followed the two veterinarians home. He had also been to the home of the two technicians who had disappeared the same night as the test subject.

It was good to know the location of the key players in this drama, but that knowledge was useless now. Galton's decision to immediately retrofit the computer security system would destroy everything Julius had done so far, like a bulldozer plowing up acres of soil in which generations of meerkats had built their underground maze of tunnels and burrows. He would have to start over.

Julius took another bite of the sandwich and chewed thoughtfully.

He was out of options. It was time to set the Sun Angels loose.

13

Bonfire Night

BRENDAN TOOK HIS SEAT in the priest's side of the confessional and prepared for a long, lonely hour to creep by. The Saturday confessions at St. Andrew's were never exactly jampacked, but since it was Christmastime, it was bound to be slower than usual. He dug his Rosary from his pocket, crossed himself, and began to pray.

It embarrassed Brendan to admit it, but he wasn't very good at praying the Rosary. The gentle repetition of the Hail Marys was meant to quiet the mind and promote reflection on the lives of Jesus and Mary, but Brendan's mind usually wandered into random areas: his to-do list, a book he was reading, the homily he was preparing for the next Sunday Mass. This time his mind drifted back to the night of his eighteenth birthday.

Brendan's parents owned a pub on the Falls Road in the Clonard neighborhood of Belfast, so they held a party for him there. Michaela and her parents had come for most of the summer, as usual, and it was now the week of the kids' birthdays: Brendan's on the eleventh of July, Nina and Michaela's on the twentieth.

The birthday party was already in full swing when Brendan arrived at the pub.

" 'Tis himself!'" someone shouted when he came in, and a few men left their seats to come and pound Brendan on the back or shake his hand. A chorus of "Happy Birthday" rang up around several raised pint glasses.

"God bless all here," Brendan said.

His father waved from behind the bar and pulled a pint of Guinness for him. "Happy birthday, son," he said as he set the brimming glass on the bar.

"Thanks, Da. Good health," he said, raising his glass.

Close behind Brendan were Connor Boone and three others: a young woman, and two young men—tough lads, as Nina called them. Connor hadn't toned down his punk look much, but since they were so accustomed to him, Brendan and his family never gave his appearance much thought. The newcomers, though, stood out glaringly in the pub full of traditionally clad neighbors. They were all in black leather, jeans and boots. The two boys had painted hair, one moussed up into a spiky green Mohawk, the other shaved close and dyed in the shape of the flag of the Irish Republic on either side. The young woman's hair was dyed black with a hint of purple, and she wore heavy black eyeliner and dark lipstick. J.J. greeted Connor and looked inquiringly at the others as they approached the bar.

Connor helped himself to a pint of Guinness. "Hello, J.J. Hope you don't mind that I brought a few friends."

"Not at all, Con." J.J. continued to fill glasses and set them on the bar. They were snapped up as quickly as he filled them.

Brendan saw Connor introduce the girl and the two boys to his father, but it was too loud for him to hear very well. No matter. It was probably better if his father forgot their names as soon as possible. They were only here to help Connor with his birthday present for Brendan, anyway. Connor had mentioned it briefly on the way over and said he would explain more when they got to the pub.

Brendan, Connor, and the others saluted J.J. with their drinks and moved off. Brendan could feel his father's eyes on his back. And no wonder. Connor's friends could hardly have been more suspicious. They might as well have stood on a bloody table in the middle of the pub and yelled, "We are volunteers for the Provisional IRA!"

On the way to the side room, Brendan met up with Michaela. "There you are," she shouted, and threw her arms around him. "Happy birthday!"

He hugged her. "Thanks, Mick." He released her and held her at arms' length. She was a bit flushed, and overly effusive, even for her. "You're not drunk, are you?"

She waved him off. "Who are your friends here? They look like Provo thugs."

Brendan sighed. She was drunk. Definitely taking advantage of the lax drinking laws overseas and her parents' total distraction—he hadn't even seen Sean and Alicia yet.

Connor broke in and introduced his friends as Danny, Mickey and Bridget.

Michaela snorted. "And I'm Marilyn Monroe. How do you do?" She shook their hands in turn. When she came to Connor she said, "At least I know *your* real name." She looked carefully at the lad with the flags on the sides of his head. "Interesting. Off to shoot a few Prods tonight?"

"Jesus, Mick, shut it!" Brendan hissed.

"Christ," Connor muttered, stifling a laugh.

Danny, Mickey, and Bridget merely grinned and thumped Brendan. They moved off into the other room, piled plates with food, and found a table. Michaela followed them and slipped in next to Brendan, knocking his elbow and spilling his beer. She grabbed his glass and took a swig.

"Go home with ye, Mick," Brendan grumbled, taking the glass away from her, then giving her a peck on the cheek.

"Bren," Michaela said. "Now that you're of age and you possess all wisdom from on high, I wonder if I could ask you a favor."

"What favor is that?"

"I want to go see the parades tomorrow."

Brendan shrugged. "So go, then."

Bridget, overhearing, gaped at Brendan. "Are ye daft? Any Prod would take one look at her and peg her for a filthy Taig on the spot."

"No, they wouldn't," Brendan retorted. "She's American. She's immune. And they don't bother with girls. You know that."

Michaela eyed Brendan's nearly full pint glass. "What's with you? It's your birthday. Drink up." She pushed his glass toward him.

Brendan touched his lips to the glass but didn't swallow. "If you go, Michaela, someone's got to go with you."

"Not me," said Nina. "And I can guarantee you Ma and Dad won't go."

"Don't even think about going alone," said Brendan. "It's too dangerous."

"I thought you said I was immune," Michaela said. "How about if I wave an American flag all the way?"

"That just might work," Nina said, with mock seriousness.

Connor leaned in. "Why do you even want to go over there, anyway? If you want to see Catholic-hating Prods, just go over to Woodvale tonight."

"I don't want to see Catholic-hating Prods. I want to see a normal parade."

"There are no normal parades here," Connor scoffed. "It's not like in America, with your July 4th and fireworks, Michaela. An Orange parade here is a chance for the Prods to flaunt their majority, wave in our faces that our unemployment rate is twice theirs, that the government, the police, and the army are on *their* side, and that their so-called freedom fighters in the UDA are legal and ours are outlawed."

"You mean the murderers in the IRA?" Michaela countered. "That's what the IRA is: a gang of losers, thugs, and murderers."

"And the Prods are all saints, I suppose?" Connor retorted. "What do you think the UDA are up to? Who do you think grabbed Timmy Murphy off the street in Derry last year and blew twenty holes in his head? Who slit Joey Moran's throat and then dragged him through the street tied to the bumper of a car? Since when has the IRA ever done anything like that?"

"The IRA killed Lord Mountbatten," Michaela replied.

"Yes, and they kill other politicians who are sympathetic to the Loyalists. The Provos have rational targets and professionally executed operations. The UDA are psychopaths. If you look Catholic, that's all the excuse they need."

Michaela snorted dismissively. "How can anyone look Catholic?"

"Maybe you have to live around here to understand," said Brendan, rejoining the conversation.

"No. Maybe you have to live somewhere else to understand," Michaela argued. "All this is just habitual and irrational. What you need to do is break the cycle of violence."

Brendan exchanged looks with Connor and his friends. Then they all burst out laughing.

Connor shook his head. " 'Break the cycle of violence' is it? And just how do you propose we do that, Ambassador?"

Nina stood up. "Come on, Michaela. Politics are boring."

Michaela stood up and followed Nina. On the way out, Nina turned around and stuck her tongue out at Brendan. He frowned back at her, pretending to be angry.

Bridget, spoke up. "Precocious, isn't she?"

"A little spitfire," Connor agreed. He picked up his glass and took a token sip. "Maybe we should take her with us tonight."

Brendan stood up. "I'll be right back."

He caught up with Michaela as she crossed the crowded pub. Putting a hand on her shoulder, he steered her out the back door. "I think you need some air," he said.

She dropped clumsily onto a beer crate.

Brendan sat down next to her. "You'll regret this in the morning," he said, putting his arm around her.

His cousin responded by putting her head on his shoulder and burping loudly into his face.

He gagged and spluttered dramatically, waving his hand in front of his face, laughing.

"Happy birthday, Bren," she said.

"Eleventh Night," Brendan grunted. "What a day to be born."

"What is it again?" Michaela slurred. "Something? The Battle of the Bulge?"

"Boyne," Brendan laughed. "Battle of the Boyne, ye daft thing. William of Orange, and all that. Why do you want to go to that parade, anyway?"

Michaela sighed. "I don't really. Load of Prod horseshit, right?"

"Right so," Brendan agreed.

The Battle of the Boyne—the victory of Protestant King William over Catholic King James—actually took place on the twelfth of July in 1690, but in the North the commemoration always started the night before, on Brendan's birthday. A lot of people were planning on getting good and drunk tonight and then going to the bonfires later, but the Collins family always made a point of staying in on Eleventh Night. J.J. and Viola had never allowed their children to go to any of the bonfires, rallies or parades because of the risk of violence. You just never knew what was going to happen.

But every year Brendan snuck out with Connor, and he had been to every Eleventh Night bonfire since the night he turned fourteen.

"Bren, you're eighteen now." Michaela said.

"And?" he said, knowing what she was going to say.

She straightened up and turned to him. "Now's your chance to get out of this place. Why don't you come to America?"

Brendan stood up. "Like your dad?" He had heard all about his Uncle Sean's miraculous conversion. It was all right for him, wasn't it? Seeing the light and running off to the promised land. He understood it, in a way. The taste of blood sometimes grew foul in Brendan's mouth, and the burden of keeping such a huge secret from his parents was wearing him down. It might be nice to live what Michaela kept telling him was a normal life.

But Brendan had responsibilities. Commitments. It was all so complicated. How could he possibly explain it to Michaela? He shook his head. "It's not so easy, Mick," he said finally, turning to her.

She looked up at him. "Bren, come on. Don't be so stubborn."

Then the back door opened. It was Uncle Sean. "There ye are," he said to Michaela. He took in her slumped posture and flushed features. "Young lady," he warned.

Michaela stood up and shuffled to her father, unable even to pretend to be sober. "I'm sorry, Daddy," she said, leaning into him. "I'm only half Irish."

Sean laughed and wrapped his arms around his daughter. "There now," he murmured into her hair.

Sean winked at Brendan. Then, remembering, he said, "Your pals are looking for you."

"Thanks," Brendan said. He glanced at his watch. It was time to go.

He looked at Michaela, and he could swear by the look in her eyes that he hadn't been able to keep his secret from her.

A little clock in the confessional chimed the half hour.

That had been his chance, Brendan realized. His chance to walk away from the IRA, from the Troubles, from all of it. Instead, he had stuck to the plan and slipped out of the pub with Connor.

They walked south on the Falls Road for a few minutes in order to get far enough away from the pub to ensure the car they lifted didn't belong to anyone attending Brendan's party. They chose a car, and Brendan removed a knife from his pocket. One of the blades was roughly serrated—the result of a few minutes' work on a grinder—and it fit perfectly into most car door locks. He inserted the blade into the lock, jiggled and pulled for a few seconds until he felt it grab, then turned it counterclockwise to unlock the door. He climbed behind the wheel and reached across to unlock the passenger door for Connor. Then he went to work on the ignition; a few seconds with the modified blade and the car started.

He pulled out onto the road and turned around, following it southeast toward the Springfield Road. Instead of turning and entering the Clonard from the south, Brendan drove straight through the intersection and made a large, clockwise detour around his neighborhood so that they could enter the Clonard from the north.

They arrived in the Woodvale district, which used to be mixed but was now almost entirely Protestant. Brendan killed the lights, drove the car carefully off the road and crossed a grassy field. He turned the car around and then backed it onto Pollard Street. Then he and Connor got out and walked up Pollard to where it joined the Springfield Road.

They were on the Catholic side of the road. On the other side were the Protestants, whose annual bonfire at this location was always huge and whose revelry was always offensive to their Catholic neighbors. Workman Avenue came down and joined the Springfield Road from the north, and it was here that the Protestants lit their bonfire. The curbs on the north side were painted red, white, and blue, the colors of the Union Jack. Numerous men in the crowd wore bright orange bowler hats.

The bonfire was already two stories high. A fire truck parked on the Protestant side sprayed water onto the roofs of the buildings nearest the fire. On the Catholic side, armed police in riot gear stood with their backs to the fire, keeping their eyes on the Catholics who had gathered to watch.

The Protestants were singing lustily. They had changed the words to *If You're Irish, Come into the Parlour (There's a Welcome Here for You)* to "If you're Catholic, stay out of the Shankill, there's a nail bomb here for you."

Brendan and Connor ignored them. They walked casually toward the fire, scanning the crowd. Then Brendan saw Tommy Morgan. He had carrot red hair cut in a mullet, and he wore parachute pants and a matching two-tone jacket. Brendan and Connor walked a few feet toward him, then stopped and leaned casually against a wall.

Connor nudged Brendan and motioned to something across the street. The young man Connor had introduced as Danny was there, swilling something from a green bottle, laughing loudly, and periodically tossing firecrackers into the bonfire. As each one exploded he would crack a joke to someone nearby and clink bottles with them, the very picture of Protestant bonhomie on Eleventh Night. His wild green Mohawk had been carefully shaven off and his clothing toned down to black denim with no chrome.

Connor pushed himself from the wall and took off south down the Springfield Road—Bridget was heading toward him. Her purse hung from her left shoulder, the signal that she had walked the gun in without any problems. When she reached the house directly across from where Mayo Street formed a T with the Springfield Road, the door opened for her and she went in. A moment later she came out, the purse now on her right shoulder, signaling that the gun was now in the house. Connor and Bridget passed each other without acknowledgement. Connor was to enter the house, and Bridget was to watch the bonfire from the Catholic side of the road. The crowd along the road effectively shielded Connor and Bridget's movements from anyone who might be watching, including the police.

Once the gun drop was complete, it was time for Brendan to make contact with Tommy Morgan. Brendan shoved his hands into his pockets and slowly approached. "Tommy, boy!"

Tommy looked over at him and grinned. He stepped forward and extended his hand. "Hey, Bren. Getting' plenty of it, I hope?"

Brendan shook his hand and then thumped him on the shoulder. "Not as much as you, Tom." He steered him away from the crowd. "Let's get out of here, Tommy. If they have an audience, it only encourages them."

Tommy shuffled his feet.

Brendan tried again. "Look, it's me birthday."

"Is it now?"

"It is. And I don't want to spend it listening to all that tripe." Brendan led Tommy south, toward Mayo Street. "Come down to Ma and Da's pub and buy me a drink."

"All right." Tommy fell into step with him. Brendan kept Tommy on the inside, close to the houses.

The house opposite the Mayo Street T-junction was chosen because its front door opened directly onto the sidewalk. As they passed the door, it opened, a hand emerged, grabbed Tommy by the sleeve and yanked him inside. Brendan followed him in and quickly shut the door behind him.

Inside, a man in a black knit ski mask slammed Tommy Morgan against the wall and hissed in his ear. "Got your attention now, have we boyo?" It was the man Connor called Mickey.

Connor—also wearing a black ski mask—stood nearby, in the shadows of the darkened house. "Take him to the kitchen," he said. Brendan knew it was Connor, but even he was chilled by his eerily calm voice.

"Hey!" Tommy blurted out. "What's this about? I done nothing! I'm on your side, you know that. Bren! Tell him! Ahhch!" Tommy cried out as Mickey slammed his head against the wall.

Brendan had no idea whose house this was, but evidently it was empty. Tommy's shouts and the scraping of heavy boots echoed in the hollow space.

Once in the kitchen, Mickey forced Tommy out of his jacket, tossed it to Connor, then pushed Tommy onto a wooden chair staged dramatically in the middle of the room.

Connor tossed Brendan a roll of duct tape. Tommy struggled as Brendan taped his arms to the chair. At one point he managed to free one of his arms and grab a handful of Brendan's hair.

Brendan wrenched Tommy's hand away and punched him full in the face. His nose snapped and blood spurted. "Hold still, you bastard," Brendan snarled and continued taping his arms down.

"Fuck you!" Tommy spat, spraying blood all over Brendan's face and neck while trying to kick him with both feet.

Brendan angrily punched Tommy full in the gut. It momentarily knocked the wind out of him and Brendan was able to tape his legs to the chair without much difficulty.

When Tommy was secured and had stopped cursing and protesting, Connor walked toward him, holding the jacket and examining it with showy curiosity. "This is a great jacket, Tom. You look right smart in it." He eyed Tommy. "And your new pants. Very flash. Latest style. You look like fucking Michael Jackson. Gonna sing and dance for us, are you? The way you sing and dance for the Prods?"

Tommy sniffed. "What're you talking about?" His voice was thick with his own blood.

Connor continued. "These are pricey clothes, eh? Nice haircut, too." He slapped his hand against Tommy's head. "How much for that haircut?"

Tommy smiled, a grotesque bloody leer. "You think I'm on the take? That I'm toutin' to the Prods?"

"We know ye'are, Tommy. People been talkin.' Quite a good find ye led them to the other night."

Tommy shook his head, talking fast. "No. No, that wasn't me. I haven't told them anything."

Connor grabbed Tommy by the hair and yanked his head back. "You expect us to believe that? The Brits just *happened* to do a random check on the house where we had three hundred pounds of gelignite stashed?"

Tommy's voice cracked. "I don't know who told them." He looked wildly around at Connor, Brendan, and Mickey. "The Brits have approached me, all right? I won't deny that. They're trying to get to me. They passed me a few quid to think it over, like, 'cause they figure I know some Provos."

"You do know some Provos, you little shit," Connor growled.

"But I didn't say anythin' to anybody."

"Then who was it, Tommy? Who told the Brits we had a cache at that house?"

"I don't know!"

Connor nodded at Brendan, who punched Tommy twice in the face. Tommy hung his head and spat blood.

The British soldiers had set wires and blown the stash, destroying adjacent buildings and rattling the surrounding neighborhood. At least they had the decency to evacuate the area first, so no one was killed, but they could have safely removed the explosives and detonated them in a remote area. Instead, they deliberately chose to blow them up in the middle of the Clonard, as an example-setting gesture, with the added bonus of causing economic hardship and disruption to Catholic business owners and residents. Every window in the Collins house had shattered and the plaster in Brendan's room had cracked floor to ceiling.

Brendan, breathing hard, stepped back. He pulled his knife from his pocket and flipped open the real blade.

Tommy's eyes widened. "Jesus, Bren…"

Mickey stepped forward, grabbed a handful of Tommy's red hair and forced his head back.

Brendan inserted his blade into Tommy's right nostril. "Remember this movie, Tommy?"

"Oh, Christ," Tommy whispered. A tear spilled from his eye and ran down his bloody and bruised face.

"Tell us who you're talkin' to," Brendan said, "and who else is talkin'." He pressed the blade against the inside of Tommy's nose. "Flick of the wrist, Tommy."

Tommy held his head rigidly still, but his eyes darted around wildly. He looked to Brendan like a man trying to think up a lie. "I don't know," he whimpered. "I don't know anything."

Connor nodded. "Make him beautiful, Brendan."

With a quick motion of his blade hand, Brendan sliced clean through Tommy's right nostril. Tommy shrieked and thrashed as blood gushed. "Jesus God!" he cried. "Jesus Christ!"

"Anytime you're done blaspheming the holy name of God, Tommy," Connor taunted.

"All right, all right," Tommy sobbed. "I told 'em about the stuff. But that's all."

"Names?" Mickey growled in his ear.

"No! I didn't tell them any names." He laughed hideously. "I don't even *know* any names, except you and Con, and I'd never...God help me, Brendan, I'm tellin' the truth!" Blood sprayed from his lips as he spoke.

Brendan walked up to Connor and took Tommy's jacket from him. He wiped his blade on the jacket, then gave a slight nod into the other room. "Have a word?" he muttered, almost inaudibly.

Connor followed him out to the front room and shut the door behind him.

Brendan folded up his knife and shoved it back into the pocket of his jeans. "I've known Tommy since we were lads. You know he's always been a bit thick."

Connor shrugged.

"Can't put things together," Brendan continued. "He's not observant. The Brits couldn't have picked a worse informant. Plus, he's so stupid he doesn't even realize that what he just told us means we'll probably kill him. He really doesn't know any names. He and his mates and their stupid hooligan stunts attract more attention than we'd like, but ever since you dropped him, he's stayed out of it. He's a civilian."

Connor sighed. "So he told us a tale? Vomited that confession expecting gratitude and mercy? 'Well, done, Tommy, for coming clean,' and all that?"

Brendan nodded. "But even if he is the one who touted, you think he'd even *look* at a peeler after tonight? Let's just knee cap him and be done with it."

Connor walked to the window and peered through the blinds. The crowd on the Springfield Road was growing. Danny—and by the sounds of it a few others—were still setting off firecrackers.

Suddenly, Connor turned around and grinned. " 'Remember this movie, Tommy?' " he said, imitating Brendan. "What happens next? He loses the whole thing?"

Brendan breathed a quiet sigh of relief. "I cut it off and feed it to my goldfish," he laughed.

When Brendan returned to the kitchen, he was unable to conceal the expression of shock that involuntarily crossed his features. Tommy Morgan was unrecognizable. His carefully styled red hair was tangled and spiky with dried blood, one eyelid was swollen shut, and his mutilated and crooked nose looked like mincemeat. Tommy peered at them through eyelids caked with blood. The front of his shirt was soaked dark red.

Connor, entering the kitchen behind him, sniffed dramatically. "What's that smell? I do believe we've made the poor bastard soil his new flash trousers."

Mickey laughed. He was standing by the kitchen door smoking a cigarette.

Connor nodded at Mickey. "Go upstairs and get ready to give Danny the signal."

Mickey snuffed out his cigarette, stomped across the kitchen and went upstairs.

Brendan took his knife out of his pocket again and flicked it open. Tommy started to whimper and struggle against the restraints, then gasped as he saw Connor standing there with a pistol in his hand.

"Relax, Tommy," Brendan said as he started slicing through the tape. "We're letting you go. Just behave yourself, all right? No more toutin' to the peelers?"

Tommy shook his head.

"There's a good lad," Connor said.

Brendan finished cutting the tape and then lifted Tommy out of the chair. He pushed him out of the kitchen and into the front hall, then held out his jacket and helped him into it.

Connor handed Brendan the gun. "Would you like to do the honors?"

Brendan took the gun.

Connor called up the stairs. "Now, Mickey."

Brendan looked up as he heard the blinds in the front upstairs room drop down with a soft clatter. He dropped his gaze and took aim at the back of Tommy's right leg.

"Wait for it…" Connor said.

"Don't worry, Tommy," said Brendan. "Best knee surgeons in the world are right here in Belfast."

Tommy finally realized what was going on and began to look around wildly. "Wait a minute, Bren! Wait!"

Connor threw Tommy face first into the front door.

Then there was a deafening burst outside as Danny saw the signal in the upstairs window and threw the whole packet of firecrackers into the bonfire.

Brendan pulled the trigger and fired a bullet into the back of Tommy's leg, aiming for the back of the knee. Quickly, he took aim at the other leg and fired. The firecrackers outside and the ensuing cheers and yells from the crowd masked the sounds of the gunshots.

With a cry of pain, Tommy slid to the floor.

"Just open the door and crawl out, Tommy," Connor said. "Somebody'll call the peelers for ye." Then he yelled up the stairs. "Let's go!"

Mickey clambered down the stairs and together the three men raced for the kitchen door. They yanked it open and ran out into the back garden. Connor and Mickey ripped off their ski masks and dropped them on the ground.

Bridget was there behind the house, on Pollard Street and heading toward the Springfield Road. She took the gun smoothly, casually dropping it into her purse and continuing her stroll, heading back toward the bonfire. Mickey fell into step with her, casually lighting a cigarette.

Brendan and Connor took off the other way. When they reached the car, Brendan drove back the way they had come, across the grassy field and back onto the Springfield Road heading west, observing what he hoped was a casual speed.

Connor turned to look out the rear window. No lights, no sign of vehicles behind them. He turned around and blew out his cheeks. Then he grinned at Brendan. "Your first kneecapping. Happy birthday, Bren."

"Thanks."

"Thought you'd enjoy it." Connor dug out a cigarette, lit it, and sat back.

Then suddenly, ahead in the distance, two sets of headlights blazed to life.

Brendan slowed the car and peered ahead. It was a roadblock. Two vehicles were parked on either side of the road and a barrier blocked their way: planks mounted on a set of sawhorses. Simple and portable. Several armed men appeared in the wash of the headlights, their automatic machine guns clearly visible in silhouette.

As they drew closer, Brendan and Connor recognized their uniforms. Connor gripped the door handle and stiffened in his seat.

"God help us," Brendan muttered. Prod paramilitaries. If they stopped here, Brendan knew that he and Connor would never be seen again. Not in one piece, anyway.

"Gun it!" Connor shouted.

Brendan punched the accelerator to the floor. The car lurched forward. He worked the clutch and slammed into high gear. The soldiers scrambled around and took aim with their weapons as the car screamed toward them. "Get down, Con!" Brendan yelled.

Brendan had been running British road blocks since he was a thirteen-year-old carjacker. He had been shot at more times than he could remember. He knew how to do this. He kept his foot down and his hand on the wheel, then ducked down, closed his eyes and roared through. British soldiers usually didn't shoot, because they never knew if they were dealing with terrorists or just stupid kids, but Brendan knew these men wouldn't hesitate.

He flinched as bullets clanged against the grill of the car and smashed through the windshield. As he crashed through the planks of the roadblock, the car lurched sideways and scraped one of the vehicles. He risked pushing himself upright so he could straighten the car, and felt a bullet whiz past his head as the gunmen peppered the car.

Brendan careened around the bend through Ballymurphy, then swerved left onto the first street he could. He took random rights and lefts, then finally shuddered to a stop in a narrow lane behind some row houses. He looked behind him. No lights. No vehicles.

"Lost 'em, I think, Con." But Connor didn't answer: he was slumped forward in his seat. "Con?" Brendan shook him, but succeeded only in pushing him against the passenger side door. Connor's head hit the window and smeared it with blood. "Bloody hell." Brendan grasped Connor's hair and turned his face toward him. He shuddered at the sight of Connor's blank eyes and the bullet hole through his face. "Shit!" Brendan shouted. He pushed Connor away from him and pounded the steering wheel.

The smartest thing to do would be to lift another car and proceed to the safe house, only Connor had not told Brendan the location. In any case, he knew he couldn't stay here. He opened the driver's side door and grunted. As pain lanced through his shoulder, he realized with alarm that he'd been shot.

Despite excruciating pain, he managed to steal another car and drive it unsteadily back to the Clonard. He abandoned it on the Falls Road and did the only thing he could think of: he staggered home.

He remembered stumbling through the back door into the empty kitchen, hearing his father call to him from the front room, footsteps and voices all around him. The room had shifted beneath his feet, tilting, turning, until darkness dropped over his eyes. Michaela had been the one who caught him as he toppled sideways.

* * *

Brendan looked at the beads in his hand, annoyed with himself. He had obliviously prayed the whole Rosary while in his head he had been an ocean away, fruitlessly reliving that night. And there was more, but the hour was up. He left the confessional, locked the church, and went back to the rectory.

Not a single person had come to confession.

14

Dirty Money

AFTER THE EXCITEMENT AT THE COURIER CAFÉ, Michaela had a hard time concentrating on her cases the next day. Every moment, she expected Adriana to arrive, raring to go with the plan to shut down Synthetic Genetics. The morning came and went, though, and Michaela was in her office finishing a lunch of Christmas leftovers when Abby came to the doorway and knocked. "Dr. Collins, there's an Adriana Munoz to see you. The woman from the other night?"

Hastily, Michaela finished her last bite and wiped her mouth. "Thanks, Abby. Ask her to come in."

Adriana came in and sat down, unnaturally straight in her chair. She had a sheaf of paper in her hand, rolled tightly into a tube, which she gripped and twisted over and over again. All enthusiasm from last night was gone.

"What's wrong?" Michaela asked.

"Some company lawyers came to Cori and me at our apartment this morning." She opened her mouth to speak, but then stopped and simply unrolled the paper and handed it to Michaela.

It was a document densely covered with legal language, but Michaela was able to decipher enough of it to understand. She looked up at Adriana and sighed.

"Cori accepted the offer. She's moving out of our apartment as we speak. She'll have enough money to buy a place of her own."

"And then some," Michaela said wryly. *Enough to wipe her conscience clean,* she thought.

"Cori told them everything," Adriana continued. "And they're really pouring it on. They've closed the lab for the holidays, given everybody a huge bonus and paid time off for an extended holiday break."

"They're buying everybody's silence," Michaela said.

Adriana's hesitation spoke volumes. "What will you do if I accept the offer, too?"

A wave of indignation swept over Michaela. "Oh, no you don't, Adriana."

"What do you mean?"

"You want to make sure I'm still going to follow through, so you can quit with a clear conscience, is that it?" Michaela said. Adriana had to know that if she and Cori both walked away, the only thing standing between Rosie and the vivisectionists at Synthetic Genetics would be Michaela and Terry's moral rectitude. "You dragged me into this and now you expect me to make it easy for you?"

Adriana's eyes widened.

"Thanks a lot, Adriana."

"They'll come to you next," Adriana said, defensively.

Michaela nodded. They had offered Adriana an astonishing amount of money. How could anyone stay strong in the face of such temptation?

Michaela was on her own now.

* * *

At the end of the day, Michaela sat down at her desk to return phone calls. She worked her way through the stack of files and was just finishing her notes on the last one when Terry walked in, carrying three rustling plastic bags. "Zorba's," he said, placing the first bag on the desk with a flourish.

"Excellent," Michaela said, attacking the bag and unloading the food. "I love you forever."

"I also got this," he said, passing her a small plastic bag from a local drugstore.

Michaela opened it and pulled out a small box. It was a pregnancy test kit.

Terry smiled. "Today would be a good day to check."

She did a quick calculation in her head. He was right. She didn't realize he had been keeping track so carefully. "You marched right up to the counter and bought this?" she said with a laugh. "Weren't you embarrassed?"

"Heck, no. The guy at the counter pumped his fist at me. Did the knuckle tap. It was a very manly moment."

"Let's hope he's right," she said, taking a huge bite of her sandwich. It was delicious.

"Michaela?"

"Hm?"

"You are so beautiful when you're stuffing your face with unhealthy food."

She tossed a sliced tomato at him. "What else did you get?"

Terry opened the third bag and removed a large capacity external hard drive. "We can digitize all the data on Rosie," he said. "We'll have it all in one place, and we can crank out copies as needed for that lawyer of David's, or whoever needs it."

"Speaking of which," Michaela said, "looks like we're on our own." She told him about Adriana.

"Wow," he said. "Must be tough to have such unshakable convictions."

"Don't be too quick to judge her. We'll be in the same position by this evening." She looked at her watch. "Dr. Sanger will be here in a few minutes. He called earlier and made an appointment for a 'consultation.' "

"Since when does a geneticist hand out the hush money?" Terry mused.

Michaela collected the sandwich wrappings and tossed them in the trash. "He's already blown his cover. Maybe they want to avoid exposing anybody else," she theorized. "Come on," she said, standing up. "Let's go check on Rosie."

Once again, the dogs in the kennel refrained from their usual cacophonous greetings. In the eerie silence, Michaela approached Rosie's cage. The dog in the run next to hers stood rigid, ears straight up, hackles bristling.

It was somewhat cool in the kennel, but not cold. Yet Michaela felt her skin prickle. She wrapped her arms around herself and shuddered.

Rosie was asleep on the floor.

Michaela whispered, "Rosie?" The dog opened her eyes and lifted her head, ears up expectantly. "Wanna go outside?" Like any normal dog, Rosie got to her feet and came toward the gate.

As Rosie got close to them, Terry grimaced. "What's that smell?"

Michaela could smell it too, a foul odor that she had encountered many times—the smell of a wound going bad. But there was something else about it, something familiar that she couldn't quite place. Michaela opened the cage and crouched down to inspect the bullet wounds, but they looked fine: no discharge or swelling, and no sign of infection or necrosis.

She gently held Rosie's head and examined her right eye. These wounds, also, were neither infected nor necrotic in appearance, but the stench was overwhelming. Suddenly it hit Michaela where she had encountered this odor before: driving past a bloated dead possum, putrefying in the sun. When a client brought in a dog for cremation that had died over the weekend when they'd been away. When she was hiking and came across a deer that had succumbed to its wounds but had not been retrieved by its hunter.

It was the smell of decay and decomposition. The smell of death. And it was coming from Rosie, not just from her wounds but from her whole body and her breath.

Michaela took Rosie's face in her hands. For an instant, she saw a normal, good-natured dog. Then, as she looked further into the depths of the dog's eyes, Michaela gasped as the life slowly drained out of them. Rosie's pupils dilated and her amber irises receded to mere margins around pools of black emptiness.

She turned to look at Terry. He looked like he was going to be sick, but his jaw was set with resolution.

Rosie stood motionless, and the breath on Michaela's face reeked like the stench from an open grave. "My God, Terry. What have they done?"

* * *

Later that evening, Abby came to tell them that Dr. Sanger was waiting for them in the comfy room.

"Thanks, Abby," said Michaela. "Go ahead and take off. We'll lock up when we're done."

Outside the door of the comfy room, Terry took Michaela's hand and gave it a reassuring squeeze. "You ready?"

She nodded, and he pushed the door open.

Garrett Sanger wasted no time with pleasantries. He held up a thick sheaf of paper. "This is a non-disclosure agreement," he said. "The company would appreciate your understanding regarding the sensitive nature of our research. We intend to compensate you fairly for your cooperation and discretion." His lines sounded rehearsed, like a little boy uttering a memorized apology. He tossed the document onto the coffee table. "The whole protocol is in there."

This was why the biotech company hadn't done anything yet, Michaela realized, even though a valuable specimen had been missing for four days. They could have pressed charges and marched in here with law enforcement. They could have broken in during the night and taken everything. Instead, they were giving her and Terry the chance to return Rosie to them, along with all the evidence, without fuss. Clean and quiet.

She and Terry sat side-by-side on the couch and paged through the document together. In painstaking detail, it outlined the conditions of their silence. They were to turn over all company property immediately. By that they meant Rosie. All images of company property, all medical records pertaining to said company property, originals and copies or facsimiles—all were to be surrendered. They were not to divulge, in conversation, in writing, or by any other means, the nature of their association with Synthetic Genetics, the nature of the work, the names or identities of its employees, or even the company's existence. If they violated the terms of the agreement, all remuneration would cease and they would be sued for reimbursement of all previous monies theretofore distributed, and on and on for several pages.

The financial offer appeared on the last page. Terry and Michaela looked at each other, trying but not succeeding to conceal their shock. Terry exhaled slowly.

Let 'em bring it, Michaela had said last night at the Courier. And they had brought it, all right. This was one hell of an opening salvo.

Michaela glanced at Sanger, who gazed at them with a satisfied smirk. It was so much money that for a moment Michaela forgot what she would have to do in exchange for it. Silence and inaction seemed like a small price to pay.

She didn't want to speak for Terry. They needed to confer, just to make sure they were on the same page. When she finally spoke, her voice cracked. "Give us a minute?"

Sanger waved his hand magnanimously. "Go right ahead, darlin,' " he said, winking suggestively.

Terry rose to his feet, hotly. "We don't need a minute, you smug son-of-a-bitch. You can take your 'non-disclosure agreement' and shove it straight up your ass." He picked up the document and threw it at Sanger's face.

The papers cascaded to the floor at Sanger's feet.

Michaela stood up. "I want to show you something."

They went to the isolation ward. Taped to the glass observation window was a note that read "Dangerous animal. Do not touch! Do not feed! Do not walk! See Dr. Collins FIRST."

Michaela unlocked the door and opened it wide.

Sanger recoiled at the smell.

"Do you get it now?" Michaela said. "Rosie's body is decomposing, but she's still alive."

Sanger folded his arms. "We want this dog back. Just give her to me, along with all the records, and you'll never hear from me again."

"No way," Michaela said. "She's had enough of you and your experiments." She pulled the door shut and locked it. "This conversation is over," she said.

They led Sanger into the waiting room and watched him shove the front door open, climb into his SUV and roar into the night.

Michaela looked up at Terry. His arms were crossed in front of him and the muscles along his jaw were clenched. He took a deep breath and let his arms drop to his sides.

She held up her fist and he tapped it with his. "Way to put your Irish on, Terry."

15

Memento Mori

"DAMMIT!" SANGER SHOUTED into the cold winter air. He unlocked his SUV and climbed in. Why had he agreed to act as Galton's errand boy in the first place? How come he didn't tell the man to deliver his precious protocol himself or go to hell? It was beneath him to be the one sent to deliver the nondisclosure agreement to those two animal doctors. Sanger was a geneticist. He had invented the damn thing, for crying out loud.

He jammed the key into the ignition and cranked it, hard. The engine's starter squealed, but Sanger didn't care. He backed out of the parking stall, yanking the wheel furiously, and tore across the lot. At a break in the cross traffic he over-accelerated and nearly jumped the curb across the street. He swore as he felt his tires scrape concrete and the rear of the SUV slide sideways. With another guttural curse, he straightened out and swerved onto the road.

He took the next driveway he came to—some strip mall— and grabbed a random parking spot. His breath came in thin, fast gasps. He had to settle down. He had to think.

Years and years of work was about to go down the tubes. Genetics was Sanger's life's work, but now he worried that it was going to kill him. It had been his lifeline, too. Once. Genetics had been everything.

Sanger's obsession with DNA began when he was a sophomore at the University of Illinois. Not in a class or a seminar. It wasn't a fascination built on knowledge for the sake of knowledge. It had begun with a pure, unfiltered instinct to survive...

It was two in the morning. He and his date were walking back to her place. Earlier, they had been to the annual Green Street celebration, a semi-sanctioned Halloween costume parade and block party that had devolved into a drinking free-for-all.

Sanger's costume was a black body suit, screen-printed front and back with a full skeleton. His mask glowed in the dark, and the gloves even had phalanges and metacarpals. When he had zipped himself into the suit that evening, he had noted with annoyance that it was tight across his chest and abdomen. He would really need to do something about that.

His date wore pink, polka-dotted flannel pajamas, big fuzzy slippers, and carried a teddy bear. They left Green Street, crossed Wright, and walked past the Alma Mater statue, heading for the gap between Altgeld Hall and the Illini Student Union.

Earlier, he had slipped her some Rohypnol, just in case, but she had made that unnecessary by drinking way too much alcohol. Sanger was buzzed, but not drunk enough to dull his senses. She was already staggering, and her huge slippers weren't helping. She was also horny as hell—one hand gripping his arm, to keep herself upright, the other clumsily attempting to unzip his body suit. Every few steps she would stop, fling her arms around his neck and kiss him lustily, which was great except that at this rate it would take all night to walk back to her room. She rented a house on Lincoln Avenue with a few other girls, but she told him she had a room all to herself.

Impatient to reach her house, he hitched her onto his back. She laughed and wrapped her legs around him. They emerged from the dim space between the Union and Altgeld and out onto the Main Quad. Garrett crossed the Quad diagonally and entered the space between Noyes Lab and the Chemistry Annex. They crossed Mathews Street, continued between the buildings, crossed Goodwin, and finally ended up in front of the Krannert Center. He set her down on a bench and pushed the mask off his face.

She looked up at him with half-closed eyes and a sleepy grin. "Are we there yet?" she slurred.

"Not quite, baby," Sanger panted. "Just catchin' my breath a sec." He leaned forward and rested his hands on his knees.

"Take me to bed or lose me forever," she drawled, then lunged for him.

He pulled the mask back over his face, turned around and picked her up again. When they reached Lincoln Avenue, she handed him her keys. He managed to unlock the back door, and they lurched inside and down the hallway to her room, shushing each other with restrained laughter. They stumbled onto her bed while pulling each other's clothes off, and in a few minutes it was over. She was relaxed and totally compliant.

Breathing hard, hovering over her, he gulped in the smell of her hair, her sweat, her pillowcase, jasmine and musk. He was ready for more. He kissed her, trying to wake her up. "Lot more where that came from, baby," he murmured, but she was unresponsive.

He frowned and propped himself up on his elbows. "Come on, darlin'. We're just gettin' started." He slapped her face and shook her shoulders. "Hey!" he said. Her eyes were closed, her mouth slack. She was totally still.

"God damn!" he hissed. He reached for the bedside lamp and switched it on. She was pale, all the color drained from her lips. He leaned over her, holding his breath. Perspiration dripped from his face onto hers. She was not breathing. He felt for a pulse in her neck.

Nothing.

"Fuck!" he yelled.

He scrambled off the bed, still cursing. He straddled a small garbage can, removed the condom and let it drop into the plastic lining of the can.

He returned to the bed and shook the girl. "Come on, come on," he urged. She was limp. Again he checked for a pulse and watched to see if she was breathing. The amnesiac effects of the Rohypnol were well known—that's why he used it. He had seen girls pass out cold with it, but this…it must be all the alcohol.

He put on his briefs, zipped himself into the body suit, then put on his shoes and socks. He looked around for the gloves. He found them on the floor and worked them back onto his hands.

Then he realized something. He was wearing the gloves when he came in. But what had he touched after peeling them off? The girl. The lamp. Had he touched the doorknob? The dresser?

The girl's roommates could come home any second.

He opened the bedroom door and crept into the hallway. The house was completely dark and silent. He found the bathroom and turned on the light. He grabbed a hand towel and ran it under the water, then returned to the girl's bedroom and wiped down every surface he might have touched, including the girl.

He was wiping her hands, when it occurred to him: her fingernails. Had she scratched him? He searched frantically through her dresser drawers and found a pair of nail clippers. He positioned the small garbage can underneath the girl's hands and trimmed her nails close. After a moment's hesitation, he dropped the clippers into the can, too. He wiped her nail beds and cuticles, scrubbed them and the tips of her fingers.

His fingerprints were everywhere. They had to be. The bedside table. The lamp. The dresser. The doorknob. He couldn't be sure what he had touched, so he wiped everything.

He went to the kitchen and rummaged around until he found a large plastic bag and a bottle of spray cleanser. He returned to the bedroom and sprayed every surface, then wiped it all down again. He removed the small plastic bag from the girl's garbage can and placed it in the large bag from the kitchen. The girl's pajamas and underclothes also went into the bag. He pulled the bedspread out from under the girl and put that in the bag, too. They had not disturbed the rest of the bedding, but he took the pillowcases anyway. He sprayed the wood floor around the bed and scrubbed it with the towel, and then jammed the towel into the plastic bag.

The house was still silent. He found a stick vacuum in a hall closet and went over the floor all around the bed, next to the dresser, everywhere. He removed the vacuum cleaner bag, wrenched the brush attachment from the bottom of the vacuum cleaner and stuffed them both in the garbage bag. He wiped the vacuum cleaner before returning it to the closet. Then, thinking the better of that, he took the whole thing apart and stuffed it into the garbage bag, too. He put two pillows under the girl's head to prop her up, then covered her with the sheet and blanket from her bed.

Sanger remembered standing back and surveying the room. The girl appeared to be sleeping peacefully.

He looked around for his mask and found it on the bedside table. He put it on, then switched off the light. As he passed the mirror, the phosphorescent, yellow-green mask seemed to float like the disembodied head of The Grim Reaper.

Slinging the plastic bag over his shoulder, Sanger hurried from the room and tiptoed out of the house.

When he got back to his frat house it was four in the morning. A Halloween bonfire on the front lawn had burned to embers and was left unattended. He threw in the plastic bag, stripped off the black body suit and stood there in his underwear, watching as the fire flared up and consumed all the evidence. When the flames were high, he threw in the mask. It fixed him with a burning stare of reproach before grotesquely melting away.

Inside, he showered in scalding water and scrubbed his skin raw.

The next day it was all over the news. The girl's blood alcohol was sky-high, with traces of flunitrazepam. Evidence of recent sexual intercourse. Typical date rape scenario. No leads. No one had seen her leave the house. No one had seen her come back. No one recalled seeing who she was with that night.

Garrett Sanger spent the next few days in a blind panic, during which he walked the fine line of lying low, while simultaneously maintaining normal frat boy behavior so as to avoid attracting attention. Every moment he expected a suit and tie at his door, a tap on his shoulder.

But as the days and weeks wore on and the investigation apparently went nowhere, his panic subsided to intense fear. He had been reading up on DNA forensics. If the hammer was going to fall, he wanted to see it coming. He devoured information, much of it reassuring. Samples were easily contaminated, especially in cases of sexual assault, because the victim's own tissues and fluids interfered with the analysis. Back then, DNA fingerprinting was still new and imperfect.

His primal fear eventually waned to free-floating anxiety. Even if they found his fingerprints and DNA at the scene, it didn't mean anything until they found a match. Sanger did everything he could to make sure he never popped up on some database. He avoided illegal drugs, he stayed out of the bars and avoided parties. He moved out of the frat house into his own apartment and drove his car like a little old lady. He knew he was succeeding when his frat brothers started calling him a pussy and regarding him with grudging admiration for his new squeaky-clean lifestyle.

He took up fitness training. He lost weight. He toned his body until it was taut and sleek like a jaguar, and he discovered that he no longer needed assistance from Rohypnol or alcohol.

His grades improved. He took the GRE and nailed it. He became a star in a select group of scientists and withdrew into the anonymity of an obscure scientific project. His background check came up clean. His fingerprints prompted no red flags.

Still, Sanger always had a sense of something following him. It was his DNA. Even though he had been careful, fastidious, his DNA had been all over that room and all over that girl—hair, skin, saliva, semen. His DNA would give him away. Even now, more than twenty years later as he sat behind the wheel of his SUV, he felt the gaze of judgment drilling through the back of his head.

He pressed his fists against his eyes and wrenched his mind back to the present.

Dr. Collins had been about to cave, he felt sure of it. Sanger had seen the wheels turning in her head and the sound of a jackpot payoff ringing in her ears. How could anyone pass up such an incredible amount of money?

That damn husband of hers, he thought, remembering the way the man had towered over him like a stupid, lumbering bear. "Smug son-of-a-bitch," Sanger muttered. He shook his head, embarrassed at the way he had flinched at the all-too-familiar sight of a man's hand flashing toward his face.

He seized the steering wheel with both hands and squeezed until his hands shook and he thought his teeth might shatter. Violence rose up like bile. He needed something to compress it, to control it. He needed a drink. He needed the girl at the gun range.

Then he would be ready.

16

Red Cross

SITTING AT MICHAELA'S DESK, Terry removed the computer disk from its packaging. It was about the size of a deck of playing cards.

Michaela looked at it suspiciously. "Everything's going to fit on that? All the X-rays and pictures?"

"Oh, yeah," Terry assured her. "This sucker's massive."

"What about the video? It's ninety minutes long."

"No problem."

First, Terry plugged the digital camcorder into Michaela's desktop computer and transferred the video. When the transfer was complete, he hooked up the camera and transferred the photos. The X-rays were already accessible from Michaela's computer, so he brought them up and stored them temporarily on the desktop screen, alongside the icon of the video and a folder containing the photographs.

Then he took Rosie's paper file, including the ECG printouts, and scanned it all, using Michaela's multi-purpose printer, fax machine, and photocopier. About a year ago, Terry had taken great pains to update her computer system with the latest and greatest, but she didn't relish the gadgetry like he did. For all she knew, the thing also had a microwave oven.

Once everything was loaded onto the desktop computer, Terry burned DVDs of the X-rays, photos, video, and digitized medical records. He labeled them and placed them into Rosie's manila folder.

Lastly, he connected the new external hard drive to Michaela's desktop computer.

Michaela leaned over his shoulder. "So that's it?" she asked.

"Not quite," he replied, pointing to the icons of all the documents created by the scanner, and all the images. "We just need to drag all these onto the external drive. As soon as I get a chance, I'll set it up so it backs up onto a cloud service."

"I think this will be a good thing," Michaela said. The more she thought about it, the more she realized that it was the right thing to do. Plus it would be nice for her and Terry to have a project in common. Their professional lives were so different that they seldom worked together on anything, especially something so crucial.

She put her hands on his shoulders, then slid her arms across his chest and hugged him from behind. "Thanks for having my back."

"That's what I'm here for." He grasped her hands and kissed them each, in turn.

Just then, they heard banging on the front door.

Normally, someone knocking after hours meant an emergency. But now, they weren't sure what to think. Was it Adriana? Sanger again?

They got up and peeked around the office door, straining to see through the waiting room windows. A car was pulled in close to the building, flooding the waiting room with its headlights. An anxious face peered in through the glass.

The person knocked again. His hair whipped around his face, and in the glare of the headlights snow swirled about.

Michaela and Terry went to the front door and unlocked it.

The figure at the door was an Asian man with glasses. "We have an emergency."

In a split second Michaela and Terry were out the door, going to the man's car. An Asian woman emerged from the passenger side of the car. The man opened the back door.

Lying on its side on the back seat was a Harlequin Great Dane. Even in the darkness Michaela could see that its abdomen was hugely distended.

Terry immediately saw it, too, and cleared his throat.

"Let's get her inside," said Michaela.

Michaela held the front door open as Terry and the man lifted the dog out of the back seat and carried it inside to the treatment area. The safest place to put a dog this size was on the floor, so Michaela quickly grabbed a large blanket from the cabinet above the cages and spread it out. They laid the dog down. It immediately sat up and tried to vomit. It retched violently, but brought up nothing but foamy saliva.

Terry took the dog's vitals, and Michaela asked the couple what had happened.

"This afternoon we got out a huge pan of leftovers from Christmas dinner," said the woman. "We set it on the kitchen counter."

The man continued the story. "Then the phone rang—something like that. Anyway, both of us left the kitchen for a few minutes, and by the time we came back, the pan was on the floor and she had eaten everything."

Terry was examining the dog's gums. He looked up and made a grim face.

"She threw a lot of it up," the man continued, "but half an hour later she was whining, pacing around, getting up and down. She just couldn't get comfortable."

"And she was dry heaving," said the woman. "We noticed that her stomach looked really big and she was panting like she was in pain."

Michaela and Terry both looked at one another: it was a classic case of stomach bloat.

Terry went to set up the X-ray machine while Michaela got the couple's names and information. They were Mr. and Mrs. Hyong and they lived in Savoy. Their dog, Chloe, was three years old.

"This is a very common condition in large breed dogs with this kind of deep-chested body type," Michaela explained to the owners. "Great Danes are especially prone to it. When they overeat like this, they also gulp a lot of air, so the stomach fills with gas and gets distended. The first thing we'll do is pass a stomach tube and decompress her stomach. We'll have to sedate her for that. We'll also need to take some X-rays, because if her stomach has twisted on itself, that's much more serious."

Mr. and Mrs. Hyong looked at one another with alarm. "How serious?" he said.

"Extremely. If her stomach is twisted, she'll need emergency surgery."

Mrs. Hyong's eyes filled with tears. "What happens if she doesn't have the surgery?"

"She'll die."

Mr. Hyong took a deep breath. "Okay, then. Do what you need to do."

They crouched down next to Chloe and stroked her head. The dog tried pitifully to lift herself up, but Mr. and Mrs. Hyong made her lie back down.

Terry came back into the treatment area. "X-ray's ready."

The couple followed Michaela down to the end of the treatment area and into the comfy room. She switched on the table lamp and the floor lamp, then reached into the cabinet above the sink and switched on a radio, which was tuned to the local classical station. The couple sat stiffly on the loveseat, looking shell-shocked.

Michaela came over and sat on the arm of the loveseat. She put her hand on Mrs. Hyong's shoulder. "It's okay."

The woman gave her a tearful, nervous smile.

Back in the treatment room, Terry and Michaela inserted two IV catheters, one into each of Chloe's front legs. Once the second catheter was in, Michaela hooked up a liter bag of lactated Ringer's solution, plugged the line into one of the catheters and opened it wide so the solution would flow quickly.

Michaela drew up one and a half ccs of gentamicin and fourteen ccs of cefazolin, calculating the dosages quickly in her head. Then she grabbed the bottle of Solu-Delta-Cortef— prednisolone sodium succinate, one of the mainstays of emergency medicine, and now allegedly the end-product of cutting-edge genetics research.

Terry seemed to have read her mind. "Too bad Chloe doesn't have a genetic crash cart. She'd already have Solu Delt coursing through her veins."

Michaela snorted. "No kidding." She tore off the plastic tab covering the bottle's stopper, drew the entire contents of the vial into a syringe, and injected the solution into Chloe's second catheter.

Then she picked up the syringe of gentamicin and injected it, followed by one cc of cefazolin. Cefazolin had to be given slowly rather than in a single push. Over the next few minutes, while they were stabilizing Chloe and taking X-rays, she would give her a cc at a time until all fourteen were gone. Chloe was panting uncomfortably and vocalizing softly.

While Michaela was giving the injections, Terry collected a blood sample from Chloe's hind leg. Then he unlocked the controlled drug cabinet on the wall. He drew up a cc of Telazol, an injectable anesthetic. He and Michaela lifted Chloe up onto an over-sink treatment grate.

"Got her?" Michaela asked, as Terry held the dog up on its chest.

"Yep."

Michaela injected the Telazol into the port on the second IV catheter and followed it with a syringe full of heparinized saline. As Chloe relaxed, Terry grasped her upper jaw in one hand and steadied her head with the other. Michaela switched on an overhead light and directed the beam into the dog's mouth. With her left hand she pulled the dog's tongue out and down to expose the back of the throat, and with her right hand she directed an endotracheal tube toward the dog's larynx. She used the end of the tube to flip the epiglottis down and out of the way, then slid the tube between the arytenoid cartilages and into the trachea. The dog gave a reflex cough, and Michaela felt a puff of air from the open end of the tube.

They lay Chloe down on her side and secured the endotracheal tube in place with a length of gauze bandage around her muzzle. Terry attached a six-cc syringe to a line in the side of the endotracheal tube and puffed air into it, inflating the cuff that formed a seal between the tube and Chloe's windpipe. Michaela attached the tubing from the anesthetic machine to the open end of the ET tube and turned on the anesthetic and the oxygen.

While she was doing this, Terry opened another bag of fluids and hooked it up to the second IV catheter. Chloe now had two IV bags flowing full speed. She would be receiving shock doses of fluids, and a dog her size would require almost six liters in the first hour.

They watched for a moment as the dog breathed in and out. The valves on the anesthetic machine fluttered gently and the bag rhythmically filled and emptied.

Terry reached under the sink and removed a large bucket and a rigid stomach tube. He slathered the tube with lubricating jelly. "Let's hope this works," he said. He extended Chloe's head and neck, slid the tube into the dog's mouth, and then passed it into the esophagus. The tube passed easily through the thoracic inlet and then to the junction between the esophagus and stomach, then it stopped. He moved it gently back and forth, but it wouldn't budge. A small amount of fluid trickled out of the tube and into the bucket.

Terry shook his head. "I was afraid of that. This thing is going nowhere." If the tube had passed successfully into the stomach, much more food and fluid would be slopping out into the bucket.

Most likely the stomach was not only distended, but also rotated around itself: *gastric dilatation volvulus*. Stomach bloat with torsion, causing complete obstruction—fluid and gas could not leave the stomach and the dog couldn't belch or vomit anything up. Passage of the stomach tube seemed impossible, so they would have to decompress the stomach by other means.

Michaela went to the supply drawer and grabbed a handful of 18-gauge needles, which she and Terry simply stuck into the dog's side, right over the distended stomach area. Gas hissed from the needle hubs and the stomach visibly deflated. Sometimes needle trocharization like this decompressed the stomach enough to allow passage of the stomach tube. Terry tried a second time to pass the tube, but it still wouldn't budge.

"Damn," said Terry. "I guess the X-rays are going to be a formality."

* * *

Michaela dimmed the lights in the comfy room and stood in front of the computer monitor with Chloe's owners. She pointed to the grossly distended, gas-filled stomach. "On an X-ray, air shows up as black. Soft-tissue and fluids are light gray, and bones and metal are white."

On Chloe's X-ray, it looked like she had swallowed a huge, black balloon: an empty black space filled most of the abdominal cavity. Projecting part of the way up from the bottom of the black balloon, though, was a light gray band, so that the stomach looked like a pillowy letter C on its side.

Michaela pointed to the gray band. "This is a portion of the stomach wall that has folded in on itself as the stomach twisted."

Mr. and Mrs. Hyong groaned. "So she needs surgery?"

Michaela nodded. "Right away."

The vascular and physiologic details were too overwhelming for most dog owners to understand. But the seriousness of the twisted stomach was easy for most people to grasp. "The twisted stomach is cutting off its own blood supply and the blood supply to the spleen," Michaela said. "When that happens, portions of the spleen and stomach can actually die. The dead tissue releases toxins into the blood."

Michaela looked at them to make sure they understood.

"When you do surgery, are you able to untwist the stomach?" Mrs. Hyong asked.

Michaela nodded. "And we remove any dead tissue in the stomach wall. If the spleen looks bad, we remove it, too."

Mr. Hyong managed a wry smile. "Is that all?"

Michaela smiled. "We also tack the stomach to the abdominal wall to make sure it never twists again."

He squared his shoulders and braced himself for the answer to his final question. "Will I have to sell my first-born for this?"

"Hopefully not," Michaela answered. "But it's not cheap."

Mr. Hyong blew out his cheeks. He looked at his wife and they both shrugged. "Better get started then."

Michaela led the couple out into the reception area. They were active clients, so she pulled Chloe's file and had them fill out a surgical consent form and an estimate of the cost. Michaela assured them she would call them after the surgery. Then she said goodnight, opened the front door for them, and watched them drive away into the snowy night.

A few minutes later, Chloe was on her back, secured to the table with ropes lassoed around her paws, prepped for surgery. Terry went to the windowsill and tuned the radio to the local country western station.

Michaela entered the surgery suite, hat, mask and surgical foot coverings in place, gowned and gloved. Terry secured the ties on the back of her surgical gown. For now, Michaela would do all the sterile work, and Terry would remain out and act as her non-sterile assistant in order to monitor and adjust the anesthetic, run the blood work, and be the go-fer between the sacred space of surgical sterility and the real world. He would scrub in later.

Terry went to the lab to run the blood tests. Michaela laid out the blue surgical drapes and clamped them in place, covering Chloe from head to foot, leaving only a narrow strip of her abdomen visible. She unwrapped a length of sterile tubing and carefully secured it to the drape with towel clamps. She plugged in the suction attachment into her end of the tubing, then tossed the other end of the tube over the drapes for Terry to plug into the suction pump.

She glanced at the surgical monitors: Chloe's heart rate was within acceptable limits, the pulse oximeter read ninety-eight, which was excellent, and her ECG tracing showed normal QRS complexes, one after another. The electrolyte derangements caused by bloat and stomach torsion—particularly depleted blood potassium—usually led to serious heart arrhythmias, but they hadn't set in yet. It wasn't terribly common for them to develop this early in the course of the treatment, but they frequently developed during surgery and especially post-operatively. Chloe would require round-the-clock monitoring for at least twenty-four to thirty-six hours after surgery, so that if the arrhythmia developed it could be detected and treated.

Michaela attached a number ten blade to the scalpel handle and stepped up to the table. "Okay, Chloe," she said, "show me a nice, happy stomach and we'll be in and out of here in forty-five." In one clean stroke, she made an incision from Chloe's sternum all the way down to her pubic bone. Michaela was not afraid to leave plenty of room to work. It took longer to close a huge incision like that, but in the end it probably saved time because it made working inside the abdomen so much easier. When training with David Brightman, he always said that a long incision takes the same amount of time to heal as a short incision. "They heal side to side, not front to back," he would say, "so don't be afraid to open them stem to stern."

The other thing David taught them was this: "Keep your hands moving." Michaela worked quickly through the subcutaneous tissue and down to the *linea alba*, the line of fibrous tissue that marked the bloodless midline of the abdominal muscles. She grasped the white line with forceps, then, with her scalpel, made a stab incision into it. She extended the incision toward the sternum, and then went all the way toward the pubic bone for maximum access to the abdominal cavity.

Terry returned from the lab with printouts from the blood analyzers. "Not bad," he called, heading for the prep room to scrub. "The 'lytes are normal." A few minutes later, Terry returned to the surgery suite, scrubbed, gowned and gloved. He turned around, facing away from Michaela. She took a large hemostat off the surgery table and carefully clipped his surgical gown closed at the back. This maneuver was necessary to secure his gown without breaking sterility. It was not ideal, but it was the best they could manage with no technical assistants. And it was certainly more sterile than the barnyard surgeries Terry did in the field.

Terry turned around and stepped up to the surgery table. "How's it look?" he asked.

"Good, I think." Michaela grasped the free edges of the abdominal incision and pried them apart so he could see. "The stomach was torsed all right, so I derotated it. The color's not as bad as it could be."

The stomach was indeed far from normal in color. Instead of the slightly pink appearance of normal abdominal viscera, the stomach was a deep red. But it was not dark—not yet— which was a good sign.

"What do you think?" Terry asked.

"The stomach is definitely congested, but not necrotic."

Terry peered into Chloe's abdomen and nodded. "Check the spleen."

Michaela reached into the abdomen. "One spleen, coming right up." She grasped the engorged spleen and carefully lifted it out of the abdomen. "Uh-oh," Michaela said. Terry saw it, too. The spleen was dark, dark purple, almost black. "This is going to have to go," Michaela said. She reached for her favorite surgical instrument: the LDS stapler. In about two minutes flat, she had severed and ligated all the vessels attaching the spleen to the stomach. A procedure that used to take her fifteen to thirty minutes was now almost trivial. The important thing was always to make surgery quicker, in order to minimize anesthesia time.

She picked up the spleen and dropped it with a thud into the biomedical waste container. Terry was looking at her, eyes twinkling above his surgical mask.

"What?" Michaela said.

"You are so in your element right now," he said. "I love it."

Turning to the damaged stomach, they discovered that derotating it had helped. It was still much redder than normal, but it looked "happy," which meant they would not have to remove any part of the stomach.

They concluded Chloe's surgery by attaching the pyloric antrum of the stomach to the inside surface of the abdominal wall. This procedure wouldn't stop the stomach from bloating again, but hopefully it would prevent it from rotating around on itself and causing another life-threatening emergency.

Michaela peeled off her gloves and retrieved three one-liter bottles of saline from the fluid warmer. She switched on the suction unit, and then, while Terry held the incision open, she poured the first liter into the abdomen. Still holding the edges of the incision, Terry jostled Chloe around to lavage the abdomen thoroughly, then inserted the suction tube and removed the fluid. They repeated this procedure three times, following another one of Dr. Brightman's adages: "the solution to pollution is dilution."

Terry began closing the abdomen, which is what he liked to do when he and Michaela did emergency surgery together. Sometimes she went out into the field with him on a large animal emergency—a dystocia or a "down cow"—in which case Terry did all the heavy lifting, literally, while Michaela assisted and perhaps stitched up. But here, among dogs and cats, their roles were reversed.

Chloe was a big dog; her incision was going to take some time to close. Terry whistled along to the radio as he sutured. Chloe's ECG was normal.

"I suppose I could make myself useful," Michaela said, "and move all the Rosie stuff onto that external hard drive. Just drag and drop, right?"

"Right." Then he looked up briefly, needle-driver poised in mid-air. "Sure you know what you're doing? Last time you tried to download pictures from the camera you deleted them all."

"Very funny, smarty. You can check to make sure I don't screw it up."

Michaela went into the office and sat down at the computer. How hard could it be? She had moved files around like this before. She used the mouse to click all the pages from Rosie's file from the computer desktop to the icon of the new external drive. When the desktop was empty, she double-clicked on the external drive. A screen popped up showing the contents of the disk—the X-rays, a video, several photos—and all the PDF files, which were the scans from the paper record. She closed the window. Then she ejected the external drive using a technique that always scared her, but that Terry assured her was quick and perfectly safe: she clicked and dragged the icon of the external hard drive onto the icon of the trash can on the desktop. She removed the cable from the desktop computer and from the external drive, and slipped the drive into her coat pocket.

She heard Terry calling her from the surgery suite.

Michaela hurried to the surgery room. Terry had finished closing and was stripping off the soiled surgical drapes. She disconnected all the equipment, untied the ropes securing Chloe's legs to the table and turned her onto her side.

Then she and Terry hefted Chloe once again onto the gurney and wheeled her into treatment. They laid newspaper on the bottom of the largest cage and topped it with a foam rubber pad, followed by large bath towels. Once Chloe was settled in the cage, they hooked her back up to the fluids—this time at a slower, maintenance rate—and to the ECG monitor. Michaela drew blood for another electrolyte analysis. She went to the lab to run the test while Terry calculated the doses for Chloe's post-op pain medications and antibiotics.

Chloe was stable, but still critically ill. Either Michaela or Terry would need to stay overnight in the hospital to monitor her. Even though her ECG had remained normal throughout the surgery, dangerous arrhythmias could develop any time. Whoever ended up staying would need to get up every hour or so to administer treatments or monitor vital signs. They had a fold-out cot in the office, along with a TV and a video game console. This last item was mostly for Terry.

They did what they always did in these cases: Terry volunteered to stay, but Michaela insisted they decide by flipping a coin. Terry won the toss and again volunteered to stay. He set up the cot for himself in a corner of the office. Michaela took a sleeping bag and pillow from the closet shelf and laid them out.

They walked back to the treatment area and stood for a moment in front of Chloe's cage, side by side. Terry put his arm around Michaela, and they watched the dog rest.

"Still think you're not doing any damn good?" Terry asked softly.

"I hear you," Michaela said. An arterial bypass system or a genetic crash cart wouldn't have helped this dog. There was no substitute for well-trained hands. Michaela realized with satisfaction that it was for moments like this that she had become a veterinarian in the first place. She wrapped her arms around Terry's waist.

He looked down at her with a mischievous grin. "Come on," he said. He took her hand and led her back to the office, rummaged through the plastic bags and handed her the pregnancy test kit.

She was surprised. "You want me to do this now?"

He nodded. "I have a good feeling about it this time." He rested his hands on her shoulders, leaned down and kissed her on the forehead.

"Wish me luck," she said, and took it to the bathroom. A few moments later she emerged and set the small plastic wand on the desk, forcing herself to walk away. Terry busied himself with the video game system. Michaela tried not to be too hopeful, because they had been disappointed several times already. The kit guaranteed absolute certainty of interpretation: a red dash meant "not pregnant," a red cross meant "pregnant."

After the allotted time elapsed, they returned to the desk and saw the result.

Michaela's breath caught in her throat. When she looked up into Terry's eyes, they shone with emotion. She sank into his embrace, wrapping her arms around him tightly. She felt like she couldn't get close enough to him.

"We did it, Michaela," he said. "We finally did it."

17

Game Over

MICHAELA WAS MUCH TOO EXCITED to go home and sleep, so she decided to spend the night at the animal hospital with Terry. He insisted, however, that he be the one to stay while Michaela went home and got the supplies they would need to get them through the long, semi-sleepless night taking care of Chloe. After all, he had won the toss, fair and square, and she had been cooped up in the animal hospital all day.

She was getting ready to leave, punching in the code for the alarm, when she realized that if she fully armed the system, the interior motion detectors would go off as Terry moved around.

She went to find him. When she passed Chloe's cage, she stopped and watched the ECG. After about a minute of normal QRS complexes, a burst of jagged ventricular premature complexes interrupted the normal rhythm. *Here we go*, she thought. The VPCs were a side-effect of the electrolyte disturbances that usually occur with bloat and volvulus. After only a few seconds, the arrhythmia corrected itself and did not reappear again, but Michaela knew that it could develop again at any moment and might not be so benign.

This was going to be a long night.

Terry was in the office, playing a video game.

"How do you set the alarm for external sensors only?" she said.

He spun his chair around and faced her. "Don't worry about that for now. I'll set it when you come back." Then he pointed the remote control at the TV and turned it off. A little smile lit up his face. "C'mere a sec."

"If you insist," she said, returning his smile. She sat down, straddling his lap. As he put his arms around her and pulled her close, she breathed deeply and relaxed, just resting against him. He rubbed her back, and under the gentle pressure of his warm hands, she felt the tension of too many tough days draining away from her.

"Better?" he asked.

"Hm," she sighed.

"Me, too," he said.

She sat up and leaned back a little, so she could look at him.

"What a team, huh?" he said. "Saving lives and making babies."

She laughed. "All in a day's work." She ran her fingers through his thick, wavy hair.

"I know," he said. "I need a haircut."

She shook her head. "I like you this way. Scruffy suits you." He hadn't shaved, so his face was rough. He had a touch of gray at his temples, crow's feet around both eyes. A scar above his left eyebrow, from Little League. A less noticeable scar on his upper lip, from a sled to the face one winter. His complexion was a bit uneven, from sunburn due to being outside so much. His blue eyes were smiling, as always.

At times like this, or like the other night when she had come home late and found him sleeping, or for no reason at all, a sensation would rise up in Michaela's heart that she couldn't describe. Love so deep it felt like hunger, except that it made her strong, not weak. It felt like the desperate longing of loneliness, combined with the comfort of reunion. It felt like unspeakable grief and uncontainable joy, mingled together in excruciating and beautiful sweetness.

He saw it in her eyes. He stroked her cheek with his thumb, studying her face as she had studied his. "I love you," he said.

She reached up and pressed his hand to her face, then turned her head and pressed her lips to his palm. Everything about her, the best and the worst, strengths and weaknesses, he knew and accepted. He knew her to her very depths, and still loved her.

Gently, as if he were afraid she might break, Terry drew her face close to his and kissed her. He was tender and re-strained, waiting for her to respond, and even then, as she op-ened her mouth to him with a faint cry, his mouth remained soft and unhurried. Without urgency, they drank deeply of one another, suspended together in timelessness.

"I wish we could just go home," Michaela sighed.

"I know," he whispered. "Tomorrow." His breath was warm on her face.

* * *

Tripod met Michaela at the door. "Hi, boy," she said, slapping his sides and tousling his ears. "Remember me?" She always felt guilty when she came home late from taking care of other peoples' pets and felt she was neglecting her own. She went outside with Tripod and spent a few minutes throwing snowballs at him, smiling as he tried to catch and eat them.

Inside, she gathered up a few things for the night: snacks and a video game Terry wanted to play. The case was on top of the TV. On the cover was an unnaturally muscled male and an impossibly proportioned female, each pointing a huge weapon, flames and bullets spraying from each cartoonish gun barrel. The title of the game was *Double Tap*. She sighed. She would never understand the appeal of video games. All she knew was that the appeal was undoubtedly sex-linked: she didn't know one woman who enjoyed them, nor one man who didn't.

She tossed the game and the snacks into a grocery bag, pulled a sleeping bag out of the closet and a pillow off the bed.

Her mind wandered as she contemplated other differences between boys and girls. She hoped she and Terry had at least one son. Then it occurred to her that if anybody could convince a daughter to enjoy video games, it would be Terry.

He had wanted to start having children right away, but she had said, no, that they should wait.

"Wait for what?" he had asked, truly puzzled.

"I don't know," she had said. And she didn't know. She could not name a single good reason to wait. Her veterinary practice was well established. He was happy with his work at the vet school. They had good friends and neighbors, and her mom lived close enough to help with the children when they came along.

It's just that people weren't supposed to start having children right away, were they?

Michaela had her doubts about herself as a mother, but Terry was obviously born to be a father. As soon as the weather warmed up, he would be out there in the street, playing catch with the neighbors and their kids. In the summer, he would invite everyone over for a car wash. He'd line the cars up, and set up teams of kids, each with a job—spraying, sponging, squeegeeing, rinsing, detailing—while he and the dads stood in the shade and drank beer. When autumn came, he organized the annual block party, complete with his Crazy Huge Pile of Leaves Contest and The Best Chili Cook-Off. He did magic tricks, silly sleight-of-hand with playing cards and quarters, holding the kids enthralled. He wasn't even a father yet and he was the most popular "dad" on the block.

Every once in a while he would say something about starting a family, but he never pushed her. Waiting a little while turned into months and then into years.

Then their friends Hank and Kath Ullman had their third baby and asked Michaela and Terry to be the godparents. After the baptism, back at the Ullmans' house, Terry and Michaela sat on the couch with newborn Charlie. The baby had a full head of red hair, just like his father. Terry held Charlie on his lap, head on his knees, feet toward his stomach. He cradled the baby's head with his large hands. The house was noisy, with friends and family milling around, talking, eating, drinking, but Charlie, Michaela, and Terry were in their own little world. The look on Terry's face as he gazed at that baby made something dissolve within her, and she thought, *why have I been so scared?*

At that moment, Terry had sensed her looking at him and turned his head. The expression on her face must have surprised him, because he looked quizzically at her, turning one side of his mouth upwards.

Sitting across from them, amidst all the noise and conversation, Kath had witnessed this tender exchange and was grinning at them. She pointed at Michaela and mouthed the words, "You're next."

That very night they threw away her pills. Over the next several months, as the hormonal fog cleared and Michaela's natural monthly cycles reasserted themselves, she and Terry noticed an almost imperceptible change. It reminded Michaela of what pet owners sometimes told her after completing long overdue dental work on their pets. Cats and dogs didn't announce that their teeth hurt, but once the periodontal disease was corrected or the abscessed teeth extracted, cats that had been hiding under the bed for two years suddenly came out and joined the family. Dogs that hadn't played fetch for months started to cavort and run around like puppies. Their owners said they hadn't realized what their pets had been going through until Michaela corrected the problem and took away their pain.

It was like that. Like healing from a wound they had not even been aware of, or lifting an invisible veil. Michaela and Terry fell in love all over again, holding nothing back from one another. He gave himself to her, body and soul, and she received him, totally. No barriers between them, chemical or otherwise. And she could give herself to Terry completely, without reserve. For some reason, to Michaela having a baby meant vulnerability, surrender, and she had never been able to do that. She realized she had been guarding her heart, even from her husband. But it had suddenly come to her, like a revelation, that she was safe and that she could trust him.

Michaela shook herself; she had been standing in the middle of the kitchen, lost in thought, remembering this morning, and the reason Terry had not had time to shave before going to work.

This *was* going to be a long night.

Michaela closed her eyes. She thought of their baby, and the sensation previously reserved for Terry alone rose up and overflowed in her heart like living water.

On the way back to the animal hospital, she forced her mind back to the problem of Synthetic Genetics. After seeing the state Rosie had deteriorated to—if this was the fate of the test subjects—Michaela was more determined than ever to see this project not only shut down, but its directors prosecuted.

Nevertheless, Michaela made an executive decision: she would not accept Garrett Sanger's hush money, but she would withdraw from active involvement in the endeavor to expose the project. She would contact David's forensic veterinarian and turn all the information over. If David were really serious about retiring, this would certainly give him something to do—a reason for getting up in the morning. She would help where she could, but with a baby on the way she could no longer be the one driving. This was why she had been hemming and hawing back at the Courier Café. For months she and Terry had seen only red dashes, but there was always the possibility she might become pregnant.

No more uncertainty now. It was time for Michaela to concentrate on her family. She would have to hire an associate to do the surgeries from now on, at least until the baby came.

Exposure to gas anesthetics posed only a slight risk, but not one worth taking.

Up ahead, she saw the red and blue flickering lights of an emergency vehicle. She pulled over to the right to wait for it. At this distance she couldn't tell if it was a squad car or fire truck. Instead of continuing to approach her in the oncoming lane, the vehicles made a left turn onto a street up ahead.

She pulled back onto the road and drove on. After a moment she realized that the emergency vehicle had turned not onto a side street, but into the parking lot of the animal hospital. She turned into the driveway and slammed on her brakes: the lot was swarming with squad cars. Another set of emergency lights dazzled her eyes as an ambulance roared into the lot.

"Oh, God," Michaela whispered. She threw open the door of her truck and jumped out. She ran toward the front door of the hospital. A police officer turned and shouted, but she had already yanked the door open and burst inside.

An officer immediately stepped in front of her. It was Hank Ullman. "Michaela, you don't want to go in there." He took her by the arm and steered her back into the lobby.

"Where is he?" she said, shaking her arm loose and hurrying past him. She rounded the corner into the treatment area.

Terry lay sprawled on his back in a pool of blood.

Two officers looked up as Michaela rushed in with a choked cry. They tried to stop her but she flung herself down at her husband's side, screaming, shaking him as if he would wake. The officers tried to pull her away. "No!" she shouted, and fell onto Terry's chest and gripped his shirt in her fists, her body heaving. Paramedics swept in and surrounded Michaela with shouts and movement.

Someone lifted her up and pulled her out of the maelstrom. She heard Hank Ullman's voice in her ear. "I've got you, I've got you."

She felt Hank's arms around her shoulders, holding her tight as she convulsed with sobs, holding her together as she shattered into a million pieces.

18

Anointing

BRENDAN DREAMT OF FIRE.

In his dream, he presided at a funeral mass, holding a huge censor from which billowed not the pure white smoke of fragrant incense, but a thick, black cloud that smelled of gasoline and burning tires. Instead of the sweet comfort of music from the pipe organ, the roar of flames was in his ears, and the angry, accusing whine of the sirens on Falls Road in Belfast. The smoke choked and nauseated him. He stood in the sanctuary of the church, and as he turned to leave, he dropped the censor. The censor tipped over and spilled its contents—black ashes on the white marble.

Brendan jerked awake. "Dammit," he muttered. *That dream again.* He sat up in bed, soaked in sweat. He flung the covers off and swore again. "God help us," he sighed.

The clock read 12:30 am.

He had tried, for years, to repress the images and memories of that night, but it was always useless.

After Connor's funeral, which Brendan missed because he was in the hospital being treated for his gunshot wound, he had finally returned to his parents' house in the Clonard. His father J.J. sat them all down in the front room. Nina, Michaela, and Viola on the sofa, Brendan in an armchair, his injured arm in a sling. Sean and Alicia stood awkwardly off to the side.

His father stood in front of him. "How dare you," he said simply.

Brendan closed his eyes. He had been waiting for this. Until now, his mother Viola had been holding her husband back, but now there was no stopping him.

"How dare you bring your IRA dirty work into this house? Into *this house* where we raised you to be a good Christian! Look at me, ye good-for-nothing *bastard!*"

"J.J.—" his mother protested feebly.

"Look at me when I'm talkin' to you!"

Brendan opened his eyes and looked up at his father placidly. "I'm sorry, Da."

"Oh, that's rich," his father snapped, throwing his hands up and pacing back and forth. "How long have you been involved? How long have you been lying to us?"

Brendan opened his mouth to answer but Viola spoke first. "What does it matter, J.J.? It's over now, isn't it? He'll get out of it. Brendan, you'll get out of it, won't you?" His mother's eyes were desperate.

"It's not so easy, Ma," Brendan whispered.

J.J. turned on him. "You'd better find a way, young man."

"He could go to the South," said Viola, quickly. "Come back when things have calmed down." She looked at Brendan for acknowledgment that this was a good idea.

But Brendan did not think it was a good idea. "I can't leave you all here. It wouldn't be safe."

Nina started to cry. "I don't see why you had to get involved, Bren." And when she looked up at him, he didn't see anger or bitterness, but disappointment and fear. Brendan had trampled her admiring heart like a rose beneath the heel of his boot.

Michaela spoke for the first time, her voice crackling with bitterness. "Go on, Bren. Run to the South. We're immune." In her red-rimmed eyes Brendan saw the bitterness that Nina couldn't seem to muster, and words no one would dare speak in the presence of his parents. Loser. Thug.

Murderer.

But he wasn't a murderer. He had never killed anybody.

After a moment, he realized that this was probably not true. His hands may not be bloodied, but how many people had been blown apart by a bomb he had constructed? How many suffocated and burned in a fire he had set?

Days later, they were all at the pub again. While Nina helped with the nightly closing-up ritual, Brendan and Michaela were in a corner, locked in a ritual of their own, a ritual of verbal combat. Dinner plates and mugs of Guinness were strewn on the table between them.

"You only come here on holiday, Mick, so you don't know what it's like," said Brendan, leaning forward intently. "Ever try to get a job around here, where half the stores are bombed out?"

"Yeah," Michaela snorted in derision. "Bombs set by the poor benighted store owners themselves, so they can collect on the insurance money."

"We can't go across the river for jobs, either," Brendan retorted, referring to the River Lagan, which separated Belfast into its Eastern and Western sections.

"Why not? Because you 'look' Catholic?" Michaela rolled her eyes.

"We look Catholic, we sound Catholic, we have Catholic names. Try gettin' a job on the docks with a name like Shamus O'Rourke."

"Why does that even matter? I thought the argument had to do with whether Northern Ireland remained part of Great Britain or joined the rest of the Republic? What does that have to do with Protestants versus Catholics?"

Even Brendan had to acknowledge that this was just a convenient label. It had always been easier to plunk people into a simple category rather than take time to explain the nuances of their political views. Most of the people in Northern Ireland were Protestant Loyalists and wanted to remain part of Great Britain, for a number of reasons. In the North, Loyalists were a majority. If the North were absorbed into the Republic of Ireland, the Protestants would instantly become a small minority in an overwhelmingly Catholic nation.

Michaela turned to Nina, who had arrived holding a tray and a damp rag. "Come on, Neens. Back me up here."

Nina sighed. "I'm tired of talking about this." She stacked all the plates and empty pint glasses on the tray. She wouldn't even look at Brendan. Nina quickly wiped the table and disappeared into the kitchen. With a look of disgust, Michaela got up and followed her, leaving Brendan alone.

When the cleaning up was finished, J.J. locked the back door and they all left the pub together through the front. Michaela stalked away from Brendan. He followed her, still wanting to win the argument. His Aunt Alicia walked quickly to keep up with them, but the others lagged behind, keeping their distance: the two brothers, J.J. and Sean, followed by Nina and Viola.

Suddenly, Nina remembered that she had left her hat inside the pub. She rushed back to the front door, unlocked it, and went in. J.J., Sean and Viola followed her back and stood in the doorway, waiting for her.

Brendan, Michaela and Alicia had almost reached the corner when he saw four people he recognized, across the street. The man Connor had called Danny leaned against the front bonnet of a bright blue Peugeot. Next to him, balancing on crutches, was Tommy Morgan. The woman called Bridget was in the front passenger seat of the Peugeot and Mickey sat behind the wheel.

They saw Brendan, and for an instant they all froze, staring at one another.

Danny pushed himself off the car and glanced down the street.

With a sudden, sickening realization, Brendan turned and ran back toward the pub.

Then, with an ear-splintering crash, the front of the pub leapt out and engulfed J.J., Viola, and Sean in a blinding explosion of stones, smoke, and glass. Brendan's parents and uncle disappeared into the slavering jaws of a beast that opened and swallowed them whole.

The shock wave knocked Brendan to the pavement and caused a car parked in front of the pub to explode.

Michaela got up and ran toward the pub, screaming. "Daddy! Oh my God—*Daddy!*"

Brendan remembered grabbing her sleeve as she tried to rush past him. "No, Michaela!" He saw a streak of blue and the muted blaring of a car horn whining past.

Michaela wrenched her arm free. "Let me go!"

Brendan wrapped his arms around her. "It's too late!"

Michaela screamed and sobbed as he held her. Then she twisted from his grip, with a snarl, and she pushed him away. "Are you happy now, Brendan? Are you? *You fucking bastard!*" She came after him and punched him full in the face, clawed him, kicked him. She hit him in the face again, and the back of her hand came away smeared with blood and tears as he dropped with a gasp. He raised his hands feebly, but made no conscious effort to defend himself. He knelt on the concrete gasping, sobbing and bleeding as she struck him again and again.

Alicia had to pull her off him, and even then he wondered why his aunt didn't join in the beating he knew he deserved. He was dazed by the flames, the smoke, and the blows. He could hear sirens wailing, but they were muted and distant to his damaged ears.

When he returned home from the hospital, hours later, his phone rang. Too exhausted to know better, he picked it up. A menacing voice on the other end said, "You and your pretty cousin are next, boyo."

Brendan suspected who was responsible for the bombing. It seemed unlikely that the Provos would retaliate so harshly for the death of Connor Boone, even though he was one of their most valuable officers. Volunteers' family members usually *were* immune, and even Brendan shouldn't have been targeted for getting caught in an unexpected roadblock. That could've happened to anyone.

The most likely scenario was that the three newcomers Connor had brought along were spies for a Prod paramilitary. They must have made contact with Tommy Morgan and learned the family's schedule at the pub. Maybe Tommy had filched a key so they could get in and plant the bomb without leaving so much as a scratched door lock to attract suspicion.

The wake was closed casket. At the funeral, his sobs came hard as he remembered Nina's last precious night on earth, and that he had been argumentative and arrogant and full of himself. Annoyed at her as he turned and watched her go back into the pub for her stupid hat. And J.J. and Viola had died not just angry with him, but dejected and convinced of their failure as parents.

Alicia and Michaela left Ireland the day after the triple funeral for J.J., Viola, and Nina. They took Sean's body back to America, and never came back.

Brendan didn't bother putting his parents' house on the market. There was no time and no one could get a good price for anything in the Clonard.

After gathering his few belongings, he too left Ireland, never to return.

* * *

Brendan was sitting on the edge of the bed in the rectory when the phone rang. He groaned. Another late night sick call, most likely. Father Angelo was already at the hospital, so this call was all Brendan's. He was not in the mood to be a priest, at the moment, but he had no choice.

He got up and crossed the room to answer the phone. "St. Andrew's. Father Collins speaking."

"Brendan? Brendan, it's me." It was his aunt, Alicia. Her voice was loud and shaky.

Brendan's heart banged against his ribs and he felt his insides contract. "Alicia, what's wrong?"

"It's Terry," she sobbed. "He's been shot."

"*What?* How?"

"At the animal hospital, Bren."

"Oh Christ," he breathed. "He's not—"

"No. No he's not dead, but—" Alicia's voice dropped to a whisper. "We're at Carle Hospital. Hurry."

Brendan swallowed hard. His eyes blurred with tears. "I'll be right there."

When he arrived at the emergency room, Alicia was waiting for him in the lobby. She got to her feet and ran to him. Brendan held her as she wept. After a moment, he released her and wiped his eyes with his coat sleeve. "Where is he?"

"He's about to go into surgery." She led him out of the lobby and signaled to a nurse in scrubs, who hit the button on a panel to open a set of double doors. "He was shot in the head, Bren," Alicia said as they hurried after the nurse.

The nurse stopped and pointed to a doorway. "Right here, Father."

Then, from around the corner behind the nurse, Michaela appeared, accompanied by a police officer. She saw Brendan and froze, for an instant, then strode toward him, fire in her red-rimmed eyes. "What's he doing here?"

The police officer grabbed her arm from behind.

Alicia stood her ground. "I asked him to come, Michaela," she said, keeping her voice low but intense. "Terry is a baptized Catholic and he has a right—"

"Get him the hell away from here!" Michaela wrenched free of the officer and kept coming. Alicia blocked her way and once again became the only thing between Brendan and Michaela's out-of-control grief. The chaos on the Falls Road in Belfast flashed into his mind, frenzied movement and activity, people all around, vehicles, firefighters, water spraying, lights flashing, but all he could see clearly was Michaela, hysterical, screaming at him as her sobbing mother held her back. He couldn't hear her, but he could read her lips.

You killed them! You bastard! You monster!

After a brief struggle, Michaela allowed her mother and the police officer to lead her to a row of chairs. Alicia looked at Brendan over her shoulder and nodded.

He turned the corner into the room and drew up short.

He had been in this hospital many times before, to give people strength before a major surgery, to pray for them when they took a turn for the worse, or to provide them with the final rites of the Church as they prepared for death. But this was the first time he had been called upon to minister to someone close to him, and the sight shocked him. Terry, shrouded in white, lay on a hospital gurney, surrounded by blinking, beeping machines. A tube protruded from his mouth and was connected by another snaking tube to the hissing ventilator. Terry's chest rose and fell gently.

Tears stung Brendan's eyes, and he clenched his teeth.

He squeezed between the machines that surrounded Terry, careful to avoid the snaking cords, tubes, and wires. All these machines to measure heart rate, body temperature, blood pressure, even brain waves. These machines were keeping Terry alive, breathing for him until the surgeons could crack open his skull and try to save him.

Afterwards, the machines would continue to keep him alive until he either recovered or the family made the decision to let nature take its course. And then what? The Church defined death as the moment at which the soul separated permanently from the body, and unfortunately no machine in the world was capable of measuring that.

Brendan removed the purple stole from his pocket, kissed it, and draped it across the back of his neck. Then, he removed a small leather case that contained two tiny vials, one of holy water and the other of blessed oil—The Oil of the Sick. He uncapped the vial of oil and tasted the scent of its perfume.

The full liturgical celebration of this sacrament included a penitential rite, scripture readings, and so on, but those things could be omitted when necessary. Terry's life depended on swift action, so Brendan skipped to the anointing and the prayer. He covered the vial with his thumb and inverted it. Then, with his thumb he traced a glistening cross on Terry's forehead, carefully avoiding the bandaging. Terry's face was the color of cold ashes.

Brendan recited the first part of the prayer: "Through this holy anointing may the Lord, in his love and mercy, help you with the grace of the Holy Spirit."

He anointed the palms of Terry's hands in the same way. They were cool to the touch. Brendan intoned the second half of the prayer in a choked whisper. "May the Lord, who frees you from sin, save you and raise you up."

He heard movement and a polite cough in the doorway behind him. Hospital personnel had arrived to take Terry to surgery. Brendan extricated himself from the web of lines and cords, then stood before the little group and traced a large cross in the air in front of him. A few of the staff, in their scrubs and lab coats, crossed themselves and thanked him.

When Brendan left the room, he found Alicia alone in the hallway, pacing. "Where's Michaela?" he said.

"She's completing her statement."

"Alicia, what happened?"

She shook her head and threw her hands up. "I don't know what happened. Nobody knows. There was this dog, some sort of experiment. Terry made a 911 call from the animal hospital, something about an intruder in the building, but by the time the police got there it was too late. Whoever it was shot Terry and took the dog. They took everything."

Brendan grasped her by the shoulders and guided her to a chair. He needed her to slow down. "Just start from the beginning."

Alicia took a deep breath and related what Michaela had told her. Somehow, Terry and Michaela had gotten mixed up in a situation involving brutal animal experiments at a biotech company and they were planning to help shut down the project. Tearfully, Alicia concluded, "I don't understand why they came after Terry."

Brendan's experience with terrorism made it obvious to him. "They're cleaning up. They went to the animal hospital to collect all the evidence—but they didn't know Terry was there. He was in the wrong place." His voice broke and he couldn't continue.

Alicia collected herself enough to gasp, "And there's something else." She looked up at Brendan, her eyes streaming. "Michaela's pregnant."

Brendan's heart dropped. It was not fair. Such happy news should not be marred by such desolation.

An officer entered through the double doors leading to the emergency room lobby. He came up to Alicia. "I want you and Michaela to stay here until morning."

Alicia's face was red, streaked with tears, her eyes frightened. She nodded.

The officer's nametag read Hank Ullman. "We'll send a team over to Michaela's place to sweep the house and secure it. We'll also send a unit over to your place." He addressed Brendan. "How are you involved in this, sir?"

Brendan extended his hand and introduced himself.

"Do you know anything about the situation with the biotech company?" Officer Ullman pressed.

Brendan shook his head.

"Just to be on the safe side, I'll request some drive-bys at your residence. Which is?"

"The rectory at St. Andrew's. In Urbana."

Alicia broke in. "Were you able to find out where this biotech company is located?"

Ullman shook his head. "No. It's not listed anywhere. No address. No hits on the Internet. It's like it doesn't exist."

Brendan realized that this was the first time he had experienced something like this through the eyes of true faith. His little brother had died when he was just a child, with a childish faith that could only ask why and then lash out aimlessly. His parents, his sister and his uncle had died during a period of his life that was devoid of faith and steeped in sin, and his response had been anger and grief.

This was different. He felt indignant at how unfair this was. He felt anger toward whoever had done this, and he felt a burning desire to see justice done. These feelings were the same ones he had felt in his childhood and in his rebellious teenage years. At each of those times, he had become lost in anger and grief, going around in circles like a top spinning and spinning until it falters and falls over.

But now he knew the truth. Those who suffered an untimely death would have their audience before the throne of God, as would the ones who sent them there prematurely. God Himself would sort out the actual believers from the actors, the innocents from the oppressors, the ones who had sought Him with a sincere heart and the ones who had coasted through life in total apathy or willful ignorance. As his mother used to say, "It will all come out in the wash."

Brendan blinked burning tears from his eyes. The justice of God was a great mystery. Even greater was the mystery of His mercy.

19

The Sun Singer

DAVID BRIGHTMAN STOOD at the threshold of Terry's hospital cubicle as if it were the edge of his grave. Last night they had performed surgery for a gunshot wound to the skull. David had heard the assessment and prognosis.

Michaela stood next to her husband's bed, with her mother. Alicia was weeping openly, but Michaela? Tears, yes. But her face was like flint.

Bloody hell, Michaela, David thought. Just cry, will you?

When his wife Joanna died, he had sobbed like a baby. He had cried out, screamed and yelled, clutching at his heart, feeling real physical pain in some deep void he couldn't describe, his grief threatening to claw its way up and rip through his chest like a wild animal. Why couldn't Michaela cry like that? Just bloody cry, and let it all out, instead of holding it in?

Michaela looked up and saw him. Instead of a strong, competent young woman at the helm of her own business and her own life, he saw what she must have looked like as a little girl. She came closer and he drew her to him. She remained huddled in his arms for a moment, her hands in front of her, allowing herself to be cradled like a child. Then she unfolded her arms and returned his embrace.

"I'm so sorry, Michaela," he said. "My God, what a dreadful business."

"What have you heard?" she said.

"Enough to know that you're in over your head."

"Way over my head." She released him and stood back, looking up at him. Her eyes and nose were red. Tears flowed freely as she said, "It wasn't just a case of animal abuse. It was animal abuse by an institution that is willing to kill to protect its secrets." She took a deep breath and lowered her glance, staring blankly at his coat collar. Then she roused herself and looked up at him again. "How's Chloe?"

David shrugged. Somehow, Michaela had retained enough presence of mind to call a member of her staff and arrange Chloe's transfer to the ICU at the vet school. David had just come from there. "She's stable."

Michaela nodded. "Good," she said.

David took her by the arm and led her out into the hallway. "I want you to walk away from this. Give me the medical data and let me hand it over to the woman in Indianapolis. Let her take it from here."

Michaela shook her head. "That is not a good idea, David. If anyone finds out that I told you anything about it…You may already be in danger."

David looked up and down the hallway. Several police officers were there, making no attempt to disguise themselves. "I think I'll be all right."

At the end of the hallway, near the elevators, a man in a long black coat stood watching, digging his fingers into his hair as he paced back and forth. David couldn't tell if the man was merely keeping a respectful distance or trying not to be seen.

David nodded towards him. "Who's that?"

"That," Michaela said, clenching her jaw. "is my cousin. *Father* Brendan."

David nodded. He knew the story. "That could be a bit awkward."

She let out a scoffing laugh, like a viper spitting venom. "You think?"

Her bitterness alarmed him. "Still, at a time like this—" he said, breaking off as a strange expression came over her face, daring him to continue but at the same time warning him not to. He reached out and put his arm around her as she turned to stand shoulder to shoulder with him. "Never mind," he said. "Families can be messy, I know."

She stepped back into Terry's ICU cubicle, out of sight of the people in the hallway. She put a hand into her pocket, withdrew something and handed it to him.

It was a portable computer disk drive.

"It's all there," she said.

"You've been carrying it around with you?"

She nodded. "It's been in my pocket since last night. They took everything else: computers, digital camera, video camera. If they had left it at that, they might have been able to sell the idea that it was a burglary gone wrong."

"But?" he prompted.

She looked up at him. "They also took Rosie and her medical record. We're not sure if they went to the animal hospital expecting to find us both there and kill us, or if they were just hoping to recover Rosie and the other evidence. Terry—" Her voice caught in her throat.

"And Terry happened to be in the way," he finished.

She mastered her emotions and continued. "When the police went to my house, my computer was gone, too."

David pocketed the disk drive, his mind racing. This situation was accelerating out of control, but he felt powerless to help her.

"The police have been taking turns watching me when they're off duty, and doing drive-bys every five minutes, it seems." She gave a wry half-laugh. "I feel like I've entered the witness protection program."

"Thank God for that," David said. Taking care of the dogs in the police canine unit had enabled Michaela to build rapport with the officers in the field, and it was now proving to be a fortunate alliance.

"I'll ask them to keep an eye on your place," she offered.

David doubted he was in any danger, but he wasn't going to argue. He stole a glance at her face. Her nose and cheeks were flushed, her eyes sunken and red-rimmed. She looked so exhausted David wondered how she was still on her feet.

He remained in the doorway as Michaela returned to Terry's bedside. Her mother stepped forward and embraced him. "Hello, David," she said, smiling at him through teary eyes. "It's good to see you again."

"A sad reunion, though," he replied.

His frown of concern for Michaela was mirrored in Alicia's face. "You and I both know how hard this is going to be for her," she said quietly.

By God, yes, he thought. Everybody knew how hard it was to grieve the loss of a spouse. But how much harder it was when you *knew* you could have prevented it. Michaela would undoubtedly blame herself for what had happened to Terry, whether he lived or died.

To err certainly was human. And to forgive? That was better left to the province of the divine. Some things were too hard for mere mortals to forgive.

Alicia squeezed David's hand and walked with him down the hallway toward the exit. Michaela's cousin was still hovering by the elevators, and as they approached, he walked toward them, his priest's collar visible at the open throat of his coat. Alicia introduced them.

"So you're a friend of the family?" Father Collins asked David, extending his hand.

David shook his hand. "Michaela and Terry were both students of mine when they were in vet school."

Father Collins looked like he was about Michaela's age, with the same dark hair and fair skin. Where her features were perfectly proportioned and classically beautiful, his were boyish and rough, but not unpleasant.

David's elevator arrived, and the two men exchanged a nod as David stepped between the doors. Outside, David walked back toward his car, which chirped to life as, out of habit, he clicked the remote entry key lock. But he realized that he didn't want to enter the confinement of his car. He needed to think, to walk, and he left the parking lot, allowing his feet to follow a well-worn path to a familiar destination.

The bitter cold of recent days had given way to blue sky and warmer temperatures. But not for long. A storm was coming. As David passed beneath a tree, a gust of wind blew a shower of heavy droplets that strafed the snow with bullet-like holes.

The temperature was dropping and David's feet were wet, his ears numb. He had arrived. He lifted the latch of the gate and entered the sacred ground, winding his way among the headstones and memorials of the small cemetery until he came to a waist high headstone with a gently curving top. He jammed his hands into the pockets of his wool coat and stood behind it. He didn't walk around to read it; he had read it a hundred times before. He had composed the epitaph and chosen the verse. It read:

Joanna Brightman.
Beloved daughter. Loving mother. Cherished wife.
Be still, my soul: the hour is hastening on
when we shall be forever with the Lord,
when disappointment, grief, and fear are gone,
sorrow forgot, love's purest joys restored.
Be still, my soul: when change and tears are past,
all safe and blessed we shall meet at last.

He remembered the day Joanna died as if it were a portrait of their entire life together, the events and feelings of decades compressed into a single day.

It was Saturday. They slept late. They ate breakfast. They took care of mundane tasks around the house. They talked to their sons on the phone. Had she been granted a premonition? Why had she felt the need to call their sons that morning?

In the afternoon they went upstairs to bed.

And then they quarreled. They were still tangled in the covers, talking, when evidently the conversation had strayed into some tricky area. He couldn't even remember. No doubt he had put his foot in his mouth. Drowsy and stupid from their lovemaking, he had probably said something flippant and British about a sensitive subject. It bothered him that he couldn't remember what they had quarreled about.

She had kicked off the sheets irritably and gotten out of bed, giving him a petulant, not quite furious look over her shoulder. This distinction was important to him. She had definitely been angry, but whatever it was, it couldn't have been *too* bad.

Then again, maybe that would have been preferable. If he had *really* blown it, he would perhaps have done what he now imagined himself doing, what he had imagined himself doing day after day ever since, as he rehearsed the scene in his mind thousands of times:

He gets out of bed and hurries to her. "Darling," he says. "I'm sorry. That was stupid. I didn't mean that." He puts his hands on her shoulders. "Come back to bed."

She pouts. "No," she says, frowning. "No more for you." And she punches him in the arm.

But he can tell that his apology has softened her. He makes a mental note—one that he has made before—apologize early. Don't mull it over too long, because if you do, she just gets angrier. Then you forget about it, which only makes her even more annoyed.

In real life he had ignored his own advice and stayed in bed, indulging his wounded pride.

But now, in his mind, he continued to play out the scene the way it should have gone. He opens the bathroom door. "Shall I draw you a bath, darling?" His smile is roguish and suggestive. She rolls her eyes, but allows herself to be led into the bathroom. They spend the rest of the afternoon in their two-person, whirlpool spa.

That evening they cook a meal together. In his imagination, this varies. Sometimes it's spaghetti, salad and garlic bread with a beefy cabernet. Sometimes it's a fancy shrimp dish with chardonnay. Sometimes it's just fried eggs and chips with pub ale. Afterwards, they might go up to the Krannert Center for a concert. Maybe nip down to the corner, rent a movie and make popcorn. Perhaps they would sit on the patio in front of their outdoor fireplace, playing backgammon or cribbage. He seemed to recall that she owed him several thousand dollars in backgammon, but that he was in the red in cribbage.

They had made plans for the next day. They were going to Allerton Park. It was October. The trees at Allerton would be gorgeous, and if the weather cooperated it was not likely to be cold.

It was an easy half hour drive from Champaign, south on Route 47, to the park's main entrance. They'd divvy up snacks, water bottles, and a picnic lunch between two backpacks and set off for the formal gardens, where they would wander around and irreverently rename the statues and attractions. *Poor, Lethargic Adam*, *The Garden of the Scary Blue Dogs,* and the *Not Lost Anymore Because We Found It Garden.* There was an immaculately trimmed boxwood hedge feature that looked like it could have been a maze, but David had renamed it *Not Really A Proper Maze Because You Can See Over The Top.*

When they had amused one another enough, they would pick up the "yellow trail" (it was a yellow line on the park map) take it about a mile past the *Creepy Little House in the Big Woods* to the *Headless Centaur*, which wasn't really headless but looked that way until you got up close, because the sculptor had, for some reason, positioned the centaur's head at an incredibly acute angle to its shoulder. From there they would follow the "brown trail" for about a mile until it came to their favorite section of the park. It was a large, circular lawn surrounded by trees, with a concrete plinth in the center for the featured statue, a huge figure by Carl Milles called *The Sun Singer*. David and Joanna had come up with numerous names for it over the years: *The Flasher, Look, Ma! No Privates, Bloody Great Immodest Git, Nothing to See Here*—and so on.

The first time they saw this statue, David had posed in front of it, holding a large leaf positioned precisely in front of the statue's crotch. This photograph amused them so much that every time they came to the park they brought something else to hold up: a teapot, a mitten, a Christmas tree ornament. After several months, it started to get out of hand. They were bringing so many strange things with them that they were running out of room in their backpacks. One day, when David insisted on bringing *Brightman and Rigg's Advanced Techniques in Veterinary Surgery*, a textbook he had co-authored—which weighed about ten pounds—Joanna created the Rule of One: they were allowed to bring one item each, they had to carry their own item, and they had absolute veto power over the other's choice. If the veto power was exercised, however, the one vetoed had the right to pick the other person's item and no counter-veto was allowed.

The day before their outing—the day Joanna died—they had set a selection of possible items on the kitchen counter, ready to pack along with lunch. In the morning before leaving, they would deliberate with mock gravity about which prop to bring. David's idea this time was to bring the stuffed, mounted head of a bobcat. Joanna had been strongly tempted to veto, but had wisely stood down. The last time she had vetoed she had been forced to hold up an empty picture frame, so that the Sun Singer's equipment was, for the first time, fully visible.

After pretending to argue about their photo op props, they would pack their lunch. Alcoholic beverages were not allowed at Allerton Park, but they always brought a small bottle of contraband anyway. After their photo shoot with *The*

Green Giant Exhibitionist, they would picnic on a blanket at the edge of the lawn, admiring the autumn foliage and envying the Sun Singer's fate of standing there, naked in the sun, for all time.

But that's not what happened.

Joanna had kicked off the covers and gotten out of bed. He had stayed right where he was, fuming.

And when she died, she had been angry with him, and he with her. Wasn't that the exact circumstance people wished to avoid—being on bad terms with a loved one who died? Weren't people supposed to make amends quickly, to always part on good terms, so that regrets like this could be avoided?

After Joanna's death, David had embarked upon the series of decisions, crossroads, and turning points that had led him irrevocably to this very moment, powerless to protect Michaela from the same species of grief that had nearly killed him.

The other day he had mused out loud to Michaela that he was thinking of quitting. But he hadn't been entirely honest with her about the reason. In truth, he loved his work. He complained about the vet students, but he actually enjoyed teaching them, and he didn't really mind going in to save an animal's life in the middle of the night. He was proud of the new surgical techniques he had invented and the fact that the boundaries of science were expanding because of his research. People came to him from all over the world for his expertise.

But everything had become so damn complicated.

David took his hands out of his pockets and set them on top of the headstone, pressing his palms flat against the frozen stone, feeling its roughness, following its gentle curve. He savored the pain of the warmth leaving his hands, and wondered how long it would take for his entire body to become as cold as the stone.

A car door slammed nearby. Footsteps crunched through the snow and a familiar voice spoke up behind him. "Is that you, Dr. Brightman?"

David turned. It was Father Collins. "Are you the pastor here?" he asked, unable to keep the note of surprise from his voice.

Father Collins shook his head. "No, I'm just the associate priest." He walked around and read the headstone. "Your wife?"

David nodded.

"I pray for her every day," said Father Collins.

David frowned. How could this priest know his wife?

Father Collins spread his arms out. "I pray for them all." He let his arms fall to his sides. "It's nice to know a little more about at least one person here."

David hesitated a moment. "Father, to be fair, I think I should tell you—"

"That you know about the bad blood between Michaela and me?"

David nodded.

"Most people close to Mick know the story."

"But they don't know yours," David offered.

Father Collins gave a wry smile. "If you know her story, you know mine."

David was surprised. He had been expecting him to come to his own defense, at least a little. "She blames you for the death of her father."

"Right so." He looked off into the distance, staring at nothing.

David knew that look. "Your own parents, too." he said. "And your sister."

"Yes." Then the priest brought his attention back to the present, eyeing him curiously. "Are you Catholic?"

David shrugged. "Yes, but not a good one."

"Why do you say that?"

"I haven't been to Mass in thirty years. Except for Joanna's funeral." After that, David had come to this cemetery more times than he could count, but he hadn't entered the church once. "I know I should be going to Mass every Sunday."

"And every holy day." A mischievous look came over the priest's face. "Let's see now. That's thirty years by fifty-two weeks. That's...fifteen hundred, give or take half a dozen holy days every year. How many's that?"

David wasn't sure what to make of this. "Almost sixteen hundred?"

Father Collins whistled. "Sixteen hundred Masses missed. On purpose?"

"I beg your pardon?"

"You didn't accidentally oversleep sixteen hundred times?"

David gave a short laugh. "I don't think so."

"Well, now. Anything else?"

"If you're trying to hear my confession, Father, I assure you we'll both freeze to death before I'm finished. They'll think we're two new additions to the statuary and plunk us on top of a mausoleum."

Father Collins pulled a violet stole from his pocket, kissed it, then draped it over his neck.

David raised an eyebrow.

The priest gestured toward the church. "The heat's on inside."

Feeling somewhat manipulated, but oddly pleased, David followed Father Collins to the front door of the church. "I don't remember how to confess. I don't even know the prayers anymore."

"Don't worry. I'll walk you through it."

As they went in, it occurred to David that much of what he had to confess would be awkward. "I should warn you. You'll probably be brain-damaged after this."

"I'll take my chances." He waved to the back row of pews. "Never mind about sittin' in the box."

David sat down, and Father Collins sat down next to him. "May the Lord grant you the grace to confess your sins with true sorrow."

Father Collins made the sign of the cross over him, and David bowed his head.

20

Corruption

GALTON FOUND SANGER hunched over a pile of papers in the recesses of his laboratory. He gripped the edge of the lab bench and towered over him. "What the hell is wrong with you?"

Sanger looked up and pulled his glasses off. "We need that dog, Frank!"

"So we break in and get everything back when no one's there! Good God, wasn't it obvious that someone was in the damn building?"

Sanger tapped his fingers on his knees.

"You mean you went in there with every intention of shooting him?" Galton shook his head. "You damn fool. That's the second time you've walked away before making sure the job was done."

Sanger stood up. "It's not my fault! I shot him in the head, for chrissakes."

"Head shots are not always fatal, you idiot. If you want to make damn sure of killing a man, shoot him right here." Galton poked Sanger in the chest, hard. "Center mass."

Sanger knocked his hand away. "Don't touch me!"

"Please tell me you had the sense to use a non-registered weapon."

"Yes," he said, like a sullen child.

"Give it to me."

"It's in my car."

The parking lot was nearly empty except for several company sedans, his own Buick, Sanger's SUV, and Julius Abayomi's Range Rover. All the other employees were blithely enjoying their well-paid holiday hiatus. No one had asked any questions. While Sanger went to his SUV, Galton stood at the edge of the lot and watched the snow. It was falling so heavily it seemed fake. From the computer surveillance room, Galton and his team monitored these grounds. In fair weather they watched the employees as they ate their lunch or played catch on the stretch of lawn bordered by the parking lot and a grove of evergreen and deciduous trees.

The light was fading. Soon the spectral trees, living and dormant, would be shrouded in darkness.

Sanger returned from his car and handed Galton a Glock 19 pistol. He hopped from one foot to the other in the cold, while Galton inspected the weapon.

It was loaded. Galton chambered a round and tucked it into his waistband. "You'd better hope her husband dies, 'cause you're not going to get a second chance. The only one who can get to him now is the angel of Death himself."

"What did the Director say?"

"The Director is spitting mad, but I'm more worried about the investors. I've got to contain this mess or they sure as hell are not going to be happy."

Reaching into his pocket, Galton removed a car key. He pressed the button on the electronic key fob. Nearby, a company car chirped to life. "Leave your SUV. Do not go home. Do not come here. Disappear. Shack up with someone and screw her until you die. I don't care." He held the car key out. "Do not be reachable except by me."

Sanger snatched it from his hand and stalked to the car.

Galton called after him. "And for God's sake, try to keep your mouth shut for once."

Sanger wrenched the car door open, got in and drove off. The car fishtailed and then skidded around the corner out of sight.

If anyone deserved a bullet in the brain it was Garrett Sanger.

The wind was picking up. If Galton didn't hurry, this damn snowstorm would strand him here. He went to his Buick and quickly stashed Sanger's Glock under the front seat. Then, inside the video surveillance room upstairs, he pulled up the parking lot camera and deleted the last twenty minutes of footage.

Then he scanned the monitors until he located Julius in the system administration section.

For a moment, he watched the young man typing away at a keyboard. Thin cords snaked from his ears to his pocket, and his head moved in time to his music. He took a sip from a can of Mountain Dew.

It looked perfectly innocent. But, like most things, it wasn't. Everything was corruptible and corrupted. He sighed and scratched his upper lip through his mustache. Galton regretted what he had to do next.

* * *

Julius angrily surveyed a large section of computer code that had taken him several hours to write. The Sun Angels system was supposed to be like tunnels burrowing underground, through which the stealthy animals could slink undetected, invisible to anyone on the surface. At the end of the tunnels, the points of access for the spiders were supposed to be even smaller, mere cracks that allowed the spiders to slip through even the most carefully guarded defenses. Most of the

system *was* like that—the code was beautiful, intricate and po-
etic. But in his recent haste he had been unavoidably sloppy.
The code he had just written was about as subtle and unobtru-
sive as an African elephant.

Fortunately, like a charging elephant, it was still unstop-
pable. And with Galton's computer retrofit about to begin,
Julius had no choice but to launch it now.

A tone interrupted the music in his ears. He pulled his
phone from his pocket. It was a text message from Galton:
please meet me in surveillance.

Julius glanced up at the surveillance camera. He extended
his palm toward it in the universal signal for *give me five minutes*.
Turning back to his workstation, he entered the final key
commands. For a moment, he hovered over the execute
command. Then he clicked it. A clock icon in the corner began its countdown.

He pushed himself back from the desk and let his hands
drop to his lap. He took a deep breath to calm himself. It was
done. No one—not Galton, not the systems administration
staff—would be able to stop the Sun Angels from scurrying
through their tunnels and delivering Anansi and his children to
their access points in the Synthetic Genetics network.

Julius bent over the keyboard one last time. He exited the
Sun Angels and Spiders screens, closed it all down, and logged
out of the computer.

He gave the camera a thumbs-up on his way out.

In the video surveillance room, Galton, seated in front of
the bank of monitors, swiveled in his chair and waved Julius
over. Every monitor was blank, and, scanning the instruments,
Julius realized that the entire surveillance system was shut
down. All the cameras were switched off.

"I want to show you something," said Galton. He typed
and clicked until he brought up an image on one of the monitors. Julius recognized the server room downstairs. He saw
himself seated in front of a maintenance terminal, working at
the keyboard. "Quarter past four this morning," Galton said.
He fast-forwarded through several minutes, until Julius got up

and exited the frame. Next, Galton clicked to the specimen storage room, where all the blood and tissue samples were stored. Julius watched himself enter one of the large walk-in refrigeration units. Galton fast-forwarded again until he came to a portion that showed Julius emerging from the unit.

Galton froze the frame. "What were you doing in there, Julius?"

Blood pounded in Julius's head. How could he be so stupid? He was assigned to a project related to the surveillance system automation. He had no business in the specimen storage room. He couldn't very well admit to Galton what he had been doing.

He had not been thinking clearly. He was too tired, too overworked, too caffeinated and too rushed. The news of the shooting at the animal hospital had shocked him, and for the first time, it occurred to Julius that he could lose far more than precious time in this endeavor. Before, it had all been a delicious challenge, a puzzle of epic scale. But fear had made him careless.

"Julius, I'm very disappointed," Galton was saying. "I'm sure you know that what you're doing is a federal crime. A direct violation of the Economic Espionage Act of 1996, not to mention just plain bad manners."

Economic espionage? Julius thought. He let out a deep breath and looked down at his shoes, secretly rejoicing, trying not to smile.

"Tell me who you're working for."

Julius saw no reason to correct Galton's mistake or complicate his pretense. "The government of Uganda."

Galton raised his eyebrows. "Uganda? You've been stealing trade secrets for them?"

Julius nodded. "Uganda is most eager to develop its economy," he said, "and biotechnology is a growing field." This was true, but incomplete. Only Julius knew what his Sun Angels and Spiders had unearthed. And no one—not even the Ugandan government—knew his true mission here at Synthetic Genetics.

"Were you working with those two technicians, Munoz and Nelson, to take one of the test subjects from the facility? Was that part of your assignment from Uganda?"

"No. Physical extraction of live subjects is not part of my assignment. Munoz and Nelson acted independently. I was unaware of their actions."

"What about those veterinarians in Champaign? Are you involved with them?"

Julius shook his head. He had been following the veterinarians and monitoring the animal hospital. But he did not inform Galton of this.

"I'm sure I don't have to tell you that you're out of a job, young man." Galton extended his hand. "Give me your key card."

As Julius dug his plastic card from his pocket and handed it over, Galton continued. "If you have a duplicate card at home or elsewhere, don't bother trying to use it, because I'm changing the codes. You could be prosecuted for what you've done, but I'm willing to play nice if you turn in all the information you've collected so far," Galton concluded.

Julius had no answer to this. He had no stash of papers, photographs, computer disks, or digital tape. All his work was firmly embedded in the Synthetic Genetics computers.

Galton sighed. "Let's go get your things, and then you're outta here."

After retrieving their coats and keys, Galton made Julius lead the way to the stairwell down to the rear parking lot. As he reached the bottom of the stairs and stepped onto the concrete floor and headed for the exit door, Julius struggled to remain calm. A net had been drawing tighter and tighter about him, and the pressure had become almost unbearable. But he was now moments away from freedom.

* * *

Galton followed Julius as he stepped down into a featureless zone between the stairway and the exterior door. The echoing space was a catchall of random junk: tools, cleaning supplies, buckets of ice melt, snow shovels.

As they approached the exit, it occurred to Galton that the young man was being suspiciously quiet and compliant.

Posing as a graduate student intern was a clever cover story for someone stealing trade secrets for a foreign government, but perhaps it was too obvious. What if Julius were posing as an industrial spy to conceal something far more damaging? A double cover story. Lies within lies. Corruption within corruption. "Julius," he said.

Julius stopped.

"What are you not telling me?" Galton said to the young man's back.

Slowly, Julius turned around, his eyes darting from side to side. His tall, wiry form tensed, like a snake ready to strike.

Galton pushed his jacket back, revealing a side holster. He moved his hand toward the grip of the gun, but Julius was an instant ahead of him. There was a flash of movement and Julius's full weight drove him backwards into the cinder block wall. Julius grabbed for the gun, but Galton drove his elbow into the young man's chin and his knee into his groin. Julius grunted but continued scrabbling for the gun holster.

Julius was strong and quick, but he was an inexperienced fighter. Galton hooked his foot behind Julius's and swept him from his feet. Julius fell, but kept his grasp on Galton and pulled him down. They fell to the floor in a heap. Galton rolled sideways, righted himself, and reached for his weapon.

Julius leapt toward him like a cat, and once again Galton grunted as he hit the wall. His hand brushed up against something leaning against the wall and he grabbed it. It was a snow shovel. He rammed the handle upward into Julius's jaw. The young man's teeth clicked together and blood spurted from his mouth, but he wrenched the shovel from Galton's grasp, stepped back, and swung the curved blade of the shovel at Galton's face.

It was an unwieldy weapon which Galton was able to duck and block with an upraised arm. Then he gripped the side of the blade and shoved hard, driving the handle once again into Julius's face. Julius staggered against a pile of equipment, hands scrambling for purchase. As he did so, he stumbled upon a better weapon, a heavy metal bar about four feet long. The bar came up as Galton finally unholstered his gun.

Galton ducked the swinging pipe and squeezed the trigger. The gun's report echoed deafeningly in the stairway. Julius's head snapped back and he dropped with a thud.

"Damn, damn, damn!" Galton hissed. Julius's face was in a pool of rapidly spreading blood. Galton squatted down next to him and rolled him over. It was a beautiful shot, right in the center of the forehead. The young man's eyes were wide open, frozen in an expression of surprise. Galton felt for a pulse. A *really* beautiful shot. Ironic, considering his earlier discussion with Sanger.

Galton was having a hard time imagining how this situation could get much worse. First, those two technicians driving off with irreplaceable company property. Then, two outsiders threatening to expose the whole project. Sanger, going completely out of bounds, and now this. He had only shown Julius the gun to scare him. And the computer retrofit had been a ruse, a set-up to see if he could flush Julius out, force him to be hasty, make a mistake.

He hadn't expected it to work so well.

Galton checked the young man's throat again. No pulse. His skin already felt cool.

He was glad he had turned all the cameras off. Looking around, he found among the untidy array of maintenance and building supplies a large tarp, and rolled Julius's body onto it. Picking up the corners of the tarp, he dragged it to the door, then outside, across the parking lot onto the snow-covered lawn toward the grove of trees.

Several times, he stopped and looked up to make sure he could still see the building through the veil of blowing snow. The drifts around the grove were already deep, piling even deeper. He pulled the tarp over the snow and through the low branches of the evergreens. This was not a good long-term place to stash a body, but it was pretty damn good for now. He could move the body later, when he had more time. Before going back inside, he looked back at the expanse of snow between the parking lot and the grove, noting with satisfaction that the freakishly heavy snowfall was already obliterating the path he had taken.

Inside, there wasn't as much blood as he expected, but it would take some time to clean up. Then he had a couple loose ends to tie off elsewhere.

Galton sighed. This was going to be a long night.

21

Storm

AS A VETERINARIAN, Michaela had learned the hard way that when offering a prognosis, it was best to err on the side of pessimism. Medicine was such an inexact science, and dealing with living beings was not like dealing with machines. Machinery had constant, quantifiable stress tolerances, failure rates, and lengths of operation, and a mechanic could tell you exactly when a part would fail, when a machine would become inoperable, or that it required the following parts and it would cost this amount and take this many hours to fix.

Living beings were not like that at all. Patients that should have lived, died. Patients for which Michaela held out no hope at all pulled through. Optimism invited disaster, but offering a worse prognosis left open the possibility of being wonderfully, miraculously wrong.

But even she had been unprepared for the stark hopelessness of Terry's surgeon. A 9mm round had gone straight through the left side of Terry's brain, in the front and out the back. The surgeons had cleaned debris from the wounds, removed some irreparably-damaged brain tissue, and then removed the left half of his cranium. They also put him into a medically-induced coma. The plan was to bring him out of the coma once the danger of brain swelling had abated, and replace the section of cranium weeks or even months later. All well and good, but the location and track of the bullet was bad. "Dr. Collins," the surgeon had said, "your husband's prognosis is very poor. You should get ready to say good-bye."

They led her to an ICU cubicle and showed her a figure covered in blankets, head swathed in white bandaging, eyes covered with patches, face obscured by an endotracheal tube and the numerous strips of tape holding it in place, tubes and wires connected to his arms, fingers, legs, ensconced in a hive of beeping, trilling, flashing monitors. Somewhere under it all was her husband, his chest rising and falling in time with a hissing ventilator.

With the surgeon's words echoing in her ears, Michaela had dropped to her knees and clung to the bedrail, afraid to cry too loud, wanting to scream, knowing she couldn't do such a thing in the hospital, blinded by tears, already feeling the emptiness of what her life would be like without him.

Terry deserved to live. Like a child, her heart cried out in simple agony, *please don't let him die!*

"Michaela, did you hear me?"

Startled, Michaela turned her head. It was dark. They were sitting in her mother's car, outside her own house. Alicia had been talking to her, but she hadn't heard.

"I'm sorry, sweetie. You're so tired. I shouldn't have said anything."

"Said anything about what?" Michaela's voice sounded weak, even to herself.

"About Brendan."

"What about Brendan?"

"He was there today."

"I know."

Her mother gave an exasperated sigh. "He kept his distance because he was waiting—hoping—for an invitation from you."

"Let him wait."

"Oh, Michaela," her mother said.

"Do we have to do this now, Mom?"

Alicia shook her head. "No. I'm sorry, sweetheart. Let's go in."

As they got out of the car, Michaela took note of the police cruiser behind them and the police officer getting out to follow them into the house.

Kath Ullman and her eight-year old son had just finished shoveling the freshly fallen snow. Kath dropped her shovel and hugged Michaela. "Just let me know what you need, Michaela." Kath released her and held her at arms' length. "Okay? Promise you'll let me help you."

Michaela's throat tightened and her eyes burned. She nodded.

It was snowing hard again. The wind was biting, blowing the snow sideways, coming in gusts that stung her face. Snow drifted against the fence. A snowstorm was coming. They were advising people to stay home, but Michaela was just here to change her clothes, and then Hank Ullman was coming to take her back to the hospital. The officer outside would be going with Alicia back to her house.

Another officer had volunteered to stay at the hospital with Terry until they returned. Even though the circumstances seemed to warrant it, Michaela couldn't help feeling a little guilty for all these officers volunteering their off-duty hours as bodyguards for her and her family.

Kath and her son took their shovels and headed home.

As Michaela and Alicia entered the house, Tripod gamboled around them. Alicia tried to shoo him outside, but he refused. The officer disappeared into the house, checking all the rooms.

The violent wind caused the house to creak and the windows to rattle. "Mom, you should go," Michaela said. "The weather." She removed her coat and draped it over the back of a kitchen chair.

"Why don't I just stay here until Hank comes?" Alicia began to bustle about. She went to the sink and put water in the kettle. "We'll have a cup of tea—"

"No!"

Alicia turned around, surprised.

Michaela had spoken more sharply than she intended. She took a breath and calmed herself. "No, Mom." Michaela dropped heavily into the chair. "I've been surrounded by people all day. Everyone's been great, but I think I just need some quiet." In truth, she needed to give voice to the grief and fear that had been hiding behind public decorum all day. She wanted to scream, let raw, crazy pain slip its leash and run wild, and she did not want her mother to hear her. "Go home and rest. I'll meet you back at the hospital later."

The officer reappeared. "All clear," she said.

Alicia picked up her keys. Michaela stood up and hugged her. "I'm sorry," she whispered. She hated this. She knew her mom felt like she was being kicked out, but Michaela desperately needed to be alone.

"It's okay, sweetie. I'll see you in a bit." Then she and her escort officer went back through the kitchen and out the back door.

Michaela went to her bedroom to change. She was still wearing the surgical scrubs from last night. She removed them and put on a turtleneck sweater, flannel-lined denim jeans, thick cotton socks. She was mechanical, deliberate in her movements, but she couldn't help thinking that Terry had given her these jeans, these socks.

Without even knowing how she got there, she found herself standing in the middle of her living room. Her eyes drifted to a photograph of Terry. She looked away. Tripod ambled over to her in his funny, three-legged way and nudged her hand with his wet nose. Michaela absently laid her hand on his head. She was finally alone, and the expected release would not come. She felt numb.

She turned her head as someone came through the breezeway. It was Hank Ullman. He stepped inside, unzipped the high, fleece-lined collar of his police parka and threw back the hood. He pulled a set of keys from his pocket and handed them to Michaela. "Your truck's in the garage."

"Thanks."

"You look tired," he said.

Michaela responded with a sigh and weak attempt at a smile.

"Ready to go?"

She nodded. "Yeah, but make yourself comfortable. Tripod needs to go out first."

Hank unzipped his parka the rest of the way and sat down on the couch. He was off-duty, so underneath his parka, he wore regular street clothes, but Michaela couldn't help noticing his weapon, holstered at his side.

Michaela went to the back door and pulled on her boots and coat. Outside, she stood with her hands in her pockets, fingering her keys impatiently. The wind was biting, coming in gusts that stung her face. Snow drifted against the fence. Tripod did his business quickly and ran to the door, pawing to be let in. As they went back inside, Tripod saw Hank in the front room and ran to be petted. Absently, she pulled her cell phone from her coat pocket and flipped it open, but then realized how absurd it was, how useless. She dropped the phone onto the kitchen table.

A moment later there was a knock on the back door behind her.

She turned and saw a policeman, bundled up to his cheekbones, just like Hank, shoulders hunched against the wind. She opened the door and let him in.

"Everything all right, Dr. Collins?" he said, pulling back the hood of his parka and unwinding his scarf. It was Hank Ullman's division commander.

Even the top brass are taking turns looking after me, she thought.

"Thanks, Lieutenant. Everything's fine," she answered, mechanically. "I'm heading back to the hospital right now." She went into the living room.

"Did your mother forget something?" Hank asked, scratching Tripod under the chin.

"No. Why?" Michaela replied.

"Who was at the back door?"

"Lieutenant Galton."

For an instant, a smile of acknowledgment formed on Hank's lips as he recognized his commanding officer. Then his expression of recognition transformed into shock. He jumped to his feet and his hand dropped to his holstered weapon, but he was too late. There were two cracking sounds, and a blood-stain bloomed over his chest as he collapsed lifeless upon the couch.

Tripod bared his teeth and charged the gunman, snarling.

Michaela spun around and cried out as Lieutenant Galton fired his weapon again. Tripod fell with a yelp, bleeding and still. Then Galton strode toward her, aiming the gun straight at her head.

His hands were swathed in bright blue, form-fitting latex gloves. When he spoke, his voice was calm and measured. "Dr. Collins, you're very upset."

"What?" Michaela said.

"You had a complete psychotic breakdown. Officer Ull-man came to check on you, but you were so distraught and disoriented by your psychosis that you convinced yourself he was the man who shot your husband."

"You're the one who shot him!" Michaela cried.

"Actually, that wasn't me."

"Why should I believe you?"

"I don't care if you believe me or not." Galton shrugged, then continued his narrative. "In a brief moment of lucidity, you realized what you had done, and sadly, in your guilt and distress, you took your own life."

A clock on the fireplace mantelpiece ticked loudly, and to Michaela it seemed like the countdown to her own personal apocalypse.

"Incidentally," Galton said with a short laugh, as if he had just gotten a joke, "this is the same gun that shot your husband, so after all this is over there will be strong evidence pointing to you as his shooter also."

Michaela clenched her fists, shaking with fury and fear. "How could you get involved in something like this? You're a police officer, for God's sake!" she shouted. She forced herself to breathe, to calm down. She raised her hands in front of her, in supplication. "Please. Leave my husband alone. Don't—" Tears streamed from her eyes. "Just don't." But she knew her pleas were futile. They must have gotten to Terry already. He was already dead.

Galton pursed his lips. "The point is, this whole situation has gotten out of hand and I need to reign it in." He leveled the gun at her.

"What about Rosie?"

A bemused expression came over Galton's face as he lowered his gun slightly. "After everything that's happened, you're still thinking about that?"

"She needs to be put down and her remains incinerated! Promise me you'll do that, at least."

"Why do you care so much about a damn dog?"

Michaela's voice shook. "She's an innocent animal. She can't make sense of suffering."

Galton snorted. "As if people can?"

Just then, the front window shattered. Galton and Michaela both flinched instinctively. The front door smashed open. Galton opened fire, but the shots went high, over the head of a figure charging low through the doorway. The figure tackled Galton, pinned him against the wall, and wrenched the gun from his hand. The gun fell to the floor and the attacker kicked it away. It spun under the couch.

Galton gasped and Michaela saw a flash of recognition on his face. The attacker, a young black man, grabbed Galton by the hair and slammed his head against the wall. He went down hard, still conscious but stunned.

The black man turned toward Michaela. His face was smeared with blood. In the center of his dark, glistening forehead was a circular wound.

A bullet hole.

A small trickle of blood flowed from the wound, pulsing slightly with each heartbeat.

22

Vigils

ALICIA PACED BACK AND FORTH in front of the window in Terry's ICU cubicle, berating herself. She should have waited and come back to the hospital with Michaela. What was she thinking? She should never have left her alone. But Michaela had always been so headstrong. It wasn't the first time Alicia had acted against her better judgment and allowed Michaela to have her way.

Like allowing her daughter to spend summers in Belfast, Ireland, in the very thick of the Troubles. Michaela's teenage sense of invincibility must have rubbed off on her mother and father, because Alicia and Sean never thought anything would happen. Why would they? J.J. and Viola were civilians. And Brendan had been an excellent liar. A good boy at home, but the minute he walked out the door...

Alicia shook her head. For more than twenty years, she had managed to steer clear of Michaela's swamp of bitterness. She was not about to wade into it now. Besides, between the two of them, Brendan and Michaela had swallowed enough guilt and gall for all of them.

Michaela had insisted on being alone, if only for a few minutes, and Alicia knew from personal experience that sometimes a person just needed solitude.

She peered outside. In the glow of a streetlamp, she could see snow blowing sideways and drifts piling up at an alarming rate. Michaela should have been here by now. She got her cell phone and called the house. The answering machine picked up, and fresh tears came to Alicia's eyes as she heard Terry's voice on the outgoing message: "Hi, this is Terry and Michaela. I think Tripod ate the phone, so we'll have to call you back." She tried Michaela's cell and got her voicemail. Why didn't she answer?

Alicia knew she wouldn't be able to sleep, so she sat in a chair by Terry's bed, wrapped in a spare hospital blanket, and turned the room's television set to The Weather Channel.

A Champaign police officer had stationed herself just outside the door. Alicia thought wryly that the weather was probably protecting everyone more than the police were.

With each failed attempt to reach Michaela by phone, Alicia's mind raced and her imagination created one disastrous scenario after another. She prayed for a simple explanation—phone lines affected by the weather, Michaela fast asleep, too exhausted to answer the phone. Alicia would even be happy to learn that she and Officer Ullman had drunk themselves into a stupor and passed out.

Alicia's eyes drifted to Terry. For a moment, she listened to the reassuring hiss of the ventilator and the beeping of the heart monitor. She took his hand. "Terry?" she said, hopefully. "Sweetheart, can you hear me?" His hand remained slack and motionless. How could something like this happen? To Terry, of all people? It wasn't fair. Alicia loved him like he was her own son. She loved the way he cared for Michaela with masculine strength and devotion, the way her daughter relaxed and smiled whenever he entered a room, the way he had softened her rough edges. And now, after years of inexplicable delay, they had finally started a family.

She tried Michaela's numbers one more time and became even more agitated when she still couldn't get through.

Alicia turned at a soft knock on the doorjamb of the cubicle. Two police officers entered. Their expressions were grim.

* * *

Brendan stood by the window in the living room of St. Andrew's rectory, watching the snow fall. In the garden, snow encased every branch and drooping blade of grass. It swathed the birdbath in a thick mound. The garden gnome, normally such a cheerful presence in the priests' garden, looked macabre, mummified in a snowy shroud.

It was cold by the window. Brendan moved closer to the fire crackling in the fireplace.

The fierce storm was shaking the house. However, the noise outside was nothing compared to the noise inside his head. Every priest, including Brendan, could hardly contain their joy when a person came to confession and began by saying, "Bless me Father, for I have sinned, it has been thirty years since my last confession." Or forty. Or fifty. Or more.

Brendan would never forget the man who had come to his confessional and said it had been *seventy* years since his last confession. In a reedy, raspy tenor, he had unburdened his soul of a thousand things that were keeping him from turning to God. Brendan had wept with the man as he humbly concluded by saying, "I've lived a long time. I've done many wicked things, but I've always felt like a little boy inside, ashamed of what I've done. I'm not running to God now just because I'm old and I don't want to go to hell. I'm not sick. I don't think I'm going to die soon. I just want to have peace inside, and I want to be happy in my life. I want to look God full in the face and see him as my loving Father."

Those were the times that made Brendan's life's work all worth it.

So Brendan's arrival at the cemetery had been propitious for David Brightman, who was now reconciled to God after many years of estrangement.

But perhaps not for me, Brendan thought, because now he had to process what the man had confessed.

Alicia once asked him what it was like to hear people's confessions. "Doesn't it bother you?" she had asked. "Listening to all those sins?" How could Brendan sleep at night, with so many sins revealed? How could he bear it?

The truth was, with a few exceptions, he didn't really remember what people told him. His brother priests had said the same thing. It seemed that God granted a special grace to His priests, the grace to forget what they heard in the confessional, which certainly was helpful: by the law of the Church, priests were forbidden to reveal anything entrusted to them in the sacrament of confession.

"Haven't you ever been affected?" Alicia had pressed. "Haven't you ever heard something that was so shocking you couldn't forget?"

Up until yesterday, Brendan would have said no.

Above the fireplace mantel was a lovely painting of Joseph leading Mary and the donkey through a waist-high field of ripe wheat. Candles burned below the painting, framing a tasteful display of religious statuary and Christmas décor. On the far left of the mantel was an object totally out of place among the others. It was a human skull, gray and dirty brown.

Brendan walked over to the mantel and picked it up. The light flickering over its eye sockets and mirthlessly grinning teeth made it look like it was laughing at him. When he was a young priest, assigned to his first parish, the pastor there also had a skull displayed on the mantel in the rectory. For months, Brendan had looked at it and thought about it, becoming more and more puzzled about its presence. Finally, when he couldn't stand it any longer, he asked, "Why do you have this thing, Father?"

The old priest had taken the skull off the mantel and turned it over in his hands. "It's to remind us of our own mortality."

"That's a pretty stark reminder."

The old priest nodded. "St. Francis used to take his followers out every day, looking for an open grave. When he found one, he would have them sit and reflect upon it for an hour." He put the skull carefully back in its place. "Imagine," he said, "if everyone in the world reflected daily on his own death. How different the world would be."

Brendan made up his mind what to do. He grabbed his coat and headed out the door.

* * *

When he got to Carle Hospital, two Champaign patrol officers stood with his Aunt Alicia at the foot of the bed in Terry's ICU cubicle.

"Any idea where she went?" Alicia was saying.

The first officer shook his head. "We were hoping you would know. She didn't contact you at all? She didn't come by or call?"

In answer to each question, Alicia shook her head, fresh tears welling up in her eyes and spilling down her cheeks.

"What's going on?" Brendan asked. "Michaela's missing?"

The second officer nodded. "But her truck is still in her garage."

"I've been trying to call her," Alicia said.

"We found her cell phone on the kitchen table," the first officer said.

Another police officer entered the room. He was not a patrol officer, like the first two. A superior of theirs, judging by his uniform and the way the two young officers took a step backward, subtly yielding the floor to him. He had dark hair, a thick mustache and a livid bruise above his eyebrow and extending down the side of his face.

"Mrs. Collins," he began, addressing Alicia. "I think you should know—"

Brendan interrupted. "Who are you, sir?"

The man took an ID badge from his jacket, opened it and displayed it. "Lieutenant Frank Galton."

Brendan lifted an eyebrow.

Galton continued. "I'm afraid something terrible happened last night at your daughter's house."

Alicia tightened her grip on Brendan's hand.

Galton continued. "Ma'am, we found Sergeant Hank Ullman in Michaela's house. He was dead. Shot."

Brendan glanced at Alicia. Her eyes were wide.

"We found a dog in the house, also shot dead."

Alicia gasped.

Brendan could tell where Alicia's mind was racing. He spoke quickly. "Not Michaela, Auntie. They didn't find her, remember? She wasn't in the house."

"No, sir, she wasn't," Galton said.

"So where is she?" Alicia cried.

"I visited your daughter's residence earlier this evening, to offer my support."

Brendan bit his lip, but kept silent as Galton continued.

"I'm sad to say that she became incoherent and violent. Officer Ullman trusted her, naturally, and in an unguarded moment she was able to produce a firearm and shoot him—"

"*What?*" Brendan and Alicia exclaimed together.

"She then assaulted me with the weapon," Galton said, indicating the bruise on his face, "incapacitating me sufficiently to make her escape. I was unconscious for some time."

Brendan let go of Alicia's hand and took a step toward Galton. The man was about six feet, two inches tall and solidly built. Brendan's voice was low and bitterly ironic. "My cousin Michaela did that to you? All five feet three inches and a hundred and ten pounds of her?"

Galton's face was stone.

"And then she made off into the night in the middle of a snowstorm?"

The officers glanced at each other. Galton stood his ground.

Brendan broke the silence. "Horseshit," he said. He knew Michaela could hit hard, but even she could not deliver a blow like that.

Galton stepped forward. He was close enough for Brendan to see the pores in his swarthy skin. "I've contacted the FBI field offices in Chicago and Springfield. As of early this morning, I'm afraid Dr. Collins is classified as a fugitive. If you knowingly harbor her or fail to inform us of her where-abouts—"

"Get out," Brendan spat.

The two officers couldn't leave fast enough—they nearly got stuck shoulder to shoulder in the door. But Galton turned and gave Brendan a final dangerous look.

Alicia turned toward Brendan. She made a feeble gesture of hopeless resignation with her hands.

Brendan shook his head. "Of course she didn't do it. But what choice do his officers have, other than to believe his story?" He sighed and dragged his fingers through his hair.

"If she's innocent, why would she run off?" Alicia moaned.

"At least we know he doesn't have her," he said, nodding toward the door. "He's still looking for her." And now Galton had the federal government looking for her, too, to arrest her for murder.

Brendan took out his cell phone and dialed the rectory. Father Angelo picked up. "Father, it's me, Brendan. I need to clear my schedule. My aunt needs looking after."

Alicia frowned at him and shook her head.

"Thanks, Father. I owe you one."

He closed the call and immediately dialed another number.

"Brendan, what are you talking about?" Alicia said. "I don't need you here to baby-sit me."

"Alicia, think about it. What's happened to just about everyone who knows about this Synthetic Genetics project?"

They both looked at Terry, still swathed, bandaged, connected to numerous machines. Behind them, the ventilator clicked and hissed in a hypnotizing rhythm, and the ECG machine beeped softly. He looked like he was sleeping, an oasis of peace in the midst of all this chaos.

"You're here to protect Terry," Brendan said. "But who's going to protect you?"

23

Spiritus Mundi

THIS WAS ALL HAPPENING TOO FAST. Only moments ago, Michaela had been preparing for an all-night vigil at Terry's side. Now, her neighbor and her dog lay lifeless on the floor of her living room, killed as casually as she would swat a fly, and she was driving rapidly through a snowstorm with a man who looked like he should be dead.

He drove his Range Rover confidently through the heavy snow, his face glowing in the blue and white lights of the dashboard. He was young, twenty at most, Michaela guessed. His eyes darted back and forth between the side and rear view mirrors. The volume on the stereo was low, but the deep bass of hip-hop music rumbled in Michaela's chest.

With a glance at Michaela, he made a quick turn into the parking lot of a darkened strip mall. He drove around the back, to the alley, and stopped among the dumpsters and detritus of business. He leaned forward and pressed the stereo button. The thrumming bass cut off abruptly.

"Who are you?" Michaela asked. "What is going on?"

"My name is Julius Abayomi." His voice was melodic, his accent beautiful and exotic. He wore low-slung black denim jeans, neon lime and orange high-top sneakers with thick black laces. Under a black leather jacket he wore an oversized tee shirt the same shade of neon lime. Emblazoned across the front of the shirt was an extreme close-up of a young black face with stern eyebrows, beads of perspiration and black-inked abstract tattoos. "I do not expect you to trust me, but I will tell you everything."

Michaela thought it over for a moment. She had no idea who this young man was, but he had saved her life, and she was completely in his power now. He didn't seem threatening.

"All right," she said. "I'm listening."

He began his story by telling her how he had been raised to be a soldier of Joseph Kony, but had run away after witnessing a massacre at one of the neighboring Lord's Resistance Army compounds. He told her how, after that, he had been raised by the sisters at St. Peter Claver's, a rehabilitation center for orphaned children in Gulu, Uganda.

Michaela vividly recalled her mother's obsession with news about the LRA several years ago, when it was getting lots of press in the United States. In Uganda, Congo, and Sudan, they were trafficking human beings—kidnapping young girls to act as sexual slaves for rebel soldiers. They took young boys, too, and forced them to join their militia. The lucky ones got away and ended up in orphanages or rehabilitation programs like the one Julius described. A madman named Joseph Kony founded the LRA, with the original goal of overthrowing the Ugandan government, but it had been many years since the LRA operated there. Kony had relocated his insanity to neighboring African countries and had somehow evaded capture for decades.

Julius told her that after university he became another kind of soldier, a clandestine one. The Ugandan civil service recruited him for a special project, not only because of his technical brilliance, but also because of his time in the Lord's

Resistance Army. His assignment was to investigate something that had troubled government officials for years: how was Joseph Kony's LRA able to function? Who supplied it with weapons, vehicles, food, and other supplies? Where did it get the resources to conduct its war against the government?

"You Americans have an expression for the task my government set for me," Julius said.

"Follow the money," Michaela said.

"Precisely," Julius said.

His task was to trace the funding to its source and find out who was financing the attempted overthrow of Uganda. The officials who hired him felt that a person of Julius's aptitude and technical training would be able to use computer savvy and knowledge of business and accounting to tease out the complex path of money that flowed into Uganda. Every corporate entity, overseas aid organization, and institute of higher education would be open to his scrutiny. They even gave him full access to government financial records, because they were willing to receive the worst news possible—that a shadow element within the government itself was paying off the agents of its own demise. Government officials were confident that Julius's mistreatment at the hands of the LRA would motivate him to be diligent. His upbringing in a well-regarded Catholic institution was also a mark in his favor, because they felt assured of his honesty.

Julius relished the challenge. He told Michaela how he spent hours on the telephone, sometimes cajoling information politely, sometimes making the person on the other end feel the full weight of the government behind his words. He spent many hours on the road, driving from place to place, hip-hop music blasting from the open window out into the bush. Other times he was hunched over piles of bank records, accessed via government-issued subpoenas and begrudgingly handed over by scowling bankers and businessmen. But the most intricate work had to be done in secret, in front of a computer monitor. Using software he designed to mimic burrowing animals and minuscule spiders, he tunneled into the deepest recesses of his targets' secrets.

His first discovery had been a relief to the Ugandan government. He flushed out a few mid-level officials and military officers who were guilty of embezzlement, but he was able to reassure his employer that no one in the government itself was funneling money to the LRA. And he was personally relieved to learn that, even though a few alumni and radical professors were sympathetic with the LRA, Makerere University itself was clean. Charitable organizations operating within Uganda also had no detectable financial ties to the LRA, beyond the inevitable LRA squads sometimes taking advantage of their generosity.

"You must have found something, though." Michaela prompted. "Something that brought you here to America."

Julius nodded. "After many months of unraveling all the ways money came into Uganda, I discovered two important things. First, for two decades Acholi Hospital in Gulu had been receiving many large endowments from an international non-profit foundation. Second, the hospital regularly made large purchase orders with a company called Accurate Construction, also located in Gulu. The invoices were paid out of the endowment accounts set up by the foundation, but no goods or supplies were ever delivered, no workers were ever hired, and no buildings were ever constructed on the hospital campus."

Michaela understood. "It was a shell. A front for moving money."

"Yes. The construction company was the key. The money went in to pay for building expenses but then disappeared into the bush. I continued following this trail, learning everything I could about the international non-profit foundation, the entity pouring money into the endowment accounts at Acholi Hospital."

Julius explained that the foundation had a subsidiary on the African continent, headquartered in Nairobi, Kenya. Ugandan officials arranged for him to pose as an independent contractor and obtain a position there as computer systems administrator. He learned that the foundation financed many areas of legitimate charitable work, but he also discovered hundreds of other companies like Accurate Construction: mere shells serving as conduits for thousands of anonymous electronic transfers from the foundation every month. Transfers of money out of those shell companies were harder to trace, but after only a few months in Nairobi, Julius happened upon a trail that led straight to Synthetic Genetics.

"So this foundation is their source of funding," Michaela said.

Julius nodded.

"But where does the foundation get *its* funds?" Michaela asked. "Who's *really* behind this project?"

"That is an excellent question," Julius said, "but what of my original assignment? The Ugandan government was still awaiting answers. Was the non-profit foundation funding the Lord's Resistance Army? I went to Gulu to ask questions."

Julius reached into the center console of the Range Rover and removed a handheld tablet computer. A moment later he showed Michaela the screen and played a video. The person behind the camera—presumably Julius—walked down a dusty street lined with low-slung, stucco buildings and the occasional traditional thatched-roof round hut. Steady pedestrian and bicycle traffic flowed in both directions. Every minute or so a motor scooter or automobile passed, stirring up a cloud of red dust.

"This is the Kidepo-Gulu Road," Julius said. He pointed to a long, low building housing several businesses. "A dental clinic here. A tailor and shoe repair shop. This one, a traditional Acholi healer. A bookshop." Finally, they came to an office at the end of the building.

The company name was affixed to the door: Accurate Construction. The block capital A was in the shape of a snow-capped mountain. Julius paused the video playback and pointed. "The letter A, here? It is made to look like Mt. Kilimanjaro. *This* was the connection," he said excitedly. "When I was a child, I saw this *same thing* on the fence of the LRA compound. You see?"

"I do see," Michaela said. "Accurate Construction didn't build anything in Gulu, but it built the LRA compounds."

"Exactly. The same foundation that funds Synthetic Genetics also funds the LRA."

"The LRA is part of the project," she whispered.

Julius opened the door of the Range Rover and got out. He stood with his back to the vehicle, hands in his pockets, looking up into the falling snow.

Michaela also got out and stood next to the young man. "How long have you known?" she asked gently. "How long have you known that you were a test subject?"

"I suspected it for some time." Julius looked down at her. "But it was not until this evening, waking up beneath the trees and the open sky, that I knew for certain."

Michaela closed her eyes. Men like Garrett Sanger weren't just conducting their genetic crash cart tests on animals. They were also experimenting on innocent boys and girls, abducted into the bush by Joseph Kony, who received money in exchange for handing the children over to mad scientists. And from Julius's account it sounded as if they were decades ahead of the research in the United States.

What was happening to the world? Everything was backward. Good people died, innocent creatures suffered, and everywhere, evil thrived. It seemed to Michaela that not just her own world was falling apart, but the whole world, whipped into a pointless, dizzying frenzy of ever-increasing offenses against life itself. She imagined a huge carousel, spinning impossibly fast, too fast for anything living to maintain its hold. Men, women, children, animals, hands shaking as they hung on, knuckles white with the effort, teeth bloodied in their gums, disintegrating cell by cell, their very DNA becoming prey to the jaws of the rough beast crouching at the perimeter of the carousel.

The young man's shoulders rose and fell as he sighed deeply. "All the African subjects deteriorated quickly," Julius said, "after their first reanimation. That is why they shot them and burned them. Because they were considered experimental failures. Because they were already dead." When he turned to face her again, his eyes glistened. "Which means I am already dead, too." The gunshot wound in his forehead was bleeding again. He used the back of his hand to wipe away the blood.

"Let me take care of that wound," she said, returning to the passenger side of the Range Rover. She opened the glove compartment and found a zippered pouch with a white cross on it.

Julius got in behind the wheel and switched on the dome light.

Michaela opened the first aid kit, opened a packet of gauze and a bottle of antiseptic solution. Carefully, she cleaned the blood from Julius's face. "How did you end up at my house tonight?"

"I have been keeping my eye on you since shortly after Rosie's disappearance. Galton had suspicions that we were working together in an industrial espionage scheme. I got to your house as quickly as I could."

She squeezed triple antibiotic ointment onto a large non-stick pad. "Julius, this project has to be exposed and shut down."

"Agreed," he said, holding the non-stick pad to his forehead while Michaela taped it in place.

"But not by me," she concluded.

The young man raised his eyebrows.

"I need to be with my husband."

Julius shook his head. "Impossible." He activated his tablet computer and quickly accessed the FBI website. On the fugitive list, under the heading "violent crimes and murders," Michaela saw her own face on the screen. The photo was cropped from the Christmas card she and Terry had sent out that year.

"That was quick," she murmured. She clicked her photo and read that she was wanted for murder, attempted murder, unlawful flight to avoid prosecution, aggravated assault and battery, and assault and battery of a police officer.

Galton had come to her house totally prepared to set up his narrative of Michaela's psychotic, homicidal-suicidal breakdown: he had worn gloves to prevent leaving any fingerprints and must have been counting on the snowstorm to wipe out any trace of his presence outside the house. His only problem now was that he had been unable to stage her suicide. But he still had the gun that he used to shoot Hank Ullman and that he said was the same gun used to shoot Terry.

With Galton's expertise, lifting Michaela's fingerprints from some object in her home and transferring them to that gun was probably easy. If he did that, the evidence pointing to her as both Terry's shooter and Hank's killer would be strong, and it could be made more convincing if Galton—a lieutenant commander in the Champaign Police Department—went public with it.

Pointing at the screen, she said, "This is all the more reason for me to turn myself in, explain myself and put an end to this." She checked the pockets of her coat, looking for her cell phone.

"Turn yourself in to whom? To Galton? That would be unwise."

"No, not Galton. Not any of the local departments. To the FBI." She couldn't find her phone.

Julius became intent. "Dr. Collins, most of the task is already completed. Before Galton shot me, I was able to complete all of my work."

"Your work?"

"Galton thought I was merely stealing information. But, in truth, I have spent many months preparing a data-destroying computer program. The Sun Angels and Spiders program will erase and irrevocably reformat all the hard drives on all the servers on-site at the main facility, and off-site at the remote backup facility."

"The program is running now?" Michaela asked.

He nodded. "I was able to launch it, and at midnight tonight, the Sun Angels will wipe the disks clean. Then, because they are very polite and well-trained, they will turn the lights out when they leave. But that is not all they can do."

"What else can they do?"

"The Spiders will follow a trail to all the bank accounts I have been able to identify, all over the world, and make every penny disappear."

Michaela gasped. "You mean bankrupt the whole project? You can do that?"

Julius chuckled. "*I* can."

She laughed wryly. "I'm glad you're one of the good guys," she said.

"All the data about Rosie will be erased," Julius continued. "Her medical records. Her genome. The laboratory protocols. Anything that might assist Dr. Sanger and the Director in reproducing their results."

"What about tissue specimens?" Michaela said. "Cell cultures and blood samples?"

"When Synthetic Genetics goes dark, the building will be completely cut off from the power grid. All biological specimens requiring refrigeration will spoil, and all samples in liquid nitrogen will thaw and denature."

"What if someone manages to get them out of the building?" Michaela objected. "If they manage to preserve Rosie's samples they could pick up right where they left off, no matter what we do."

Julius shook his head. "That thought occurred to me, so I personally disposed of them."

"Sounds like you've thought of everything, but I have to ask: what about samples preserved in formalin? Those won't be affected by a power outage."

"Everything is destroyed," he said.

"Everything except Rosie," Michaela concluded. If her tissues or data remained intact anywhere, including on her microchip, the project could be easily resurrected.

"Dr. Collins, we must find her."

He was right. Michaela knew she couldn't just leave Rosie in Garrett Sanger's hands without making at least some effort to put an end to her suffering. "We can track her with the microchip, right?"

"Yes, but we need her chip number."

That damn microchip. Who would have imagined that a simple string of numbers and letters could be so crucial? "I used to have the number," Michaela said, "in Rosie's chart at the animal hospital, but it was taken, along with everything else. You didn't find the number with all her other information?"

"In that regard, I was perhaps too thorough." Julius absent-mindedly tapped out a beat on the steering wheel. "I saw the number once, briefly," he said, "but without an eidetic memory it is not possible for me to recall the sequence." He turned the stereo on again, and the thrumming bass of the rap music resumed.

Michaela remembered some of the number. The first letters were SGG: Synthetic Genetics Group. What were those blasted numbers, which she had repeated to half a dozen phone reps from the pet microchip companies?

She put her head in her hands and listened to the rap music. The rhythm started to lull her into a stupor. She could hear herself reciting the chip's letters and numbers in time to the beat, except she had no idea what the numbers were. She rubbed her face, trying to clear her head.

Even if she and Julius found the chip number and discovered where Rosie was, how were they going to get to her? Breaking and entering? High-tech burglary? Julius's warnings notwithstanding, Michaela still wondered if the most logical thing to do was turn herself in to the FBI and take her chances.

But if she did that, she could be tied up for days or even weeks. She needed to see Terry sooner than that. And her mother. "My mom's probably going crazy worrying about me," she muttered under her breath. *Going spare*, as David Brightman would say. Then it hit her. "Wait a minute," she said out loud. "I made a copy of Rosie's records. On a portable computer drive. I gave it to a friend for safekeeping." She turned to Julius and cocked an eyebrow.

Julius grinned. He turned the key in the ignition and the Range Rover roared to life.

24

Absolution

AFTER JOANNA DIED, and years before Terry entered the scene, David and Michaela had loved each other. It seemed ridiculous—a young veterinarian and her former professor, something people would make lewd jokes about. But for some reason it worked. The large age difference didn't seem to matter. After all, he had also been several years older than Joanna.

Perhaps it was because Michaela was older than her years. Or maybe, as she used to kid him, it was because he was incredibly immature for his age. As an illustration, Michaela liked to tell the story of a certain evening at his house, when the phone rang and she had answered it. After listening for a moment, she had handed the phone to David, saying, "It's The Portrait Center in Urbana."

He had taken the phone and put on the most toffee-nosed, upper-crust English accent he could muster and said, "Yes, this is David Brightman speaking…a portrait sitting, eh? Well, before you get into the pricing and all that, I feel compelled to inform you that my family and I are not very photogenic at the moment... Yes, you see, we had a recent house fire and I'm afraid we're all rather horribly disfigured."

David had never seen anyone spew their drink in real life—only in the movies—but that's exactly what Michaela had done. Then she had grabbed the phone from him and thrown it across the room, red-faced and spluttering with laughter.

They enjoyed each other immensely, but there was always a veil between them, barely noticeable but still impenetrable. It was more than his simply missing Joanna and needing to work through the grief. To most people, David Brightman seemed to be working through it just fine. He was getting on with his life. He had a beautiful young woman at his side, a stellar career. Plenty of reasons to get up in the morning.

But it was Michaela—and only Michaela—who noticed the harder edge creeping into David's personality. Cynicism replaced his good humor and he became increasingly prone to bitter self-deprecation. She alone sensed that something was deeply troubling and tormenting him, but even with all her love and support, she couldn't help him.

He usually did a good job of sequestering his pain, hiding behind that incredibly useful shield of biting British humor. But sometimes he caught a glimpse of his own eyes in a mirror and saw such anguish it shocked him. No matter how much Michaela tried to coax it out of him, he could never bring himself to divulge what was tormenting him. David had loved her. He really had. But he was hiding something he couldn't bear to tell her. Something he couldn't tell anyone.

Until this afternoon.

And now David Brightman was absolved. Ironically, the burden upon him now was almost as great as the one he had just released: what to do next.

David lifted his hands from the computer keyboard and leaned back in his chair. The wind was picking up again. He listened to it buffet the house.

He was still trying to sort out how Michaela's cousin had managed it—David hadn't been to confession in well over thirty years. He had omitted nothing. He had dutifully come home and performed his penance, which had required locating and dusting off an ancient prayer book from his parochial youth. He had thought long and hard about his purpose of amendment—the interior resolution to do everything possible to stay on the right track, to maintain this newfound spiritual equilibrium in which the account balanced in his favor.

He turned his attention back to the computer screen and was just making up his mind about what to type when he heard an insistent knock at the back door. "Crikey," he muttered. Someone stuck in a snowdrift, perhaps? He left his study, crossed through the kitchen, and opened the back door.

It was Michaela. The wind swirled around her in the threshold. He opened the door wide and ushered her in, quickly closing the door behind her. "Michaela, what on earth? Why aren't you at the hospital?"

"I need to talk to you, David. I'm sorry it's so late."

"Good Lord, no," he said. "Don't worry about that."

She unbuttoned her coat, handing it to him, like she always used to. He hung it up in the hall closet.

"I need that disk I gave you," she said. "I need some information."

He studied her face. She was haggard and pale, sickened by grief and exhaustion. "Michaela, I thought you were going to let that go."

She closed her eyes. "David, can I please have the disk?"

He sighed at her stubbornness. "It's in the study." He led her across the hall and opened the top drawer of his desk. He removed the portable drive from the drawer and plugged its cable into the port on his computer. After a moment an icon of the device appeared on his computer desktop. He double-clicked on the icon. The resulting window was empty. A legend at the bottom of the window read *Zero items*.

Michaela gaped at the screen. "*Zero* items? It's blank?"

David chewed at his bottom lip.

She put her hand on the mouse and clicked hopelessly in the empty window, then pounded her hand on the desk.

"Dammit!" She straightened up violently and stalked away from the desk, her back to David.

"Was that your only copy?" he said.

She whirled around. "Yes, David, once my house and office were ransacked, that was my only copy!"

David winced, but kept silent.

Michaela sighed. "I'm sorry, David. It wasn't your fault. I must have done it wrong. I thought I was transferring files to the drive but—" Her voice dropped to a whisper. "I'm hopeless at computers. Terry always takes care of that sort of thing."

She took two unsteady steps to the couch and sat down. Quickly, he poured some scotch into a tumbler, pressed it into her hand, and watched with alarm as she drained the glass. She gasped and leaned forward, pressing the empty tumbler against her forehead.

David could see her fighting for control. It had always embarrassed her to cry. He sat down next to her and put his arms around her. Always the fighter, she stiffened and resisted. "Michaela…" he whispered, gently taking the tumbler and setting it on the coffee table. "It's okay." She inhaled sharply and covered her face with both hands. Her shoulders shook. Finally, she let go. She turned toward him and clutched his sweater, sobbing into his arms. He held her tightly, shushing and murmuring, his heart breaking for her.

David's secret had driven him and Michaela apart, like ice floes on an arctic sea. After almost two years, he had broken it off with her. It was one of the toughest decisions he had ever made.

But fortunately, not long after that, there was Terry. It had been a beautiful thing to watch, those two falling in love with each other. Terry changed everything for her. Even her relationship with David changed for the better, and they were able to be good friends. In time, an unspoken pact arose between David and Terry that, together, they would protect her. What she needed protection from was never quite defined, because Michaela was strong and independent. She knew how to make things happen in her life. How else could she have built a thriving veterinary practice on her own? The only thing a self-sufficient person like Michaela needed protection from was herself. Her tendency to brood and take her work so seriously that she forgot to enjoy life.

David had always been able to make her laugh. That was easy. But Terry was the one who could get Michaela to "lighten up," as the Americans put it. To live in the moment instead of constantly looking ahead to the future. Or dwelling on the past.

But Terry was powerless to help her now. It was up to David.

And he didn't have a bloody clue what to do.

When Michaela's sobs subsided, she looked up at him and he recognized the grief and guilt of a spouse drowning in self-recrimination. He could almost hear her painful inner monologue. *Why did I leave him there alone? Why didn't I transfer the dog to the ICU at the vet school right away? Why did I agree to get involved in a corporate whistle-blowing scheme? What was I thinking? Didn't I realize how dangerous that could be?*

"Let's think this through," David said, trying to sound business-like. "Are you *sure* you don't have copies of those files somewhere?"

Michaela shook her head, and began ticking off items on her fingers. "The dog's original medical record at the animal hospital—clinical findings, X-rays, photographs, ECG, and the video. Gone. The scans and copies Terry put onto the computer. Gone. The only complete record was supposed to be on that damn disk!" Her anger was rising again. "How could I be so stupid? I can't even copy files to a drive, for crying out loud."

"The only *complete* record? Is there a partial record somewhere?" David asked.

Michaela stopped and considered for a moment, but finally she shook her head. "I don't know."

He looked closely at her. She looked ill. She closed her eyes and dropped her face into her hands.

This has to stop, David thought. Now.

He reached out his hand to smooth the hair on the back of her head. "Are you all right?"

"I'm fine."

David was about to say what a load of rubbish *that* was, when Michaela lifted her head, her eyes wide, mouth slightly open.

"A partial record," she whispered.

"What?"

She stood up, quickly. "David, I have to go. I'm going to find that dog and put an end to this."

He tried to grab her arm and make her stay seated, but she escaped his grasp. She left the study and went to the hall closet.

"I don't think you should be going anywhere in this weather," he said, following her into the hall.

She took her coat from its hanger and crossed through to the kitchen. "I need to borrow your key to the Basic Sciences Building."

"What for?"

"I need access to the incinerator."

David followed her. He found his key card and gave it to her. "Michaela, just stay here, will you? Or let me come with you to the hospital."

She shrugged her coat on and opened the back door. "I really have to go, David."

"Michaela, this is madness!"

But she had already left.

For a moment he stood, frozen, staring stupidly at the door. Then he returned to his study. He poured himself two fingers of scotch and downed it in one gulp, coughing and grimacing as it burned his throat. Then he returned to the hall for his coat and keys.

25

How Death Came Into the World

EARLIER THAT DAY, when his body lay cold in the snow and his soul drifted untethered, Julius had dreamt of when he was a child, arriving in Gulu town with the Abuja family, Nicholas, Imena, and their two sons. Walking with the sisters to St. Peter Claver's and meeting Jacob Otoye. Going to school. Playing on the playground with the other children.

One day, while they were eating lunch, Sister Mary Emmanuel told a story—a traditional African folktale about the request Man sent to the Supreme God, whom the Acholi people call Jok.

"At the beginning of the world, Jok created all the animals and all humankind," Sister began. "He made the earth to be beautiful and fertile, full of growing, living things good for humankind to eat. He wanted them to be busy and industrious, but most of all, he wanted humankind to be happy. He especially did not want the people to die. 'I do not desire the sadness of death to afflict my people,' Jok said to himself. 'I want the people to live. But,' said he, 'I will wait for the people to think about it for a time, and allow them to decide what they want.' And so Jok waited.

"After a long time, the first people began to die. And they were very sad to lose their loved ones, and they began to talk amongst themselves. 'Death is very unpleasant. Could we not ask Jok to take it away? Could we not ask Jok to allow these dead to come back to life and to never again permit any one of us to die?' They all thought this was a very good idea. So they made plans to deliver this request to Jok.

"The people asked themselves, 'Whom shall we ask to deliver this request to Jok?' "

A boy next to Julius piped up. "Dog took the message."

A little girl nearby said, "Lizard took the message."

"No," said Sister. "It was Hare they chose to take the message, because Hare is fast, and they wanted to have their loved ones back with them as soon as may be. So they told Hare: 'We are displeased with Death. Please ask Jok to take it away from us forever, so that none of us will ever die. And also ask him if those who have died may come back to life.' And so Hare bounded off with the message for Jok. But, although Hare is fast, he is forgetful, so in order to help himself remember the message, Hare repeated it to himself over and over again."

Julius recalled Sister Mary Emmanuel with fondness. She was skilled at the craft of storytelling—she made Julius and the other children laugh as she imitated Hare breathlessly repeating the message: " 'Take Death away from us, that none of us may ever die, and let those who have died come back to life. *Pant pant pant pant.*' "

Julius pulled his jacket tighter around him and snugged his knitted cap down over his ears. It was bitterly cold outside, and Michaela was taking longer than he expected.

"As Hare was running through the bush on his way to deliver the message to Jok, he brushed against a branch on which Tick was waiting. When Hare passed by, Tick jumped off and burrowed himself into Hare's neck. Tick listened to Hare repeating the message over and over again, and he wondered what Hare was up to. 'Hare,' Tick said, shouting up into Hare's ear. 'What is it that you keep repeating over and over again?'

"Hare answered, 'It is a message to Jok from all humankind. They are displeased with Death and they are asking Jok to take it away from them so that none of them will ever die and those who have died will come back to life.' "

Sister gazed around the circle of upturned faces. "Now Tick was a spiteful creature, as you know. He thought to himself, I do not want humankind to live forever! What would become of me if that should happen? Whenever a human being sees me, he tries to crush me. So Tick said to Hare, 'Surely, that is not the message. Are not human beings troublesome to one another? Do they not vex one another? Why should they want to prolong such vexations as they endure from one another? Should they not long for death, and be relieved when their annoying friends and relatives pass away? Humankind cannot possibly want to live forever or to have their loved ones back. You must have garbled the message.'

"Hare was a sweet-natured and trusting creature, so he listened to Tick. He had certainly seen the way humans quarreled. But he had also seen the good in humankind. Did they not love one another, man and woman, mother and child, brother and sister? Did they not help one another, friend and neighbor? Did they not weep when their loved ones died? Surely Jok does not desire the people to be sad? He said as much to Tick, but Tick was determined to ruin humankind's happiness. He confused poor Hare, so that he could not remember what the true message was and became afraid that he would come before Jok and be unable to speak. Then Hare had an idea. 'Friend Tick,' he said, 'you seem so much more sure of yourself than I. Perhaps, if I take you, will you speak the message to Jok?'

"This is exactly what Tick had been hoping for. He agreed to deliver the message of humankind to Jok. Hare was delighted. He bounded the rest of the way to Jok's dwelling, and said to Jok, 'My Lord! The people have finally decided about death!'

" 'Oh ho,' said Jok. 'I have been eagerly awaiting their choice.'

"Wicked Tick spoke up. 'My Lord Jok, the message of humankind is this: we are pleased with Death because it puts an end to this troublesome thing called Life with which you have burdened us. Please let us keep Death always. And as for our family and friends who have died, we beg you to keep them as they are. We do not wish for their return, for they were always getting on our nerves anyway.'

"Now Jok was very surprised at this. He thought the life he had given the people was very good, and he had seen how they wept when the first people experienced death. But he was willing to let them make their choice. Jok said to Tick, 'Do the people understand that the choice they make today is irrevocable? They will not be able to come back to me later and change their minds.'

" 'Oh, yes, My Lord Jok,' said Tick. 'They know that what they choose will be the permanent state of things.'

" 'Very well,' proclaimed Jok. 'It shall be as they wish. They will die, whether from disease, or old age, or war, or accident. No one shall escape Death. And when a person has died, they will never be permitted to return to the land of the living.' "

Sister Mary Emmanuel raised her voice dramatically. "And with a mighty clap of thunder from the hand of Jok, it was done!" She struck her hands together, and the children jumped, even Julius, who had heard this story many times before.

Sister continued. "Hare thanked Tick for helping him deliver the message. Tick said, 'Believe me, friend Hare, the pleasure was mine alone.' And with a malicious grin on his face, Tick jumped from Hare's neck onto a branch.

"Hare hopped back to the people and said, 'Behold, I have delivered your message to Our Lord Jok and he has agreed to do as you requested. From this day forward, all people will be subject to Death. They shall take their leave of this harsh world at the time appointed and will never be forced to return. Are you not delighted, O people?'

"The people were angry and said, 'What have you done, you foolish Hare! It was not our wish to die! You got the message backward! Now we will never see our loved ones again and the grave will have the last word.' The people wailed and cried out in anguish at their sad fate, and they chased the Hare from their presence, pelting him with sticks and rocks. That is why, to this day, Hare runs when he sees a person coming.

"Poor Hare realized then what an evil trickster the Tick was. He ran back to Jok and explained what had happened, but Jok could not be persuaded: he had spoken. If he were to relent, that would damage his reputation as the Supreme God. Jok gave Hare a gift, though, to prevent such a thing from happening again. He gave Hare very long ears, which he felt would assist Hare in being able to hear the difference between the truth and a lie.

"As for Tick, Jok summoned the nasty creature and said, 'You have spoiled the most perfect part of my creation. You will be punished. From now on, all will despise you, animals and men, yet you will be completely dependent upon them for your life; you will have to drink their blood for your nourishment. In this way, you will be unable to speak, for you will always have your mouth full. When any human being sees you, he will tear you out of his flesh, leaving your mouth behind, so again you will be unable to speak. You have done enough damage for all time. You will never do any more.' "

Julius started the engine of his Range Rover and turned up the heat. Jacob Otoye and the sisters at St. Peter Claver's had saved his life. They had given him a second chance.

On his last trip to Gulu, he had stopped by to see them. He stopped at the market on the way there. Men and women lined the street behind their displayed goods, some items on rough wooden tables beneath canopies, others simply spread out on blankets beneath umbrellas. He bought bananas, toma-

toes, and some dried fish for the sisters, and a bag of pepper-
mint candies for the children at St. Peter's.

Returning to his rented open-topped SUV, he took the
Gulu-Arua Road and drove until he came to the walled structure he knew so well, the one that always needed painting, the
wide metal gate that was always scored with rust. He stopped
the SUV, got out, and banged on the gate near the little window with its sliding cover.

After a moment, the cover screeched open and a familiar
face appeared, like a portrait in a frame. The face grinned.
"Julius!" It was Sister Mary Emmanuel. "Just a moment." The
cover clanged shut, then a commotion ensued on the other
side as the gate was unlocked and manhandled open by several
boys.

Julius got back into his vehicle and drove through. Boys
and girls swarmed around him, shouting, jumping up and
down, ignoring the fruitless shooings and cluckings of Sister
Mary Emmanuel, another sister, and a couple of men whom
Julius did not recognize.

Sister Mary Emmanuel worked her way through the
crowd and hugged him. "Welcome, Julius, come in! Children,
this is Mr. Abayomi. He was a student here many years ago."
She introduced Julius to the other sister and the men, who
were all teachers and counselors at the center. They went back
to their classrooms, and Sister led Julius toward the veranda of
the school building. She commissioned some older boys to
fetch refreshments.

"Where is Jacob?" Julius asked.

As if in answer, Jacob Otoye's broad voice boomed from
the doorway of the school office. "Julius Okene Abayomi!
Welcome back!" He hugged Julius warmly and sat him down.

"It's wonderful to see you again, Julius," began Sister
Mary Emmanuel. "We were happy to hear of your graduation
from university."

"Thank you, Sister. I was grateful to receive your con-
gratulations. I am sorry I have not returned sooner. I accepted
a position immediately and it has required all of my attention."

"A position with whom?"

"The civil service."

"In Kampala?"

"Technically, yes, but I have spent little time there, as my responsibilities required extensive travel."

"And what of this visit?" Jacob asked. "Is it business or pleasure?"

"As of this moment, pleasure," he said, grinning broadly.

When Julius had first met Jacob Otoye, his mutilated hands had frightened him. As Julius suspected, Jacob had also come to the St. Peter Claver Rehabilitation Center from the bush, many years ago, as a child, an escapee from an LRA encampment, just like Julius. Unlike Julius, he was caught the first time, and punished. Undaunted, he had tried again, and the second time he was successful.

Julius calculated quickly in his mind and determined that Jacob was most likely too old to be a test subject.

After his education at St. Peter's, Jacob had stayed on as a volunteer, and after signing up repeatedly for extensions, he had given up pretending he wanted to do anything else and announced that he would stay on full-time. The sisters in the convent wrote to their benefactors overseas and arranged a stipend for him—a family in Burlington, Vermont started sending $250 per month, which was more than enough for Jacob to live on. He gave most of it back to the sisters, requesting only that they earmark the funds for helping pay the tuition of children who went through his rehabilitation program.

The LRA abductees who came to St. Peter's were scarred, many of them physically, like Jacob, all of them psychologically. Most of the girls—some as young as thirteen—had given birth, and most of the boys had blood on their hands. Jacob's program of rehabilitation was simple: nutritious food, wholesome exercise, proper sleep, basic education. In short, a normal life. He obtained a degree in psychology, which enabled him to devise effective therapies for the children, ranging from conversation to re-enactment and role-playing.

As Julius got older and began assisting in the rehabilitation programs, Jacob and the sisters often remarked to him how resilient these children were. Girls who had been forced into sexual slavery, and boys who had been forced to kill—somehow they found their innocence again, suppressed but not conquered.

Sitting in a rickety chair on the veranda with his old mentors, Julius watched the children playing in the rough dirt and on the dilapidated playground equipment. They were full of life and joy, and despite their laughter and squeals of delight, he was powerless to suppress the image that came to mind—his friend Jonathan and the other boys being herded like sheep to the clearing, doused with gasoline, shot, hacked to pieces with machetes, and, finally, immolated.

It seemed to Julius that there was a spirit of death in this world that pitted the powerful against the weak. The powerful, who granted to themselves the right to decide who should live and who should die, who is "wanted" and who is "unwanted." Jacob and the sisters didn't even realize that they stood between that spirit of death and the innocent ones who were its intended victims. According to African legend, death had come into the world by trickery. But human beings had been its willing agents ever since. Would there ever be enough people to stand in the breach and push the spirit of death back to where it came from?

He turned to Jacob and Sister Mary Emmanuel, a maimed middle-aged man and a diminutive older woman, who would never think of themselves as soldiers in a war, yet that is what they were. "May I express to you how grateful I am?" he said. "For everything you did for me. For everything you continue to do for all these children."

They looked at him quizzically, shrugged, and said he was welcome. Their embarrassed self-effacement made Julius smile broadly. "Perhaps, when I have completed my assignment, I can return and assist you in your work."

"I think it will be many years before we have a great need for advanced computer programming here," Jacob said, chuckling.

Julius laughed. "Until then, I will help with the dishes."

Sister Mary Emmanuel spoke up. "Jacob is right. You are always welcome here, of course, but with your gifts, I believe you could do much more for us out in the world."

Julius knew she was right. But he wanted to make a return for all the goodness he had received from these dear old friends.

He had promised himself that he would find a way to do it.

* * *

Julius looked up and saw Michaela hurrying toward him. He unlocked the door and she climbed in. He started up the Range Rover. "Have you the disk?"

"No. The chip number's not on it."

"This is an inauspicious beginning."

Michaela shook her head. "We need to get to the animal hospital."

"Why?"

She turned to him excitedly. "The microchip scanner. It always saves the *last number scanned*." Then she shook her head, uncertain. "I don't remember if I used it to scan any pets since Rosie, but it's the only thing I can think of." She buckled her seat belt. "The easiest way to get there from here is to take 74 to Mattis. Do you know the way?"

He nodded. In a few minutes they were at the intersection of University Avenue and Route 130. He turned right onto 130 and then took the ramp onto Interstate 74 Westbound.

The snow had stopped. Once they were on the Interstate, Michaela seemed to relax. Julius had noticed that Americans often took comfort in long, lonely stretches of highway. They seemed to enjoy sitting behind the wheel of a car, listening to music and driving for hours. In Africa, a long cross country trip by automobile was a harrowing experience, often punctuated by tire damage due to the poor state of the roads, or mechanical trouble from the dilapidated condition of most automobiles, but in this country it was a pastime as enjoyable as going to the mall, or attending a team sporting event in a large stadium with thousands of people.

Julius took the ramp off the interstate toward Mattis Avenue. "Dr. Collins, I am with you in your worry for your husband."

She took a deep breath. "Thank you," she said, her low voice nearly a whisper.

Julius turned his head slightly to look at her.

She returned his look. "You can call me Michaela," she said, and smiled. It was a gentle, sad smile, and even though she was tired and burdened with grief, her expression was warm.

They drove on Mattis Avenue for a short distance, then, following her directions, drove into a residential area.

Just then they heard the wail of a police siren, and seconds later the interior of the Range Rover was awash with flashing red and blue lights. Julius tensed and tightened his grip on the steering wheel, and he felt her hand on his arm as he slowed down.

Ahead of them, a second squad car turned the corner, lights flashing.

Walls of snow, created by the plows, had narrowed the street. In a moment the second squad car would hem them in.

"Julius…" she warned.

He wondered what happened to FBI fugitives when they were caught by a police department that was clean, let alone one that had corruption in its highest ranks.

Julius gunned it. The massive tires dug in to the street and the Range Rover shot forward, a plume of snow and ice fanning out behind them. The approaching squad car attempted to swerve into their path to block their way, but as it braked it went into a skid and ended up askew in the street. Julius quickly maneuvered around it, scraping the wall of snow and clipping the squad car's bumper. He caught a glimpse of the astonished cop at the wheel, and in the mirror saw the first car leap forward to give chase.

He careened left at the T-junction, then took the next left.

Michaela twisted in her seat to watch out the back window. "They saw us turn!" she cried.

In his mirror, he saw the emergency lights of only one vehicle following them. The second squad car was most likely on a route to cut them off from the other direction.

He made a hard right at the next street, then another right. He slapped his hand against a button on the dashboard, killing all the Range Rover's lights.

"Turn left here!" Michaela cried. "Don't use the brakes!"

Julius gripped the wheel and wrenched it left. The truck fishtailed wildly, but Julius threw the wheel to the right and corrected it.

"Right! Right there!" she yelled, pointing to an alley.

They slid into the alley and Michaela shouted, "Quick! All the way through." The snow was deep here, rutted and only partially plowed, but the Range Rover tore through it easily.

Julius looked behind him and saw the squad car attempt the same turn into the alley, but get bogged down in the deep, rutted snow. Julius jammed the accelerator down and thundered through the alley. There was no way out except the egress ahead of them.

Before they reached the end of the alley, a police car appeared and blocked their way. It moved into position, but slid on the ice, leaving a narrow space behind it. Julius aimed straight for the opening and pressed the accelerator down.

"Oh, Jesus." Michaela braced herself with both hands against the dashboard.

They smashed into the rear quarter panel of the squad car and spun it ninety degrees. The Range Rover skidded, then righted itself, bounced out onto the street and careened into a snow bank.

Julius yanked the wheel and hit the accelerator again, breaking free from the snow bank. Michaela ordered him through a series of quick turns until he was completely lost, but no new police cars appeared on their tail. Then she directed Julius onto a side street and into a small strip mall. He pulled in behind a building, out of sight. They clambered out of the Range Rover.

Julius grabbed his tablet computer from the center console and shoved it into the inside pocket of his coat. "How far to the animal hospital?" he asked.

"Not far. Hurry!"

Michaela led the way. They climbed a fence and waded through deep snow across several residential backyards, invisible from the street. Police cars crisscrossed back and forth, lights flashing. They came to a street with a bank, a convenience store, and a few restaurants. They hopped another fence, and suddenly they were in the back parking lot of the animal hospital.

Michaela waded through deep snow, slowed down and finally stopped in front of a Jeep, buried to its bumpers. Silence descended upon them like a shroud.

She dug into her pocket and pressed a button on the fob keychain. The Jeep chirped and the lights flashed. "Can you dig it out while I go inside and get the scanner?"

Abruptly, Michaela turned away from the Jeep and forced her way through snow to the back door of the hospital. She ripped through the yellow and black police tape, unlocked the door, and disappeared inside.

Julius brushed armfuls of snow off the Jeep. With every exhalation, fog obscured his vision. Beneath the trees and the open sky, when the fog cleared, he could see the stars above him.

His friend Jonathan fell under a burst of machine gun fire. Julius stood over him. "Help me, Julius," the boy whispered.

Then Sister Mary Emmanuel was calling him for class. "Julius!" she cried. But he ran. Sister caught up with him, grabbed him and spun him around. "And that, my child, is the story of how Death came into the world. We did not choose it. It was a trick of the Devil."

No. It wasn't Sister Mary Emmanuel. It was his mother. "Julius!" The heat of the African sun was intense. And it was so humid. The air itself seemed slick with sweat.

He felt strong hands grip his upper arms and shake him. "Julius!"

He blinked, then looked down into Michaela's wide, frightened eyes. She swallowed hard, composed her features, and let go.

The cold hit him powerfully and he realized what had happened. *So soon?* he thought.

She held a small plastic carry-all. "Come on," she said. She reached into the snow on the Jeep and pulled the door open. She started the ignition, retrieved a snow scraper from under the front seat and finished clearing off the windows. With a glance at Julius, she took the driver's side.

Then she rummaged through the untidy interior of her husband's Jeep, through the glove box, the sun visor and under the seat. In the center console, she found his smart phone. It was powered on. A red icon on the screen indicated that the battery was almost dead. She powered the phone down, then, after a moment's hesitation, slipped it into her coat.

She left the headlights off and drove carefully out of the parking lot, avoiding the use of her brakes. She took the first turn she could, entering a darkened residential area. She took her foot off the gas and let the Jeep creep along. Two police cars, lights whirling, sped by on the main road.

Watching in the side mirror, Julius saw them turn into the parking lot of the animal hospital. Michaela continued to coast, lights off and no brakes, until she judged they could not be seen from the main road. Then she switched on the headlights and drove the long way back to Mattis Avenue.

"Do they know what kind of car your husband drove?"

She nodded. "And it won't take long for them to figure out what happened."

After driving on Mattis Avenue for a few moments, Michaela surprised Julius by turning into the parking lot of a darkened store and driving behind it. She turned off the Jeep's lights, and in the darkness, turned to face him. Her expression was soft, full of sympathy and concern, her features slipping into it naturally and without affectation or disguise. Julius could imagine her, the animal doctor, having just analyzed the results of some tests, delivering unhappy news to a family about their beloved pet. As the bearer of the news, she would be just as heartbroken as the ones who received it.

"It might be different for you, Julius," she said. "I only know what I've seen with Rosie."

"What have you seen with Rosie?" he pressed.

Michaela met his eyes again, but when she spoke she retreated into clinical detachment and scientific precision. "Apparent partial seizures. Intermittent lapses into catatonia. Tissue breakdown suggestive of post-mortem cellular autolysis." She looked away.

"Is that what will happen to me?" he said.

"I don't know, Julius. I don't know what's going to happen. But I'll stay with you, I promise."

All those years ago, Julius had seen what Jonathan and the other boys looked like, and how heavily-armed grown men had been afraid of them. Would he become violent? Dangerous? "How long do I have?"

She reached toward him and grasped his hand. "I'm not sure, but I'll be right beside you." In her eyes, he saw a protective intensity that reminded him of his mother, and his throat tightened.

He squeezed her hand in reply. "Then we should hurry," he said. He let go of her hand and reached into his inside coat pocket, bringing out his handheld mini-tablet computer. As it blinked to life, he handed her the carry-all and she removed the hand-held microchip scanner. He saw that she had also packed various emergency medical supplies.

Julius brought up the GPS software while Michaela flipped the switch on the scanner and cycled through its menu. Then she showed him the small LCD display. "This looks like Rosie's number. I recognize the letters at the beginning."

The scanner read SGG-068-19H5-7465-87Y.

Julius thumbed the sequence into the GPS prompt window and clicked the search button. Two seconds later, a set of GPS coordinates appeared. He highlighted and copied the coordinates, then quickly brought up a reverse geocoder and plugged in the numbers. This time it took a bit longer, but soon an address appeared, along with a map.

Michaela leaned in. "She's in Urbana."

Julius zoomed the map in, getting closer and closer to street level.

"Can you pull up a photograph?"

Julius switched the viewer to satellite mode. He recognized the University of Illinois campus, with all the buildings labeled. The red pinpoint icon hovered over West Gregory Drive between the Morrow Experimental Plots, the Animal Sciences Laboratory and the Institute for Genomic Biology.

This was puzzling. "Rosie's in the middle of the street?" he asked.

"I don't think so." She smiled and turned the key. The Jeep rumbled. "Let's go."

* * *

Garrett Sanger did as he was told. He found a place to lie low, in the girl's apartment above the gun range. Her place was like a mama bear's den. As long as he cleaned up after himself and pitched in for groceries, he could eat, drink, and enjoy the fringe benefits.

At the moment, she was in her kitchenette cooking and he was in the shower. The water was hot, the pressure perfect. He turned slowly in the spray, rotating from scalp massage to face massage, opening his mouth and letting the water in. He turned and leaned forward so the spray would hit the back of his neck and his trapezius muscles. He moved forward, pulling his shoulder blades back.

Sanger turned off the water and grabbed a towel. He wiped the steam from the mirror and examined himself. From his corded shoulders to his well-defined waist and abdomen, his torso was a perfectly proportioned V. His musculature was lean, not bulky like those body-building freaks at the gym. He had excellent definition between his deltoids, biceps, and triceps, and his rectus abdominus muscles formed a symmetrical six-pack. Tattooed on his lower abdomen, just inside his hip bone, was a small skull. It was black, with empty eye sockets.

Keep your mouth shut for once, Galton had said.

I can keep my mouth shut better than you'll ever know, Sanger thought bitterly.

His cell phone buzzed from the pocket of his jeans on the floor of the bathroom. He dug it out and answered it.

It was the Director.

Time to come out of hibernation.

26

Darwin's Playground

BEHIND THE WHEEL OF TERRY'S JEEP, Michaela made her way to Kirby Avenue and headed toward the southeastern edge of the University of Illinois campus. Terry's scent was in the upholstery and in the air—the smell of earth, cotton, mint. She breathed in the fragrance of evergreens, heard the gentle crunch of fresh pine needles beneath their feet as they hiked through a forest in early spring. She closed her eyes for a moment only, just to feel his breath on her face...She started and opened her eyes as the Jeep jerked back into the right lane. Julius's hand was on the wheel.

She shifted and straightened in her seat, trying to stimulate her body with movement and avoid lulling herself into a trance.

Kirby Avenue became Florida Avenue. She turned left onto Lincoln and drove north, skirting the eastern boundary of the University campus. In a moment they had reached their destination on West Gregory. Julius consulted the screen of his computer. The icon showing Rosie's location hovered over the Animal Sciences Building, to their left. To their right was the Institute for Genomic Biology. The street was deserted.

Michaela shifted the Jeep into park and drummed her fingers on the steering wheel. "Why here?" she said.

Julius looked at her.

She raised her hands, indicating the general area the chip had led them to. "This makes no sense. Why didn't they just take Rosie back to Synthetic Genetics?" And as she asked the question, the answer became obvious. "Damn," she muttered.

"Do not be dismayed," said Julius.

"Why not?"

"They knew you would have compassion for her, and that you would come looking for her. Do not be dismayed that your character was so easy to discern."

"How could they be so sure I would actually find her?"

"Because you are with me, naturally!"

Michaela smiled and shook her head. Was she this confident and cocky at his age?

"Do you wish to continue?" he said.

"Knowing that we may be walking into a trap? Are you giving me the chance to bail out?" she asked.

"The chip is programmed to send an alert if it is moved."

"An alert to whom?"

"Galton."

"So he won't be onto us until we find Rosie and take her somewhere?"

"Correct."

"The vet school's not too far," said Michaela. "Depending on where Galton is right now, we might be able to get Rosie inside to the incinerator before he catches up to us."

"These buildings will all be locked at this time of night."

"Yes, but look." Michaela pointed to the large building to their right, the Institute for Genomic Biology. Lights were on, and people were moving around inside. "A true scientist is not deterred by a little snow." She pointed again. "Or even a lot of snow." Two people on the street clambered over the curbside heaps left by the snowplows, then hurried toward the large plaza in front of the IGB building.

"How does that help us?" Julius said. "Rosie is not in that building. She is in this one." He pointed to the red icon on the screen of the tablet, then out the window at the Animal Sciences Building.

"Aha," Michaela said slyly. She grabbed the plastic carrying case. She used it for house calls, so it was loaded with miscellaneous basic medical equipment—needles, syringes, rubbing alcohol, cotton balls, microchip syringes, blood tubes, sterile culture swabs, even a small laceration repair kit. She could bring it to a house call and deal with anything from administering vaccines to stitching up small lacerations. She had also packed a large bottle of sodium pentobarbital.

The sidewalk was icy—Michaela slipped and nearly fell, but Julius caught her elbow. They both proceeded more cautiously, stepping gingerly past the IGB building along its southern exterior wall, then turning right into the wide, paved plaza leading to the main entrance. On the plaza was a large public sculpture. It was a triptych of large, abstract forms, all identical in shape but different in scale and color, one red, one yellow, and one green. Each piece looked to Michaela like a larger-than-life lump of Play-Doh, squeezed and shaped by a giant hand and plunked down in the snow. She and Terry had come to the IGB's grand opening. They had taken a tour of the building and seen the sculptures unveiled. That day had been sunny and pleasant, but now the sculptures were nestled in a deep carpet of virgin snow, each coated with ice, all glistening in the moonlight. The smallest piece, the yellow one, was half submerged.

The sculpture was entitled "Darwin's Playground." Michaela had thought about this many times. What did that mean, anyway? During the media hubbub surrounding the sculpture's installation, students and scientists at the IGB theorized that the elements were supposed to be proteins, or perhaps, ribosomes, the little factories within living cells that manufactured proteins. Perhaps it was meant to be merely whimsical. Perhaps it was meant to express something more. What was the whole field of genetics and genomics, if not a playground for molecular biologists? That particular area of scientific endeavor had evolved beyond simply studying and cataloging the genes of living tissues to actually manipulating and changing them. To people like Jan Mueller and her colleagues at the vet school, it was all play, a great adventure of discovery.

But to men like Garrett Sanger and Frank Galton, it was deadly serious.

One thing that bothered Michaela about this was the implication that Synthetic Genetics Group had its tentacles entwined in the University of Illinois. This section of the campus—the Animal Sciences Laboratory, Turner Hall, Bevier Hall—was the domain of the College of Agriculture, and many other life sciences departments throughout the University had facilities in the multi-disciplinary IGB building. The sources of funding for all the projects were numerous and various; huge grants came from pharmaceutical and biotechnology companies, the State of Illinois, and Uncle Sam. She hoped the dirty money Julius had tracked down hadn't made its way here. Maybe Sanger still had some connection and access to one of these buildings and that's why Rosie was here.

They waded through deep snow past the three-part sculpture, then split up so they could each cover one of the entrances to the IGB building. They didn't have long to wait. After only a couple minutes, someone came out the door on the far side of the plaza and Michaela hurried to grab it before it swung closed and locked.

Julius joined her and they went inside, entering the gleaming lobby of the IGB. Ahead of them towered a two-story pillar decorated with scientific images—beautiful grayscale electron micrographs, colorful immunofluorescence studies, maps of metabolic pathways. The images spiraled up and around the pillar, forming a model of the DNA double helix.

Julius removed his tablet from his pocket and pressed, swiped, and thumbed the keyboard for a moment. Then he showed Michaela the screen. There was a schematic of the IGB building, where they were. Inside the Animal Sciences building across the street there was a blinking red dot.

She pointed toward a doorway to their left. "This way."

They followed the blinking pixel through the door and down a flight of stairs to the lower level. They crossed a large space that housed a café. Two men sat at a table, talking excitedly to one another in biotechnical jargon that Michaela could not follow. The doors to several laboratories were wide open. People moved freely about the building, and they either ignored Julius and Michaela or smiled and said hello politely.

She led the way along a hallway until they came to another door with signage pointing to the Animal Science Building. "The buildings here are connected by underground tunnels," she explained. They entered a dimly-lit underground passageway of bare concrete. "We're under West Gregory right now." Their steps echoed as they followed Julius's schematic around corners and through doors. Finally, they came to a glass-fronted door with a darkened laboratory space beyond it.

As soon as Julius swung the door open, Michaela knew they were in the right place: she could smell it.

They saw Rosie immediately—she was the only animal present in a long row of dog runs. Rosie saw them, too, and Michaela's heart lifted as the dog recognized her, pricked her ears, and wagged her entire back end. Michaela crossed the room and opened the wire door of the run. She knelt down in front of it and Rosie came to her. "There's a good girl, Rosie," Michaela said, petting the dog and ruffling the straight, golden fur on her head and neck. "What happened to you, huh?"

Rosie turned her attention to Julius. She smelled his outstretched hand and recoiled, shrinking from the young man's attempt to pet her.

Michaela looked up at Julius. "Animals can sense it." They needed to hurry. She led Rosie out of the run into the middle of the room. "Can you hold her for me, Julius?"

Julius returned his tablet computer to his jacket pocket and grasped Rosie's collar. "Why can we not simply remove the microchip and leave it here? Then we will not be tracked when we leave the building with Rosie."

She shook her head. "I considered that, and it sounds simple enough to do. But that chip is about the same size as a grain of rice, and it's embedded in the fatty tissue under the skin in the scruff of her neck. Or it may have migrated down one shoulder blade or the other." When Michaela had heard the manufacturers' assurances that, once implanted, a microchip was impossible to remove, she had been skeptical. She had done an experiment and tried to find the microchip on a deceased patient, just to see if it could be done, but even with an X-ray to guide her she couldn't find it. "We'll just have to do this fast and hope we get to the incinerator before Galton does."

Julius crouched on the other side of the dog and held her in place. Rosie looked askance at him, then looked stoically in front of her.

Michaela prepared a 20-gauge IV catheter and a syringe of heparinized saline.

Instructing Julius how to hold the dog's front leg, she clipped the hair away, exposing the region of the cephalic vein. Then she slipped a tourniquet over Rosie's paw and tightened it above her elbow. She inserted the catheter, taped it in place and flushed the catheter with the saline. From the bottle of sodium pentobarbital, she drew up ten ccs.

She put the syringe on the floor and took Rosie's face in her hands and stroked her ears. "Are you ready, girl?"

Rosie stopped panting and closed her mouth.

Michaela was about to uncap the syringe of euthanasia solution when Julius stopped her.

The young man gazed at her intently. "Let me do it," he said.

They switched places, Michaela gently restraining Rosie from the side, Julius sitting cross-legged in front of her. The young man took a deep breath and laid his hand on Rosie's head. He and Rosie were at eye level with one another. He held the dog's gaze for a moment, and ran his hand down Rosie's neck.

But Rosie was already gone. Her body had become still and rigid and her eyes unfocused. Julius looked down, inserted the needle into the catheter's injection port, and depressed the plunger. When the syringe was empty, Rosie's body relaxed. Michaela laid her head on her paws.

Julius placed his hand on Rosie's recumbent form. "Man, for all his splendor, lacks wisdom," he murmured. "He is like the beasts that are destroyed."

The syringe slipped from his fingers and his hand slid listlessly to the floor. His jaw twitched open with a gulp. The color drained from his slackened lips and his eyes emptied themselves, like clay vessels overturned and unstoppered, and when he exhaled, the air flowing past his flaccid vocal chords rattled and groaned, the way Rosie's had done on that day that seemed an age ago. Then he was motionless.

Involuntary revulsion pulsed through Michaela, but she felt for a pulse in his neck. His skin was cold, his pulse absent.

Then Julius inhaled sharply. His rigid frame relaxed, and he looked around in alarm, blinking, confused. An instant later, his eyes filled with tears and he began to weep.

Michaela took him into her arms, like a child, cradling his head on her shoulder as he cried. In a few moments, he straightened and wiped the tears from his cheeks. He picked up the bottle of euthanasia solution and took a breath to speak.

"No," Michaela said, flatly, shaking her head.

"Why not?" he protested, his voice hoarse. "You do it every day with animals."

"That's not the answer."

"What is the answer?" he protested, his whisper almost inaudible.

And now we come to it, Michaela thought. The question that, as a veterinarian, she had always been able to avoid. Animals could be put to sleep when necessary to relieve their suffering, or even for less noble reasons like economics, when pet owners simply couldn't afford the diagnostics and treatment. But what about human beings?

Despite Garrett Sanger's efforts, medical science could only do so much. People didn't live forever, and in the end the human body was still a fragile thing. It aged. It succumbed to disease. It could be damaged beyond repair. Sometimes even the most heroic medical interventions proved fruitless.

For now, a ventilator was keeping Terry alive, but Michaela knew that his brain might be irreparably damaged. She believed in giving a living, breathing person every chance to recover, to heal, to respond to treatments. But Terry might never breathe on his own again. If his brain was so damaged that the most basic function of life was beyond its ability, then keeping him on the machine was nothing more than refusal to accept reality.

But there was a big difference between letting someone go and pushing them away.

She took the bottle of euthanasia solution from the young man's hand. "There's a line in the sand, Julius," she said, "and I won't cross it, even if I can."

"What if a human being is suffering? Is it not compassionate to relieve the suffering of that person?"

"Yes, but by sharing the person's pain and relieving the pain as much as you can. You don't relieve human suffering by eliminating the ones who suffer."

"But why can you not put a person out of his misery the way you do with animals?"

"Because you can put a person out of his misery without ending his life!"

Julius sighed and dropped his shoulders.

"Synthetic Genetics is trying to cheat death by artificially avoiding it. It's also possible to cheat death by artificially hastening it. Playing God goes both ways."

She put the bottle of sodium pentobarbital back into the carrying case. "We have to get out of here," she said, scooping up the other supplies and tossing them haphazardly into the case. Michaela looked behind her. "If we get caught and separated..." She didn't even want to finish the thought. If Synthetic Genetics captured Julius, what would they do to him? Stuff him in a cage and study him until the flesh fell from his bones?

She knew there was no point in meaningless reassurances. Everything wasn't going to be all right. After this, she would be preparing to accompany this young man on a ghastly journey toward death.

* * *

In the darkened cab of his vehicle, Frank Galton took a sip of coffee. On the screen of his tablet computer, a small dot pulsed gently, motionless. A moment later, the dot started to move.

"Come to papa," he whispered.

* * *

Michaela drove as quickly as she dared back to the veterinary school. As they made the right turn onto Lincoln Avenue and headed south, away from the University's main campus, Julius spun in his seat to look behind them. A glance in the rear view mirror confirmed that they weren't being followed.

Michaela took the road that looped around the teaching hospital and ended up behind the Basic Sciences Building. This huge edifice was the home of first- and second-year veterinary students, research professors and their labs, but, more importantly, the pathology department. The building's drop-off area was to their right.

A little fleet of four University pick-up trucks, each equipped with a front-mounted snowplow, sat in the middle of the parking lot, an empty expanse of ice and freshly-plowed snow. Otherwise, the place was deserted.

She slowed the Jeep to a crawl as they drew near to a loading dock with two pairs of heavy double doors above it. One was labeled ANIMALS FOR DISPOSAL ONLY, the other ANI-MALS FOR NECROPSY EXAMINATION. The double doors opened to refrigerated holding areas large enough to accommodate several large animals. The exterior doors were kept unlocked so that anyone from the community—veterinarians, farmers, even pet owners—could drop off deceased animals for cremation or post-mortem. Every morning, fourth-year vet students and pathologists, charged with the grim but fascinating task of determining cause of death, would unlock the interior doors and see what cases had arrived during the night.

There was a standard, street-level entrance door nearby. The broad concrete apron in front of it was flanked on each side by towering piles of snow pushed up against a metal utility enclosure on one side and a heavy-duty fence on the other.

Michaela parked the Jeep in front of the utility enclosure. The vehicle slid a few feet on the ice and the front-mounted plow crunched into the pile of snow in front of them.

Julius was subdued. He sat with his head bowed, hands resting in his lap.

"I know you're afraid, Julius," she whispered. "But I'm here. I'm not going anywhere."

"What if I try to hurt you?"

"You won't," she said instinctively. Then she thought of Rosie, who had remained placid and trusting throughout her ordeal, and she knew it was true. "You won't," she said again. "You are who you are, Julius, no matter what. Until the end."

"What about you? What about your husband?"

It was agony to admit it, but Michaela knew she would not be able to turn herself in or go to the hospital yet. Julius was dying. One of the side effects of this project was that post-mortem changes began before the test subject was really dead. Decay would eventually reach a point where bodily structures completely lost their integrity. Multiple organ failure would occur. Julius wouldn't be able to move. His body would just rot. Michaela had no idea at what point true, clinical death could be declared, but this process would be gruesome and horrifying.

Michaela had to see this through to its grim conclusion. Underneath the expert hacker and the experienced government operative, Julius was still just an innocent boy who did not deserve to die this horrible death alone. "I will stay with you until the end," she said, "whatever that entails."

Julius lifted his head. He looked at Michaela with a sad, gentle smile.

Michaela reached out and took his hand. "We'll take Rosie inside to the incinerator, and then get you the hell away from these people." They would have to find somewhere quiet, somewhere far away. She gave his hand a final, emphatic squeeze. "Okay?" she said.

Julius brushed away a final tear. "Okay." He gave her a characteristic toothy grin.

They went to the back of the Jeep, where Michaela opened the tailgate and Julius picked up Rosie's body. She shut the tailgate, locked it, and led the way to the entrance, walking carefully on the ice between the tall piles of snow. When they reached the door, Julius put Rosie on the ground while Michaela fumbled in her pockets for David's key card.

Suddenly light blazed behind them and they whipped around. Michaela raised a hand to shield her eyes.

It was one of the University pick-up trucks, roaring straight at them. The blade of its raised plow jutted out like the jaw of an animal.

They were trapped between the huge piles of snow. The high beams of the headlights blinded Michaela, and as she attempted to dive clear, she felt her feet slip out from underneath her. Julius instinctively grabbed her arm, preventing her from upending completely. He braced himself and shoved her away from him.

Michaela fell into the snow bank a few feet away.

An instant later, the plow slammed into Julius, pinning him to the concrete exterior wall with a sickening thud. His legs went limp and his upper body slumped forward grotesquely, his cheek resting on the edge of the plow blade. The truck backed away, and in the glare of the headlights, Julius divided in two. His legs fell away from Michaela, his torso toward her, and she found herself simultaneously looking at the soles of his shoes and the top of his head. Both of his legs twitched, and the fingers of one outstretched arm scraped the ice on the pavement.

Michaela screamed.

Then the blood came, steaming in the cold night air, liquefying the ice beneath it as it seeped toward her, bringing the stench of death with it. Michaela gagged and vomited into the snow.

Rough hands grabbed her and hauled her off the snow bank. Her head spun and Galton's face lurched into view. He regarded her coolly, his eyes flickering up and down. He shoved her contemptuously to the ground, removed his weapon from its holster, and chambered a round.

Michaela's senses were completely overwhelmed—nausea, grief, pain, confusion, a raw wetness in her throat. Cold air stung her teeth as she inhaled sharply, awaiting her annihilation. Yet, as Galton took aim, she looked him square in the eyes, determined to go bravely to her grave with no regrets.

She heard a sharp pop and she flinched. A spray of blood gushed from the side of Galton's face and his body collapsed to the ground.

She turned, and there was Garrett Sanger, arm outstretched, gun in hand.

Michaela exhaled, shuddering.

Sanger approached and shot two rounds into Galton's chest. "How's that for center mass, asshole?" He kicked the corpse and holstered his weapon. Sidestepping Galton's sprawled form, he went over to Julius's body. It was still moving, both hands scrabbling in the gory slush, guttural sounds coming from his throat. "I'll be damned," said Sanger. He prodded Julius with the toe of his boot.

"Don't touch him!" Michaela shouted.

With a dismissive look, Sanger dragged Galton's body next to Julius's twitching torso. He stomped to the University pick-up truck, which was still running, and backed it up until it cleared the space between the snow banks and the building. Then he wrenched the spare gas can from the rear mount. He unscrewed the cap as he approached the bloody mire where Julius and Galton lay. He tossed the cap to the ground and upended the can, emptying its entire contents on them.

He grabbed Michaela by the arm and dragged her away. She staggered for a second, but she regained her footing.

Sanger flipped open a Zippo lighter and dialed the flame high. Stepping far back, he tossed the lighter. Michaela turned away as the flames roared and the heat struck her. The orange light penetrated her closed eyelids. She refused to look.

Above the hissing noise of the flames she heard Sanger's voice. "Too bad about your husband."

When she opened her eyes and looked at him, his face twisted into a depraved smile. "Maybe y'all can still use him for spare parts."

Something in Michaela's abdomen contracted, blood rushed to her face, and the darkness receded. Weakened as she was, she swung her fist as hard as she could and felt it crack against Sanger's jaw.

He staggered, but quickly regained his balance and came at her. He bared his teeth and dealt her a ferocious backhand that knocked her to the ground. Her cheek throbbed and she tasted blood in her mouth.

"Where's the dog?" he growled.

She nodded toward the door to the pathology section. "Over there."

"Get it," Sanger ordered.

She staggered to Rosie's body and, with difficulty, picked her up. Sanger kept his pistol trained on her, as if she were in any shape to escape or attack.

He waved the gun toward the Jeep. "The Director wants to talk to you."

27

Valley of the Shadow

SANGER DROVE TERRY'S JEEP along rural back roads. Despite the cold, he had lowered both front windows, but the smell emanating from Rosie, lying motionless in the back, was thick and choking.

Michaela hunched in the passenger seat.

Sanger spoke suddenly. "Aren't you dying to know how I did it? How I created such a complex genetic system?"

From what her friend Jan Mueller had told Terry, splicing genes into complex organisms and expecting them to work was ridiculous. Functional genes were riddled with sequences that were never activated, or coded for something unrelated to the gene in which they were embedded. She didn't understand how it was possible to do what Sanger had evidently succeeded in doing. But none of that mattered now. He wanted to boast, so Michaela let him talk.

"We did it without germ line manipulation of any kind. We wrote our own goddamn genome, a whole chromosomal system, and put it on a custom-built matrix of nano-fibers. It contains the shock-arresting array, the genetic crash cart, everything. Then we encapsulated it into its own little magic bullet and implanted it in the abdomen."

So that was what she had seen on the X-rays, the metal object in the abdomen that she mistook for another gunshot round.

Sanger laughed. "It's like a whole new organ system, a plug-and-play mini-me. Imagine the potential applications."

Michaela shook her head in disbelief. "Just answer me this. Please tell me our government is not involved."

"Of course it is. But you're thinking too small."

"What do you mean?"

"Use your imagination, Dr. Collins. Who *wouldn't* want a whole army of soldiers who can withstand prolonged hypoxia, are impervious to circulatory shock, and have a physiologic self-repair mechanism?"

Whoever they were, Michaela thought, they had to know they were funding renegade research that would never be sanctioned by any legitimate company, university, or institute. "Adriana believed the project was funded by dirty money," Michaela said.

"Not just dirty money. Filthy money. We have a non-profit that funds the various branches of the project. It gets funding from all over the world, from anybody who's willing to pay. Organized crime rings, drug cartels, multinational terrorists, extremist militias, rebel armies. And just a few government treasuries."

"Including ours?"

"Heavily laundered through layers of innocent-looking shell companies, of course."

Our tax dollars at work, Michaela thought. It made sense, though. Any of the groups Sanger just named would want a piece of this research, if it kept their foot soldiers alive for one more battle or one more assignment. The company accepted money from anybody and would make the results available to anybody. It was pay to play on a global scale. Equal opportunity evil.

"Know what people die of in a bomb blast?" Sanger asked.

Michaela closed her eyes, remembering the blast at the pub. "Concussive organ failure, mainly. Penetrating wounds and fractures caused by flying debris. Second and third degree burns." A single tear spilled from one eye and ran down her face. Embarrassed, she hastily wiped it away.

Sanger didn't even notice. "With the arterial bypass systems and the genetic crash cart? No problem. They'd bounce back like characters in a video game." He spread his hands in a gesture of concession. "Okay, granted, if the blast is strong enough to separate limb from limb, blow internal organs out of the abdominal cavity—"

Michaela stopped listening. Thoughts of the bombing triggered others about her family. Her father. Nina. Terry. She rummaged through her pockets for Terry's cell phone.

"The hell are you doing?"

"My mother has no idea where I am. I need to call her."

Sanger frowned for a moment, then his face relaxed and he shrugged. "Go ahead," he said, but he made a point of shifting his gun slightly, just to remind Michaela that it was there.

* * *

Alicia, half-asleep in the chair next to Terry's bed, watched a slideshow of family portraits and snapshots, old and new, on her tablet computer. Herself and Sean as students, wearing their Illini orange and blue. Michaela's first day of school. Michaela and Terry's wedding day.

An old photo from Belfast appeared on the screen, one of Brendan and Michaela as children. Before the bombing.

Brendan was in the hallway, pacing, making another frantic phone call.

Alicia's cell phone rang. She scrambled to dig it out of her bag. She felt her stomach twist when "Terry Adams" appeared on the caller ID screen. She answered it quickly, hoping Brendan hadn't heard her phone ring. "Michaela?"

"Hi, Mom. It's me." Her daughter's voice sounded forced, unnaturally casual.

"Michaela, where are you? What happened?"

Suddenly, Brendan entered. He pointed at the phone, shaking his head.

"I can't talk long, Mom," Michaela said. "I just wanted you to know that I'm all right."

"Why can't you talk? Are you in trouble?" Alicia caught Brendan's eye and motioned for him to stay back. "Tell me where you are and I'll come get you." With one hand she worked the touch screen on her tablet.

There was a long pause. Alicia sensed what that meant. She had had her share of awkward phone calls like this, unable to speak freely because someone else was nearby. Except this call was more than just awkward.

"Get her off the phone," Brendan hissed.

Alicia mouthed the word *no*. Brendan had warned her earlier that the police, or even the FBI, would be monitoring Michaela's phone, and presumably Terry's as well. But she knew that two could play at that game. As long as Terry's phone was powered on this would work. He had one of the new phones and Alicia could locate it with an app on her tablet. All she had to do was keep Michaela talking. "You can't tell me where you are because someone is with you who's threatening you?"

"No, Mom," her daughter said. "I just wanted to call and...check on Terry...how is he?"

Alicia froze. She heard mortal fear in her daughter's voice. "He's okay. Still on the ventilator, but he's stable. Sweetheart, what's wrong?" Alicia said, working quickly on her computer. "Come on, come on," she muttered.

When Michaela spoke again, her voice was shaking. "Don't leave him, okay? When he wakes up, tell him that I love him. And I love you, Mom. Good-bye."

The call went dead.

The app gave her the phone's location. An icon of a miniature smart phone screen hovered over what looked like a blank screen. She zoomed out and saw that the icon was on a rural road south of Champaign-Urbana, apparently in the middle of nowhere. She turned the computer around so Brendan could see it.

He studied the screen for a moment and nodded slightly.

There was a soft knock on the door behind him. A man stood in the doorway. He was about six four and built like an offensive lineman.

"Jack, thank God," Brendan said, hurrying forward to shake his hand.

"Sorry it took me so long to get here, Father."

"Alicia, Jack is one of the deacons at St. Andrew's."

Jack's huge hand engulfed hers. He wore his National Guard uniform. Alicia thought that was a nice touch.

Brendan filled Jack in on the important points: that the police were not to be trusted, and under no circumstances were they to leave Terry unattended.

The big man nodded. "I think I've seen this movie. What if some doctor or nurse comes in saying there's a patient transfer, or he has to go get X-rays or something?"

Brendan looked up at the towering figure. "That's why I called you—to be as uncooperative as possible and make sure that doesn't happen."

The deacon took off his coat and slung it over a chair, then took up his position next to Terry's bed. "Don't worry, Father. If they want to get to Terry, they'll have to go through me first."

Alicia stood up. "And me."

Brendan's mouth twitched, and it occurred to Alicia that she and the hulking deacon made an unlikely pair of bodyguards, standing there on either side of Terry's bed.

Alicia looked at the screen of her tablet computer and re-freshed the image so she could get Michaela's current location. The icon for Terry's phone had turned black. "Damn," she breathed.

Brendan held out his hand. "Let me see that."

She handed Brendan her tablet computer. "The phone's offline. It's too late, Brendan."

"We'll see," he said.

Alicia frowned, but before she could ask him what he meant by that, her nephew stooped to kiss her on the check. She gripped and squeezed his hand, then let him go.

* * *

Michaela's hands were slick with sweat. She could feel it dripping down her forearm as she held Terry's phone to her ear. She let the phone drop and pressed the button to end the call. There was nothing more to do. Nothing more to say.

They drove in silence. Michaela held the phone in her lap and looked at the image on the screen. It was a photo of her and Terry. She kept her eyes on his face. No matter what happened next, this was the vision she wanted to take with her. Terry smiling up at her. She was able to savor the vision only for a few precious seconds, before the phone's battery died and the screen went black.

She looked out into the darkness. Tall hedges, flocked with snow and ice, flashed past the window. She thought about Julius. From the first moment of his existence, a di-abolical cadre of vivisectionists had owned him. They were supposed to end his life, coldly observe and record his reani-mation, then gun him down and immolate his remains. But he had confounded them all. He had escaped. He had survived. He had spent months in the shadows discovering their secrets, then come out of the shadows to hide in plain sight and exe-cute a brash plan that would bring to nothing the men who had marked him for death. Then he had burst into Michaela's house and delivered her from a situation that was careening toward her violent death. He was proud of what he had accomplished.

His last seconds played in her mind—the snowplow bearing down on her, the blinding headlights dazzling her eyes, her pulse pounding in her throat. His hand gripped her arm and she felt herself falling. Time slowed. And then time stopped. In that moment of stopped time, just before the blade of the snowplow sliced through Julius's body, Michaela looked up and met the young man's eyes, and in them she saw not terror or regret, but exultation. He had saved her life again. He had won. Even in his last moment, Julius Abayomi remained an icon of the victory of life over death.

Sanger braked violently and turned left. A long, dark driveway opened at a parking lot. Tall lamp posts poured pools of light onto the glittering surface of freshly-fallen snow. Sanger pulled the Jeep into the parking space closest to the building and killed the engine. He got out and crunched in the snow around to Michaela's side. He opened her door and waved her out with the gun.

Michaela hesitated. The building Sanger had brought her to looked completely out of place. Normally, the rural outbuildings she saw every day were blocky, nondescript structures with muted aluminum siding and corrugated metal roofs. They were usually plunked in the middle of a field somewhere, surrounded by a weedy gravel lot, and accessed by a bumpy drive. The endless fields of cultivated farmland were flat, which made these types of buildings easily visible from the numerous rural routes that crisscrossed the county in a checkerboard grid. This building, on the other hand, was completely hidden from view. Its builders had chosen a parcel of land with a grove of mature trees, and sited the building in their midst. They had further screened the building from sight by planting a mixture of tall evergreen and deciduous shrubs. Michaela was hemmed in.

The building looked like something from a suburban research and development corridor. It was a sweeping, two-story structure made of dark brick and black-tinted windows. On the bottom level, the ten-foot high windows were low to the ground. The façade was slick and shiny like a city skyscraper, except for a cantilevered metal overhang looming over the entry.

Out here in the country, Michaela had often noted with satisfaction that even the most austere rural utility building had a pair of planters lining the front door, or at least some shrubs to soften the harsh lines. But this building was bare. It seemed to rise up out of the ground like a marble and glass mausoleum. Not a single piece of vegetation disturbed the flat expanse of snow around it.

Michaela knew that if she went inside that building she would never come out.

She followed Sanger to the back of the Jeep. He swung the rear window up, then lowered the tailgate with a clang. Michaela grimaced as the smell hit her. Rosie had reanimated again. She was on her feet, tail down, head lowered. Her eyes were luminous in the yellow glow of the parking lot.

Sanger reached in toward her. Rosie emitted a low growl and her upper lip flicked upwards, exposing her fangs. Sanger backed away.

"Let me try," Michaela said. She picked up Rosie's leash from where it lay in front of her. When Michaela approached, Rosie's posture did not change, but she didn't growl. Michaela held out her hand. "Here, girl." Rosie stepped halfway out and allowed Michaela to clip the leash to her collar. Michaela rubbed her ears. "Good girl, Rosie."

Sanger backed farther away.

Rosie jumped down into the snow.

Michaela shut the tailgate and the rear window. She turned and watched Sanger crunch across the snow to the entryway of the building, where he swiped a card through a scanner and entered a code on a keypad. A green light flashed. He pulled the door open and held it.

She approached the door, Rosie following obediently. The letters SGG were painted in plain white letters on the glass next to the door.

Sanger motioned for Michaela to lead Rosie inside, then came in behind them.

Michaela jumped as the heavy door slammed shut behind them. She followed Sanger into a small reception area. Dim lights emitted an anemic glow from recesses in the ceiling. The interior walls were the same dark brick as the building's exterior. The maroon and black floor tiles added to the feeling of catacomb-like gloom.

They took a snaking route through the hallways. Here, the walls were white and the overhead lights were bright, but the black and maroon color scheme appeared in accent tiles on the floor and the doors.

Sanger walked quickly, swiping his card through various secure doorways and finally stopping in a large open area. "Welcome to the kill floor," he said, gesturing expansively.

It was a two-story space with a maroon metal walkway high above, encircling the room. There were doors off the walkway and windows giving glimpses into the offices overlooking the procedure floor. A metal staircase connected the walkway to the main floor. Skylights pierced the ceiling above.

At first glance, the procedure floor looked like a typical veterinary hospital's treatment room, with six open stations evenly spaced around the area. Each station had an over-the-sink grate table, a bank of shelves stocked with supplies, and a mobile cart with an anesthesia machine, ECG, and pulse-ox monitor. An oxygen hose snaked up from each anesthesia machine to the ceiling. Each cart also had two auxiliary oxygen tanks.

But a more careful perusal left Michaela with the sensation of being in a modern torture chamber. There was a locked cabinet labeled "FIREARMS. RESTRICTED ACCESS." Stretcher-like boards with leather straps leaned up against one wall. Two of the tables were fitted with restraints to hold a dog's head in place, with a system of pulleys and heavy weights above.

Two walls were lined with cages, all empty.

Michaela led Rosie to the bank of cages. The smell coming from her was almost unbearable, but Michaela knelt down in front of her. "Good-bye, girl," she said. Rosie perked up a little and wagged her tail. Michaela nearly gagged at the putrid smell, but she stroked the dog's face and allowed her to lick her fingers.

"Ain't that sweet," Sanger drawled.

"Promise me that you'll put her down and destroy her remains. It's not right to leave her like this."

"I can't make any promises. We may want to study her further."

"For what possible reason?" Michaela turned to look at Sanger. "Hasn't she been through enough?"

"Just insatiable curiosity." He winked, a perverse gesture. "You know how we scientists are."

Michaela shook her head. "No, I don't know how scientists are, if this is what passes for science these days." Michaela turned away from him and opened a floor level cage. "Go on, Rosie." Rosie went in, inspected the cage briefly, then lay down.

"I want to know what went wrong," Sanger said.

She stood up, still with her back to Sanger. "You went wrong," Michaela said with a scoffing laugh. She pushed the cage door shut, and then heard a noise she recognized: the slide lock of a handgun. She straightened and turned around. Sanger was aiming his gun at her. She was looking directly into the barrel. With difficulty she shifted her gaze to his eyes, and in them she saw a mixture of bravado and uncertainty. "Is this the part where you explain everything to me and then kill me?" she asked.

"No. This is the part where I blow your fucking head off!"

Sanger's shrill outcry echoed throughout the high-ceilinged chamber. Before it died, another voice broke in from above, deep and resonant, with quiet authority: "Garrett."

Michaela looked up and gasped. Standing on the metal walkway, his hand on the banister of the stairs, was David Brightman.

28

The Kill Floor

"GARRETT, FOR GOD'S SAKE," David said. "Put that gun down. What do you think you're doing?"

"I'm protecting your precious research, Dr. Brightman."

Michaela looked at David in disbelief. "*Your* research?"

Sanger snorted. "Meet the director of the project, honey."

David started down the stairway. "Yes, and as the director of the project, I don't need a rogue geneticist with delusions of grandeur thinking he needs to protect it." He reached the first landing. "Now, put the gun down, before it goes off and you hurt yourself," he concluded, finally reaching the main floor.

Michaela walked slowly up to David.

He returned her unwavering stare.

Without warning, she struck him full in the face. "You son of a bitch," she said evenly, fighting back tears.

She took another swing at him, but this time he was ready and caught her arm. "Now, Michaela—"

She wrenched her arm out of his grasp. "I trusted you. You have a friend in animal forensics? Like hell! You erased that disk and left me with nothing!"

"Michaela, listen—"

"And now Terry is fighting for his life. Because of your precious project." Angrily, she wiped her eyes with the back of her hand. "I hope it's worth it to you."

"Michaela, would you please just listen to me?"

She pointed at Sanger. "Call off your dog."

"Garrett, put the gun down," David said. "Why don't we go into my office and talk about this like civilized people?"

"Over a goddamn cup of tea, I suppose?" Sanger snarled.

"Well," David said with a weak smile, "you can hardly go wrong with a cup of tea."

* * *

David's office was basic and unadorned. His desk was in the corner near the windows, piled with papers, journals and files. A sofa, two armchairs, and a low coffee table took another corner. Floor to ceiling bookcases lined one wall, but most of the shelves were empty. Cardboard boxes, packed with books and office supplies, were strewn about the room, perched on the edge of the desk, or stacked, teetering, in a corner.

David had prepared tea at a sideboard against the opposite wall. Michaela sat stiffly on the couch, wrapping her hands around a steaming mug.

Sanger had refused tea, and stood with his arms crossed, leaning against David's desk.

It was a corner office with a view, but the blinds were closed against the dark outside.

David sat in an armchair. "You must have loads of questions, Michaela," he said.

"That's quite an understatement, David," she said. The mug was starting to burn her hands, so she set it down on the coffee table.

"Let me help you. I'll ask you some questions. Play professor for a bit." He sipped his tea. "Do you know exactly what makes an animal die? Not just in general, but precisely, on the cellular level?"

Michaela shrugged. "Lack of oxygen to the vital organs."

"Specifically?" David prompted.

Michaela shook her head. She didn't feel like playing this game.

"Why can you live for only four or five, eight minutes perhaps, without oxygen?" he said. "Because after four to eight minutes of oxygen deprivation, the lysosomes inside the cells can't hold themselves together anymore, and they burst."

"So?" Michaela said.

"Lysosomes are little packets of enzymes," he said.

Michaela sighed. "Yes, David, I know. Enzymes digest things. Break other substances into smaller pieces."

"Prolonged oxygen deprivation causes the lysosomal membrane to lose its integrity, and the lysosome bursts, at which point the enzymes inside the lysosome spill out into the cell."

Sanger came forward and sat down on the edge of the other armchair. "The cell digests itself from the inside out." He snapped his fingers. "Dead cell. Once enough cells die, you've got organ failure. If that happens all over the body, you've got multiple organ failure, and you're toast."

Michaela looked from David to Sanger. "I assume you're telling me this because the reanimations have something to do with lysosomes."

"You bet it does, honey," quipped Sanger. "I've been studying membrane stabilizers my whole life, and we're talking about the mother of them all. It's a large sequence of base pairs that codes for a very complex protein. This protein's job is to stick its finger in the dike and keep the lysosomes from bursting, even in the total, prolonged absence of oxygen. The cell doesn't die. It just sits there until…" Sanger shrugged.

David continued. "We call it Lysosomal Stabilization Factor. LSF. It stabilizes the lysosomes long enough to allow the crash cart and the airbag to work. The cells slow down considerably as a result of oxygen deprivation, but they live, because the lysosomes stay intact. Then, once the circulatory bypass systems and the shock-reversing array kick in, oxygen delivery to the cells resumes."

"And Rosie's Lysosomal Stabilization Factor worked better than you thought it would," Michaela concluded.

"Quite," said David. "We've been observing the same phenomenon in the African test subjects. The lysosomes *never* lose their integrity. The cells never undergo autolysis. They go into some kind of hibernation and are able to wait a long time for the body as a whole to stabilize. The exact mechanism of reanimation is still a mystery."

"Ever heard of people being revived after being immersed in near freezing waters for hours?" Sanger said. "I'll bet it's something like that. It's fantastic."

Michaela looked at David. He swallowed uncomfortably. Then she addressed Sanger again. "Is this another one of your brilliant inventions, Dr. Sanger? More tinkering with the genetic code? Part of the genetic crash cart and the intra-abdominal implant?"

Sanger shook his head.

David answered, "When Garrett boasts about the mother of all membrane stabilizers, he doesn't mean he invented it."

"What does he mean, then?" she asked.

"It's naturally occurring, Michaela."

"*What?*" Michaela said.

"Lysosomal Stabilization Factor is not part of the genetic crash cart. It's on the seventh chromosome, in both dogs and humans."

Michaela frowned.

"You see what this means, don't you?" said David. "The power to return from death is *in our DNA*. It's hard-wired into us. It's the resurrection gene, Michaela."

She gave a short gasp of amazement. "How did you discover it?"

Sanger shrugged. "By accident. Know what proteomics is?"

Michaela shook her head. "Not really."

"Proteomics is like reverse engineering the genome. If you can learn the amino acid sequence of a protein, you can deduce the mRNA sequence, and then from there find a string of complementary base pairs on the DNA."

Michaela could hardly believe this. The sheer number of proteins created by a living organism was literally astronomical, because they were the main components of every physiological pathway.

"How is this possible?" Michaela protested. "How can you study the amino acid sequence of a gene that's never expressed? I mean, with one glaring exception, no one has ever come back from the dead, and his DNA isn't exactly in the public domain."

Sanger shook his head. "You'd be surprised, Dr. Collins."

"By what?"

"The reason most people don't come back from the dead is that LSF's natural state is to be turned off."

"And?"

Sanger continued. "Discovering Lysosomal Stabilization Factor wasn't enough." He turned to David. "I hate to be contrary, professor, but the sequence that *activates* LSF—that's the real resurrection gene. That's the gene that really decides who lives and who dies. So we had to study people who had the active form of the gene."

Michaela said nothing, inviting Sanger to continue.

"We were talking about Lazarus Syndrome the other day," David reminded her.

"You've been doing proteomic and genomic research on people who claim to have returned from a state of clinical death?" she asked.

"Yep," Sanger concluded smugly.

"It's not working too well, is it?" Michaela scoffed. "Julius Abayomi turned into a walking corpse before my eyes, and Rosie looks like she's about to go into rigor mortis. Whatever it is you've discovered, it's not life after death. It's a nightmare. It's a reanimated body—"

"—with no one upstairs, I know," Sanger finished. "But that dog is Patient Zero. She's priceless. Not only does she have the surgical bypasses and the shock-arresting array, somehow her Lysosomal Stabilization Factor is permanently *switched on*. She can reanimate multiple times, instead of going all 'dawn of the dead' after only one, like the African subjects. We need to study her and figure out the mechanism for LSF's activation." He shrugged. "I admit, we've got a few glitches to iron out—"

Michaela laughed bitterly. "Iron out? At what cost? How many living beings have you tortured like this? Helpless animals and innocent children! What are you trying to prove?" She turned to David. "You taught medical ethics, for crying out loud. What on earth made you get mixed up in something like this?"

David's face was flint. He then turned to Sanger. "Garrett, would you give us a moment, please? There's a good chap."

Sanger hesitated for an instant, then got up and left. David followed him to the door and locked it behind him. "Do you understand the importance of what we've discovered here, Michaela? What the Lysosomal Stabilization Factor is? It's the resurrection gene."

"Yes, I got that David."

"Do you know how my wife died, Michaela?"

Of course she knew. But she let him go on.

"It was the stupidest thing you can imagine," he said. "She was going to take a bath, you see, in our luxurious whirlpool spa. Relax. Listen to music. But she slipped. When she fell, she hit her head on the edge of the bath and was knocked unconscious. She sank underneath the water. Before she could regain consciousness from a nasty but not fatal blow to her head, she drowned."

Michaela knew all this already. She could see how painful it was to him, still, to recount the details. "David," she began, trying to stop him.

But he plowed ahead. "How do you suppose I know what happened?"

"You came home and found her, David. You found your wife dead, and it was a horrible shock, but—"

"No, dammit! I didn't come home and find her! I was in the next room the whole *bloody* time! Thumb on the remote, flipping mindlessly through the channels, sulking because we had just had a row," he said. "Heard a bit of a noise but thought nothing of it. Forty-five minutes later, she was still in the bath, so I called to her. No answer. Here the brilliant professor finally cottoned on that something was amiss. I got up and knocked on the door. Still no answer. Now, finally, truly concerned, I opened the door. *That's* when I found her, God damn it!" he cried, his voice breaking. "Forty-five bloody minutes."

Michaela's eyes burned, but her anger and sense of betrayal restrained her from reaching out to him.

"How beautifully ironic," he continued, "that my groundbreaking work in cardiovascular surgery would draw the attention of a company doing equally cutting-edge work in tissue regeneration. Imagine my surprise when they approached me. Can you understand why this kind of research would appeal to me? Why the idea of finding the gene responsible for resurrection would fascinate me to no end?"

"This is your reason for getting up in the morning?"

David laughed. "It is a bit barbaric, isn't it?" he said. "Circulatory bypass systems. Genetic crash carts. Still, how ideal it would have been for my dear wife to have been equipped with the activated form of Lysosomal Stabilization Factor. It would have kept her alive for three quarters of an hour, just long enough for her idiot husband to get off his indignant ass and check on her—" He broke off and looked away, angrily wiping tears from his face. "What we're learning to do could have saved her."

Michaela stood. "What you're learning to do is the reason my husband is on life support at Carle Hospital," she said coldly.

"Another bitter irony."

Michaela pressed her fingers to her temples. Unbidden, a vision of Terry filled her mind, unconscious and bloodied on the floor of the animal hospital. A circulatory bypass system might have come in handy then. Maybe if Terry had had his own genetic crash cart, he could have stabilized himself while his own genetic cell phone dialed 911.

She stepped closer to David. His eyes, when they met hers, were stricken with that same desperate anguish that, years ago, had driven them apart. "David, it's too late for Joanna. She's gone," she said. "We can't bring her back."

He closed his eyes and tears spilled from them. He turned away from her for a moment. Then he whirled around and took her hand. "Come on." He led the way out onto the walkway above the kill floor. Their shoes clattered on the metal staircase as they descended to the main level. They crossed the space, toward the corridor that led to the main entrance.

"David, what are you doing?"

"I'm getting you out of here."

"And then what?"

They passed the bank of cages and Michaela stopped in front of Rosie. "Look at her, David," she said.

David sighed. "Michaela, come on." He took her arm and tried to lead her away.

Michaela stood her ground. She opened the cage door and led Rosie out. "Look at her! Look at what you've done."

Rosie's coat was dull. In her collar area the fur was missing, and the skin was chafed and pitted. When Rosie looked up at them, Michaela noted with alarm that her pupils were dilated. The corners of her mouth were dry and cracked and her tongue was ashen.

Without any prompting, Rosie went back into her cage and lay down. David closed and latched the cage door. He stood looking at the dog for a moment and then, with difficulty, he looked away and stared at the floor.

Michaela grasped his hands and shook them slightly. "David, this is evil."

He met her eyes. He had a slightly bemused expression, as if considering this possibility for the first time. It amazed Michaela that his academic brilliance, his keen intelligence, and his unparalleled skill as a surgeon had been unable to protect him from falling headlong into a moral crevasse that seemed obvious to her.

"Promise me you'll put a stop to this," she said.

He sighed deeply and looked down at the floor again. "How?" he muttered. "Now *I'm* the one who's in over my head."

"How would Joanna feel if she knew you had gotten involved in something like this, especially to assuage your guilt over the way she died? It's not rational, David. Joanna was a good and gentle person. This doesn't honor Joanna's memory. It's an insult to her memory."

He met Michaela's gaze, looked hard at her for a moment, then clenched his jaw muscles. He squeezed her hand.

"I knew it!" a voice boomed.

David and Michaela turned at the sudden sound.

It was Sanger. "I knew it," he said again.

"Knew what?" David asked.

"That you'd get cold feet. You're not really a man of science are you? Matter of fact, you're just a glorified plumber. You're no director. Know who the real architect of this project is? Me! This is my life's work, professor, and I'll be damned if I let you and your little girlfriend shut it down." Sanger produced his gun and aimed it at them.

Slowly, Michaela reached behind her and, as quietly as she could, lifted up the latch of Rosie's cage.

"Are you finished?" said David. "You know this project is a failure, don't you?"

"A failure? It's exactly the opposite. It's a resounding success. We bring the dead back to life!"

"It doesn't work!" Michaela cried. "You reanimate them—but look what happens!"

"What's the difference between what we've done and what doctors do every day—keeping people alive with machines? Nothing."

"Nothing?" Michaela couldn't believe what she was hearing. She thought of Terry, sustained by a machine that breathed for him until he could breathe on his own, but still very much alive. Even a person in a coma or a vegetative state didn't putrefy before your eyes. "Look at this dog. Can't you smell it?"

Sanger angrily swiped perspiration away from his eyes. "Life from death. Isn't that what medical science is trying to achieve, ultimately? Isn't that what all religion is about? Immortality? Raising the dead to life?"

"How can you possibly compare what you do to legitimate medicine or religion?" Michaela argued. "The resurrection of a dead body is a miracle of God, not a triumph of science. The fact that you can accomplish some kind of physical reanimation is meaningless if the end result has more in common with the bodies in the morgue than with the living."

Sanger waved his gun dismissively. "Technicalities, Dr. Collins. They can all be worked out."

Michaela edged away from David, enabling Rosie to see Sanger through the bars of her cage. Rosie got to her feet and growled. "You disgust me," Michaela said.

Sanger blinked. "Excuse me? Helluva thing to say to a man with a gun to your head. Oughta shoot you where you stand."

"Then what are you waiting for?" Michaela took another step to the side. She continued to maintain eye contact with Sanger as she edged sideways. *Please*, she prayed. *Just a moment more.*

"Stand the fuck still!" Sanger was breathing hard and his voice cracked as he spoke. "People don't want to die. People are afraid to die. This work is a triumph of science over superstition," he spat.

Rosie now had a clear view of Sanger through the bars of her cage. Her growl was low and threatening.

Michaela laughed. "Did they teach you how to grandstand like this in grad school? Make these little speeches like you're in a movie?"

"You little—" Sanger swiftly stepped toward her, gun upraised to strike.

Before Michaela could stop him, David stepped between them and grabbed for Sanger's hand. They struggled briefly, but Sanger managed to squeeze the trigger and the gun discharged.

David dropped at Michaela's feet, his hands clutching vainly at a rapidly spreading bloodstain over his heart. He coughed and blood spewed from his mouth.

Michaela dropped down beside him, helpless to do anything but grasp his hands and hold on. "David!" she cried.

For a second, his darting eyes met hers, then he seemed to gaze right through her. Incredibly, his mouth formed into a slight smile and for an instant she saw *joy* in his eyes. "There you are," he whispered. Then his face went slack. His pupils widened to dead blackness, and with shocking swiftness, David Brightman was gone.

Regaining his balance, Sanger came at her again, pistol raised. Michaela stood up to meet his attack and he flung her backward against the bank of cages. Michaela felt the cage door against the back of her legs. Rosie growled, but she couldn't get out.

The latch of a top cage brushed Michaela's ear. She reached over and released the latch, then, before Sanger could pin her, she ducked her head, grabbed the bottom of the cage door and threw it open, straight into his face. His glasses flew off and he staggered backward with a curse.

Michaela dove sideways onto the ground and rolled away. With a savage snarl Rosie launched herself against the unlatched cage door. It swung open and Rosie leapt out. Sanger lost his footing as Rosie charged, and they both went down in a snapping, flailing heap. The gun discharged once before Sanger dropped it and it skittered away.

Then, with a loud *thunk*, the lights went dead and everything went black.

"Shit!" she heard Sanger say, then rustling and scrabbling on the floor.

Michaela could see nothing. Even the emergency exit signs were dark.

It was midnight. Julius's computer program had just completed its work. Synthetic Genetics was dead, its data banks emptied, and from thousands of bank accounts all over the world, billions of dollars of dirty money winked of existence.

Michaela felt her way along the bank of cages, as silently as she could. She bumped into something and couldn't help crying out in alarm. It was Rosie. Michaela reached down and held her collar. The dog's fur was slick and warm with blood.

"Come on, Rosie," she whispered. "Get us out of here."

Rosie moved off. Michaela had no idea where they were going. She winced as Rosie's toenails clicked against the floor. Low light filtered in through the snow-covered skylights overhead.

Sanger clattered up the metal staircase and raced along the walkway above.

She heard a gunshot and felt something whiz by her head. Sanger had found his gun.

Instinctively, Michaela dropped low and ducked her head, crouching as she moved, still gripping Rosie's collar. The gun went off again and she felt Rosie flinch, but the dog kept moving.

Sanger continued to clatter around above her on the metal walkway, blindly shooting into the treatment area below. What happened next was too fast for Michaela to track. More gunshots. A sharp impact in her midsection, as if she'd been kicked in the side with a steel-toed boot. A flash of light and a *whump* as a fireball leapt to the ceiling—an exploding gas tank from a stray bullet. Then something dropped onto her from above, and she fell under its weight. It was Sanger. They each lay dazed for a moment, then he grabbed her.

He was enraged beyond reason, his face inches from hers, his hot breath on her tear-stained face. With sheer horror Michaela realized that he was becoming aroused, forcing her legs apart and thrusting his pelvis against hers like a rutting animal, hands scrabbling for her throat. She knocked his hands away, tried to twist her body out from underneath him, searching with her hands on the floor around her, trying to find something anchored to grab onto and pull herself free. She closed her fingers around metal that was not anchored down, so she swung it like a hammer at Sanger's head. In that instant, she realized that she had found Sanger's gun and was holding it by the barrel, hitting Sanger with the grip. He grunted in pain, but he, too, realized what Michaela had and tried to wrest it from her.

Michaela's hands closed around the grip. Her finger found the trigger and she squeezed. There was a sharp bang and a recoil that drove her shoulders and elbows into the floor. Sanger's throat burst open in a gush of hot blood and he collapsed on top of her.

Michaela pushed his body off and crawled away, spitting blood from her mouth. She slumped and rolled onto her back. Directly above her, a section of the ceiling was on fire. The orange, flickering light cast an eerie illumination on the floor.

Then Rosie's cold, snuffling nose was in her hair.

She reached up and wrapped her hand tightly around Rosie's collar. "Let's go, girl," she gasped.

Rosie took off across the kill floor. Michaela kept slipping in blood as she scrambled along on her hands and knees. She was starting to feel light-headed.

As they rounded the corner, another gas tank exploded.

Michaela knew it wouldn't take long for the fire's heat to reach the large oxygen tanks that fed into the hoses all over the building. How ironic that she should die like this, amid explosions and fire.

Seconds later, she passed out.

29

Joyride

THE HIGH BEAMS BLED OUT INTO NOTHINGNESS on this interminably straight rural highway. Brendan started as the voice from the GPS app on Alicia's tablet computer shattered the silence. "In a quarter of a mile," it intoned, "you have reached your destination."

He slowed down.

"In two hundred yards, you have reached your destination."

He slowed to a crawl, looking for a building, a road, a turning—anything.

"You have reached your destination."

Brendan pulled over. He got out of his car, looking in every direction, leaving the gravel shoulder and walking into the field of corn stubble next to the road. A feeling of dread filled him. According to Alicia's computer, Terry's phone was in this exact spot before it went dark. Michaela's last words had been to say good-bye.

Brendan stopped, afraid that if he took one more step he would stumble over his cousin's dead body. He stared into the black southern sky.

There was a flash of orange in the distance. A heartbeat later he heard a muffled bang. Treetops stood out in silhouette against dancing yellow light.

He got back into his car and drove toward the trees, making right and left turns on the rural roads, always keeping the flickering light before him. As he got close he scanned the edge of the road. A driveway came into view on the left, with red reflectors marking each side. There was another explosion and flames shot up over the tops of the trees. He followed the driveway to a parking lot, driving past a large utility truck covered in snow.

There was a Jeep in front of the building. In the back window was a decal with the insignia of the University of Illinois College of Veterinary Medicine. Next to the Jeep were three sets of footprints in the fresh snow, two human, one dog, leading to the main door. He surveyed the building. Every window was darkened, but flames rose from the rooftop. He tried the front door. Locked.

He went to his car and fetched a tire iron from the trunk. He came back and started hammering the front door. It was made of bulletproof security glass. It would eventually break, but there was no time.

He looked around frantically for something heavy enough to break the glass or destroy the door handle, but there was nothing. No large rocks—nothing. Only a smooth, perfect blanket of snow around the featureless foundation of the building.

Brendan checked his belt. He was relieved to discover that by force of habit he had clipped his phone to its usual place. He dialed 911. He talked to the dispatcher and reported a fire. He didn't know the official address, but he tried to describe where he was. The operator instructed him to stay on the line until the emergency vehicles arrived, but that seemed utterly foolish to him. He left the phone on, placed it on the hood of the Jeep and kept looking around for something to help him get inside.

Another explosion boomed inside the building. He flung the tire iron at the window. It bounced uselessly against the glass. Angrily, Brendan spun away and glared helplessly across the parking lot and into the darkness.

Then his eyes alighted on the utility truck, parked in the far corner of the lot.

He retrieved the tire iron and hurried across the lot. When he reached the truck he swung the tire iron over his head and smashed the window with two swift blows. He climbed up on the running board and reached in to open the door. He quickly climbed in, checked the visor, under the seat and in the glove box—no keys.

He reached into his jacket and pulled out his penknife. He flipped open the jagged blade, the one he had used daily as a teenager, but never since leaving Ireland. He hoped he could remember how to do this. He stuck the blade into the ignition and jiggled it until it felt right, then turned it. The engine came to life.

Brendan looked up and scanned the building. Orange light flickered above the rooftop and the skylight blew out under a plume of smoke and flame.

He threw the truck into gear and rocketed across the parking lot, straight at the exterior ground-level windows of the building. For a moment he experienced a brief memory of the many times he had done this on the streets of Belfast, running through British military checkpoints, never knowing if the soldiers were going to open fire or just stand back and let him through.

Right before impact, Brendan threw himself sideways onto the truck's bench seat.

There was a tremendous crash, a lurch and a jolt. Something hit the left side of his head.

He opened his eyes. It was dark and something was draped over him—some kind of fabric. He pushed it aside; it was the spent airbag. Looking up through the windshield, he saw planks, bricks, debris and dust.

The engine had cut out, but he shifted the truck into park and turned off the ignition. He tried to open the door but it was blocked by something. He ripped open the glove compartment and found a flashlight, then slid across the seat and exited through the passenger side.

The truck had smashed into a conference room and partially destroyed a wall leading into the hallway. Brendan pushed aside crumpled chairs and kicked away shards of glass. Then he climbed through the defect in the wall and scanned the hallway with his flashlight. He set off into the interior of the building. It was immediately apparent that he was going to get lost very quickly. The air was thick and smoky.

He rounded a corner and stopped short. Two figures lay on the cold tiles of the corridor, with a large smeary trail of blood behind them. One was a large, yellow dog.

The other was Michaela.

Her hand was tangled in fur and grasping the dog's collar. The dog was utterly still. Its lifeless eyes were open and glazed over.

The smell made him gag, but he laid his hand briefly on the dog's head. Brendan grieved in his spirit that such a thing should happen to a trusting, innocent animal, but he was thankful the dog's instincts had led them this far. They had almost made it.

He freed Michaela's hand from the dog's collar and shone the flashlight briefly over her—she was covered in blood.

"Oh, God," he whispered.

Brendan picked up Michaela and carried her toward the front of the building. Smoky hot air seared his throat, making him cough. Tears streamed from his burning eyes. Michaela's blood was warm, soaking through his shirt. She was losing too much blood.

He came to the hallway where he had entered, but instead of going back through the wrecked conference room, he carried Michaela straight to the door that led to the reception area. He hit the crash bar with his foot, crossed the lobby and exited the building.

Gently, he set Michaela down in the snow, pulled off his coat and slid it under her.

He felt her neck. The pulsation beneath his fingers felt weak. Thank God he had called 911. He listened, hoping to hear sirens.

A huge explosion blew out the building's second story windows. Brendan threw himself over Michaela to shield her from the rain of splintered glass and debris. It pelted his back like hailstones. The flames towered over the building. There was a deafening crash as a section of the roof caved in.

Brendan heard the faint sound of approaching sirens. He watched Michaela breathe in and breathe out.

There was a roar overhead, driving wind, and flashing lights. A red and white helicopter burst into view over the trees, then dropped down onto the parking lot. The word Air-Life was painted in red on the side. Two paramedics got out and came directly to Brendan, carrying a stretcher and emergency supplies.

"She's bleeding. From somewhere here," Brendan said, indicating her abdomen. "I don't know what happened."

One of the paramedics lifted Michaela's sweater and swabbed away a large mass of congealed blood. Beneath it was a perfectly circular wound, something else with which Brendan was all too familiar.

The blaring sirens were close. Red and blue lights lit up the trees. Three fire trucks rumbled around the last bend in the driveway and ground to a halt.

Two firefighters raced over. "Is anyone inside?" one of them asked.

"I think so," Brendan said. "I don't know how many."

More fire trucks arrived and firefighters rushed about. Brendan had a vague sense of seeing ladders going up into the air, water spraying down onto the building.

The paramedics lifted Michaela onto the stretcher. Brendan followed them as they carried her to the back of the helicopter and put her in. Brendan also climbed up and one of the paramedics gave him a look.

"I'm a priest," Brendan said.

The paramedics exchanged a glance, then secured the door. The pilot fired up the rotors and lifted off.

Brendan squeezed in next to Michaela, trying to keep out of the way. The paramedic fixed a mask over her nose and mouth and opened the oxygen tank valve. He set an IV catheter into Michaela's arm, lifted her shirt and attached the ECG monitoring disks.

He took Michaela's vital signs and fed the information to the pilot, who in turn repeated it through a radio handset. "Pulse is thready and weak. Mucous membranes are pale, CRT three and a half seconds. Lips and face show noticeable pallor. PLRs are sluggish."

The paramedic affixed a blood pressure cuff to Michaela's arm and pumped it up, taking a reading. "BP is..." he hesitated. He glanced at Brendan.

"Sweet Jesus." Brendan always carried a small vial of holy oil in his pocket. Never had he imagined using it on his cousin in a situation like this. He fished the vial from his pocket. His hands shook as he uncapped the tiny bottle and he spilled it, trying to get a small amount onto his thumb. He grasped Michaela's hands and traced the sign of the cross in oil on each palm, then he did the same on her forehead, choking out the words of the prayer: "Through this holy anointing and His most loving mercy, may the Lord assist you by the grace of the Holy Spirit, so that, freed from your sins, He may save you and in His goodness raise you up."

Michaela cried out.

"She's coming around," Brendan shouted. "That's a good sign, isn't it?"

"Yeah, but extremely painful with a bullet in your abdomen."

Michaela tried to sit up.

"Hold her!" the paramedic shouted.

Brendan put his hands on Michaela's shoulders as the paramedic cinched a restraint strap across her chest.

Michaela tried to thrash, but the paramedic had tightened other restraint bands at key points.

Brendan took her hand and clenched it. "Michaela, can you hear me?"

Her frantic eyes darted around, not seeing him.

He put his face directly over hers. "Mick, it's me. Look at me."

Michaela found his eyes at last. Even his experiences of violence and terrorism could not prepare Brendan for what he saw when he looked into her eyes. He had never seen that kind of pain before. The helicopter noise, the radio transmissions and the beeping of the ECG machine sounded wildly in his ears. He felt like he needed to shout to be heard. "Just listen to me. We can get through this!"

Michaela squeezed her eyes shut and gripped Brendan's hand with astonishing strength. Brendan brought her hand to his forehead and pressed it against him, praying. He prayed without words, lifting up his tortured emotions in a silent petition.

"BP's dropping," the paramedic said. He called to the pilot, "What's our ETA?"

"Two minutes," came the reply.

"Make it one."

Brendan suddenly noticed that the beeping—Michaela's heart rate—had slowed. Her grip on his hand had lessened.

Then the beeping stopped.

"Asystole!" the paramedic shouted.

Brendan looked at the heart monitor. It was a flat green line.

The paramedic reached into a drawer and drew up something into a syringe. "1 cc of epi IC." He drove the needle into Michaela's chest and drew back on the plunger. Bright red blood flowed back into the syringe. Then the paramedic depressed the plunger and administered the contents, blood and all, directly into Michaela's heart. He watched the heart monitor for a second. Nothing. He drew up another cc of epineph-rine and injected it. This, too, had no effect.

The paramedic took off Michaela's oxygen mask and switched to one that was connected to a bag. He handed the bag to Brendan. "Press the mask snugly to her face and squeeze this bag every time I count to five."

The paramedic centered himself over Michaela, put the heel of his right hand on her sternum, and the heel of his left hand on top of his right. "Beginning cardiac compression," he called out.

"Almost there!" shouted the pilot.

The paramedic pumped down on Michaela's chest with both hands and counted aloud to five. "Squeeze the bag!"

Brendan obeyed. Under his breath, unconsciously in time to the paramedic's cadence, he prayed, "Hail Mary, full of grace. The Lord is with thee." *Squeeze the bag.* "Blessed art thou amongst women and blessed is the fruit of thy womb, Jesus." *Squeeze the bag.* "Pray for us sinners." He squeezed the bag again and wiped his eyes with his sleeve. "Pray for us sinners."

"Come on," the paramedic grunted, counting to five under his breath. "Bag her!"

Brendan squeezed the bag, and whispered, "Now and at the hour of our death."

The helicopter lurched to a stop. The side door flew open. Someone reached in to remove the stretcher, someone else took down the IV bag and laid it next to Michaela. Hospital personnel wheeled a cot over and they put the stretcher onto it. A paramedic jumped onto the cot and rode it to the rooftop elevator, continuing cardiac compressions. Brendan was edged aside by someone who took over squeezing the bag. Down-stairs in the ER, they rushed Michaela inside, through a swing-ing door, into an emergency bay. Brendan tried to stay along-side her, but they stopped him.

"Sorry, sir. You'll have to wait out here." Curtains swooshed shut in front of him. He heard them saying, "Clear!" and then the weighty *chunk* of a defibrillator.

He grabbed onto a chair, smearing it with blood, and knelt down on the floor.

"Clear!" someone called again. Brendan winced at the violent sound of the machine trying to restart Michaela's heart. In his mind he cried out: *Don't do this!*

But it was too late. She had already bled to death.

30

Between the Spirit and the Dust

FOR THE SECOND TIME since Sanger's stray bullet had ripped through her, Michaela lost consciousness. This time, she knew she was dying. Her heart pumped frantically to maintain blood perfusion to her vital organs, but each contraction only pumped more blood uselessly into her abdominal cavity. She was in hypovolemic shock, and soon her oxygen-deprived brain would shut down.

But to her it was a relief. The pain of a bullet puncturing her peritoneum and lodging in the muscles of her back was like being wrenched inside out. She heard herself cry out. She caught a glimpse of Brendan's face over her, his shocked eyes, felt something wet splash onto her face. She heard his voice: *We can get through this!*

Then she was gone.

At first she was aware of the heaviness of her body, but then she felt it dissolve. Her spirit lifted and expanded to infinity. She floated and fell, and waited in immeasurable darkness.

After what seemed like a thousand years, or perhaps only a moment, the utter darkness retreated and some kind of place formed. Bare ground surrounded her, spreading out in every direction toward a distant, brown horizon. Grit and rocks bit into her feet. The air was foul, hot, and filthy like smoke.

She heard low voices, and sensed people all around her, shadowy figures she could barely discern. She felt them behind her, in front of her, on every side, but as she moved across the blackened slag, the figures moved away from her like oil separating from water. When she stood still, the figures came closer and she could hear them speaking.

Somewhere nearby a man was saying "...how could you blame me? She had been letting herself go, and it was getting worse and worse every year. I'm only human after all. Was I supposed to put up with her coldness forever? When someone came along who actually knew how to love me, how could you blame me?"

A woman's rough voice muttered, "Nobody ever appreciated what I did for them. I gave up my career so he could pursue his. I stayed home and raised the children. And for what? So he could go 'find himself' at forty? So those ungrateful children could finish college and go live abroad in their fancy houses and drive their big cars? Whose sacrifice do they think got them where they are today?" she scoffed.

Michaela heard other stories. A son misunderstood his whole life by overbearing parents. A soldier who was just following orders. A politician who played the game just like everybody else.

"What is this?" she said.

Just for an instant, the murmuring voices all around her went silent. Bone scraped against bone.

Then the voices started up again, repeating themselves.

"...how could you blame me? She had been letting herself go, and it was getting worse and worse every year. I'm only human after all."

"Nobody ever appreciated what I did for them. I gave up my career so he could pursue his. I stayed home and raised the children. And for what? So he could go 'find himself...?' "

Michaela stumbled away, splinters of rock biting into her feet, harsh whispers and hot breath in her ears.

"Oh, it's so easy for him to be the good guy, to be the hero. *He's* the one who takes them to Disneyland and on cruises. Did he ever take *me* on a cruise? Not a chance."

"Nothing happened that she didn't ask for. Simple cause and effect! If she's going to behave like that, I had no choice but to dish out the consequences."

"It was all in good fun. I never actually hurt anyone. I'm basically a good person."

Then she heard a voice that stood out from the rest: "You know where you are." Michaela couldn't tell if it was a man or a woman.

She turned toward the new voice. A shadowy figure emerged from just outside her peripheral vision.

"What did you say to me?" Michaela asked.

The voice snarled with malice. "You know where you are. And you can't get away."

She tried to turn toward the voice, but she couldn't position herself in front of it. The shadowy figure kept sliding off to the side. It was maddening, like a dream.

"You hear that?" the voice sneered.

Michaela heard it. The muttering and whispering voices continued all around her, a dissonant chord sung over and over again by a choir of countless throats, all hoarse from their recitations.

"That is music to my ears, Michaela...Marie...Collins."

"Who are you?" Michaela cried. "What do you want?"

"Every single solitary soul in this place *wants* to be here," the voice hissed. "They are *happy*, Michaela...Marie...Collins."

"Stop calling me that!"

"Want to know why they're so happy? Because this is what they all wanted, more than anything else in the world: they wanted to be *right*. Here, they get to be right, and no one will argue with them. Ever again. You're right about your cousin. You're right about everything." The voice paused and then spat out her name like a curse: "Michaela…Marie… Collins."

Terror rose up in Michaela's throat and she screamed. Her own script started to form in her mind. It came easily, because she had been reciting it daily since she was seventeen years old. *Somebody has to remember what he did. Somebody has to make him pay. He can't be let off the hook. Forgiving him would be an insult to their memory, an insult to my mother's grief, and to mine. He took my father away from me! Nina was the sister I never had! He will not get away with it. Does he think having some "conversion" makes it all okay? Somebody has to remember what he did. Somebody has to make him pay…*

But nobody in this place cared. No one was listening, because they were all too busy talking about themselves, alone, standing in their places, chanting their stories, their reasons, their justifications. Their excuses. Over and over again, for all eternity.

Michaela ran. She felt something cold rip down the center of her back and catch in her spine, but still she ran. She fell. The knife-like shards of splintered rock sliced her hands. Heat ran from her wounds. She knew that she deserved to be here, but still she ran. The murmuring chorus chided her, clawed fingers tore at her, the howling screech and hot breath and heavy jaws closed around her neck and she screamed again.

Abruptly, on the wind, she heard a new voice, not hot and gravelly but pure and clear.

Don't do this.

A prayer. And in a mysterious way she could see the words and the fervent soul uttering them. She saw words in the air above her head.

She understood that her refusal to forgive Brendan had infected everything in her life. That her life-long bitterness and rage had led her here.

But why? Why couldn't she forgive?

Think, Michaela. What did you say to David?

David had refused to forgive himself, and it had driven him into isolation and a crazy scheme to genetically engineer a way to cheat death. Was that any more ridiculous than what Michaela had been doing? Is this the impossible bargain she had been holding onto? The twisted logic that told her refusing to forgive Brendan meant she didn't have to acknowledge that her father, Nina, J.J. and Viola were really gone? Did holding onto resentment somehow tether the dead to life so that she would be able to reel them back in some day?

Michaela felt ashamed. The only one she had tethered was herself.

She looked around and saw that she was now somewhere different. On the horizon, a spectacular light glowed like a white-hot sunrise. The light flashed, and a deep rumbling rolled toward her and reverberated in her chest. The light was too brilliant to look at, so she closed her eyes and felt its warmth on her face. From the deepest part of her, from her very essence, that sensation of beautiful agony arose. Michaela experienced the indescribable sensation that she had for Terry, for their unborn child, that feeling of inconsolable longing—except that this was even more powerful, endless, and unquenchable. All the earthly love she had ever given or received was a mere taste of what she was experiencing now and what awaited her over that horizon.

But then her physical awareness began to return. Her body collected itself from the farthest flung corners of space, as if the universe were drawing back together into the singularity that it had been before time began. Grass prickled the bottoms of her feet and brushed her ankles. Blue sky and a green hillside with daisies resolved into view.

Daisies? she thought to herself, and gave a little laugh, as if it were a joke. The silhouette of a figure appeared and walked toward her. Michaela shaded her eyes and watched the figure approach. When she recognized who it was, she broke into a grin. "Daddy!"

Her father ran to her, and she to him, until she fell, laughing, into his arms.

Michaela was surprised at how real and solid he was. After a moment, she held him at arm's length and looked up at him. "Where are your wings?"

He laughed. "Oh, Michaela, we don't have wings."

"I know. But this..." She cast her eyes all around her. "This isn't quite what I expected. Is this an actual place, or is it a dream?"

"Yes."

"Very funny." She looked behind him into the distance, hopeful expectation in her eyes.

Her father shook her head. "Just me at the moment. But they're looking forward to seeing you again." He smiled, with a glance down at Michaela. "Both of you." He took Michaela's hand and they walked toward the horizon. Michaela took a deep breath, exhaled and melted into contentment. Her legs were strong, striding through the grass. She squeezed his hand. "Daddy?"

"Yes?"

"Seriously. What is this? Where are we?"

Her father furrowed his forehead. "I'm not exactly sure. An in-between place, I think." He looked up and closed his eyes. "Can you hear him?" he asked.

Michaela listened. A light breeze blew up the hillside, ruffling the grass, tousling her hair. On the wind, she heard the pure, clear voice that had brought her out of the place of darkness. "Brendan?"

He nodded. "I've a question for you, my dear."

"What is it?"

"Are you willing to let God be God?"

"What is that supposed to mean?"

Her father let go of her hand.

"Daddy?"

He spread his hands in a mischievous gesture of mock helplessness, and took one step closer to the horizon.

31

Confession

BRENDAN KNELT by the emergency room gurney, Michaela's hand in his. Her flesh was cool, smooth, sticky with her own blood and damp from his tears. The doctors had pronounced Michaela dead, then let Brendan in and discreetly withdrawn, pulling the privacy curtains closed. The floor to ceiling fabric encircled him like a confessional.

He was weak. His chest ached and his eyes stung. His throat was raw. And he was furious. He felt a wave of anger rising from his chest. Instead of vocalizing it, he pushed himself violently to his feet and grabbed the edge of the gurney. He gripped the rail so hard his body shook.

How could You let this happen?

Brendan bit his lower lip and made himself look. Michaela was stripped to the waist, her underclothes drenched in blood, her chest, abdomen, pelvis, and thighs slick with it. Fluid still dripped uselessly into her veins from the IV bag, and wires draped across her to the silent ECG machine. Her face was grayish white, her lips colorless. The one mercy was that her eyes were closed. Brendan had seen more sightless eyes than he cared to.

His own eyes grew heavy again, tears spilling out and down his cheeks. He could barely see, but he reached out with his right thumb and traced a cross on his cousin's forehead. A cross of blood. His mind was blank. He couldn't remember the official words, the ones he had prayed over hundreds of souls whom he had conducted into the hereafter. All he could remember were the words he had grown up hearing every night from his parents at bedtime: "May the Lord Jesus bless you, and may the prayers of the angels and saints preserve you, now and forever."

He laid his hand on her head.

Then he sat down, heavily, in a chair next to the gurney. The ECG machine's flat green line seemed to him a mocking sneer. He rested his elbow on the arm of the chair and covered his eyes with his hand. The sounds of hospital activity crept in through the curtains. Muted voices. Ringing phones. A crying child.

In the cubicle next to him, he heard the faint sound of an ECG machine starting up. The irony of it struck Brendan like a blow to the face. Michaela had been pursuing a mystery concerning this very thing. Man in pursuit of immortality, dodging the sword of the angel at the gate and tearing fruit from the Tree of Life. Man playing God.

But God will not be mocked. He is the author of life, and He holds the keys of death. The verse of a psalm came to his mind: *the ransom of man's soul is beyond him. He cannot buy life without end, nor avoid coming to the grave.* How much more nonsense would the Lord tolerate before He simply closed camp? How long before He rolled up the veil between Heaven and Earth like a celestial Venetian blind and put a stop to Man's tampering arrogance for all time?

Brendan sighed and let his hand fall from his eyes.

Then he sat straight up. The beeping of the ECG machine was not in the cubicle next door. It was in this one. The flat line was gone. In its place were regularly spaced, jagged little spikes.

Michaela's chest rose and fell.

He jumped up and flung his chair backward across the floor. "Hey!" he yelled. He grabbed the curtain and ripped it open, accidentally dislodging it from its hooks. It cascaded to the floor like a spent parachute. "Somebody! Quick! Over here!"

Nurses came running, doctors in green scrubs and white lab coats, swarming around Michaela with exclamations, shouts of profanity and wonder. They hooked her up to oxygen, shouted orders to each other, injected things into her IV line.

"Get the surgical team back here, stat!" somebody yelled.

Brendan ran his bloody hand through his hair. Did people really say *stat*? A nurse emerged briefly from the swirling chaos, her eyebrow cocked at Brendan, questioning, and pointed up.

Brendan splayed his hands and shrugged.

She gave him a thumbs-up and returned to her work.

A moment later they wheeled Michaela away. Brendan followed, keeping pace with the gurney, holding his cousin's hand. She was conscious and trying to say something, but an oxygen mask obscured her face and he couldn't hear her. Brendan stroked her hair away from her forehead and looked into her eyes.

They reached a set of automatic doors and someone took Brendan by the arm. "We'll take her from here, sir. "

It was the nurse of the thumbs-up. This time she winked and handed him off to a young man in scrubs, who led Brendan to the waiting room. He glanced over his shoulder and saw the doors swing closed.

He sat down and leaned forward in the chair, putting his head in his hands. "Jesus, Mary and Joseph," he sighed. His body was shaking and his mind was a jumble, completely overloaded with information, confusion, and emotions, feelings he hadn't experienced since he was young. Exhilaration, terror, grief. But also joy like he had never known. He would never forget the sight he had just seen: the light of Heaven in Michaela's eyes.

Then he remembered another verse from scripture: *O Lord, your love for me has been great. You have saved me from the depths of the grave.*

* * *

After the bullet punctured Michaela's abdomen, it slid past her intestines, barely missed her liver, slammed through her left kidney, and had almost come out through her back. It remained partially buried in the muscles to the left of her spine.

Her left kidney was shredded. It had been the source of her hemorrhaging and was too badly damaged to salvage. The surgeons had ligated the renal artery and removed the entire kidney. The bullet was nestled between two of the major nerve roots that peel off the spinal cord, and it had not damaged either one. Its removal was straightforward.

What the surgeons couldn't figure out was how this patient was even alive in the first place. After completing the surgery, the chief surgeon had studied the notes left by the ER staff: *Patient was pronounced dead at 12:38 am by attending physician Dr. Marc Greensmith. At approximately 12:53 am spontaneous reestablishment of cardiac function occurred, followed shortly by spontaneous respiration.*

The rumors quickly spread through the hospital. *The guy who came in with her is a priest. He brought her back from the dead.* Hospital personnel, who had no business in Michaela's room, kept coming in with lame excuses.

"Just checking her IV line, sir."

"Just making a notation in the record, sir."

They would come in and look at Michaela, look at Brendan, flip through the chart without so much as uncapping a pen, then leave, shaking their heads.

Brendan was immune to annoyance, though. He was content to just sit and watch her breathe. Watch the color return to her face as life's blood dripped into her arm from the transfusion bag.

During the surgery, Brendan had gone upstairs to check on Terry and tell Alicia everything that had happened. After surgery, Father Angelo had come over and together he and Brendan had given Michaela the sacrament of anointing. Police had come to ask Brendan questions. What did he know about Frank Galton? Had he ever met Garrett Sanger? What about David Brightman? They also asked him about someone named Julius Abayomi. But Brendan had no answers for them.

Michaela's breathing changed, and she stirred. Brendan sat up and leaned closer, taking her hand. She opened her eyes and blinked, then looked around anxiously.

"Over here, Mick," Brendan said.

She turned her head toward him and smiled weakly. " 'Tis himself."

Brendan returned her smile.

"Terry?" she said.

"Still on the ventilator. But he's stable."

Michaela sighed, visibly relaxing. "Where's my mom?"

"Upstairs with Terry. We've been taking turns watching both of you." Brendan looked down at her hand. Her skin was pale, like porcelain. He stroked her thumb. Urgency burned in his throat, something he had been desperate to say for more years than he could count. "Michaela," he began.

But she interrupted him. "Brendan, I'm sorry."

"No, Mick. I'm the one who's sorry." He squeezed her hand. She squeezed back, weakly. He looked in her eyes and said the words he had waited over two decades to say. "I knew better than to get involved with the bloody IRA, but I was a stupid, angry boy. I can understand why you haven't been able to forgive me for all these years."

She shook her head. "I was the only one in the family to hold a grudge." Tears filled her eyes. "I'm the only one who didn't come to your ordination." Her voice broke, and she had to pause before continuing. "Bren, I was angry because I thought you'd become a priest only out of guilt. That you wanted to hide yourself away and make some kind of ridiculous atonement." She let out a bitter, self-recriminating laugh. "I hated you so much that it never occurred to me that you actually believe in what you do."

A sob escaped Brendan's throat. She reached up and put her arms around his neck. He leaned into her and put his head on her shoulder.

When they had cried enough, she released him and wiped her eyes with the sleeve of her hospital gown. "I could hear your voice, Brendan," she said. "You were the one calling me back."

"Beggin' for your life is what it was, Mick. I was in a blind panic. I just prayed from me' gut."

Michaela smiled, her eyes still closed. "Always trust your gut," she said, with a passable Northern Irish burr.

Brendan smiled. He had always liked the way she teased him about his accent.

Michaela opened her eyes. "How did you know where to find me?" she asked, frowning.

"That was your mother," Brendan answered. "She ran an application on her computer to find Terry's phone."

"Terry's always misplacing that phone," she said quietly. Then she frowned. "But I don't understand. The phone went dead long before we got to Synthetic Genetics."

Brendan shrugged.

For a while, she remained lost in thought. Then she said, "Mom said she introduced you to David."

Brendan nodded.

"Did he tell you about the project? Is that how you knew where to go?"

Brendan hesitated, keeping his eyes on the floor. Only a short time ago, in the back pew at St. Andrew's, David Brightman had told him everything.

Then, after receiving absolution, David had extended his hand, and Brendan had taken it. "Thank you, Father." He had opened his mouth to say more, but choked on his words.

"It's all right, my son," Brendan had said. "Go in peace."

Brendan raised his eyes to Michaela's.

Her face softened. "You heard his confession."

Brendan remained silent, his eyes impassive, and neither nodded nor shook his head.

Michaela considered this for a moment. "Will you hear mine?" she whispered.

32

Love's Purest Joys Restored

TERRY HEARD QUIET VOICES, but he couldn't understand the words. He had no idea where he was. He panicked and tried to thrash, but he couldn't move.

Slowly, the fog in his mind dissipated, like early morning mist evaporating in the heat of the rising sun, and he realized what had happened and that he must be in the hospital. He had to warn Michaela that she was in danger, that Sanger had come and taken everything and was running around with a gun.

He felt someone come close to him and a soft hand grasp his. Before she spoke, he knew it was her.

"Terry, it's me. Can you hear me? Can you squeeze my hand?"

He tried with all his strength, but he couldn't even twitch his fingers. He heard dismay in her voice. "Are you sure he can he hear us?"

An unfamiliar male voice answered. "I believe so." The male voice came closer. "Terry, can you blink your eyes?"

He tried, and he was able to open and close his eyelids a little.

"Neural connections and brain structure are unique to each individual," the voice continued, "so there's no way to predict just how much disability a wound will leave. We'll run some tests later to assess his brain function, but he's no longer comatose, and for now I would just assume the best and get him up to speed. Tell him what happened."

"Do you remember when you told me to get ready to say good-bye?" she said.

The male voice chuckled. "I do. And in this case, I'm glad to be wrong."

Holy crap, Terry thought. *What happened to me?*

Footsteps retreated, and Terry felt her hands on his face, her lips on his mouth as she kissed him tenderly. "Terry, don't worry," she said. "You were shot in the head, and you've been in a coma. But you're awake now, and as soon as you're better, we'll go home."

He tried to put his arms around her, but all he could do was lie there like a speed bump. Tears streamed from beneath his closed eyelids.

Her hands gently wiped them away. Holding his face in her hands, she leaned in close and kissed him. "Terry, it's okay," she whispered. "I love you. Everything is fine." She paused. "The baby is fine. Just hold onto that, and we'll get through this."

They did brain scans and an electroencephalogram. The conclusion was that he was conscious. And not just minimally conscious, which was its own category, but fully conscious. *No kidding*, Terry thought wryly. *If I weren't completely paralyzed, I could tell you that myself.*

That had its own category, too. Fully conscious but paralyzed meant that Terry was "locked-in."

And that's exactly what it felt like. He would strain with all his strength to sit up, and the attending nurses would remark that he had moved his head a little. He would try to speak, but would hear his voice making only garbled noises.

Within a few days, he didn't need the ventilator to breathe anymore, so they removed the tracheostomy tube. They fed him through a stomach tube. The bullet had done some damage to the bones around his eye socket, so he had surgery to fix that. Eventually, they did another surgery to put the left half of his cranium back. They bent and straightened his arms and legs, and repositioned him often—on his back, on his side, sitting up, lying down.

And still, he could only blink. But he felt stronger somehow.

Every week, Brendan came and gave him the sacrament, anointing his head and hands with that sweet smelling oil, and giving him a taste of consecrated communion wine on his tongue with an eyedropper. Alicia came by often, too, and listened to audio books and podcasts with him. Michaela came to see him twice a day, once at lunch time, and then again after work. She brought music, and read to him, and told him about her day, about how the pre-natal visits were going.

Sometimes he could open and shut his eyes on command, but that was the only glimpse he could provide into his fully active mind. If he could talk he would have told Michaela everything he was thinking. He felt the heat and the humidity. He smelled morning coffee and the lunch Michaela brought everyday. It made him angry to be stuck like this, unable to move or speak. He especially hated it when he got an itch he couldn't scratch.

When he sensed Michaela hovering over him, those were the times when he tried his hardest to open his eyes, so he could see her beautiful face. When she smiled down at him, he felt like he'd received the favor of a goddess, and he wondered what she ever saw in a guy like him. He would have apologized for going way overboard with the "for better, for worse, in sickness and in health" thing.

Questions burned in his mind, too. Synthetic Genetics was finished, at least here in Illinois, but was there another arm of the project somewhere else? Were more dogs suffering like Rosie? What about the research going on in Africa? That young man, Julius, made the money go away, but what would happen to all the human test subjects? Most of all, Terry wanted to ask Michaela if it was all worth it. Hank Ullman and David Brightman were dead. Julius was dead. Even their dog was dead. And Terry knew that he might be flat on his back for the rest of his life. It had to be worth it. *Please tell me we managed to save at least some of them*, he thought.

One day Michaela came over and, with the help of the nurses, propped him up in the bed. Then she sat next to him and put his hand on her abdomen, which was getting bigger every day. Then he felt it! A little kick, a flutter of new life.

He wanted to jump up and down, shout for joy, but all he could do was twitch his hand a little, and it made him angry. How could he love his wife like this? How could he be a father? What was he? Had he been reduced to the level of an animal—or worse? He was there, but he was stuck. He was no different from the person he had been as a boy and as a young man. His thought patterns hadn't changed. His sense of humor hadn't changed. His preferences hadn't changed.

But what if they had? What if the damage to his brain had made him unable to think or had impeded his ability to hear and comprehend what occurred all around him? Would he still be Terry Adams? What if he were only "minimally conscious" or in a "persistent vegetative state?" What the hell did that mean, anyway? Did a human being suddenly become a potted plant?

He reflected on this deeply, for many weeks, and finally confronted head-on the question of what it meant to be human. When and where did he truly begin, and when and where did he end? He had not yet discovered the answer to that question. All he knew was that, even though his body was paralyzed, his mind and heart remained free. It was good to be alive! Every breath felt like a gift, and he wouldn't waste a single one. He would be the best husband and father he could be, just as he was. He would love Michaela and their baby from here, in silence and stillness. His longing for her was so intense he could hardly stand it, but he knew he just had to be patient. Months, years, decades? In this life or the next? Either way, it was okay. They would be together again eventually.

* * *

Terry woke up from a deep sleep, and he felt different, as if he had been only half awake up until this moment. He had been placed on his side, and he didn't want to be on his side, so he rolled over onto his back.

He heard Michaela's voice. "Terry?" In her question there was urgency and hopefulness, something he hadn't heard in months.

He turned his head toward the sound, lifted his hand and felt her take hold of it. In response to the gentle pressure of her hand, he squeezed back, and she gasped. "Terry, can you hear me?" she said. "Can you open your eyes?"

After so many months of catching brief glimpses of the world through eyelids that fluttered open only for a second, he blinked and opened his eyes fully. The first thing he saw were those beautiful green eyes, filling with tears of joy. He reached out to her and touched her face. She was even lovelier than before, if that were possible.

Ever since he had known her, all the way back to when they were undergraduates at the University, she had worn grief like a shield, and once he heard the story about Brendan and the IRA and the bombing, he understood. True, sometimes the grief manifested itself as bitterness and anger, but who could blame her for that? It was just part of who she was, a natural defense mechanism that he always chalked up to her fiery Irish heritage. Gradually, she had allowed him past her outer defenses to the feminine inner strength and fierce compassion that were the root of the toughness he so admired.

Soon he discovered the fragile treasure the walls were meant to protect: Michaela's broken heart. It was as simple as that. All Terry could do was love her as much as he could, and hope that she would mend over time.

She and Brendan had told him about their reconciliation, how forgiveness had restored and healed them both. But now, Terry could see it for himself, with his own eyes. Michaela was completely changed. His wife was no longer a fortress bristling with defenses. She was a palace overflowing with new life, not because she was expecting a baby, but because, in a way, she had already given birth. Her broken heart had become brand new.

He realized he was gaping, in awe.

Michaela blinked, and gave him a quizzical smile. "What is it, Terry?"

His voice was weak and hoarse. "Wow, Michaela," he whispered. "Let me look at you."

Acknowledgments

The author gratefully acknowledges all the people who were so generous with their time and valuable input:

- Hearty thanks to Paul McComas. As my advisor for a Master of Science degree in Written Communication, he skillfully shepherded the novel through its first draft as the thesis project for that degree. I also thank Joanne Koch for her encouragement.
- Friends, family members, and colleagues eagerly read and provided helpful feedback on the later drafts of the novel: Annie Walker-Bright, Richard Walker, Liz Whiteacre, Brian Bartley, Tom Buonincontro, Debbie Buonincontro, Sue Gibson, Aaron Foege, Stephanie Foege, Andrew Billing, Colleen Billing, Yvonne Costa, Lisa Connor, DeAnn Chamberlin, and Melissa Lantro. Thank you!
- I'm grateful to several experts who helped with technical details about police work, cutting-edge science, life in Africa, and surgery, on both humans and animals: Officer Jim Schlicker, Dr. Ned Hahn, Dr. Herb Whiteley, Charles Batte, Telima Olungwe, Dr. Don Waldron, and Dr. Craig Reckard. I'm grateful to them all for sharing their expertise with me. Nevertheless, I take full responsibility for any errors of fact or procedure that snuck into the book despite their best efforts to enlighten me.

Also, many thanks to the editing and publishing professionals who worked on the book. Copy editor Sheryl Fujimura corrected my typographical errors and tried to rein in my verbosity. Story editor Drew Downing kept the story on track. Creative designer Tom Buonincontro designed the cover and title page. I am deeply appreciative of your excellent work!

I should note that for Michaela's terrifying vision of Hell I am indebted to Samuel Beckett's *Play*, especially the film version directed by Anthony Minghella and starring Alan Rickman, Juliet Stevenson, and Kristin Scott Thomas. I also found John Conroy's book *Belfast Diary* extremely helpful for understanding what it was like to live in Northern Ireland during the height of the Troubles.

And finally, I want to thank my daughters. They read early drafts of the manuscript and provided honest, helpful feedback. They brainstormed titles. They accompanied me on research trips to east central Illinois, where we explored the tunnels under the campus of the University of Illinois, took goofy pictures at Allerton Park, and sampled Dagwoods and Green Rivers at the Courier Café. Hannah and Teresa, I am grateful for how each of you helped me and encouraged me throughout this project, but mostly I am simply in awe of the beautiful young women you have both grown up to be. This book is dedicated to you!

About the Author

CLARE T. WALKER is a practicing veterinarian and an independent author who writes fiction and non-fiction.

Want news of upcoming releases?
Snippets from works-in-progress?
Behind-the-scenes exclusives?
Announcements of special promotions?

Join the Reader's Club at **www.ClareTWalker.com**!!

CPSIA information can be obtained
at www.ICGtesting.com
Printed in the USA
LVOW12s2054171217
560113LV00001B/9/P